"Welcome to your home away from home for the next ten days," Lia said.

Magliore cast an appraising glance over the cozily furnished room, then looked back at her. "You mean we're to share this cabin...alone?"

Her pulse reacted to the low, velvety timbre of his voice. She cleared her throat briskly. "The other agents will be less than fifteen feet away in the next building. You'll be more than safe."

Magliore chuckled low in his throat. "Believe me, Miss Charles," he drawled, trapping her in the smoldering beam of his gaze, "that was never my concern. No man in his right mind would ~~~~~~~ forced confinement with such an exq~~~~~ beautiful woman as yourself."

Lia's heart thudded.

Damn. She was losin~~~~ herself. In the six ye~~~~~~~~~~~~~~~~ ~~cret Service, not once had ~~~~~~~~~~~~ ~ine with a protectee. She'd never ~~~~~~~~~~ But Armand Magliore, with his dark g~~~~~~~s and raw animal magnetism, was the living, ~~eathing embodiment of temptation. This was a man who would persuade a nun to cross the line into sin with one little crook of his finger. Lia doubted he'd ever met a woman he couldn't bend to his will.

Books by Maureen Smith

Kimani Romance

A Legal Affair
A Guilty Affair
Secret Agent Seduction

Kimani Arabesque

With Every Breath
A Heartbeat Away

MAUREEN SMITH

is the author of ten novels and one novella. She received a B.A. in English from the University of Maryland with a minor in creative writing. She is a former freelance writer, and her articles were featured in various print and online publications. Since the publication of her debut novel in 2002, Maureen has been nominated for two *Romantic Times BOOKreviews* Reviewers' Choice Awards and twelve Emma Awards, and has won the Romance in Color Reviewers' Choice Awards for New Author of the Year and Romantic Suspense of the Year.

Maureen currently lives in San Antonio, Texas, with her husband, two children and a miniature schnauzer. She loves to hear from readers and can be reached at author@maureen-smith.com. Please visit her Web site at www.maureen-smith.com for news about her upcoming releases.

SECRET AGENT
SEDUCTION

Maureen Smith

Dedicated to Mavis Allen, an extraordinary editor
whose vision made this book possible

 KIMANI PRESS™

ISBN-13: 978-0-373-86082-1
ISBN-10:   0-373-86082-X

SECRET AGENT SEDUCTION

Copyright © 2008 by Maureen Smith

Dear Reader,

I hope you enjoy following Lia and Armand on their dangerous trek through a dark Caribbean jungle and finally to a secluded cabin retreat in Maryland's Catoctin Mountains, where they fall in love. I was thrilled to receive an invitation to write a story for the ROMANCE ON THE RUN series, which allowed me to combine two of my favorite plot elements—romance and suspense. My mission was to deliver pulse-pounding action balanced with an emotional, sizzling romance. I hope you discover that the mission was accomplished.

What I also enjoyed about this story was being able to dabble in the paranormal by giving Lia the ability to read minds. But rather than giving her access to Armand's wicked mind, I let her find out the good, old-fashioned way what he was thinking about her. It was a lot more fun that way!

I'm seriously flirting with the idea of giving Armand's twin siblings, Felicite and Henri, their own stories. What do you think? Drop me a line and let me know if you'd like to read more about the Magliore family!

Long live the ROMANCE ON THE RUN series!

As always, I love to hear from readers! Please e-mail me at author@maureen-smith.com, and visit my Web site at www.maureen-smith.com for news and updates on my upcoming releases.

Until next time, happy reading!

Maureen Smith

Chapter 1

Friday, September 5, 2008
1900 hours
Muwaiti
West of the Dominican Republic
Day 1

Secret Service Agent Lia Charles lay in a thicket of mangrove trees surrounding a ramshackle cabin thirty miles off the coast. The cabin had a palm thatch roof that sloped low over the porch, so at night it blended with the surrounding jungle. The building served as the base of operations for a small cadre of rebel soldiers led by political revolutionary Armand Magliore.

Though night had fallen, the oppressive heat and humidity had not. Lia inhaled; the air was hot, heavy and thick, pushing its way down her throat and into her lungs. Sweat ran down her sides, back and arms, causing her camouflage BDUs to stick to her skin. She briefly fantasized about an air-conditioned hotel room with a shower, a clean bed and a mini-fridge stocked with ice-cold beers.

First things first, she reminded herself.

From the deep cover of jungle, she observed the cabin through her military-issue night-vision goggles. The base camp had been under surveillance by her special ops team for the past six days. During that time, they had observed approximately nineteen soldiers armed with enough AK-47s and Uzis and RPG-2 grenade launchers to fortify a small army. From sunup to sundown, the men had arrived in dusty, open-topped jeeps and departed in what appeared to be four-hour shifts.

But on this particular night, the camp was deserted.

Conspicuously so.

"Damn it," Lia swore softly under her breath.

There was a faint rustling in the bushes behind her. She tensed, then relaxed as she was joined by Matt "Dutch" Connelly, one of the six members of her team, returning from his reconnaissance of the lowland area of the jungle.

Dutch, a Navy SEAL, was built like an NFL linebacker—big, burly, but surprisingly quick and agile. He and Lia had worked together for five years. Dutch, unlike many of his ex-military comrades, didn't subscribe to the mind-set that women don't belong on the front lines of battle. He'd always treated Lia as an equal. If he had any reservations about her role as team leader, he hid them well.

Lia began her Secret Service career as an anti-counterfeiting grunt in Financial Crimes. After distinguishing herself in there, she had been transferred to the protection detail, where she became responsible for protecting foreign heads of state and other visiting dignitaries. Her fluency in six foreign languages—Arabic, Chinese, Farsi, French, Italian and Spanish—made her a natural choice for these assignments. It hadn't hurt that she also possessed a black belt in aikido and had graduated at the top of her class from an elite military academy for girls.

At twenty-eight, Lia was already considered one of the best agents ever to be recruited by the Secret Service. Her superior fighting skills combined with a razor-sharp mind and the innate ability to remain cool under pressure had earned her the respect of agents twice her age.

But what her colleagues didn't know about her was that she could also read minds.

Lia had spent most of her life trying to avoid physical contact with others to keep from invading their private thoughts—which meant her love life was virtually nonexistent. But she had to admit that the gift had its perks. For example, she didn't have to speculate about whether or not the grinning auto mechanic was trying to rip her off. All she had to do was shake his hand and intercept his thoughts. She didn't have to wonder if a rude waitress had spit in her food to get even with her for sending it back as unsatisfactory; she'd know the moment she "accidentally" brushed against the waitress's bare arm as she set the plate on the table. And nowhere had Lia's psychic ability proved more useful than in her line of work. In some cases, being able to read a suspect's mind during an interrogation had made the difference between setting a guilty man free or detaining an innocent one.

Lia's military training gave her the clearance to participate in clandestine assignments that took her beyond the scope of the protection detail. One week ago, she had been summoned to the office of Bill McManus, assistant director of the Office of Protective Operations. She was briefed on her latest assignment, which was to lead a covert special operations unit into the jungles of Muwaiti, a war-ravaged Afro-French province in the Caribbean. Her mission was to extract revolutionary leader Armand Magliore from Muwaiti and escort him safely to the U.S., where, in ten days, he was scheduled to testify before the United Nations about a high-level assassination plot devised by his government.

Magliore had been a fearless, loyal soldier in the Muwaitian army until the assassination of the much-beloved president ushered in a new regime. President Alexandre Biassou had wasted no time establishing himself as a corrupt, ruthless dictator who disposed of anyone who dared to defy him. From innocent civilians to members of his own political party, no one was spared from his brutality.

Which made Armand Magliore something of a legend among his people.

He'd not only risked death and dismemberment by defecting from the Muwaitian army two years ago, but then he'd formed an underground resistance movement. Over the past year, he had led demonstrations and violent revolts against the government, amassing powerful enemies who would stop at nothing to keep him from leaving the country alive.

Which was what made the utter stillness of the base camp that night so unsettling to Lia.

Where are Magliore's men? she wondered.

When Magliore first brokered a deal with the United States—political asylum for his family in exchange for his testimony before the UN—he'd been instructed not to alter his routine in any way that would arouse the suspicion of President Biassou and his mercenaries, who'd been vigilantly monitoring the revolutionary leader. On the date of his extraction, Magliore and his resistance fighters were to report to the remote cabin as usual and remain there until the arrival of Lia and her tactical unit. Once Magliore was safely in custody, his men were to disband and go into hiding for their own protection.

But where the hell were they? Had Biassou's hired assassins gotten to them first?

"All clear," Dutch whispered, as he resumed his position on the muddy forest floor beside Lia. Dressed in identical camo gear, he trained his night-vision binoculars on the silent cabin. "Any movement yet?"

Lia shook her head. "It's quiet." She frowned. "Too quiet."

"Think we're walking into an ambush?"

Lia's frown deepened. Without answering, she scanned the thick jungle canopy shrouded in darkness and mist. The four remaining members of her team were strategically hidden in the surrounding brush, watching the camp's perimeter, awaiting her signal to advance.

During childhood hunting trips, Lia's father, a retired foreign service officer, had taught her to look from the corner of her eye for improved night vision, as well as to "see" with her other senses.

Reading minds won't help you much out here in the wild, he'd told her. *It's just you against nature.*

Lia listened now for the approach of enemy footsteps, swift and stealthy, but all she heard were the distinct night calls of exotic birds and the raucous wing-beats of mosquitoes and other nocturnal insects. Nearby a large snake curled around the lower branches of a tree eyed them suspiciously, but made no move to attack.

Not that Lia was concerned. The only kind of predators she needed to worry about were on foot.

Keeping her gaze trained on the cabin, Lia reached inside her field pack and pulled out a satellite phone and her GPS tracking device. Three earlier attempts to connect with the command post had failed, so she was relieved when at last she heard a crisp, familiar voice on the other line.

"We've been waiting for your call."

"I couldn't get a good signal," Lia said.

"What is your position?"

Lia rattled off the latitude and longitude coordinates from her GPS.

The high-tech surveillance systems used by the U.S. military, CIA, Secret Service and other intelligence agencies had been designed to minimize casualties in dangerous rescue missions such as these. From a height of 40,000 feet and a distance of 150 miles, the radar systems could detect a human being under cloud cover on the forest floor or inside an underground bunker.

"We have one body inside the cabin," came the report.

"Just one?"

"Yes. And you may have company soon. I count twenty bodies moving in your direction."

"On foot?"

"Negative. Judging by the rate of approach, I'd say there are three vehicles."

"How close?"

"Fifteen miles. You'd better—"

The satellite connection fizzled.

But Lia was already on her feet and hefting her M16 rifle. As Dutch followed her lead, she clicked her three-way radio. "It's showtime, boys."

They erupted from the deep cover of jungle and sprinted across the clearing toward the dark cabin. Lia led the way up to the porch. Beneath the sheltering overhang of the palm thatch roof, she held up two fingers, signaling that two of her men should stand guard outside.

Dutch kicked the locked front door, and with a loud splintering crack, it crashed inward. Leading with her M16, Lia swept into the cabin. It was pitch-black and as silent as a tomb.

At her signal, Dutch and the others separated to search the premises, moving soundlessly from room to room to check for trouble from alternate vantage points. Lia figured that Magliore was hiding somewhere, keeping himself out of sight just in case Biassou's mercenaries arrived before her team.

Or maybe he's not hiding. Maybe he's hurt, or dead.

Moving slowly and stealthily, Lia advanced farther inside the cabin. Her night-vision goggles transformed everything into a world of green phosphor and shadows. The timber walls were covered with old maps, charts and diagrams, and a shortwave radio sat on a small table near the window, the lone item of furniture in the main room.

As Lia rounded the corner to another room, she felt a prickle of awareness on the back of her neck. She whirled around just as a dark, masked figure dropped from an opening in the beamed ceiling and landed on the floor with the agility of a panther. Before she could react, the crouching menace swung his leg in a roundhouse kick that knocked the M16 cleanly from her hand. The rifle flew from her grip and was snatched up in midair as if it weighed no more than a plastic water gun.

With an android twist of her body, Lia delivered a high, powerful kick that caught the right side of her opponent's face. He grunted, his head snapping backward. Not missing a beat, Lia kicked again, but this time he anticipated her move. Without releasing the M16, he caught her leg at the height of the kick and pulled her other leg out from under her. She fell to the floor, momentarily stunned by his speed and dexterity.

He wasted no time, giving her no opportunity to recover. Standing above her, he jabbed the butt of the rifle at her head. Lia rolled quickly to her side, evading the vicious blow. He swung downward again and she rolled away, onto her back, narrowly escaping the second jab.

With lightning-quick reflexes, she reached for the 9mm clipped to her waist and pointed the gun between his eyes.

"Drop the weapon!" she shouted above the clamor of heavily booted feet pounding in their direction. She repeated the command in French.

Her assailant hesitated, his head tipped slightly to one side as he regarded her through the narrow slits in his black mask. He seemed a little surprised.

"Who are you?" he demanded in English.

Despite the perilous situation, Lia couldn't help noticing the deep, smoky timbre of his voice, tinged with the lazy lilt of the island. He was over six feet tall, solid power and muscle covered in black from head to toe.

"I'm not going to ask you again," Lia said, low and controlled. "Drop the weapon."

When he continued watching her in silence, her finger tightened on the trigger. "Don't try anything stupid. You're outnumbered."

He sent an unhurried glance over his shoulder. He seemed unfazed by the three M16s pointed unerringly at the back of his head. From behind the mask he chuckled—a low, husky rumble that made Lia's belly clench. "It appears that I am outnumbered."

Unnerved by her body's reaction to him, Lia said tersely, "Put the gun on the floor, then slide it toward me. *Slowly.*"

When he had complied and stood with his hands behind his head, his long legs braced apart, Dutch quickly patted him down for weapons. He confiscated a Glock 10mm, a 9mm with a sixteen-round clip, an AK-47 and a .45 caliber pistol.

Lia holstered her own Glock and slung the strap of her M16 over her shoulder, then sprang nimbly to her feet, aware of the minutes ticking by. The radar system had detected three vehicles fifteen miles from their location. If her team was to make it back through the jungle for their rendezvous with the chopper, they would have to leave very soon.

Every time Lia went on these assignments, she took great pains to conceal her femininity, though even a loose T-shirt and cargo pants still managed to accentuate her lithe, curvaceous figure. Her body armor concealed her frame under her camo gear, while the helmet she wore obscured her exotic features and long black hair, knotted tightly at the back of her head.

As Dutch shone his small but powerful NiCad light into the room, Lia removed her military-issue Special Forces helmet, complete with night-vision goggles and headlamp, and tucked it underneath her arm. Guided by Dutch's light, she walked over to their captive and unceremoniously ripped off his mask.

The face that stared back at her was the same one that appeared in the dossier she'd received last week, but nothing could have prepared Lia for the searing intensity of amber-colored eyes that reminded her of a tiger's, heavy-lidded and rimmed with a thick fringe of black lashes. The photographs had revealed a darkly handsome man with hard cheekbones, a square jaw and mahogany skin, but the camera lens had not captured the overwhelming sensuality of his mouth, the lush fullness of his bottom lip.

Lia cleared her throat, feeling strangely off balance. "Armand Magliore, I presume?"

He nodded once. Those feral eyes watched her with a kind of probing intensity that made her want to place her hands over vital body parts, as if he could see through her body armor.

"And you are?"

She quickly recovered her composure. "Special Agent Lia Charles. This is my team. We're here to—"

She broke off in midsentence at the expression on Magliore's face. As she watched, he looked incredulously at her and the other three agents.

And then, without warning, he threw back his head and roared with laughter.

Lia bristled. Under normal circumstances, she might have enjoyed the deep, sexy, rumbling sound—if it wasn't coming at her own expense, as she suspected.

"What's so funny?" she said through gritted teeth.

"No offense, Mademoiselle Charles," Magliore drawled insolently. "But your government must not be serious about stopping Biassou if they have sent a woman to keep me alive until the hearing."

Dutch and the others took umbrage. "Hey! What the hell—"

Lia held up a hand. "That's all right, fellas," she said in a mild tone. She refused to give Armand Magliore the satisfaction of knowing his sexist remark had gotten under her skin. Besides, it wasn't the first time someone had underestimated her because she was a woman, and it certainly wouldn't be the last.

"Mr. Magliore is entitled to his opinion," she said coolly. "However asinine it may be."

Dutch snickered. "And speaking of asinine, ask him why he attacked you a minute ago. Doesn't he know we're the good guys?"

"Apparently not," Lia said wryly.

Magliore met her gaze unflinchingly. "I had to be sure you weren't Biassou's henchmen. I apologize if I hurt or frightened you, Miss Charles. Although," he drawled, reaching up to touch the fresh wound above his right eye where Lia's boot had connected, "it would seem that *you're* the only one who came away from the skirmish unscathed."

"Too bad I didn't inflict more damage," Lia muttered under her breath.

Magliore laughed. "Now *that's* what I want to hear from the woman who's been entrusted with my life."

His words, though teasing, sobered Lia at once. What the hell was she thinking, threatening the man? Armand Magliore was her protectee. No matter how infuriating he may be, or how utterly attractive she found him, she had to remain focused and behave like the trained professional she was. His life—*and* her career—depended on it.

"Where are your soldiers?" she asked him.

"They're not here."

"I can see that," Lia said levelly, striving for patience. "They were supposed to be here with you this evening. That was the plan."

His gaze turned coolly belligerent. "I sent them away."

"Why?"

"There was no need for them to be here. *I'm* the one you were coming for, not them."

"Which is why you were instructed not to alter your routine in any way that would compromise the extraction," Lia said tightly. "The sudden absence of your men would arouse suspicion in anyone who's been monitoring the cabin over the last several months—namely Biassou."

Magliore's expression hardened. "My men have been

fighting for me, and alongside me, for the last two years. They've repeatedly put their lives on the line and risked the safety of their families for a war *I* started! I instructed them to stay away from the cabin today because I didn't want to risk their lives any more than I already have. If I die tonight trying to leave Muwaiti, there's no earthly reason they should perish with me."

Lia stared at him, torn between two warring emotions. On one hand she admired his unselfishness and fierce devotion to his men, but on the other hand she was furious that he'd willfully defied their instructions and possibly compromised the entire operation.

"We've got company," Javier Garcia announced from the open doorway of the cabin. "We just spotted three jeeps heading down the road."

Galvanized into action, Dutch and the others rushed out of the cabin, weapons at the ready. When Magliore moved to follow them, Lia reached out quickly, grabbing his arm to detain him.

He scowled down at her. "What are you doing?"

"I need to get you out of here," Lia said authoritatively. "Unless I'm mistaken, those are Biassou's mercenaries approaching the camp, which means we're going to be under heavy fire in less than five minutes."

"You think I don't know that?" Magliore growled, anger and impatience radiating from his body. He tried to shake off her hand, but Lia held fast. His expression turned ferocious. "Damn it, woman! Give me back my weapons so I can help your men fight!"

"No! I can't risk your life like that! It's too dangerous." When he tried to charge past her, Lia tightened her grip on his arm. She had the sensation of wrestling with a wild tiger.

"Look," she ground out. "My men are highly trained operatives with over twenty years of combat experience among them. The fact is, they don't *need* your help, Magliore. But your family does. And so do the people of Muwaiti, who've

been suffering under the brutal dictatorship of Alexandre
Biassou for years. You owe it to them to make it out of this
country alive. You're their only hope, the only one who can
ensure that Biassou is removed from power and punished for
his crimes. Are you going to let them down?"

Their gazes locked in a silent battle of wills. Leashed fury
simmered in Magliore's amber eyes. A pulse throbbed at the
base of his jaw, and beneath Lia's hand, his muscles were
rigid, primed for action. She understood, even sympathized
with his predicament. He was a soldier, trained to fight and defend his territory. He was born for battle, not to watch passively
from the sidelines. It would be hard for him to surrender his
power to another, let alone a woman. But that's the way it had
to be.

At least for the next ten days.

"We have to go," Lia said, quietly but firmly. *"Now."*

Magliore held her gaze for another tense moment, then re-
lented. "We can leave through the back door. This way." As he
grasped Lia's hand in the calloused warmth of his own, a flutter
of heat ignited in the pit of her stomach.

But she was too distracted by the jarring discovery she'd just
made to dwell on her reaction.

As Magliore led her quickly through the dark cabin, Lia
realized that for the first time in her life, she had met someone
whose mind she couldn't read.

Chapter 2

The sounds of machine-gun fire and men yelling peppered the night air as Lia and Magliore crept stealthily away from the back of the cabin. After scanning the surrounding brush to ascertain that Biassou's mercenaries were not lying in wait to ambush them, Lia signaled to Magliore, and together they quickly struck off into the deep jungle.

Lia had returned Magliore's weapons to him so that he could defend himself if they came under attack. He brought up the rear as she navigated through the thick foliage, her rifle set to burst pattern, her eyes fixed on the green-tinted shadows in her night-vision goggles as she searched for signs of other men on foot. She knew the mercenaries would be in hot pursuit once they realized that Magliore had managed to escape undetected from the cabin.

All around them the dense, sultry jungle throbbed with plant and animal life. The air was damp and heavy with the scents of fecund earth and flowers that bloomed only in the dark. There was little visibility to the sky above, except where natural openings and thin spots in the forest canopy let in shards of moonlight. Wet leaves on the ground absorbed their footfalls, but the clay mud beneath the leaves made their footing tenuous, and every slime-covered log posed a hazard. Although Lia had been to Muwaiti once before, never could she have imagined the sheer vastness of the jungle.

As they traveled farther away from the base camp, the sounds of the firefight grew quieter. Lia didn't allow herself to contemplate, even for a second, the fate of her team members. She had to remain focused on the mission that had brought her to Muwaiti: to get Armand Magliore safely to the United States. That was her first, and only, priority.

Glancing over her shoulder, she saw that Magliore was still shadowing her, his fingers clutching the barrel and stock of the AK-47 slung across his chest, ready to neutralize any threat. The rifle seemed an innate extension of him, as familiar to him as the rugged jungle terrain they were traversing. Lia could easily imagine him leading an army of brave soldiers into battle, conquering his enemy with a ruthlessness borne of pride, not cruelty.

Catching her eye, Magliore inclined his head in a nod, barely perceptible. Lia turned away, irritated with herself for romanticizing the man, as if she had nothing better to do.

She pulled out her GPS to check the approximate coordinates of the site where the chopper was to pick them up. The intermittent GPS readings on the incandescent screen confirmed that they were heading in the right direction. They should arrive at their destination in twenty minutes, barring any complications.

No sooner had she completed the thought than Lia heard a faint rustling in the trees to their right.

She froze, her heart thudding in her chest. Her finger tightened on the trigger of her M16.

Had the rest of Biassou's mercenaries caught up to them?

Or had her team members made the rustling noise as they crept through the dark jungle to meet her at the rendezvous site?

A quick glance at her GPS revealed that Dutch and the others were nowhere nearby. Which could mean only one thing.

Behind her, Magliore had stopped walking. Glancing over her shoulder, Lia signaled for him to remain silent. He nodded once.

Turning around slowly, Lia took three steps. Again she heard movement in the trees. This time the noise sounded as if it was coming closer.

Spurred by instinct, she spun around and dove in front of Magliore, knocking him to the ground just as a bullet singed the air above them. Before he could recover from the bone-jarring impact, Lia raised her rifle and fired into the dense foliage. A man's gargled scream told her she'd hit her mark.

Anticipating the return of gunfire, she sprayed the trees with three more rounds of ammo. There were more screams and angry shouts.

Taking advantage of their opponents' confusion, Lia and Magliore scrambled to their feet and ran through the thick undergrowth, keeping low to the ground as shots rang out over their heads.

They took cover behind the broad trunk of a massive tree strapped with vines. The dark jungle was lit with the deafening, staccato blasts of automatic weapons firing into the night.

Magliore returned fire, buying Lia time to reach inside her field pack and pull out a 40mm single-shot grenade launcher. With practiced ease, she attached the device under the barrel of her M16, loaded it with a high-velocity grenade and cocked the hammer. At Magliore's signal, she reached around the tree and fired into the dense brush shielding their enemies. The explosion upended a small patch of trees and sent two mangled bodies hurtling through the air. They were dead before they hit the ground.

"Let's go!" Lia shouted to Magliore.

They took off at a full sprint, slowed only by the tangle of branches and vines and slippery spots on the muddy forest floor. They ran until they reached a clearing in the jungle that stretched approximately sixty feet across, wide enough for a helicopter to land. On the opposite side, at the edge of the clearing, a small rock formation protruded from the ground. It would serve as a shield while Lia set up the flares to signal their readiness for pickup.

"We'll take cover there," she whispered to Magliore, pointing at the rock formation.

He nodded, and together they started off across the moonlit clearing, keeping their weapons drawn. Adrenaline pumped through Lia's veins, and the fine hairs at the back of her neck tingled. The night had grown unnaturally still and silent, save for the call of birds soaring above the jungle canopy.

Lia clicked her three-way radio. "Dutch, do you read?"

Dead silence greeted her.

She clicked the radio again. "Garcia, what is your position?"

Nothing.

Lia's mouth went dry. Glancing up, she found Magliore watching her, his expression unreadable in the shadowy moonlight.

Looking away, she forced herself to continue walking. She refused to speculate about whether or not her team members had been captured or killed by Biassou's mercenaries during the shootout. Her men were trained professionals who knew the risks involved in such a dangerous operation. They knew, as did Lia, that every time they embarked on one of these assignments, there was a chance they wouldn't make it back home.

Understanding the risks had never stopped any of them from accepting the call of duty.

"We can go back and get them," Magliore said in a low voice.

Lia gave her head a vigorous shake. "No. My orders were

to get you out of that cabin and safely onto the chopper, and that's what I'm going to do."

"What happens if your men don't make it here on time?"

Lia hesitated. "There's a second chopper on standby. We anticipated the possibility of getting separated."

When they were halfway across the open stretch of jungle, they heard the noisy rumble of an approaching engine. They whipped around in time to see an open-topped jeep erupt from the dense foliage, as if it had been spewed from a cannon. There were six men inside the vehicle, all dressed in camouflage gear. All but the driver were armed with submachine guns.

As the jeep roared toward Lia and Magliore, the mercenaries stood and began firing at them.

They hit the ground, returning fire as they rolled. Shots cracked in the night air and bullets thudded into metal. Magliore picked off the front passenger, whose bullet-riddled body pitched sideways and toppled from the jeep.

Lia steadied her rifle and squeezed off two three-round bursts. One of her shots shattered the windshield and took out the driver.

Out of control, with no one manning the accelerator or clutch, the jeep veered sharply off course, skidding into a tailspin as the men's panicked shouts rang out.

Not wasting a second, Lia and Magliore hurried to their feet and raced toward the rock formation less than thirty feet away.

They ducked for cover as the jeep, manned by a new driver, made a tight U-turn and began speeding toward them again. Three remaining gunmen in the rear deck fired at Lia and Magliore in rapid succession, the bullets peppering the rock they were using as cover.

Crouching beside Lia, Magliore opened fire, his AK-47 spraying a line of holes in the hood as the jeep barreled closer. Keeping her head down, Lia quickly loaded her grenade launcher, sweat rolling down her face and into her eyes, stinging them.

She had one shot, one chance to make it count. She couldn't afford to miss.

When the jeep was within twenty feet of their position, Lia peered around the rock, trained her sights on the target and pulled the trigger.

The 40mm grenade covered the distance in a split second and detonated against the jeep's fuel tank.

The explosion shook the ground, sending flames and black clouds of smoke billowing up into the sky.

Magliore grabbed Lia, instinctively using his body to shield her from flying shrapnel and debris. They lay motionless for several moments, but there were no more sounds of enemy gunfire.

After another moment, Magliore lifted his head and peered into Lia's face. "Are you all right?" he demanded.

She nodded, pulling out of his arms. Her ears were still ringing from the explosion and her right shoulder hurt like hell from knocking Magliore to the ground earlier. But other than that, she was none the worse for wear.

She peeked around the rock at the flaming remains of the jeep. "They're all dead."

"Thanks to you." Magliore's crooked grin was a slash of white in the shadowy gloom. "Nice shot."

Lia shrugged dismissively, ignoring an absurd twinge of pleasure at the compliment. After all, this was the same man who'd ridiculed her government for sending a woman to retrieve him.

In the distance she heard the whirling rotors of an approaching chopper, cutting across the dark jungle canopy as it closed in on their location.

Lia let out a long, inaudible breath.

The cavalry had arrived. Thank God.

But where were her men?

Armand Magliore stared out the window of the sleek government helicopter as it swept over the black jungle, heading away from the small island. *His* island. The only place he'd ever called home.

His chest tightened at the thought of never seeing his country again.

Armand had no illusions about what would happen if he failed to ensure Alexandre Biassou's removal from power. He could never return home, nor could his family. Biassou would have them murdered the moment their feet touched Muwaitian soil, and he would brazenly display their mutilated corpses to send a message to all others who dared to challenge his dictatorship.

Armand suppressed a shudder at the thought. Even though he was willing to be martyred, he couldn't let anything happen to his mother and twin siblings, whom he'd been responsible for since his father died eighteen years ago.

Armand had been only fourteen years old when Jacques Magliore was killed by an armed robber on his way home from work. Armand, the oldest of three siblings, had assumed leadership of the family, knowing this was what his father would have wanted—and expected—of him. It had forced him to grow up fast. Faster than any of his friends, who couldn't understand why Armand had to work in the tobacco fields instead of joining them for a leisurely afternoon of swimming at the beach. Filling his father's big shoes hadn't been easy, and Armand had often felt overwhelmed by the sheer enormity of his responsibilities. But somehow he'd survived, and so had his family.

He'd be damned if he would let anything happen to them now.

Armand took comfort in the knowledge that, for the past two weeks, his mother and siblings had been sequestered in a federal safe house outside Washington, D.C., thousands of miles beyond Biassou's reach. The Secret Service, in brokering the deal with Armand, had insisted that keeping him and his family at separate locations would be safer for everyone because Armand was Biassou's primary target, and his proximity to his family only endangered their lives more. Putting aside his own misgivings, Armand had consented to the arrangement. He'd do anything to keep his mother and siblings out of harm's way. Even if it meant staying away from them for a while.

After he testified before the United Nations Security Council and Alexandre Biassou was found guilty of his crimes, Armand would be reunited with his family. And then he would return to Muwaiti to help rebuild and restore his war-ravaged country to the idyllic paradise of his youth.

But if Biassou somehow managed to escape punishment, Armand would deliver justice for his people.

One way or another, Biassou would pay.

Until then Armand would bide his time, swallow his pride and entrust his life to the United States Secret Service.

Specifically, to the woman seated beside him in the chopper.

Lia Charles wore a calm, meditative expression as she gazed out at the dark expanse of jungle below. Her black hair was pulled back tightly from her face, except for a few stray wisps that clung to the damp skin of her forehead, cheeks and neck. To look at her, one would never suspect that she could kill with lethal precision and force. With long-lashed, dark eyes that tilted exotically at the corners, high cheekbones and a lush, sultry mouth that appeared sweeter than the ripe mangos he had devoured as a boy, Lia Charles looked more like an angel than an assassin.

Other than to answer a few questions about their travel itinerary, she'd spoken very little since they had boarded the helicopter. Armand had known she was worried about her men, though she'd tried her best to hide it. When she had finally received confirmation that they were safe and would be picked up by the second chopper, she'd closed her eyes for a moment and whispered shakily under her breath, *"Thank God."*

Armand had been intrigued by the trace of vulnerability he'd glimpsed beneath her steel veneer.

And now as he stared at her, he had to resist the urge to touch the smooth curve of her cheek, to caress the slender column of her throat, to loosen the austere knot at the nape of her neck and work his fingers through the thick, lustrous strands of her hair.

He didn't think she'd take too kindly to being touched—even by the man whose life she'd just saved.

In his thirty-two years on earth, Armand had never known another woman like her. Not only was she exquisitely beautiful, but she was also strong and fiercely courageous. She fought like a warrior and led with a confidence that dared anyone to defy her just because she was a woman.

He'd been stunned when she had removed her helmet inside the cabin and he had realized that she was the same beautiful, alluring woman who had haunted his dreams for the past eight years, ever since the first moment he had first laid eyes on her.

He remembered it as if it were yesterday. He'd been a brash young soldier in the Muwaitian army, stationed in his hometown of Port le Duc. On that fateful afternoon, he and a fellow soldier had been on their way to a neighboring military base to deliver medical equipment and supplies. They'd taken a detour through the bustling port city and found themselves stuck in a traffic jam caused by an accident that had just been cleared.

While their truck was idling at an intersection, waiting for the light to change, Armand had glanced out the passenger window.

And that's when he saw her.

She was standing with a group of peace corps volunteers who had set up a booth outside the town clinic to administer free vaccines to children from the village. A long procession of mothers, with infants balanced on tired hips and small children in tow, inched along the narrow, winding road lined with palm and banana trees.

The moment Armand saw the beautiful young American, a

hot rush of need swept through him, taking his breath away. Her long black hair was caught up in a loose ponytail, her smooth brown skin glowed beneath the Caribbean sun and her long shapely legs poured from a pair of khaki shorts that hugged her lush, round bottom.

He couldn't take his eyes off her.

His heart constricted as he watched her interacting with the children, who were terrified of the scary-looking needles. Lia distracted them while they were getting vaccinated, telling jokes and making funny faces that coaxed shy giggles from them.

Armand had silently willed her to look his way, but she never did. As the truck lurched away, he watched her through the side-view mirror until she disappeared from sight. When he returned to the clinic the next day to find her, he was told that the American peace corps volunteers had left the island that morning. He felt an acute sense of disappointment.

And loss.

He never forgot her.

Even in the dark years that would follow, as his life became consumed with fighting Biassou's reign of terror and violence, at night the beautiful American girl with the exotic Gypsy eyes and entrancing smile would come to Armand in his dreams.

And now, by some incredible stroke of fate, she was back in his life.

Armand had never been one to indulge in sentimentality. Life's harsh realities had robbed him of any such tendencies. Yet he couldn't dismiss the fact that Lia's sudden reappearance in his life was nothing short of a miracle. And he couldn't banish the uncanny sense that she had been sent there for a reason, one that transcended any political mission.

As the chopper swept out over the black ocean, bringing him closer to a foreign land, Armand realized that his destiny was irrevocably intertwined with the woman who sat quietly beside him.

Only time would reveal what that destiny was.

Chapter 3

Saturday, September 6, 2008
1900 hours
Thurmont, Maryland
Day 2

Dusk had fallen by the time an armored stretch limousine carrying Armand Magliore, Lia and three additional Secret Service agents approached an electronic gate manned by unsmiling marine guard patrols. After clearing the final security checkpoint, the limo began its gradual ascent up a steep hill that overlooked ninety forested acres nestled deep in Maryland's Catoctin Mountains. The secluded retreat, located some seventy miles northwest of Washington, D.C., featured several comfortably furnished cabins, scenic mountain views, miles of hiking trails and a stocked trout lake.

But this was no idyllic retreat for lovebirds seeking a romantic weekend getaway. The rural property was one of several owned by the U.S. government and reserved for foreign heads of state, as well as other visiting dignitaries and high-level persons under Secret Service protection. Its proximity to Camp David all but guaranteed that there was no safer place on earth to stash a revolutionary leader pursued by a ruthless, bloodthirsty despot.

Or at least that's what the Secret Service was counting on.

After the hot extraction in Muwaiti, the sleek, powerful chopper transporting Lia and Magliore had arrived at an undisclosed military base along the Gulf of Mexico just a little after 3:00 a.m. There they had been met by various top-ranking Secret Service officials, including Lia's boss, Bill McManus. He had thanked Magliore for cooperating with the United States government and conveyed a personal message from the president, who lauded Magliore for his "remarkable courage and commitment to ensuring liberation and peace for the people of Muwaiti."

While they had waited for the chopper carrying the rest of Lia's team to arrive, she and Magliore had been fed and given clean clothes. A young medic had tended to the small wound above Magliore's right eye, raising a censorious brow when he was told that Lia—not one of Biassou's mercenaries—had put it there. She hadn't bothered to defend herself, even when Magliore insolently referred to her as G.I. Jane.

Two hours later her team had arrived at the base—bedraggled, bleary-eyed, foul-tempered, but glad to be alive. When Dutch had hoisted Lia into his arms and spun her around in a dizzying circle, Magliore had watched them through cool, assessing eyes.

After an initial group debriefing with the brass, Lia and her men had been dispatched to their separate assignments—they went back to Washington, D.C., for another round of debriefing, while she was headed to the mountain retreat in rural Maryland.

Now she watched as the limo drove past a nondescript lodge used for clandestine intelligence briefings, and continued up the road before pulling into a circular driveway shared by two rustic cabins.

Lia remained inside the limo with Magliore while both buildings were checked by the other three agents who comprised the protection detail, tall men wearing dark suits, white shirts, subdued ties, dark sunglasses and the requisite earpieces. They wore microphones on their wrists and carried automatic weapons under their jackets. Lia had worked with all three men before and was satisfied that the assistant director had chosen the best for this protection detail.

While she waited for the agents to give the all-clear, Lia glanced over at Magliore, who'd been mostly silent during the ninety-minute drive from Andrews Air Force Base. He'd gazed out the window at the passing scenery, seemingly oblivious to the exchange of light banter between Lia and her colleagues. As she stole glances at him, she couldn't help wondering what he was thinking about—which, of course, would have been unnecessary if she'd been able to read his mind.

Between extracting him from Muwaiti and sitting through hours of debriefing, Lia had had little time to dwell on the startling discovery she'd made back at the cabin. But once they were comfortably ensconced in the limo, bound for their new destination, the questions had resurfaced. Her inability to read Armand Magliore's mind completely baffled her. She had never met anyone whose thoughts she couldn't intercept, and the fact that Magliore was the first made him that much more intriguing to her. Was he the yang to her yin? she wondered. Did he possess some sort of rare gene that worked as an antidote, counteracting her psychic ability? Did such a thing even exist? If her great-grandmother Genevieve were still alive, Lia definitely would have asked her. After all, she reasoned, the notion of such an antidote couldn't be any crazier than the phenomenon of mind reading.

At various intervals during the ride Lia had found herself studying Magliore's handsome profile, admiring the strong bridge of his nose and the sensual curve of those full, masculine lips before she realized what she was doing and jerked her gaze away.

This time, however, she was startled to realize he was staring right back at her. Those unusual, amber-colored eyes roamed across her face in a way that trapped the air in her lungs.

"You've had a long day," he murmured softly.

Lia glanced away, cognizant of her travel-worn appearance. "So have you. I'm sure you'll want to lie down and rest after we have dinner."

"Will you be joining me?"

When her eyes flew to his face, a hint of a wolfish smile curved the corners of his mouth. "For dinner," he clarified.

Of course that's what he meant! Get your mind out of the gutter, Lia!

She swallowed. "Yes. I mean, if you want me to."

"I want you to," he said huskily.

She nodded, shaken by the masculine heat and energy that surrounded him like a crackling force field. She averted her gaze. "All right."

After what seemed an eternity, the other agents returned from securing the premises. Lia was almost as relieved to see them as she'd been to see the approaching chopper in the night sky over the jungle.

It had been agreed that Lia, as head of the protection detail, would share the two-bedroom cabin with Magliore while the other three agents would occupy the larger cabin next door. What had seemed like a perfectly logical decision at the time— *before* Lia had met the potently virile Magliore—now sent a whisper of alarm through her as the door closed behind them.

To mask her unease, Lia gestured airily around the living room, which featured rustic pine furnishings, a high ceiling supported by rough-hewn cedar crossbeams and an enormous brick fireplace carved into the wall above a raised hearth.

"Welcome to your home away from home for the next ten days," Lia said.

Magliore cast an appraising glance over the cozily furnished room, then looked back at her. "You mean, we're to share this cabin…alone?"

Her pulse reacted to the low, velvety timbre of his voice. She cleared her throat briskly. "The other agents will be less than fifteen feet away in the next building. You'll be more than safe."

Magliore chuckled low in his throat. "Believe me, Miss Charles," he drawled, trapping her in the smoldering beam of his gaze, "that was never my concern. No man in his right mind would protest forced confinement with such an exquisitely beautiful woman as yourself."

Lia's heart thudded.

Damn. She was losing control of the situation, of herself. In the six years she'd worked for the Secret Service, not once had she ever crossed the line with a protectee. She'd never even been tempted. But Armand Magliore, with his dark good looks and raw animal magnetism, was the living, breathing embodiment of temptation. This was a man who could persuade a nun to cross the line into sin with one little crook of his finger. Lia doubted he'd ever met a woman he couldn't bend to his will.

But Lia wasn't just *any* woman. She was a highly trained Secret Service agent who'd been assigned to protect him. To do that, she needed to remain focused, professional. Detached.

And the first step would be to establish some ground rules.

Magliore was watching her, his eyes alight with keen interest. "Is something wrong, Miss Charles?"

"No. *Yes.*" Exasperated, Lia blew out a deep breath. "Look, Mr. Magliore—"

"Armand."

"Excuse me?"

His mouth twitched. "After everything we've been through in the last twenty-four hours, don't you think we've earned the right to be on a first-name basis with each other?"

Lia gave him a cool, measured look. "What I think, *Mr. Magliore*, is that I'm not here to amuse or entertain you or to keep your bed warm at night. I'm here for one reason and one reason only. To keep you alive until the date of your hearing before the United Nations. I don't expect you to like the fact that your life has been entrusted to a woman. I think you made your feelings known back in Muwaiti. You may not respect my qualifications, but I *do* expect you to respect my authority and judgment—as well as my boundaries—for the duration of our stay here. *Comprenez vous?*"

Magliore held her eyes for several long beats, as if deciding whether to even answer her.

"Do you understand?" Lia repeated in a deceptively soft tone.

After another moment he inclined his head. "*Oui.* I understand perfectly, Miss Charles."

"Good." Lia nodded briskly, then glanced at her watch. "Dinner will be here shortly. Everyone usually walks to the main lodge for breakfast, lunch and dinner, but since we arrived so late this evening, we're getting our meal delivered right to our front door. I hope you're hungry, because it's going to be quite a spread. One of the top White House stewards is on staff for the duration of the summer."

"I look forward to it," Magliore murmured. "Are there many others on the property at this time? It seems a little deserted."

"It is—for now. Sometime tomorrow we're expecting a delegation of high-ranking military officials for a three-day intelligence summit that couldn't be rescheduled. We tried to keep the number of guests as low as possible, to minimize the risk of your exposure. Only a few people know that you're here, and we'd like to keep it that way."

Magliore smiled faintly. "Am I to wear a disguise for the next ten days? Dark sunglasses and a fake mustache?"

Lia chuckled softly. "That won't be necessary. We've managed to keep the story out of the media, so even if someone were to recognize you over the next several days—which is a very remote possibility—they wouldn't know why you were here anyway. Like I said, your presence in the United States is highly classified information that only a select few are privy to."

When Magliore nodded wordlessly, she said, "If you'd like to shower and change before dinner, you'll find everything you need in your bathroom. Towels, soap, toothpaste, shaving cream—whatever you need."

Again he nodded, already starting toward one of two doorways that opened off the living room. Suddenly he stopped, looking expectantly at her over his shoulder. "Aren't you coming?"

Lia stared at him, nonplussed. "Where?"

He frowned a little. "I was under the impression you would be guarding me at all times." He paused. "Even when I'm taking a shower."

Lia felt her cheeks grow warm at the thought of herself posted outside his shower stall, trying not to peek through the steamy glass door as ribbons of water sluiced down his hard, sculpted chest and taut abdomen before rolling down those long, powerful legs.

Her mouth went dry. "I, ah, don't think that will be necessary. I'll be right outside your bedroom door if you, ah, need me."

Magliore nodded, a ghost of a smile playing at the edges of his mouth. "I won't be long."

"Take all the time you need," Lia muttered to his retreating back.

When the bedroom door had closed firmly behind him, she let out a long, shuddering breath.

At that moment, with her pulse hammering wildly and her knees shaking, she realized that extracting Armand Magliore from the dark, treacherous jungles of Muwaiti had been the easy part.

Resisting her attraction to him would test the very limits of her endurance.

Dinner, as Armand discovered that evening, was everything Lia had promised it would be.

The lavish meal—prime rib, lobster, herbed potatoes and exotic pasta dishes he'd never heard of before—was far more palatable than anything he'd eaten in the past year during his self-imposed exile to the jungles of Muwaiti. And being seated at a table draped in fine linen made him feel almost civilized again.

The only thing that would have made the meal perfect, in his opinion, was having Lia as his only dinner companion.

He'd wanted her all to himself, but she'd made sure that they were joined by the other three Secret Service agents—no doubt to serve as a buffer between her and Armand. He didn't know whether to be offended or encouraged by the fact that she thought she needed a buffer from him.

After she put him in his place earlier, he couldn't help wondering if he'd only imagined the attraction between them, the powerful connection he'd sensed back at the cabin in Muwaiti.

But then he'd watched her reaction when he had asked her whether she would be guarding him while he took a shower. It was an outrageous question, one he'd fully expected to receive another tongue lashing for. But she hadn't berated him. Instead he'd watched as a telltale flush spread across her cheeks, as those luminous, dark eyes turned smoky with desire while she tried her damnedest not to imagine him naked.

He'd grown instantly aroused.

And he'd reveled in the knowledge that she felt it, too. An explosive chemistry between them that promised unparalleled heights of ecstasy.

Now, as he watched Lia laughing and conversing with the

other three agents, his irritation grew. It was the same way he'd felt that morning when he had watched one of her men, the big one they called Dutch, pick her up and swing her around the briefing room. Armand had been seized with a fierce, primal urge to march over and snatch Lia out of his arms, then give the man a vicious left hook that would have made him wish he were back in the jungle fending off Biassou's mercenaries. Armand knew he had no right to feel so damn possessive over Lia, but he couldn't help himself. She'd haunted his dreams for so long, he felt that she already belonged to him.

Never mind that, until about a week ago, she hadn't even known that he existed.

The sound of her soft, smoky voice pulled him out of his reverie. "Would you like more potatoes?"

Armand looked at her. She held the serving spoon, poised to give him another helping of potatoes. Oddly touched by the simple gesture, he nodded, though he'd already stuffed himself and couldn't conceive of swallowing another bite of food.

"Do you like sports?" asked the agent to his right, a black man with a smooth, bald head who'd introduced himself earlier as Will Cosgrove.

"I don't follow American football, if that's what you're asking," Armand replied, because they'd been talking about their favorite football teams throughout dinner. Lia, Armand noted, not only *watched* football, but was an avid fan who could hold her own when it came to analyzing and discussing the various teams' strengths and weaknesses.

"You must like soccer," Cosgrove said to Armand, determined to engage him in conversation. "Isn't that the most popular sport in Muwaiti?"

"It is." Armand hesitated, then, making an effort to be sociable, he added, "But basketball's catching on there, too. There's been talk about forming an Olympic basketball team."

"No kidding?" Cosgrove and the other two agents exchanged vaguely amused glances. "No offense, but it'll be a long while before your team could compete with ours. We've still got the best players in the world, I don't care what *anyone* says."

"I applaud your confidence," Armand said blandly. "If nothing else."

The others laughed at the subtle barb.

"Yeah, well, we'll see who's laughing after the Olympics," Cosgrove grumbled.

"I'm sure Mr. Magliore has better things to do with his time than watch sports," Lia said quietly, meeting Armand's steady gaze across the table. "Like doing his part to ensure a better future for the people of Muwaiti."

"Good point," Cosgrove said sheepishly.

When they finished eating, Lia invited Armand and the other agents to join her in a friendly game of poker. Recognizing the ploy for what it was, Armand politely declined. Before he retired to his bedroom, however, his eyes met hers in a look that silently communicated to her that she couldn't run from him forever.

She glanced away quickly.

Now, as Armand lay in bed, staring up at the darkened ceiling, a slow, satisfied smile curved his mouth.

Lia Charles challenged him like no other.

And nothing fueled Armand more than a challenge.

But pursuing her was more than a game to him. Contrary to what she believed, he wasn't looking for a meaningless diversion or merely passing the time until the United Nations hearing. He wasn't interested in having just *any* warm, willing body in his bed.

He wanted Lia because she aroused and captivated him, and he knew that they could bring each other indescribable pleasure.

He wanted her because she'd been embedded in his soul ever since he had first laid eyes on her.

He wanted her because he no longer knew what it was like *not* to.

Armand was a patient man. He'd dreamed about Lia for

eight long, torturous years, never imagining that he'd see her again.

Eight years.

He could definitely wait a few more days—hell, even a week—to break through the barrier she had erected between them.

He knew that what awaited him on the other side would be nothing short of paradise.

Chapter 4

Saturday, September 6, 2008
0100 hours
Muwaiti
Presidential Palace
Day 2

Alexandre Biassou could not sleep.

He paced up and down the vast marble floor of his private sanctuary—the only section of the palace that servants dared not tread without his permission.

It had been nearly two hours since he'd received word that the mercenaries he'd contracted to assassinate rebel leader Armand Magliore had been killed.

All but one man had been annihilated by the Special Forces unit sent by the American government.

Even after ordering the beheading of the lone survivor—

who'd whimpered and pleaded for his miserable life—
Alexandre was still seething with fury. According to the information he'd obtained from the sniveling man, the American extraction team had been led by a woman, of all things.

A woman.

The very notion that he'd been thwarted by a mere female curdled Alexandre's stomach. That's what was wrong with the godforsaken country in the first place. It was run by women!

First they had allowed one of them to serve as secretary of state. But they hadn't learned from that mistake, promoting yet another woman to the same position nine years later. As if that weren't grievous enough, they'd allowed two successive women to preside on the nation's highest court for nearly thirty years. And then, to add insult to injury, the country had elected a woman to become president!

Imbeciles.

And they considered themselves a respectable superpower? Nonsense!

With less than two years remaining in her current term as president, the old shrew had trained her sights on Muwaiti. To strengthen her bid for reelection, she'd had the unmitigated audacity to petition the United Nations to impose tougher economic sanctions on the country if Alexandre did not end what she called his "bloody reign of terror and violence." Like the ceaseless harping of a fishwife, her shrill demands for justice for the people of Muwaiti had finally gotten the attention of the international community. Within the last year, exportation of Muwaitian goods had declined drastically as a result of aggressive trade sanctions imposed by spineless leaders who sided with the American president. Muwaiti's economy was suffering, and tourism was at an all-time low.

All because of one interfering woman.

And now, to learn that he'd been foiled by yet another female was almost more than Alexandre could stomach.

Thanks to that whore, Armand Magliore had made it safely out of Muwaiti—the very thing Alexandre had wanted to prevent!

"She fought like a warrior," the wounded mercenary had whispered before he died. He had been with the men who pursued Magliore and the warrior-woman through the jungle. Six had been on foot, six had arrived minutes later in a jeep. And then there were the eight men who'd stayed behind at the cabin to fend off the Americans.

How had twenty assassins been taken out by an army of six? *Merde!*

Jaw clenched, Alexandre stood at the windows with his hands clasped tightly behind his back and surveyed the dense jungle canopy that stretched for miles beyond the impenetrable walls of his fortress, a sprawling palace built of stone and glass and furnished with all the trappings of wealth. Far grander than anything inhabited by even the richest man on the island.

The thought brought him no consolation on this dark night.

Armand Magliore had been a thorn in his flesh for the past two years, ever since he'd defected from the Muwaitian army and formed an underground resistance movement to oust Alexandre from power.

For as long as he lived, Alexandre would remember the day of Magliore's treacherous defection. It was the same day Alexandre had nearly lost his own life.

Long before Alexandre was introduced to Armand Magliore, he'd heard of the brash young warrior. The other soldiers had grumbled about his brooding intensity and maverick ways, while infatuated young girls whispered about his dark good looks every time he passed them on the street. Magliore, the firstborn son of a tobacco farmer, had joined the Muwaitian army at the age of seventeen to help support his family, whom he'd looked after since his father's death. Though he possessed the keen intelligence of a scholar, Magliore had lacked the means to pay for an education. For-

tunately for him, Francois Seligny, the former Muwaitian president, had believed in overcompensating soldiers for serving
their country. Magliore had received a degree in engineering
from the local university and kept his family afloat with the
generous stipend he earned from the military.

Seligny, Alexandre later learned, had taken the promising
young soldier under his wing, treating him like the son he'd
never had. It was even rumored that Magliore would eventually marry the president's eldest daughter, a match undoubt-
edly conceived by Seligny himself.

When Alexandre had stopped to consider all that he had
taken from Armand Magliore, he realized it was no wonder the
rebel leader despised him so much. Not only had Alexandre
killed the man Magliore regarded as a mentor, but in so doing,
he had ruined Magliore's chance at happiness with the beautiful young woman he'd reportedly loved. After Seligny's assassination, his wife and daughters had fled the country,
vowing never to return. Magliore, Alexandre had assumed,
must have been heartbroken.

He'd known all of this on the day he had ordered Magliore
to drive him into the village on a personal errand. He'd wanted
to exercise his authority over the surly young man, teach him
that no matter what he thought of his new president, he had to
honor, respect and obey him—or suffer the consequences.

But more than anything else, he'd wanted to break
Magliore's spirit.

When they had arrived at his mistress's home that afternoon,
Alexandre had forced Magliore to stand outside in the swel-
tering heat while he entered the inviting coolness of the house.
After making love to his mistress several times and enjoying
a sumptuous meal fit for a king, Alexandre had emerged hours
later to find Magliore standing in the same spot where he'd left
him—his posture erect, his uniform still dry, his face expressionless.

Alexandre had been enraged.

Watching from the open doorway, his mistress—that faithless whore!—had laughed and joked that Magliore, who'd demonstrated remarkable stamina, should join them in bed the next time.

Alexandre had wanted to strangle her. If he hadn't thought Magliore would intervene, he would have.

During the long ride back to the palace, he'd deliberately taunted the young soldier, denouncing everything from his family to his blind devotion to Francois Seligny. Throughout the vicious verbal attack, Magliore had kept his eyes on the road and his hand steady on the steering wheel. The longer he remained silent and aloof, the more abusive Alexandre had become.

But no matter what he had said, no matter how offensive the slur, he could not goad Magliore into retaliating.

So he'd let down his guard.

Filled with good food and wine, and drowsy from hours of kinky sex with his mistress, he'd eventually dozed off in the backseat of the limousine.

He had been awakened by the cold, razor-thin blade of a knife pressed against his carotid artery. And the demon eyes that bored into his had been filled with lethal retribution.

It had been like something straight out of Alexandre's worst nightmare.

He'd swallowed convulsively, feeling the sharp blade of the knife dig deeper into the soft folds of his flesh. "W-what are you doing?" he had demanded.

Magliore had smiled, cold and deadly. *"Je vous déteste,"* he had said, his voice a silky, dangerous caress that razored along Alexandre's nerve endings. "I could slice your throat right now, from ear to ear, and not think twice about it. You deserve no less, you filthy son of a bitch."

"You would never get away with it," Alexandre had said with an implacable calm that disguised the shameful trembling in his knees. "My men would find you and kill you, then hang your rotting corpse from a tree in the town square."

Unfazed, Magliore had arched an amused brow. "Before or after they pillage your palace and make off with all your riches?"

Alexandre had clamped his lips together, not even bothering to defend his militia. He knew all too well about their reputation as "gun-toting hooligans masquerading as soldiers," as one acerbic American journalist had described them. Lawless, undisciplined men, who strutted around town brandishing their big weapons, lording their authority over everyone, stealing whatever they pleased and terrorizing poor farmers and merchants who were merely trying to provide for their struggling families.

Alexandre had known that his soldiers' loyalty to him was based on fear, not respect or admiration. He had also known that if Magliore killed him and installed himself as de facto leader, the Muwaitian soldiers would fall under his command as easily as they'd fallen under Alexandre's in the wake of Seligny's assassination.

All this had gone through his mind as he stared into Magliore's cold, feral eyes and saw the promise of his own death mirrored there.

Through the window to his left, Alexandre could see that they were parked along a narrow, deserted road flanked by dense jungle, miles from his estate. Magliore could have cut his throat and dumped him out here and no one would have ever found his body—at least not before the wild animals did their work.

Had that been Magliore's plan? Had he been plotting this all along? Had Alexandre unwittingly facilitated his own murder by ordering Magliore to drive him into the village that afternoon, leaving himself alone and at the complete mercy of a madman?

After what had seemed an eternity, Magliore had finally spoken again. "I'm leaving your godforsaken militia," he said, low and icy. "If you try to stop me, or if you harm a single member of my family, I will hunt you down and kill you. If you think for one minute that I could never make it past your armed guards, think again. Recognize this knife?"

Alexandre's gaze had dropped to the pearl-handled knife at his throat, and his stomach plummeted sickeningly. He had recognized it. It had once belonged to Francois Seligny—one of many things Alexandre had stolen from him.

The irony of him being murdered with Seligny's weapon had not been lost on him, nor on Magliore.

A malevolent gleam had filled the young rebel's eyes. "I took the knife from under your bed last night—while you were sleeping."

Alexandre had felt a chill at his words. The knowledge that Magliore had been prowling around in his bedroom while Alexandre slept—oblivious to the presence of an intruder, oblivious to the mortal danger he was in—had sent fear lancing down his spine, along with a healthy dose of outrage.

How had Magliore invaded the palace so easily? Where had the palace guards been? If Alexandre survived this terrible ordeal, he had vowed, heads would roll!

Magliore had leaned down and whispered softly in his ear, "Remember this every time you lay down to sleep, *diable*. I spared your life not once, but *twice*. I promise you that the next time we meet, I will not be so generous."

Alexandre had closed his eyes, refusing to give Magliore the satisfaction of seeing the immense relief he felt reflected in his eyes.

When he opened them again, Magliore had vanished. Taking Seligny's knife—and Alexandre's false sense of security—with him.

To this day, he could not climb into bed without hearing Magliore's threat whispering through his mind, taunting him. He'd never breathed a word of his near-death encounter to anyone. It sickened him to realize how close he'd come to losing his life, simply because he'd underestimated the extent of Magliore's hatred for him.

He would not make that mistake again.

Not that it really matters anymore, he thought bitterly. If Magliore were allowed to testify before the United Nations on September fifteenth, Alexandre would be ruined. Not only would he be removed as president of Muwaiti, but he'd also be imprisoned—possibly executed.

He couldn't let that happen.

He wouldn't.

Alexandre had worked too hard to get where he was to have it all snatched away by some traitorous dissenter. He had no intention of relinquishing control of Muwaiti.

Not without a fight. A fight he fully intended to win.

Through the high arched windows, Alexandre watched as a small brigade of armed guards patrolled the vast grounds of the estate. After the nightmare ordeal with Magliore, Alexandre had tightened security measures at the palace, taking no chances. He knew there were others, like Magliore, who opposed his regime and would do anything to overthrow him, even if it meant taking his life.

Since illegally seizing control of Muwaiti four years ago, Alexandre had not fared very well in the court of public opinion. He was vilified as a ruthless dictator. An uncivilized brute. A greedy, bloodthirsty tyrant who was unable, and *unwilling,* to heed the counsel of others, especially if it threatened his own agenda.

So against his better judgment, Alexandre had followed the advice of his political advisor, who'd warned him that assassinating Armand Magliore would plunge the already beleaguered country into a state of pure anarchy.

Magliore's brazen defection from the Muwaitian army two years ago had earned him thousands of loyal followers—weak, pathetic souls who came to regard him as their hero, their modern-day savior. Magliore represented everything Alexandre Biassou did not have—righteousness, integrity, goodness and valor. As long as the charismatic rebel leader remained alive, valiantly fighting for the cause of the Muwaitian people, they could hold on to their futile hopes and dreams for a brighter, more prosperous future.

As Magliore's popularity grew, as he successfully mobilized a growing number of dissidents, Alexandre had wanted nothing more than to capture and publicly execute the insolent traitor, making him an example to anyone who dared to defy Alexandre's authority.

But his advisor had warned him against taking such action. *"If you kill him, he will become a martyr. And nothing destroys a kingdom faster than the looming specter of a martyr."*

So Alexandre had proved his critics wrong, and heeded the man's counsel.

For over a year he'd allowed Magliore and his coarse band of freedom fighters to lead their demonstrations and revolts, many of which ended in violent clashes with members of the Muwaitian army. Although he had lost several comrades along the way, Magliore had never backed down. If anything, he seemed to grow more defiant, more relentless in his crusade to overthrow Alexandre. It was as if the loss of each soldier strengthened him, giving him a renewed sense of purpose and commitment to his cause. And instead of blaming him for the senseless deaths of their sons and brothers, the Muwaitian people simply handed over more of their men to help in the fight.

Alexandre was infuriated. He had been severely tempted to disregard his advisor's counsel and strike out, crushing Magliore beneath the heel of his boot like nothing more than an annoying insect. It didn't help that in the back of his mind lingered a secret fear that Magliore would come back to finish what he'd started in the backseat of that limousine two years ago.

Get him before he gets me, Alexandre had often thought to himself.

And then the unthinkable happened.

Jean-Claude Baptiste, a high-ranking official in Alexandre's party who was disgruntled over his limited share in Alexandre's coffers, had turned on him. He'd gone straight to Magliore and told him everything he knew about Alexandre's illegitimate presidency, including the most damaging part of all—Alexandre's plot to assassinate the president of the United States.

By the time Alexandre had learned of Baptiste's unspeakable treachery, it was too late. Magliore had already contacted the U.S. government and brokered a deal. His testimony against Alexandre in exchange for political asylum in America for his family.

Enraged, Alexandre had reacted swiftly and without mercy. He and his men had taken Baptiste out to the deepest, darkest bowels of the jungle and castrated him, leaving him there to slowly bleed to death. When Alexandre had returned an hour later, Baptiste had been gasping his last breath. Alexandre had spat in his face, then sliced open his chest and ripped out his heart. Baptiste's mutilated remains had been left behind for predators to feast upon. His heart had been delivered to Armand Magliore with a note attached: *This is what happens to traitors.*

And then, for good measure, Alexandre had put a bullet between the eyes of his advisor.

If he had not heeded the foolish man's advice in the first place, Magliore would have been dead and buried a long time ago. Instead he'd been allowed to run rampant, spreading his message of dissent among his oppressed countrymen, solidifying himself as one of Alexandre's most formidable enemies.

Alexandre clenched his jaw. As evidence that Baptiste had been secretly devising his downfall for several months, he'd kept for himself indisputable proof of the assassination plot. After he was killed, a search of his residence had revealed a locked safe filled with taped phone conversations and audio recordings from clandestine strategy meetings that had taken place right inside the presidential palace. It was not known whether he had furnished copies of these items to Magliore before he died. In all likelihood, he had not. If the U.S. government were already in possession of irrefutable evidence of Alexandre's guilt, he would already be in prison. No, they did not have the proof, he assured himself once again. They needed Magliore to appear before the United Nations Security Council and testify against Alexandre. Magliore was their secret weapon, their surprise witness. Without his official testimony, no charges could be brought against Alexandre.

He not only intended to keep Magliore from making it to that hearing, he intended to silence him permanently. As he should have done two years ago.

If only he could find capable assassins worthy of the task.

Alexandre ground his teeth. The bitter acid of bile churned in his stomach, rising in his mouth. His hands fisted so tightly that his nails dug into the calloused flesh of his palms. He didn't so much as flinch.

There were two things on this earth Alexandre Biassou could not abide. One was cowardice.

The other was failure.

He may not have succeeded in his first attempt to eliminate the defector who posed the biggest threat to his future.

But Alexandre would not fail again. As far as he was concerned, failure was not an option.

Chapter 5

Lia awakened at 4:00 a.m. to work out with the free weights and pull-up bar she'd set up in her room before going to bed the night before. As she went through her sets and reps, pushing her aching muscles to the limit, she watched as dawn broke over the Catoctin Mountains, spreading vivid flame in hues of orange and pink across the sky. It promised to be another beautiful day, one that almost made her wish she were at the scenic mountain retreat on vacation, instead of on assignment.

When she finished her workout, she showered and dressed in a crisp white button-down shirt and a pair of tan slacks. She'd washed her hair and blown it dry before she'd gone to bed. She now twisted it into a loose knot atop her head, then surveyed her reflection in the full-length mirror in the bathroom. She looked neat, sensible and professional—exactly what she'd been going for. God knows she didn't want to give Armand Magliore any reason to find her attractive. Although, she noted grimly, her travel-worn appearance hadn't seemed to make a difference at dinner last night. Every time she'd glanced across the table, she'd found Magliore watching her with that bold, possessive gaze. The heat he sent through his penetrating eyes surrounded her, leaving her with a liquid rush in unspeakable parts of her body.

She'd been secretly relieved when, after the meal, Magliore had not joined her and the others for poker, going to bed early instead. She'd waited until she could be sure he was asleep before she'd sent her colleagues on their way. And then she'd lain awake for hours, trying her damnedest not to think about the irresistibly sexy man in the room beside hers, trying not to imagine whether he slept in the nude. Of course, the more she tried not to imagine this, the more her mind wandered. She fantasized about sneaking into his room and sliding beneath his bedcovers to press her naked body against his hot, muscled flesh. He groaned huskily with pleasure and reached for her, cupping her buttocks and holding her tightly against his throbbing erection. She shivered, her clitoris swelling with arousal. She kissed his soft, sensuous lips and slipped her tongue inside his mouth as they writhed against each other.

Without breaking the kiss, Lia rose about him, straddled his hips and lowered herself onto his long, thick shaft. He swore hoarsely and began thrusting into her so hard and fast she nearly lost her balance astride him. But she held on tight for what would become the ride of her life.

The fantasy was so carnal, so *real,* that before long Lia found herself gasping for breath, two fingers pushed deep inside her body as she brought herself to a shuddering orgasm.

It had been a *long* night.

With a sigh of disgust, Lia slipped on a pair of low-heeled pumps and holstered her sidearm before heading out of the room.

It was still early, barely five-thirty. She hoped she had a few more hours to herself before Magliore woke up. She needed at least that much.

But as she stepped from her room, she noticed that his door was halfway open. She felt a slight twinge of disappointment.

So much for having a few hours to myself.

She paused in the doorway for a moment, listening for sounds of movement or running water within the room. It was silent.

She knocked softly. "Mr. Magliore?"

There was no answer.

Lia hesitated, then pushed the door all the way open and slowly entered the room. The large master suite had the same cozy, rustic furnishings as her own room, but it also featured a fireplace and a private seating area with two overstuffed chairs and an ottoman.

One half of the king-size bed was rumpled, the heavy comforter thrown back across the undisturbed side. On a wooden bench at the foot of the bed, a sturdy leather suitcase sat open, filled with the tasteful articles of clothing that had been purchased for Magliore before his arrival.

As Lia ventured farther inside the room, she prayed she wouldn't stumble upon the man naked, or worse, answering the call of nature. How embarrassing would *that* be.

"Mr. Magliore?" she called out.

Still no answer.

The bathroom was empty.

The entire suite was empty.

Lia turned and headed quickly from the room. With a mounting sense of alarm, she checked the living room and the rustic, utilitarian kitchen near the back of the cabin.

Magliore was nowhere in sight.

Cursing under her breath, Lia reached for her sidearm and

hurried toward the front door, adrenaline pumping through her veins. Her mind raced with possible scenarios of what had happened to him, foremost that he'd been kidnapped by Biassou's mercenaries in the dead of night and taken somewhere to be tortured and killed.

Oh, God. Please not that!

Lia threw open the front door and burst onto the wraparound porch.

She was brought up short by the sight of Armand Magliore standing at the wooden balustrade that curved around the wide porch. His back was turned to her, his hands shoved deep into the pockets of his dark jeans, as he stared out at the forested hills and mountains in the distance.

At her sudden appearance, he glanced over his shoulder. His lazy gaze ran the length of her, skimming over the service revolver gripped in her right hand before returning to her face.

"Good morning," he said softly.

The adrenaline ebbed from her system, replaced by an overwhelming surge of relief—and anger.

"Good morning?" Lia echoed in disbelief. "Is that all you have to say for yourself?"

He arched an amused brow at her. "I beg your pardon?"

"I thought you'd been kidnapped by Biassou's men," she burst out. "I thought they'd broken into the cabin in the middle of the night and snatched you out of bed. I thought you might already be *dead!*"

A ghost of a smile lifted the corners of his sensuous mouth. As he turned slowly to face her, Lia couldn't help noticing how nicely his jeans fit him, riding low on his lean hips and clinging to the hard, sculpted muscles of his thighs and buttocks.

Did the infuriating man have to be so damn sexy?

"As you can see," he murmured, "I'm very much alive."

"Yes, I can see that," Lia snapped. She holstered her

weapon, glaring at him. "What the hell are you doing out here by yourself, anyway?"

"I wanted to watch the sun rise. It's a simple pleasure I haven't enjoyed in over a year."

Something in the quiet admission made Lia feel guilty for yelling at him. Which only angered her more. "Yeah, well, I hope it was worth risking your life for," she said testily.

"Oh, it was, believe me. It was the most beautiful thing I've seen in a long time." Gazing at her, he added huskily, "Second only to you."

Her heart thumped, and she swallowed with difficulty. Refusing to yield to the jagged need suddenly flooding her system, Lia returned his gaze steadily. "In the future," she said, her voice carefully controlled, "please refrain from leaving the cabin unattended. My job is to protect you, but I can't do that very well if you insist on wandering off alone."

Magliore inclined his head. "Fair enough."

"Thank you."

Slightly mollified that he'd acquiesced so easily, Lia made her way across the wide porch to join him at the railing. She felt his eyes on her as she took a deep breath of cool, clean air, scented with pine and cedar and the soft perfumes of a dozen wildflowers in late-summer bloom. In the distance, the sunlight spilled over the shoulders of the Catoctin Mountains like liquid gold. Halfway up the side of the mountain range, an eagle soared above the tops of the Douglas fir and pine trees, wings outstretched as it climbed higher and higher in the air.

Lia watched in silence, letting the peace and beauty of her surroundings seep into her, if only for a few moments.

"Just for the record," she murmured, "it *was* a breathtaking sunrise."

Out of the corner of her eye, she saw Magliore smile at her. "You watched it, too?"

"Yes. *I* watched it from a window in my room. I believe yours has one, too. A window, I mean."

He chuckled softly. "Touché."

"I don't even know how you slipped past me," Lia grumbled irately, unwilling to drop the subject. "I've been up for over an hour. I didn't hear you get up or sneak past my door."

He flashed a mischievous grin. "I can be very stealthy when I want to be."

Lia frowned. "That may be true, but what about the security alarm? The control panel is supposed to emit a signal every time someone leaves or enters the cabin." Her eyes narrowed suspiciously on his handsome face. "I read in your dossier that you're very adept at taking things apart and putting them back together. Did you do something to that alarm?"

Again he chuckled. "I assure you, Miss Charles, I didn't touch the alarm."

Lia's frown deepened. She'd secured the cabin before going to bed last night, and the alarm had been working just fine. Had someone else tampered with it? She and the other three agents were the only ones who had access to the cabin, and she couldn't imagine any of them sneaking over in the middle of the night to disable the security system.

Don't overreact, Lia. Maybe there's a simple explanation for what happened. Maybe one of the wires had a short circuit.

"Let's go back inside," she said to Magliore, who was watching her intently. "I can make some coffee before we walk down to the lodge to have breakfast in an hour."

"Sounds good," he murmured. Gently he cupped her elbow and steered her toward the open doorway of the cabin, the warmth of his strong fingers penetrating the thin cotton of her blouse. Lia was too distracted by the mystery of the malfunctioning alarm to notice.

Or at least that's what she told herself.

A thorough inspection of the alarm control panel revealed nothing amiss.

After questioning the other agents, who were equally

baffled by what had happened, Lia got on the phone with her immediate supervisor in Washington. Nancy Janikowski was in charge of protective services for foreign heads of state, ambassadors and other visiting dignitaries. As team leader, she also served as liaison for agents in the field.

"Given how old those cabins are, you're bound to have some issues with faulty wiring," Janikowski said after hearing what had happened.

"How soon can you get someone out here to look into it?" Lia asked.

"It may take a day or two. I'll put in a call as soon as I get off the phone with you."

Lia nodded. It wasn't quite the answer she'd been hoping for, but she knew there was nothing she could do about it.

All thirty cabins on the property were equipped with high-tech security systems that were networked to an off-site central command center. The alarms were largely viewed as a last line of defense, and a thin one at that. The rationale was that if any unauthorized person, such as a terrorist, somehow breached all the security protocols and made it past the marine guard patrols stationed at various checkpoints on the property, an alarm would be sounded long before the intruder reached any of the cabins.

For that reason, no one at headquarters would consider it a priority to dispatch an electrician to investigate faulty wiring at a cabin that would be vacated in less than ten days anyway.

Lia knew it, and so did Janikowski.

"Try to relax a little, Lia. You're at one of the safest places in the world."

"I know," Lia murmured.

The rural mountain retreat was so secure that most agents felt comfortable giving their protectees more freedom and privacy. During a previous assignment, in which Lia had been a member of the protection detail for a Lebanese sheikh and his wife, the couple was allowed to go on long, leisurely walks while Lia and the other agents followed at a distance of a hundred yards. As long as the couple remained in their sight, the agents believed they were more than safe.

The difference between then and now, Lia reminded herself, was that Armand Magliore was no visiting dignitary. He was a hunted man. Hunted by a ruthless tyrant who would stop at nothing to keep Magliore from testifying against him. It would be foolish to underestimate Alexandre Biassou, to think the danger had passed simply because they were no longer on his turf. Lia had been trained to anticipate the impossible, to leave nothing to chance. As long as Magliore remained in her custody, she would do everything in her power to keep him safe.

Nothing less would do.

As if reading her mind, Janikowski said, "President Fordham expects us to take very good care of Magliore, to make sure all of his needs are met. Whatever he wants, we're to give it to him—within reason, of course. Do you understand?"

"Yes, ma'am," Lia said.

"Good." There was a light tapping on the other end, and Lia could imagine Janikowski seated in her tidy little office back in D.C., drumming her lacquered fingernails on the glass-topped surface of her equally tidy desk.

Even before she spoke again, Lia braced herself to receive news she wouldn't like. "You know Fordham will be traveling a lot over the next two months," Janikowski began. "Giving speeches, making her rounds at all the party conferences and caucuses, meeting with the labor unions, making her final push before the November election."

Lia shook her head at the beamed ceiling of her bedroom, where she'd retreated to make her phone call after breakfast. "Don't tell me. You're pulling the other agents from this assignment."

"Just for a few days. McManus says they're needed back on the presidential detail. You know how this works. It's an election year, and we're already stretched pretty thin as it is. What can you do?"

"Not much, apparently," Lia muttered.

But she knew Janikowski was right. Burdened by the White House's wartime security needs and the persistent threat of terrorism, the Secret Service had been showing considerable strain even before the current election year. Since September 11, the number of individuals granted Secret Service protection had doubled to include top White House aides such as the chief of staff, and national and Homeland Security advisors. In recent years, the agency had taken on additional Homeland Security jobs, which forced it to cut back on traditional financial fraud and cybercrime investigations. The reality was that the Secret Service's duties had grown faster than its funding, which meant that the agency's already stretched personnel and resources were going to be stretched even further in the years to come.

"If I didn't think you'd be okay on your own for a few days, believe me, I'd have gone right back to McManus and raised hell. But you're one of our best agents, Lia. If anyone can keep Armand Magliore alive and well, *you* can."

Lia snorted. "With all due respect," she said dryly, "resorting to flattery is *so* beneath you."

Janikowski laughed. "You're right. I'm sorry. I couldn't resist trying, anyway. And it's not like I was stretching the truth. You *are* one of the best, which is why you were handpicked for this assignment. We both know—" Just then her secretary's voice could be heard in the background. Janikowski's answer was muffled as she covered the mouthpiece with her hand.

She returned to the phone a moment later. "Hey, Lia, I've gotta run to a meeting. I'll get someone out there to look into the faulty wiring as soon as possible. I promise. If you need anything else, you know how to reach me."

"Thanks," Lia said, before disconnecting.

When she opened her bedroom door and stepped back into

the living room, she found Magliore standing near the fireplace, his posture rigid as he stared hard at the television,
which was tuned to the twenty-four-hour cable news network.
As Magliore watched the news broadcast, he wore an expression of lethal fury mingled with stark anguish. Lia was so
startled by his appearance that it took her several moments to
realize what the reporter was talking about, and when it finally
registered, she had to suppress a horrified gasp.

*"…Once again, I'm reporting live from the capital city of
Port le Duc, where early this morning Muwaitian soldiers
opened fire on a group of civilians, killing eight and wounding
two. According to Muwaitian officials, the soldiers were provoked into violence by an angry mob of protesters issuing
threats against President Alexandre Biassou—"*

"That's a damn lie!" Magliore exploded. In a fit of violent
rage, he swept his arm across the fireplace mantel, sending a
glass bowl of pine potpourri and a collection of wooden knick-
knacks crashing to the floor.

Lia held herself perfectly still. "Mr. Magliore—" she began quietly.

"They're lying through their goddamn teeth," he roared,
upending the heavy wooden ottoman and scattering a stack of
glossy coffee-table books. "Those soldiers weren't *provoked*
into anything. They killed those innocent people because that
sadistic son of a bitch *ordered* them to do it—to send a message
to me!"

Lia's heart constricted with sympathy and a shared sense of
outrage. "I'm sorry," she murmured gently. She hesitated, then
took a step toward him. "I wish there was something I could do."

Magliore met her concerned gaze, his eyes cold and hard
with controlled rage. "I have unfinished business with Alexandre Biassou," he said in a low, flat tone that spoke volumes
about violence and retribution. "Can you get me on the next
plane to Muwaiti so that I can finish what I should have done
a long time ago?"

A faint shiver passed through Lia. "You know I can't do that," she said softly.

A shadow of cynicism twisted his mouth. "Then there's nothing you can do for me." Without another word, he stormed past her and slammed out of the cabin.

Chapter 6

Lia waited a full minute before going after him, wanting to give him a moment of privacy, hoping that he wouldn't venture beyond the porch.

She should have known better.

By the time she caught up to him, he was heading away from the cabin and down a densely wooded walking trail.

She fell in step beside him, lengthening her strides to match his own. He cut her a hard sideways glance.

"I'd like to be alone for a while." He bit off his words.

Lia shook her head. "I can't leave you alone. Not while you're out here."

He clenched his jaw, but said nothing more.

They lapsed into silence, punctuated by the faint rustling of leaves, the soft chatter of birds in the trees and the occasional piercing cry of an eagle soaring overhead.

After several minutes, Lia hazarded a glance at Magliore's stony profile. "I'm a very good listener," she offered quietly.

He gave her a mocking glance. "I don't need a friend or confidante, Miss Charles. And unless I'm mistaken, neither of those duties fall under your job description."

Lia ignored the barb. "You've had a terrible shock. I can only imagine—"

"Yes," he growled, suddenly whirling on her, his tiger eyes flashing with fury. "That's *all* you can do, Miss Charles. You don't know what my people are going through, or how much they're suffering. You can only imagine. So do us both a favor, and spare me the empty rhetoric."

As he started away again, Lia reached out quickly, grabbing his arm. The look he impaled her with would have sent Goliath running for the hills, but Lia stood her ground.

"You're right," she said solemnly. "Beyond what I've read in the papers or watched on television, I *don't* know what your countrymen are going through. I've witnessed their suffering from a safe distance, through the cloudy lens of an outsider. But believe me when I tell you that I am truly saddened by what is happening in Muwaiti. I would not trivialize your pain, or that of your people, with empty rhetoric."

Magliore fell silent, a muscle ticking in his jaw as he stared at something over her head. He gave no indication he'd even heard what she said.

Lia had a sudden impulse to reach up and touch his face, to soothe his restless spirit, to ease the bitter torment reflected in his thick-lashed eyes.

Instead she dropped her hand from his rigid arm and nervously moistened her lips. "You may be surprised to know that I once visited Muwaiti," she told him casually.

His gaze flicked to hers, but he didn't speak.

"It was about eight years ago," Lia continued, undaunted by his brooding silence. "I was twenty years old, on my second summer tour with the peace corps. We stayed at this cozy little hotel in Port le Duc that served the best rum punch on the island—which was an important selling point to us, being college students and all." She gave a soft, reminiscent chuckle.

Magliore didn't even crack a smile.

"Anyway," she forged ahead, "we were only there for two weeks. Long enough for me to fall in love with the beautiful island, the gracious people, the rich, vibrant culture. And the food. God, I loved the food. We divided our time between volunteering at the clinic and delivering medications to elderly people in the village who couldn't get around on their own. It was a wonderful experience. I met an old Creole woman, who reminded me a little of my grandmother, and when I spoke French to her, she swore I was her long lost granddaughter!" Lia laughed at the memory, and this time she noticed a slight softening in Magliore's expression as he stared down at her.

She was suddenly determined to break all the way through that impenetrable mask. "No matter how late it was when we returned to our hotel," she continued, "I never missed dinner. I'm telling you, I must have gained at least fifteen pounds during those two weeks alone!"

Wry humor tugged at the corners of his mouth. "I doubt that very seriously."

Lia grinned at him. "Well, not for lack of trying, that's for damn sure. Anyway, I didn't want to leave Muwaiti. I was very sad when it was time for us to go. Don't laugh, but I felt like something was *compelling* me to stay, almost like I'd be leaving a part of myself behind if I left the island."

She felt, rather than saw, Magliore stiffen imperceptibly at those words. He studied her in a silence that vibrated like electricity between their bodies, his eyes probing hers, searching for something she couldn't begin to decipher.

Inexplicably, her palms grew damp. "As our plane took off that morning," she said, unable to break eye contact with him, "I looked out the window and, right then and there, I vowed to return to Muwaiti someday."

"And you did," Magliore said, ever so softly. "You did return."

Lia nodded. "I did. Though not exactly in the capacity I'd always envisioned," she said ruefully.

"Life can be that way sometimes," Magliore murmured. "Unpredictable."

Again she nodded, feeling strangely off balance. It was a feeling that had become all too familiar within the last two days—ever since she'd met Armand Magliore.

"Needless to say," she continued, finally dragging her gaze away from his and focusing on a point beyond his right shoulder, "I was stunned when, four years later, I learned about the assassination of President Seligny, who had so graciously welcomed us into his country. The news came as a horrible shock to all of us who had met him personally during our stay there. To know that Alexandre Biassou may have been responsible—"

"There's no *may have* about it," Magliore interrupted curtly. "He *was* responsible for murdering Seligny. And I intend to make him pay."

Lia met the lethal intent in his gaze, and a fine chill ran through her. "You'll get your chance at the hearing," she reminded him.

Magliore smiled, a cold, predatory smile that sent a whisper of warning through her. "Oh, I *will* get my chance. Hearing or not."

Lia held his gaze unflinchingly. "I hope you're not planning anything foolish. Alexandre Biassou is not worth losing your freedom over—or your life."

Magliore shook his head slowly at her. "That's where you're wrong, Miss Charles. Because of Biassou, I've already lost my freedom. And my life… Well, my life bears no resemblance whatsoever to the one I knew before he seized control of my homeland. So the way I see it, I've got nothing to lose, and everything to gain, by ridding the world of him once and for all."

"You have nothing to lose?" Lia challenged hotly. "What about your family?"

Something like pain flickered in his eyes, disappearing as swiftly as it had appeared. "My family," he said evenly, "has been through more than you could ever imagine. No matter what happens from now on, they will survive."

Before Lia could respond, he gently placed a finger against her parted lips. Heat shot through her veins as he said silkily, "Let's not continue this unpleasant conversation, *chère*. I can see that it's troubling you, and that's the last thing I want to do."

Lia jerked her head away, dangerously close to overheating from his touch. "I'm fine. You're the one I'm concerned about."

Magliore's eyes glinted with amusement. "If I didn't know better, Miss Charles, I would think you actually care whether I live or die."

"Of course I care," she grumbled. "It's my job to care."

"Your job. Right. Of course. And I suppose it's also because of your job that you looked positively terrified this morning when you thought I had been abducted and murdered by Biassou's henchmen."

"That's right." Unnerved by the knowing gleam in his eyes, Lia added glibly, "Besides, I don't want to go down in Secret Service history as the first agent to lose a protectee on only the second day of the assignment."

Magliore threw back his head and laughed, a strong, deep sound that rumbled up from his chest and made her toes curl inside her pumps.

Clearing her throat, Lia averted her gaze, staring down the path of the wooded trail they'd been following. "Would you like to continue walking, or are you ready to return to the cabin?"

"You mean, I have a choice?" Magliore asked, managing to sound both skeptical and amused.

This time Lia laughed. "Of course you have a choice! You're not a prisoner, Mr. Magliore. I don't intend to keep you locked inside the cabin for the next nine days. In fact, you may go anywhere and do anything you want on these grounds—as long as you remain in my sight at all times. Do we have a deal?"

"Absolutely," he murmured, his eyes searching hers. "You say I can go anywhere and do anything I want?"

Lia nodded.

"In that case, do you know what I'd like to do now?"

Lia could feel her pulse hammering at the base of her throat. She was almost afraid to ask, but she did anyway. "What would you like to do now?"

His gaze slid down her modest white blouse and simple tan slacks before easing back up to her face like a long caress. In a low, husky voice he said, "I'd like for you to remove that prim and proper outfit—"

Lia gasped.

"—and slip into something more comfortable so that we can, you know, go fishing."

It took several moments for the rest of his words to register. *"Fishing?"* Lia echoed dumbly, staring at him. "You want to go fishing?"

Magliore nodded. "What did you think I was going to say?"

Her eyes narrowed suspiciously on his handsome face, but his expression was innocent. Too innocent.

"Miss Charles?" he prompted, watching her expectantly. "Would you rather we do something else?"

"Oh, no!" Lia said so vehemently that he raised an amused brow at her. "We can go fishing. I don't mind at all. I used to go fishing all the time with my father. It was fun. I'll make the arrangements as soon as we get back to the cabin."

As she fell in step beside Magliore once again, Lia took comfort in the knowledge that fishing was probably the only activity that not even this man could turn into a sexually charged undertaking.

With his arms folded behind his head and his long legs stretched out before him, Armand watched with a lazy smile as Lia, standing at the opposite end of their small motorboat, closed her eyes for a moment, whispered a quick prayer, then cast her fishing lure overboard. The bait-hook hit the water with a soft *plop,* setting off gentle ripples in the clear, sun-dappled lake.

"Come on, come on. Come to mama," Lia muttered under her breath. Her lovely face was a study of concentration as she stared into the water, as if she were channeling all the trout beneath the surface of the lake to take the bait and come meet their demise.

"Third time's the charm," Armand called encouragingly to her.

Turning her head, she gave him a withering look. "I don't need *you* to remind me that I've already failed in two previous attempts to catch any fish."

Armand smothered a grin at her open hostility. "I was just trying to be supportive. But if you'd rather I didn't, I'll just sit here and enjoy the view."

The view he was referring to had nothing to do with the idyllic beauty of their surroundings—the shimmering lake surrounded by lush green forest, set against a vivid blue sky. While impressive, the scenic landscape paled in comparison to the sight of Lia in a pair of dark blue jeans that showcased the lush swell of her bottom and molded those curvaceous, impossibly long legs of hers. They were the kind of legs that could wrap around a man's waist and lead him straight to paradise, something Armand had fantasized about often enough over the past eight years.

She'd changed into a snug red T-shirt that offered enticing peeks of her midriff whenever she bent over or reached for something—which, thankfully, she'd been doing a lot during the last hour. Armand was hypnotized by the sliver of smooth, brown flesh that covered her flat, softly muscled belly. He wanted to touch her, wanted to run his fingers over her silky skin and cup her high, round breasts in his hands. He imagined leaning down and capturing a tight, dark nipple in his mouth, making her moan with pleasure as he suckled and caressed her with his tongue before lowering her body to the—

"Why is it," said Lia, breaking into his steamy musings, "that *I'm* the one doing all the hard work when it was *your* idea to go fishing in the first place?"

Armand chuckled, trying like hell to ignore the throbbing ache in his groin. If he didn't think she'd look over and catch him, he would have reached down and adjusted his jeans to relieve the straining at his zipper.

"Because we only have one fishing rod. And unless I'm mistaken," he drawled, "*you're* the one who kept bragging about what a skilled fisherman you are, how your father taught you everything he knew."

"I am," Lia insisted, scowling. "And he did. I'm just having an off day, that's all. It's been a while."

She looked so adorably frustrated that Armand took pity on her. He started to sit up. "Here, let me hel—"

"No, no," she said firmly. "I can do this. *I'll* catch the fish, and *you* can clean and cook them for dinner. How does that sound?"

At the mention of dinner, Armand felt a surge of anticipation that had nothing to do with enjoying a delicious meal. He had another—far better—reason to look forward to dinner that evening.

He and Lia would be completely alone.

Earlier that morning, she'd informed him that the other Secret Service agents were being recalled to Washington to join the president's protection detail. Armand had been thrilled to realize that he would have Lia all to himself for the next three days. Morning, noon and night, she would be his only companion, just as he'd wanted all along. It was almost too good to be true.

"I think I've got something!" Lia cried out excitedly.

Pulled from his pleasant contemplation of the evening ahead, Armand sat up, watching as Lia quickly reeled in her fishing lure.

Sure enough, she had hooked a large silver trout weighing at least five pounds, a thing of beauty. But before she could haul it in, the fish wriggled free of the hook and splashed back into the water.

Lia watched, with an expression of abject dismay, as her prize catch swam away valiantly.

Armand waited a beat, then offered the first thing that came to mind. "At least you're making progress. That trout was even bigger than the one you almost caught before."

Lia gave him a look that told him, in no uncertain terms, just what he could do with his unsolicited feedback. Armand swallowed a bark of laughter.

"If Dad could see me now," she grumbled, glaring at her fishing rod as if it were the source of all her troubles, "he would disown me."

"Oh, I doubt that very seriously," Armand drawled, reaching into the cooler on the floor beside him and pulling out two frosted beers. He twisted the cap off each bottle, then held one out to her. "Why don't you take a short break? Sometimes all you need is a little time to regroup before getting back on the horse."

Lia eyed the proffered beer for a moment, then, with a resigned sigh, she set down her fishing rod and came toward him.

Their fingers brushed as she took the cold bottle from his hand. Heat shot through his veins at the satin warmth of her skin. His body stirred with desire.

Oblivious to his reaction, Lia plunked down on the seat beside him, lifted the bottle to her lips and took a healthy swig of beer.

Armand studied her profile with a knowing grin. "It kills you, doesn't it?"

"What?" she mumbled sullenly.

"Not being the best at something. It's eating you up inside, isn't it?"

She scowled. "I wouldn't go that far."

"I would. You've got steam coming out of your ears. Ouch! It just burned me."

Her lips twitched, fighting the tug of a grin. "All right, so maybe I am a *little* annoyed."

"Just a little," Armand said, smiling.

Lia huffed out an indignant breath. "We've been out here for over an hour, and I haven't caught anything!"

"What's the rush?" Armand murmured. "The day's still young. We've got all afternoon."

"At the rate I'm going," she grumbled morosely, "it's going to take us *all night*."

Armand took a long sip of his beer, thinking of at least two other things he'd rather be doing with Lia all night. Fishing was not one of them.

"I don't understand what the problem is," she continued in exasperation. "I've never had this much trouble before. The first time I went fishing with my father, I was only seven years old, and I caught plenty of fish the first hour we were out there! Same as every other time we went fishing. Now I'll be lucky if I catch just one before we leave."

Armand leaned back on his elbows, a soft, whimsical smile playing about the corners of his mouth. "Maybe I'm the problem," he mused. "Maybe I'm bringing you bad luck."

Lia shot him a dark look. "Now that you mention it, the same thought had occurred to me."

When Armand roared with laughter, Lia grinned at him. With her long, black hair scooped into a ponytail, she looked so much like the spirited young beauty who'd captivated him all those years ago that for a moment he almost forgot they weren't back in Muwaiti. But the sight of the Glock 9mm sidearm holstered at her waist served as a sobering reminder that things were not the same as they had been eight years ago.

In more ways than one.

Determined to keep reality at bay, at least for a while longer,

Armand smiled gently at Lia. "When was the last time you went fishing with your father?"

"Six years ago," she answered. "He and my mother took me on a two-week cross-country trip the summer I graduated from college, before I started my job at the Secret Service. Dad said it would probably be a long time before we could all go on another vacation together, so he wanted to make it really special."

"And was it?"

Lia nodded. "Most definitely," she said, smiling at the memory. "We rented an RV and drove from our home in Arlington, Virginia, all the way to California. Along the way, we visited just about every national historic landmark we could, including a number of slave houses and presidential museums, Churchill Downs, the Saint Louis Arch, Rocky Mountain National Park, the Grand Canyon, the vineyards in Napa Valley and Alcatraz Island. We ended our trip at Lake Tahoe, where my father and I went camping, hiking, sailboating and fishing while my mother mostly stayed behind at the cabin and tried to recover from our travels."

Armand chuckled. "I don't blame her. It sounds like quite an adventure you had."

"Oh, it was," Lia agreed, her smile widening as she warmed to her subject. "I'd never been to any of those places before, so it really was a treat."

"Your family didn't travel a lot during your childhood?"

She laughed. "On the contrary. We traveled *all* the time. Just not in the United States. See, my father was in the foreign service, so I grew up mostly overseas. While most American kids spent their summer vacations at camp or amusement parks, I was moving all over Europe and Africa. By the time I was thirteen years old, we had lived in England, France, Germany, Italy, Japan, Senegal and South Africa."

Armand whistled softly through his teeth. "Quite the world traveler, weren't you?"

Lia grinned ruefully. "You could say that. Now don't get me wrong. I had a very fun, exciting childhood. I was constantly exposed to different people, languages and cultures, and I wouldn't trade those wonderful experiences for anything in the world. But the downside of moving around so much was that I never really felt rooted anywhere. We were always on the go, like a Gypsy caravan. In fact, that's what one of my tutors called me—her little American Gypsy."

Armand smiled softly. "You have eyes like a Gypsy. Did she ever tell you that?"

Lia nodded, chuckling. "All the time."

"Too bad," Armand said huskily. "I was hoping to be the first."

Lia met his gaze, her smile fading. Armand could tell by the way her eyes narrowed slightly that she'd caught his double meaning. Afraid that she'd put an abrupt end to the conversation and resume fishing, he smothered a wicked grin and returned to the original subject.

"Of all the places you lived, what was your favorite?" he asked.

Thankfully she took the bait. "Hmm. Let me see…" She pursed her full lips, pondering the question for a moment. "It's hard for me to pick a favorite. Each place was so unique and different from the rest, and of course, they all had their pluses and minuses. But if I absolutely had to choose a favorite place, I would say Senegal. I'll always remember the breathtakingly beautiful beaches, the exotic food and music, the vibrant people and customs. Come to think of it," she said with a surprised little smile, "I loved Senegal for many of the same reasons I loved Muwaiti so much."

Armand felt a thrill of pleasure at her words, similar to the way he'd felt earlier when Lia had revealed to him that she hadn't wanted to leave Muwaiti eight years ago, that she'd felt as if she were leaving a part of herself behind. To know that she loved his homeland even half as much as he did made his chest swell with pride and satisfaction. It also made him feel ridiculously euphoric and hopeful for the future. Because if Lia truly loved Muwaiti and wanted to see the country restored to the peaceful paradise she remembered, then just maybe—

Armand stopped himself, shaken by the direction of his thoughts. *Don't get ahead of yourself, Magliore. Concentrate on surviving the next nine days before you go making any plans for your future, let alone someone else's.*

"Because we never stayed anywhere longer than two years," Lia was saying, "I tried not to become too attached to any one country. Like I said before, it was hard to feel rooted to a place when you knew you'd be packing up and leaving at any time. Thankfully, I had the kind of parents who made anywhere we lived feel like home."

Armand noted the softness that filled her voice and the warm glow that lit her dark eyes whenever she spoke about her parents. He wanted to keep her talking, wanted to learn everything there was to know about her. What made her happy? Or angry? What was her favorite novel? Did she live alone or with a roommate? Had she ever been in love or lost her heart to anyone?

Okay, Armand amended, maybe he'd rather *not* hear the answer to those last two questions.

"Do your parents still live in Virginia?" he asked instead.

Lia nodded. "My father is retired from the foreign service, and he and my mom spend most of their free time putting around in their garden, traveling—no, they haven't had enough—and doing a lot of community outreach and fundraising. They like to keep busy, which works out fabulously for me. The busier they are, the less time they have to worry about me and my dangerous job." She chuckled wryly, leaning back and propping her booted feet up on the opposite seat. "Never mind that the kind of upbringing I had pretty much guaranteed that I could never settle for a safe, boring desk job."

"Naturally." Armand grinned, giving her a deliberate once-over. "And somehow I can't see you confined to a safe, boring desk job anyway."

She gave a husky little laugh that made his pulse leap. "Thanks. I will definitely take that as a compliment."

"You should," he murmured. "It was."

When Lia took a sip of her beer, Armand forced himself not to stare at the sight of her lush, pretty lips wrapped around the rim of the bottle, forced himself not to groan when the pink tip of her tongue flicked out to swipe a droplet of beer from her lower lip. She was a lethal combination of innocence and eroticism, strength, beauty and intelligence. It took his breath away.

Even though her posture was relaxed, he'd noted the way her dark, watchful eyes periodically scanned the surrounding forest, searching for any unseen threat.

The things a man could accomplish with a woman like her by his side, Armand thought.

Nursing their beers, they lapsed into companionable silence, lulled by the warmth of the afternoon sun on their faces, the lazy drone of a hummingbird hovering nearby, the gentle rocking motions of the boat as it bobbed in the water. Armand couldn't remember the last time he'd ever felt so relaxed and at peace with himself and his surroundings.

It had been far too long.

At length, Lia broke the silence between them. "So what about you, Magliore? What was it like growing up on a tropical island?"

He gave her an amused sidelong glance. "I can guarantee you it wasn't half as exciting as your globe-trotting childhood."

She smiled easily at him. "Let me be the judge of that."

"All right," said Armand, setting aside his empty beer bottle and hooking his hands behind his head once again. For a moment he idly surveyed their booted feet, which were propped side by side on the opposite seat. He noted the differences in their shoe sizes, struck by how much larger his own feet were. Lia Charles may be a fierce warrior, but she was also a warm, beautiful, undeniably feminine woman.

"As you might imagine," he began, "I spent much of my childhood on the water. Just to give you an idea of how much the ocean was a part of me, I learned how to swim before I could walk. I went swimming every day after school and on the weekends as soon as I finished my chores. My friends and I used to go deep-sea diving all the time. We spent hours exploring rock formations and the coral reefs, which were pretty amazing. But even when I wasn't *in* the water, I had to be *near* it. I would walk up and down the shoreline, studying tide pool after tide pool until my parents called me inside. They usually had to send my younger brother or sister to get me. That's when I would know I was in big trouble," he added with a soft, reminiscent chuckle.

Lia smiled, listening to him with an expression of such rapt absorption that his chest expanded a little. "Did you get in trouble very often?" she asked.

"Not at all," Armand lied with a straight face.

Lia didn't buy it for a second. "Yeah, right!" she said laughingly.

He feigned an affronted look. "Now why would you say that?"

Lia rolled her eyes at him in amused exasperation. "One thing I've learned about you over the last two days is that you don't follow rules very easily. Right or wrong, you march to the beat of your own drum, and something tells me you always have. So if you were even half as stubborn and maddening as you are now, then you must have *stayed* in trouble when you were a little boy."

Armand grinned at her. "You think I'm stubborn and maddening?"

"Are you kidding? I've met mules that were more cooperative than you."

He threw back his head and laughed.

Trying to hide her own smile, Lia lifted her beer bottle to her mouth and took a long sip.

As his mirth subsided, Armand shook his head slowly. "I don't think I've ever been compared to a mule and come out on the short end of the stick," he lamented. "That must be an all-time low for me."

"Don't feel bad," Lia told him cheerfully. "At least one of those mules I was referring to had been given a mild sedative before I arrived, which made him a little less ornery."

Mouth twitching, Armand arched a brow. "Are you saying you might need to sedate me in order to ensure my cooperation from now on?"

Lia laughed. "Of course not! Don't be…" She trailed off as a sudden gleam of inspiration lit her dark eyes. "But now that you mention it, that's not such a bad idea."

He shook his head, chuckling. "I'll have to keep a close eye on you, woman, just to make sure you don't slip something into my drink."

She grinned mischievously. "You shouldn't have put the idea in my head."

"*Me?* You're the one going around drugging poor mules to make them less ornery."

"What? I did not *drug* any mules," Lia laughingly protested.

"Well, then, you were an accessory," Armand said accusingly. "Which makes you just as guilty."

Lia gaped at him in comical disbelief for a moment, then burst out laughing again.

Armand grinned at her, enjoying their nonsensical banter more than anything he'd enjoyed in months. He wished they could stay out there longer, keep the rest of the world at bay forever. But he knew better.

Eyes glittering with mirth, Lia said to him, "Enough about mules. I want to hear more about Muwaiti, what it was like when you were growing up."

"How about I tell you more over dinner?" Armand proposed.

She nodded. "All right. Speaking of dinner, I'd better get busy catching some fish or we're going to starve tonight."

Armand nodded. "I have every confidence in your ability to catch the biggest trout in this lake. But if at any time you need my help, I'm right here."

Lia hesitated, then nodded. "All right."

Armand watched her get up, retrieve her fishing rod and resume her position at the opposite end of the boat. Before casting her lure over the side, she glanced back at him almost shyly.

He gave her a gentle smile of encouragement.

Her answering smile was as radiant as the afternoon sunshine. His heart thudded.

And at that moment Armand decided he would do whatever it took to make Lia Charles his.

Chapter 7

Sipping from a long-stemmed glass of white wine, Lia watched as Magliore used a spatula to turn over the large trout sizzling on the fired-up grill. Flame and smoke billowed, the savory aroma of grilled fish mingling with the scents of pine, hibiscus and night-blooming jasmine.

Two hours after returning from the lake that afternoon, she was still basking in the glow of her big catch—an eight-pound rainbow trout she'd needed help hauling into the boat, a feat for which Magliore had been more than generous in his praise. Afterward, with the prize trout slung over her shoulder, Lia had walked back to the cabin with a cocky swagger that made Magliore laugh uproariously.

Upon their return, she'd tossed a salad while he had cleaned, gutted and seasoned the trout. As they had worked alongside each other, Lia had found herself enjoying their relaxed domesticity. She couldn't remember the last time, if ever, she'd felt so comfortable with a man, especially one who did such dangerous things to her nervous system. Armand Magliore was not only the sexiest, most compelling man she'd ever known, but he was also charming, intelligent and unselfish, with a wicked sense of humor that offset some of his brooding intensity. The more time Lia spent with him, the more she wanted to learn about him—beyond what was reported in his dossier. Although a nagging voice in the back of her mind warned her that getting to know Magliore wasn't part of her mission, as the day wore on, she found it harder and harder to maintain her professional distance.

They decided to dine outdoors on the private deck that overlooked the lake and surrounding mountains. Lia felt incredibly feminine as Magliore pushed in her chair at the table, topped off her wine and served her meal with a gallant flourish.

"Thank you," she said with a soft, grateful smile.

"You're welcome," he murmured, taking a seat across the table from her.

The round wooden table had been covered with linen and adorned with a single white candle in a glass holder, which Magliore had found in the kitchen. He'd also located a small portable stereo and some reggae, calypso and steel drum CDs that Nancy Janikowski had sent in an effort to make him feel more at home. Lia had secretly watched as he crooned softly to the music while manning the grill, his hips moving in perfect time with the melodic island beats, fueling lascivious thoughts that left her feeling decidedly hot and bothered. Her one and only consolation was that Magliore couldn't read her mind any more than she could read his.

"Mmm, this is heavenly," Lia said after sampling her first bite of the tender, succulent trout. She ate another forkful and made an appreciative sound. "Cooked to perfection."

Magliore smiled. "I'm glad you like it. I can't take all the credit, though. You're the one who did all the hard work catching it."

She shook her head, smiling a little. "It was a team effort."

Remembering the way he'd fought alongside her in Muwaiti, helping her fend off the mercenaries in the jungle, she said without thinking, "We make a pretty good team, don't we?"

Something soft and intimate filled Magliore's eyes. "I was just thinking the same thing," he said huskily.

They gazed at each other for a long, electrified moment before Lia glanced away, becoming absorbed in the task of adding salt and butter to her baked potato. She racked her brain for a safe topic of conversation and said the first thing that came to mind. "Do you cook often?"

One corner of Magliore's mouth quirked. "If heating up MREs and roasting fish over a campfire count as cooking," he drawled sardonically, "then yes, I do cook often."

Too late, Lia realized her gaffe. How could she have forgotten, even for a moment, that the man seated across from her had spent the last year living in exile, holed up deep in the jungle in a ramshackle cabin that he shared with at least nineteen other men? She couldn't imagine that such a living arrangement afforded him many opportunities to hone his culinary skills.

Seeing her embarrassed expression, Magliore chuckled softly, taking pity on her. "Don't worry, you're not alone. Over the past twenty-four hours, even *I've* forgotten once or twice what my life has been like for the last year." His voice softened as he gazed at her. "Being here with you, in this beautiful place, makes it easy to forget that the rest of the world even exists."

Lia felt her insides melting at his words. *Oh, no,* she thought weakly. *I'm in deep trouble.*

Clearing her throat self-consciously, she reached for her glass of wine and took a long, fortifying sip, acutely aware of Magliore still staring at her. At that moment it occurred to her how romantic the scene might appear to the casual observer: the two of them enjoying a candlelight dinner against a scenic mountain backdrop, sipping wine from crystal glasses while

Caribbean music played softly and invitingly in the background. For one insane moment, Lia allowed herself to imagine what it would have been like if different circumstances had brought them to that secluded mountain retreat, if they were two lovebirds simply enjoying a romantic getaway instead of two strangers being hotly pursued by a vicious madman. If things had been different, she and Magliore might have watched the sunset after dinner, then melted into each other's arms to slow dance under the glittering stars. Afterward they might have slipped back inside the cabin, holding hands and wearing the dreamy smiles of lovers cocooned in their own private world. Magliore would build a fire, and they'd sit by the cozy hearth, sipping good wine and talking in low, intimate tones until he leaned over and kissed her, leaving her breathless and wanting more. More of his taste, his touch, his—

"Miss Charles?"

The sound of Magliore's deep voice brought Lia's forbidden daydream screeching to a halt—and not a moment too soon. A few seconds more, and they would have been tearing off each other's clothes and going at it in front of the fireplace.

When her startled gaze flew to Magliore's face, she found him watching her expectantly, the corners of his mouth twitching. Her face flamed, and for the second time that evening she thanked her lucky stars that the man couldn't read her mind.

Drawing in a shaky breath, she reeled in her dangerous thoughts. "I—I'm sorry," she stammered. "Did you say something?"

"Nothing important," Magliore murmured. "I asked if you could pass the butter."

"Oh! Yes, of course."

After the exchange, he asked softly, "Where'd you disappear to a minute ago? You had a faraway expression on your face. What were you thinking about?"

"MREs," Lia lied swiftly.

One dubious brow sketched upward. "MREs?"

"Yes."

MREs—meals, ready to eat—were prepackaged food rations given out to U.S. soldiers during times of war or conflict. Lia knew from firsthand experience that the meals had the soft, unappetizing consistency of room-temperature baby food, but they provided necessary sustenance to soldiers who found themselves in field conditions where organized food facilities were not available.

"I, uh, was wondering where you and your men got them?" Lia asked.

"There was a soldier in the Muwaitian militia who believed in our cause," Magliore answered, using his fork to cut into his trout. "At great risk to his own life, he provided the MREs to us, as well as some other supplies we needed."

"Does that include weapons?"

Magliore gave her a brief, enigmatic smile. "Let's just say he was willing to help our cause any way he could. Which is why he remained in the militia. He knew he could be of more use to us from the inside rather than the outside."

Lia nodded, agreeing with the rationale. "There's no question *he* was taking a huge risk. But what about *you?* How did you know you could trust him? Weren't you afraid he might turn on you at any time? If he'd been caught helping you, surely Biassou would have tortured him until he revealed critical information about your operation."

"He wouldn't have revealed anything," Magliore said with calm, implacable resolve.

Lia frowned. "How do you know?"

Magliore took a leisurely sip of his wine before answering, "Because I knew him to be an honorable, fiercely loyal man. He would have died before giving Biassou any ammunition to use against us. And," he added, gazing at his twinkling wineglass, "he had his own personal reason for wanting to destroy Biassou."

Lia waited a heartbeat. When he didn't elaborate, her curiosity got the best of her. "What was his reason?" she asked, almost dreading the answer.

Magliore slowly lifted his gaze to hers. "His younger sister was one of Biassou's many mistresses. She had the misfortune of becoming pregnant with his child. When he learned about the baby, he was furious and demanded that she get an abortion. He told her he didn't need *nor* want another one of his bastards running around the island. When she refused to get rid of the baby, saying that she loved him and wanted to bear him a son, Biassou became enraged. He beat her to within an inch of her life."

Lia let out a horrified gasp. "Oh, my God," she breathed, staring at Magliore.

His expression hardened. "By the time her brother found her that evening, she was lying on the kitchen floor in a pool of blood, barely conscious. Biassou had beaten her so badly her face was hardly recognizable." His jaw tightened. "She lost the baby. Which was what the sadistic bastard wanted, of course."

Lia shook her head, a lump of sorrow and compassion wedged in her throat. "H-how old was she?"

"Nineteen," Magliore said, his teeth clenched so hard his voice was like a growl.

Lia swallowed. "Is she…is she still alive?"

"She survived. But the injuries she sustained left her paralyzed from the waist down. She'll never walk again, nor will she ever have children."

"My God," Lia murmured hoarsely. "That monster's cruelty knows no bounds."

Magliore's lips twisted bitterly. "You don't know the half of it."

Lia suspected he was right. What she'd already read and heard about the unspeakable atrocities committed by Alexandre Biassou left her with a sick feeling in the pit of her stomach, along with a healthy dose of outrage.

Angrily she said, "No one would blame the girl's brother

for wanting to get even with Biassou, or at the very least, defecting from his damn militia."

"You're right. No one would blame him." Magliore paused. "He remains in the militia so that he can take care of his sister and make sure all of her medical needs are met. The only reason he has not torn Biassou to pieces with his bare hands is that his sister begged him not to. Even bound to a wheelchair for the rest of her life, she still managed to show mercy to the one who put her there." He shook his head, adding in a low, cynical voice, "That bastard has been shown more mercy than he could ever deserve."

Lia said nothing, fragments of their earlier conversations whispering through her mind. *I have unfinished business with Alexandre Biassou...I intend to make him pay...I've got nothing to lose, and everything to gain, by ridding the world of him once and for all.*

Lia knew a threat when she heard one, and those had all been threats with a capital *T*. But what the hell was she supposed to do? If she had reason to believe that Armand Magliore was a loose cannon plotting to assassinate the president of Muwaiti, and she failed to alert her superiors, there'd be hell to pay. As universally reviled as Alexandre Biassou was, his assassination at the hands of Magliore—while he was in the custody of the United States government—would be nothing short of a diplomatic nightmare. Not only would the Secret Service come under fire for facilitating vigilantism and the assassination of a foreign leader, but Lia would be reprimanded, possibly fired, for her perceived negligence.

But that wasn't even the worst outcome, Lia realized. If the United Nations Security Council failed to prove its case against Biassou, and Magliore decided to take matters into his own hands, he would be captured and imprisoned, or worse, killed. The idea of him suffering a slow, torturous death made her chest squeeze with an emotion akin to fear. What happened to this man mattered to her. Mattered more than she cared to admit, even to herself.

Lia frowned. If only she could get inside his head, find out what he was thinking so that she could at least *try* to talk some sense into him.

But it was no use. Since his violent outburst earlier, she'd already tried several times to read his mind, casually allowing her hand to linger on his arm, brushing against him as they walked back to the cabin. But all she got for her trouble were scorched nerve endings. No dark, brooding thoughts about revenge or assassination plots. Nothing.

For whatever reason, the inner workings of Armand Magliore's mind eluded her.

Since her gift had failed her, Lia realized that the only way to get him to confide in her was to gain his trust. In order to accomplish that, she had to befriend him, convince him that she was on his side. Which she was. She wanted nothing more than to see Biassou punished for his horrific crimes against the people of Muwaiti. Hell, if she were anything but a federal agent, she might have loaned Magliore her gun to put an end to Biassou's sorry life.

But she *was* a federal agent, which meant she couldn't stand by and do nothing if Magliore decided to seek out justice on his own.

She was so absorbed in these grim musings that she didn't notice him studying her over the rim of his wineglass until he murmured, "Time to change the subject."

Lia snapped to attention. "What? Why?"

"Because you're frowning. Which means whatever you're thinking about is upsetting you. And it would be a shame to waste any more of this meal, or this wonderful view," he said, gesturing toward the mountains, "on such an unsavory topic as Alexandre Biassou. So I propose that we change the subject. And the sooner, the better."

"All right," Lia agreed, managing a smile as she lifted her glass to her lips. "What would you like to talk about?"

"You."

She chuckled wryly. "How'd I know *that* was coming?"

"I don't know," Magliore said with a lazy smile. "Maybe you can read minds."

Lia choked on a sip of wine and began coughing.

Magliore frowned, leaning forward a little. "Are you all right?"

She nodded quickly, dabbing at the corners of her mouth with a linen napkin. "Went down the wrong way," she said hoarsely.

He eyed her a moment longer, as if trying to determine whether or not she needed the Heimlich maneuver.

"I'm fine," Lia assured him. To demonstrate, she ate a forkful of her baked potato, chewing and swallowing without incident. "What, uh, would you like to know about me?" *Besides what I can't actually tell you. Like the fact that I* can *read minds. Just not yours!*

He gave her a lopsided grin that somehow managed to be sexy and boyish at the same time. "To throw your previous question back at you, do *you* cook often?"

This time it was her turn to grin. "That, er, depends on your definition of *cooking*," she hedged.

He raised an amused brow at her. "Meaning?"

Lia's grin turned sheepish. "I can boil water, heat up frozen dinners and toss a mean salad, but that's pretty much the extent of my culinary talents."

Magliore chuckled. "And why is that?"

"Well, for starters, I'm not home very often. I've grown accustomed to eating on the go, at restaurants, hotels, airplanes, presidential retreats or wherever my various assignments take me." She shrugged, spearing a cherry tomato with her fork and popping it into her mouth. "I guess you could say I've spent the last six years, more or less, eating on my employer's dime."

Magliore smiled a little. "I guess the least they could do is feed you, considering that you put your life on the line for them every day." As he picked up his fork and resumed eating, he remarked, "You must love your job."

"I do, very much," Lia agreed without hesitation. "There's no such thing as a typical day. My job is challenging, diverse, rewarding in ways I could have never imagined. I've had the pleasure of meeting so many different types of people, from all walks of life. I have the utmost respect for the smart, dedicated people I work with. Well, *most* of them, anyway," she amended with a wry grimace.

Magliore smiled, his gaze never leaving hers. She'd noted that about him from the very beginning, the intensity with which he zeroed in on her face whenever she spoke, as if what she were saying was of immense importance to him.

A woman could get lost in those beautiful, mesmerizing eyes.

"So what are the drawbacks?" he asked.

Lia blinked. "Drawbacks?"

He nodded. "To being a Secret Service agent. What are the drawbacks?"

"Hmm." Lia pursed her lips thoughtfully. "Well, as an agent on protection details, you sort of learn the hard way that you can't make any future plans because when the time comes, there's a pretty good chance you might be halfway around the world. The reality of the job is that you're forever on someone else's schedule, and that can take some getting used to. Fortunately for me, moving around so much during my childhood prepared me to handle the transient nature of my job."

"Still," Magliore said, "it can't be very easy on your social life."

Lia gave a humorless laugh. "Social life? What's that?"

"My point exactly."

Poking at her salad, Lia lifted one shoulder in a flippant shrug. She didn't bother explaining to Magliore that even before she'd joined the Secret Service, her social life had been practically nonexistent. Being a freak of nature had a way of keeping one isolated from others.

"You're a very beautiful, desirable woman," Magliore murmured. "You can't expect me to believe you don't have someone special waiting at home."

Lia briefly considered, then decided not to berate him for asking such a personal question. Instead she met his knowing gaze with subtle defiance in her own. "What if I told you I don't?"

"Don't what? Have someone special waiting at home?"

She nodded.

A glimmer of satisfaction shone in his amber eyes. "Then I'd have to conclude that there's something seriously wrong with the men in this country."

Lia told herself it was *not* a twinge of pleasure she felt at his words. Surely she wasn't that susceptible to male flattery— even from the mouth of a gorgeous, incredibly virile man like the one seated across from her.

"How do you know the men are the problem?" she countered mildly. "How do you know *I'm* not the one who's not interested in a relationship?"

Magliore held her stare. "Are you?"

"Am I what?"

"Interested in a relationship?"

Lia pursed her lips for a moment, pretending to consider the matter. "Maybe," she said enigmatically. "Maybe not."

His gaze darkened. "That's not an answer."

"I know." Against her better judgment, Lia found herself enjoying the heady sense of playing with fire, as if she were dangling a raw steak in front of a ravenous wolf. "At any rate, what I may or may not be interested in has no bearing on this conversation."

Subtle challenge glinted in his eyes. "Doesn't it?"

"No," Lia said matter-of-factly. "It doesn't."

Instead of responding, Magliore tipped his head slightly to one side, regarding her in thoughtful silence for several long, unnerving moments. The longer he remained silent, the more Lia found herself wanting to squirm under his intense scrutiny.

Just when she thought she couldn't take it anymore, he said softly, "You know what I think?"

Lia shot him an aggrieved look. "No. But I'm sure you'll tell me."

His mouth twitched. "What I think," he said, "is that you're very young."

Lia made a strangled sound. "*Excuse* me?"

He held up a hand. "Hear me out. I'm not implying that you're immature. I'm saying that you're young. You're only twenty-eight. Young, like I said."

"What's your point?" she said through gritted teeth.

"My point," Magliore said, "is that you haven't really lived long enough to know what you want."

Lia bristled, her eyes narrowing sharply on his face. "Are you suggesting that I don't know my own mind simply because I'm still in my twenties? That is pure nonsense—an insulting, ridiculous and unfounded generalization. And besides, you're only four years older than me. That's nothing!"

A shadow of a smile touched his mouth. "I've lived a thousand lifetimes in one, *ma petite.*" In his voice Lia heard sorrow, regret, anger and the terrible pain of loss. She heard the voice of experience from a world-weary, battle-scarred soldier who'd witnessed too many atrocities and lived to tell about them.

Although her indignation had been justified, she felt small and petty for challenging him, for inadvertently diminishing the horrors he'd experienced under Biassou's brutal regime. He was right. He was a lifetime older than she, and wiser in more ways than she could ever imagine. She'd traveled around the world, immersed herself in different cultures and embarked on dangerous missions, but she'd never faced the level of adversity he had. She'd never been forced to endure the kind of hardship and suffering he had eaten, slept and breathed every day of his life for the past four years.

Before she could formulate a response, Magliore, his eyes roaming across her face, said huskily, "As to the other matter, don't think for one moment that I don't know exactly what *I* want."

Lia swallowed, ensnared by the heat of his intoxicating gaze while her heart thudded uncontrollably in her chest. Although she knew she should keep her distance from this dangerous man, she was hopelessly drawn to him. Intrigued.

Captivated.

She could not speak as he continued, "One day you're going to fall in love. Maybe not soon, but one day. Head over heels, helplessly in love. The kind where your thoughts are consumed by that person, and after a while you find yourself unable to remember what your life was like before he entered the picture. And one day, *chère,* like it or not, you're going to be forced to make a difficult choice between the job you love and the man you love. I wonder what choice you will make?"

Lia was so mesmerized by his words, and the uncanny sense that he'd looked deep into her soul and discerned her innermost desires, that it took several moments before his question sank in. When it did, she felt a fresh wave of indignation.

Her chin shot up, her eyes narrowing. "Who says I'd have to choose?" she challenged hotly. "Who says I can't have both? The man *and* the career?"

Magliore gave her a look that told her she should know better. "It doesn't really work that way."

Lia scowled. "You're only saying that because I'm a woman. I know you wouldn't have asked me that question if I were a man."

"If you were a man," he drawled blandly, "I wouldn't be remotely interested in your response."

Ignoring this remark, Lia pinned him with a direct look. "Just what do you have against women in the Secret Service?" she demanded bluntly.

Magliore frowned. "Didn't I tell you earlier that I couldn't see you confined to a safe, boring desk job?"

"Yes," she said impatiently. "But ever since we met, you've made it perfectly clear that you don't think women belong in the Secret Service, working as agents."

He opened his mouth to respond, but Lia wasn't finished.

"Look, I realize that we come from two different cultures. I've heard that Biassou is a notorious misogynist, and while I'm not putting *you* in that category, I understand that you, too, may have grown up with certain views and expectations of women. But things are different here in America. Women balance families and demanding careers all the time. We're decorated soldiers who leave behind our husbands and children for months at a time to fight overseas. We're doctors, lawyers, scientists, politicians, police officers and firefighters. We hold top-level positions in academia, business and government."

"I noticed," Magliore murmured, his mouth twitching.

"Good. So it should come as no surprise to you that when, and *if,* I find a man deserving of my love, I fully expect him to respect and support my decision to continue working as a Secret Service agent."

"And if he doesn't?" Magliore asked in a low voice.

Lia met his gaze unflinchingly. "Then he's not the one for me."

Even as the uncompromising words left her mouth, the names of over a dozen other agents who were either divorced or going through a divorce ran across her mind. Her own boss was a casualty of a failed marriage.

There was no denying the fact that the divorce rate was particularly high among those in law enforcement. Lia had no illusions about the amount of compromise and sacrifice that would be required of her and her partner to make any relationship work. She'd learned that firsthand by watching her parents. Because the family had moved around so much, her mother had never worked outside the home. She'd sacrificed her own career in finance in order to support her husband's, and although it couldn't have been easy for her, she'd never once complained—not to Lia's knowledge, anyway. Her parents had, and continued to have, the happiest, healthiest marriage she had ever known. Their relationship was based on the abundance of love, admiration and respect they'd always had for each other.

Lia knew that the demands and pressures of her job would make any future relationship challenging, but she also believed that if she found the right man, together they could make it work.

Not that finding Mr. Right would be on her radar anytime soon, she reminded herself.

Watching as Magliore took a sip of his wine, she shook her head ruefully. "I guess I should have warned you that, in addition to being a supercompetitive fisherman, I hate losing arguments," she joked, trying to inject some levity into the conversation.

The remark wrung a grim laugh from Magliore. "I would've never guessed."

Her lips twisted into a wry, self-deprecating smile. "One of the things you learn as a Secret Service agent is how to be diplomatic when diplomacy is called for, and how to be a good negotiator when diplomacy doesn't work. That said, there are certain issues I feel very strongly about, and in the process of defending my position, I've been known to come across as a bit, ah, combative."

Magliore's mouth curved in a lazy smile. "Never apologize for being passionate about your beliefs, Miss Charles. God knows I never have." He raised his glass to her in a toast. "Truce?"

Lia grinned. "Truce." They clinked glasses lightly.

Gazing across the table at him, she admired the smooth perfection of his mahogany skin in the soft candlelight, watched as the flickering flames danced across the hard angles and planes of his face. Her eyes traced the line of his thick, black brows and lingered on the sensual contours of his lips. As desire stirred within her, she looked away, her gaze settling on his strong hands clasped lightly on the table. She remembered their calloused warmth against her skin, leading her from the cabin in Muwaiti, passing her a cold bottle of beer on the boat, giving her a high-five when she caught the eight-pound trout.

She'd thoroughly enjoyed his company that afternoon, arguments or not. A part of her didn't want the day to end.

A very big part of her.

It was now dusk, the sky muted and purplish against the darkening landscape of trees. A pair of citronella torch lamps, along with the candle, cast a warm, inviting glow over the table and kept the mosquitoes at bay while fireflies flickered on and off around them. Lia felt the tranquility and beauty of her surroundings seep into her, lulling her into a state of relaxed contentment.

As she and Magliore finished their meals, they laughed and talked, picking up where they'd left off earlier at the lake. Lia listened in rapt fascination as he regaled her with stories about growing up in Muwaiti, tales that included spontaneous forays to sugarcane fields, exploring caves and chasing iguanas with his twin siblings, and going hunting and fishing with his father. Although Lia knew from his dossier that Jacques Magliore had been killed when his oldest son was only fourteen, Magliore chose not to mention this, dwelling instead on happier childhood memories. He reminisced about lying on the floor of his fourth-grade classroom and reading from his favorite book while he listened to the ocean waves crash against the rocks outside the window. That was his reward for completing his assignment early, along with the sweet treats his teacher used to sneak to him. Lia's mouth watered when he talked about how he and his friends would lie in the sun after hours of swimming and gorge themselves on luscious mangos, guavas, pineapples, pomegranates and carambolas.

She was so enthralled by the colorful sights and sounds he was describing that she didn't think to protest when he suddenly rounded the table, took her hand and pulled her gently out of her chair.

"Dance with me," he said as a reggae song with an upbeat tempo began playing on the stereo.

Lia's response was part laugh, part groan. "Do I really have—"

"Just one dance." Magliore smiled as he led her out to the

middle of the deck, the calloused warmth of his big hand sending shivers up and down her spine. "Ahh, this is one of my
favorite songs," he said as he began swaying his hips to the
music.

When Lia stood still before him, he chuckled and reached
for her, pulling her lightly into his arms. She resisted, her body
stiffening beneath his hands on her waist.

"Relax," Magliore murmured, subtly guiding her movements. "I won't bite, I promise."

"It's not that." Although it should have been. "It's just
that…I'm afraid I'm not much of a dancer. I missed most of
the high-school parties and dances, including my prom, which,
as you probably know, is the single most important social event
in any American teenager's—"

"Wait." Amber eyes searched her face. "You missed your
high-school prom?"

Lia nodded ruefully. "My father was rushed to the hospital
an hour before I was supposed to leave. He was having severe
chest pains. We thought he was having a heart attack. Thankfully it turned out to be nothing more serious than angina—
scary, but treatable."

Magliore shook his head at her. "So you spent your prom
night in a hospital emergency room?"

The compassion in his deep voice nearly brought tears to
Lia's eyes. Which made her feel like a complete fool. "I didn't
tell you that to make you feel sorry for me," she said almost
defensively. "I just wanted you to understand why your dance
partner may have two left feet."

"You're doing just fine to me."

"I—" With a start, Lia realized that they had been swaying
rhythmically to the music the entire time they were talking. The
moment she became cognizant of it, she stumbled.

"It's okay," Magliore said softly. "Just relax and absorb the
music. Your body will do the rest."

He was right. Before long Lia felt her limbs loosening as

she emptied her mind of everything but this moment. As one song segued into another, she felt herself surrendering to the music, keeping her upper body relaxed and steady while her hips undulated to the edgy, pulsing rhythms. Magliore held her gaze as they danced, and there was something so powerfully intimate about the connection between them that Lia felt naked, her soul stripped bare before him. It was like nothing she'd ever experienced in her life.

Watching her through heavy-lidded eyes, Magliore said huskily, "I knew you had it in you, *chère*. I knew the moment we met, when we crossed swords at the cabin back home, that you had this fire in you."

Lia felt herself flush, immeasurably pleased by his words. She smiled demurely at him. "You're not too bad yourself, Mr. Magliore."

Which was an understatement. Lia had watched enough movies and music videos to know that Caribbean men, generally speaking, were supposed to be amazing dancers. Armand Magliore was no exception. The languid sensuality of his movements hypnotized her. Just the way he danced left no doubt in her mind that he would be a superb lover—intensely passionate, skilled, unselfish.

Imaginative.

When her body grew hot and flushed, she knew it had nothing to do with her exertions on the dance floor.

Just then the uptempo reggae music faded into a slow love song. As Magliore drew her into his arms, bringing her flush against his body, her pulse hammered and her blood heated.

"It's getting late," she whispered shakily. "We should probably clean up and—"

"Shh. Just close your eyes and dance," he murmured, the velvety timbre of his deep voice caressing her senses, seducing her.

Although she knew she shouldn't, Lia did as he told her, curving her arms around his neck and resting her head on his shoulder. She could feel his heartbeat, strong and steady. She was breathtakingly aware of every inch of his body against hers: the strength of his arms around her, the hardness of his chest and abdomen rubbing her tingling breasts, the firm, muscular glide of his thighs against hers as they swayed to the slow, sensuous music. His heat penetrated her flesh, scorching her nerve endings. He smelled like smoke and fire from the grill, but beneath that was his own clean, uniquely male scent. Suddenly she wanted to press herself more fully against him, crawl inside his skin, touch everything, taste everything.

As if sensing a shift in her, Magliore drew back his head and looked down at her.

Their gazes locked, and for one intense moment the world swirled around them in a rush of smoky sound and dancing shadow. The smoldering heat in his eyes made her breath lodge sharply in her throat. In that instant Lia knew he was going to kiss her.

And she wasn't going to stop him.

In the far recesses of her mind, an alarm sounded, but her body was beyond heeding the warning.

As his dark head slanted over hers, her pulse quickened with anticipation. The first touch of their mouths was like an explosion in her brain, in her body. All her senses roared to life. Her breasts throbbed, heat pooled between her legs, her thighs trembled.

His soft, warm lips moved slowly and sensually over hers, drawing a helpless moan of pleasure from her. Dizzy with need, she ran her hands along his muscled upper arms, then over his broad shoulders to pull him even closer. With a low, husky groan of approval, he deepened the kiss, parting her lips so that the tips of their tongues met, making her shiver.

His tongue slid inside, exploring her mouth in silky, tantalizing strokes that sent currents of sensation whipping through her. He ate at her mouth, tasted and licked inside her as if she were made of his favorite confection and he couldn't get enough. She fell headlong into his fierce, marauding kiss, intoxicated by the taste and feel of him. The experience of him holding her, crushing her against the solid warmth of his chest, was unbearably arousing. A liquid warmth coiled inside her, drawing tighter and tighter until she thought she'd come apart in his arms. She wanted him with a desperation that terrified her—or would have, if she'd been thinking at all clearly.

But Magliore made her forget everything in those forbidden moments—she lost awareness of time, of where they were and even who she was. All she knew was that she needed him closer, deeper, tighter…his touch, his taste, his mouth devouring hers.

She nibbled and suckled his lush bottom lip, and he made a harsh sound deep in his throat, his arms tightening around her with steely strength. She trembled as his lips moved against the corner of her mouth, jaw and chin before sliding along the arch of her throat, trailing a fiery pathway of nerves.

His hands slid to her bottom, kneading her, grinding her into his pelvis so she could feel the thick, rigid length of his erection.

That was when Lia realized she'd let things go too far.

As if she'd been doused with a bucket of cold water, her body stiffened with shock. Her eyes flew open.

Magliore groaned, tightening his hold on her as she tried to pull away. "Don't go," he entreated her raggedly, his lips rasping against her throat. "Please don't go."

Lia shivered in response even as she forced herself to step out of his arms. "No," she whispered breathlessly, shaking her head. "I-I'm sorry. This is wrong. We shouldn't have done that."

Magliore was breathing as hard as she was, his chest rising and falling rapidly. He reached for her, his eyes glittering with need and frustration. "No one has to know."

"It doesn't matter," Lia said, struggling against the pleasure of his touch. "*I* know. And that's more than enough for me."

"Damn it, Lia—"

She held up a hand, cutting off the rest of his argument. She was so shaken by the explosive kiss they'd just shared that she didn't bother correcting his use of her first name. What would be the point? After what had just transpired between them, they could never return to any semblance of formality, anyway.

"Maybe you should go inside," she said, marveling at her ability to keep her voice steady when her legs were quivering uncontrollably. "I can stay out here and clean up."

A muscle worked in Magliore's jaw. He held her gaze for a long, charged moment, then abruptly turned away. "No. You go inside. I'll clean up."

"We can both—"

"You don't want to be anywhere near me right now," he said, low and dangerously controlled. "Take my word for it."

Lia swallowed, her heart thundering. Not trusting her voice, she turned without another word and beat a hasty retreat, wishing she could run all the way back to Washington, D.C., and as far away as possible from Armand Magliore.

Chapter 8

After Lia disappeared inside the cabin, Armand unleashed the brunt of his anger and frustration upon the grill. He cleaned and scrubbed the damn thing until it gleamed like new, fighting to control his raging libido as he worked.

He had kissed Lia.

After eight long, torturous years of dreaming about her and waking up in a cold sweat only to realize he might never see her again, he'd finally gotten his wish. He'd held her in his arms and he'd kissed her.

And she'd run from him, denying both of them what could have been the most spectacular night of their lives.

With a savage curse, Armand next attacked the dishes on the table. He'd been obsessed with Lia for so long, he'd almost convinced himself that the reality of holding and kissing her could never compare to his fantasies.

He couldn't have been more wrong.

Remembering how it had felt to kiss her, to taste her lush,

sweet lips and caress her warm, silky skin, Armand felt desire threatening to boil up inside him once again.

Although he'd spent the past year living in celibacy, Armand was no monk. He'd enjoyed his fair share of island beauties—women who were as appealing and diverse as the many different shades of his people.

Once upon a time, he'd even given serious thought to marrying the daughter of former president Francois Seligny. Nathalie was strong, beautiful and compassionate, and she'd loved Armand wholeheartedly. But as much as he cared for her and admired her father, Armand knew he could never belong to her as long as his dreams were haunted by visions of a beautiful young American with Gypsy eyes and a bewitching smile. Nathalie had known, too. Although he'd never told her or anyone else about Lia, Nathalie had sensed his unavailability. She'd often accused him of saving his heart for another woman, a creature of such mythic proportions mere mortals could never measure up to her, she'd said laughingly. But beneath her teasing remarks, Armand had always sensed her pain and disappointment, which made him feel guilty. He'd wanted to fall in love with her, wanted to forget his secret dreams about a woman he never expected to see again. But he couldn't. When Nathalie and her family had left Muwaiti after burying President Seligny, Armand had known it was for the best. He'd hoped, in time, that Nathalie would find someone to spend the rest of her life with, someone who would love and cherish her the way she deserved.

As for him, he'd all but resigned himself to a future of obsessing over a beautiful mystery woman he could never hope to have.

And then one day, against all odds, she had come back into his life.

The more time Armand spent with Lia, the more convinced he became that she held the key to his destiny. And now that he'd finally had a taste of her, he had to have more.

When he'd finished clearing the dishes and straightening the deck, he went to take a shower—a freezing one—to cool the fire still raging in his blood. He wanted Lia so badly he ached, wanted her more than anything he'd wanted in years.

But as he stood beneath the cold spray of water, he began to realize that all was not lost. The passion he'd experienced that night with Lia had not been one-sided. Far from it. She'd responded to his kiss with an explosive hunger that rocked him back on his heels and took his breath away. No matter what she said or did from this point on, she could no longer pretend to be immune to him. He'd tasted her need, seen the passion in her eyes, felt her surrender in his arms.

He now knew, beyond a shadow of a doubt, that she wanted him as much as he wanted her.

Which meant there was hope.

One way or another, Armand was going to have her.

How could she have been so stupid?

Several hours later as she lay in bed, Lia was still berating herself for succumbing to temptation and kissing Magliore. She couldn't believe she'd been so irresponsible, so down-right reckless. Armand Magliore was her protectee, the man whose life had been entrusted to her. Locking lips with him did *not* fall under her scope of duties.

Cursing viciously under her breath, Lia punched her pillow in frustration and flipped over, onto her back. Clasping her hands behind her head, she glared up at the darkened ceiling in angry disgust.

She had always prided herself on being a consummate pro-fessional. But there was nothing remotely professional about the way she'd behaved that evening. As if dancing with Magliore hadn't been inappropriate enough, she'd had to go and kiss him!

What the hell had she been thinking?

That's easy, her conscience mocked bitterly. *You were think-ing about his soulful bedroom eyes, his sexy mouth, his deep, mesmerizing voice. You were thinking about the way his big,*

*powerful hands would feel caressing your body, and the way
his soft, sensuous lips would feel against yours. You were thinking about everything but doing your damn job.*

Lia groaned as a fresh wave of shame engulfed her.

For all her lecturing and pontificating about the importance
of maintaining boundaries, she'd gone and done something
crazy like this. Cosgrove and the other agents hadn't even been
gone an entire day. The moment she and Magliore were completely alone, her resolve to keep him at arm's length had
flown right out the window, along with her common sense.

Lia wished she could blame her lack of self-control on too
much alcohol, but she knew better. She'd only had half a bottle
of beer and one glass of wine, hardly enough to impair her judgment. When all was said and done, she had no one but herself to
blame for what had happened that evening. Magliore hadn't
forced himself upon her. She could have refused to dance with
him, and she definitely could have stopped him from kissing her.
But she hadn't. She'd allowed him to kiss her because she was
incredibly attracted to him, and had been from the moment they'd
met. If she was completely honest with herself, she would admit
that she'd wanted this, wanted *him,* ever since she had pulled off
his mask back at the cabin in Muwaiti. One look at his mouth and
she'd known that kissing him would be an unforgettable experience.

At the memory of his hot, plundering kiss, a wanton
pleasure settled between Lia's thighs and brought another low
groan to her lips. She squeezed her eyes shut tightly in a desperate attempt to block out the forbidden images, but it was no
use. She couldn't get that mind-blowing kiss out of her mind.
She'd never experienced anything like it before, although, ad-
mittedly, her experience with men was woefully limited.

Her ability to read minds had always made the dating scene
something of a challenge—even more so than for other women.
What could be worse, Lia had often thought, than knowing the
guy she was kissing was either thinking about the basketball

game he was missing, or calculating how quickly he could get her clothes off?

Lia had often been so turned off by her dates' thoughts that they hadn't progressed beyond kissing. And *no* man had ever come close to making her feel the way Armand Magliore did.

She snatched her pillow off the bed and buried her face in it to muffle the loud, agonized groan that erupted from her mouth.

For the first time in her career—hell, in her life—Lia considered the possibility that she was in over her head. With ruthless mercenaries on the prowl, she couldn't afford the distraction of becoming romantically involved with Magliore. She needed her wits about her, needed to be alert and ready to respond to any threat. But how was she supposed to put aside her powerful attraction to Magliore and carry out her responsibilities when she couldn't stop aching for his touch, his next kiss?

She thought about calling Janikowski and asking to be reassigned. But what would Lia tell her? That the man she'd been assigned to protect was too damn sexy for his own good? For *her* own good? That Magliore wasn't the one who needed protection—*she* was?

Lia could only imagine how her supervisor would respond to such an explanation, and it wouldn't be good. Even if Janikowski granted her request to be reassigned—which was highly unlikely at this critical juncture—the damage to Lia's reputation and career would be devastating. She'd be permanently branded as the agent who had allowed her raging hormones to interfere with her ability to do her job. Everything she'd ever worked for and fought to establish for herself would be tarnished. And those who believed that women had no business working as agents in the Secret Service would feel vindicated.

And if, God forbid, something were to happen to Magliore because Lia failed to protect him, she would never forgive herself. Ever.

No, she told herself resolutely. She could not let that happen. She wouldn't abandon her post. She had to see this through. Too much was at stake. Not only her career, but a man's life—and the future of an entire country. If she continually reminded herself of just how much was riding on her shoulders, surely that would give her the strength to withstand any temptation that came her way.

Because when it came to resisting Armand Magliore and the seductive power he had over her, Lia knew she would need all the strength she could get.

Monday, September 8, 2008
0700 hours
Thurmont, Maryland
Day 4

"Rough night?" Armand murmured the next morning as he and Lia sat across the table from each other in the main lodge, where breakfast was being served. Although it was barely seven o'clock, nearly every table in the large dining room was occupied. The air hummed with clinking glasses and silverware and the low murmur of conversations.

Lia glanced up from her plate to meet his speculative gaze. "Not at all," she said quickly—too quickly. "You?"

Armand gave her a slow, lazy grin. "I slept like a baby."

"That's good." Her eyes dropped with a sweep of her long, black lashes. "I'm glad to hear it. I slept well, too."

Liar, Armand thought, his grin deepening. Even if Lia hadn't been sporting small bags under her eyes, he knew for a fact that she was lying through her pretty teeth about getting a good night's rest. He'd heard her through the wall that connected their rooms, tossing and turning restlessly in bed before getting up to work out with her free weights. Sometime in the middle of the night, he'd been awakened by the sound of her prowling around the cabin, presumably under the guise of checking locks on the doors and windows. He'd drifted back to sleep with a satisfied smile on his face, basking in the knowledge that she was as rattled by the kiss they'd shared as he was.

Reaching for his cup of coffee, Armand continued conversationally, "It's hard *not* to sleep like a baby at this place. All this clean mountain air, the peaceful sounds of nature. And those beds are amazing. Of course," he added wryly, "*anything* beats sleeping on a cold, hard floor with nineteen other men— at least half of whom snored like pigs."

"Mmm, hmm," Lia murmured noncommittally, not glancing up from her plate. It was obvious she hadn't heard a word he'd said.

Deciding to have a little fun with her, Armand said huskily, "The only thing that would make the nights more perfect is having a soft, warm body to cuddle up with. Don't you agree?"

"Definitely."

Armand waited a beat, watching as comprehension belatedly dawned on her face, causing a deep flush to crawl across her cheeks.

Mortified, her eyes flew to his face. Seeing his mischievous grin, she scowled. "Very funny."

Armand chuckled. "I thought so. You've been silent and brooding all morning. I thought you could use a laugh."

Frowning, she stirred cream and sugar into her previously untouched coffee. "I *haven't* been brooding," she grumbled.

"No? What do you call it then?"

She said nothing, carefully setting aside her spoon before lifting the cup of coffee to her mouth. She drank slowly, staring over his shoulder as she monitored traffic at the entrance to the dining room.

When they'd arrived for breakfast half an hour ago, she'd walked straight to a table in the rear corner and slid into the chair with its back to the wall, giving her a view of the whole room, just as she'd done yesterday morning. *Force of habit,* she'd admitted when Armand had commented on it. As a man who'd spent the last four years of his life looking over his shoulder for enemies, Armand had cultivated the same habit, the same need to keep a close eye on everything in his environment. But rather than claiming the chair beside Lia—which he hadn't thought she would appreciate—he'd sat down across the table from her. Which meant he had nothing to stare at but the wall—and her.

Not that he was complaining.

Finishing his breakfast, Armand leaned back in his chair, stretched out one leg and contented himself with imagining Lia in something other than the blue-and-white pinstripe blouse and pleated gray slacks she wore. Something light and gauzy, he mused. Or tight and clingy, like those snug-fitting jeans she'd changed into yesterday when they went fishing. He imagined her hair loose and tousled, as if she had just risen from bed—his bed. He imagined her lips soft and wet from his kisses, her eyes half-closed and smoky with desire.

At that moment Lia met his gaze, then glanced away quickly when she saw the naked hunger in his eyes.

Needing an excuse to relieve the sudden straining at his zipper, Armand got up, stretched his arms above his head for a moment, then rounded the table and dropped into the chair beside hers.

Her entire body grew as taut as a wire. "What are you doing?" she demanded, staring at him as if he'd lost his mind.

He gave her an unfazed look. "Changing seats."

"Yes, I can see that," she snapped. "Why?"

He lifted one shoulder in a careless shrug. "I felt like it. Is that a problem?"

"There are only two of us at this table," she ground out. "There's no reason for both of us to sit on the same side."

"Then why don't *you* move?" Armand suggested.

"Because I was sitting here first!" When he grinned at her, she must have realized how juvenile she sounded. She made a strangled noise in her throat, then clamped her mouth shut and turned away.

After fuming for several moments, she said tersely, "You're supposed to be keeping a low profile. Sitting with your back facing the room is the best way for you to do that."

"The best way for me to keep a low profile," Armand countered mildly, "is for us to eat all of our meals at the cabin. Alone." He paused, searching her taut face. "But I don't think you want that, do you, Miss Charles?"

Her eyes flickered before she jerked her gaze away. "Just try not to draw too much attention to yourself," she muttered.

He grinned, leaning back in his chair and stretching out his long legs once again. "Just call me the Invisible Man."

Lia snorted. "As if."

"Meaning?"

"As if *you* could ever be invisible. I think every female head at that table whipped around when you walked into the room this morning."

Armand smiled at her surly tone. "I didn't notice," he said honestly.

"Yeah, right. You expect me to believe that?"

He shrugged. "Believe whatever you want."

"I intend to."

As they lapsed into taut silence, Armand sipped his black coffee and idly surveyed his surroundings. The floor was thickly carpeted. Moose, elk and bear trophies were mounted on the pine walls alongside rustic wood-framed paintings that captured vintage scenes of the American West. In one corner of the room, a sedate fire crackled in the stone fireplace, warding off the morning chill in the mountain air. Several tables had been pushed together to accommodate a large group of army generals, their uniforms crisply pressed and their shoes polished to a high shine. Seated at several nearby tables were smaller, quieter groups comprised mostly of women—the secretaries and assistants, Armand assumed.

At that moment his gaze collided with a pair of dark, alluring eyes that belonged to an attractive caramel-toned woman in her early thirties. She had shoulder-length dark hair, and she wore a navy-blue pantsuit with a scooped neckline that hinted enticingly at ample cleavage. Her lips were painted a deep shade of red, curving in a bold, feline smile as she stared across the room at Armand.

He inclined his head, winking at the woman before returning his attention to Lia. He watched for a few minutes as she absently picked at her omelet, which had to be cold by now.

"Is something wrong with your food?" he finally asked.

"No," she murmured. "I'm just not that hungry."

"Eat anyway." When she arched a brow at his commanding tone, he added, "You need your strength in order to protect me, don't you?"

It was the wrong thing to say.

Lia bristled, her nostrils flaring slightly. "I don't recall asking *you* to remind me what *I* need in order to do my job, Magliore."

Realizing that he'd inadvertently struck a raw nerve, Armand pushed out a long, deep breath. "Look, if this is about last night—"

Lia flinched. "It's not," she said stiffly. "And if it's all the same to you, I'd rather not talk about last night."

Armand frowned. "You'd rather pretend it didn't happen?"

She inhaled a sharp breath and glared at him. "I'm not pretending anything. I'd just prefer not to rehash it. It happened, it was a mistake, now let's move on."

Anger stirred in his chest at her dismissive words. "What if I don't want to move on?" he challenged in a deceptively soft voice. "What if I can't?"

"That's too bad!" Belatedly remembering that they were not alone, Lia lowered her voice to a conciliatory murmur. "Look, what we did yesterday was a big mistake. I shouldn't have crossed the line with you like that. I'm sorry for giving you mixed signals. Believe me, if I could undo what happened—"

"You wouldn't."

She blinked. "Wouldn't what?"

"You wouldn't undo what happened. And do you know why?" As Armand leaned toward her, he felt a perverse twinge of satisfaction when he saw her eyes widen, heard her breath quicken. Bringing his lips close to her ear, so that anyone watching them would think he was merely sharing a joke, he said silkily, "You wouldn't change a damn thing about that kiss, because you enjoyed it as much as I did. I know it, and you know it. So please don't insult my intelligence by suggesting otherwise."

Lia swallowed hard, her pulse beating erratically at the hollow of her throat. He could feel the tension emanating from her body, matching his own. "This is neither the time nor the place to have this discussion," she said shakily.

Armand gave a harsh, mirthless laugh as he drew away from her. "Something tells me you'd say that even if we were completely alone at the cabin."

She looked at him, her eyes dark and stormy. "You don't under—"

"Excuse me, sir."

Armand and Lia glanced up sharply in unison. A member of the dining staff stood at their table balancing a drink on a silver serving tray.

He offered a sheepish smile to Armand. "I don't mean to interrupt, sir, but I was asked to give this to you."

"What is it?" Armand asked.

"A mimosa, sir. And a note. From the young lady at table nine." He lifted the tall champagne flute from the tray and set it down on the table with an elaborate flourish.

Armand chuckled softly as the steward passed him the note. "For your eyes only, she wanted me to tell you."

"Thanks," Armand said as the man bowed gracefully before departing.

Deliberately ignoring Lia, who'd remained coolly silent throughout the brief conversation, Armand unfolded the piece of paper and read the note: *A group of us are going horseback riding after lunch. I hope you can join us. My name is Tiffany, by the way.*

Lifting his head, Armand looked across the room and found the pretty woman in the navy blue pantsuit staring at him with a soft, inviting smile. He winked at her, his lips curving in a lazy half smile.

Out of the corner of his eye, he saw Lia frown as she watched the two-way exchange. "You shouldn't drink that," she said tightly.

"Why not?"

"You don't know where it came from."

Armand chuckled dryly. "It came from the kitchen."

"You don't know that for sure."

Breaking eye contact with Tiffany, Armand arched a brow at Lia. "Are you suggesting that someone is trying to poison me?" he drawled.

She met his dubious gaze unflinchingly. "It's highly possible."

"Hmm. Well, then, I guess I'll take my chances."

Before he could reach for the champagne flute, Lia snatched it away from him.

He watched in amused disbelief as she sniffed delicately at the glass, then dipped her pinky inside and sampled the cocktail.

After a long moment, she passed him the glass without a word.

"I'm touched," Armand said, half-seriously.

"By what?" she grumbled.

"By your continued willingness to risk your life for me. This mimosa could have been poisoned, as you said. You were willing to be the first to find out. I'm touched. Deeply."

Lia scowled, rolling her eyes at him. "You don't have to be a smart-ass, Magliore. I'm just doing my job."

"Right," he murmured. "Your job. How could I forget?"

She reached for her cup of coffee and took a long sip. As she did, Armand saw her trying very hard *not* to peek at the note in his hand.

His mouth twitched. "You're dying to know what it says, aren't you?" he teased.

She shook her head, quickly averting her eyes. "Not at all. It's none of my business."

"You're right about that." Armand set the glass down on the table without taking a sip. And waited.

After a prolonged moment, Lia said very casually, "Unless, of course, you're planning to do something I wouldn't approve of. Like sneaking off to be alone with your new secret admirer." When Armand said nothing, her eyes narrowed suspiciously on his expressionless face. "You *do* know that I can't allow that."

"Allow what?"

"Allow you to be alone with that woman."

"Her name is Tiffany," Armand supplied.

"Whatever. You can't go off to be alone with her. You have to remain in my sight at all times."

Instead of responding, Armand idly stroked his chin between his thumb and forefinger, feeling the rasp of bristly whiskers. Now that he'd returned to civilization, he needed to get back in the habit of shaving on a regular basis.

"Do you understand?" Lia prompted, staring at him. *"At all times."*

"If that's the way it has to be."

"It is."

"In that case," he drawled, "we've been invited to go horse-back riding this afternoon."

Lia frowned. "I really don't think it's a good idea for you to become friendly with any of these people. What if Tiffany recognizes you from old news clips, or starts asking too many personal questions?"

"I think I can handle myself."

"Of course," Lia said sardonically. "Men have perfected the art of lying and evasion."

Armand smiled. "Exactly."

"Be that as it may—"

"Aren't you the one who told me yesterday I could go anywhere and do anything I want while we're here?"

Lia hesitated, then nodded curtly.

"Well, what I want," Armand said, meeting Tiffany's gaze across the room once again, "is to enjoy the company of a beautiful woman with no strings attached. No guilt, no recriminations. No muss, no fuss."

"In other words," Lia said bitingly, "you want to have a fling."

He turned his head to look at her. "What can I say?" he murmured, deliberately baiting her. "It's been a long time."

Her mouth tightened, but she said nothing more.

Hiding a smile, Armand reached for the champagne glass and raised it in a toast to Tiffany, who beamed with pleasure before shooting a triumphant look at Lia.

Lia scowled.

And Armand downed his drink, realizing he'd just been handed his ace in the hole.

Chapter 9

For the first time in six years, Lia hated her job.

No amount of training could have prepared her for what she would endure over the next several hours.

After kissing Magliore the day before, she'd told herself that things couldn't possibly get worse.

She couldn't have been more wrong.

In hindsight, Lia realized she should have expected the worst when Magliore told her that he'd been invited to go horseback riding. He might as well have asked her to go skinny-dipping in the lake.

Although Lia had always loved animals, they'd never particularly cared for her, sensing, perhaps, that something was different about her. Whenever she approached horses they became restless, whinnying nervously, stamping the ground and trying to back away from her. Their spooked reaction to her had always made her cry as a child, but as she grew older she learned to accept that animals, like people, sometimes rejected that which they couldn't understand.

When she had first joined the protection detail, she had been required to take advanced riding lessons from the U.S. Park Police. The horse she had worked with every day for two months was an adaptable, highly trained animal that managed to put aside his own misgivings about Lia in order to help her become an adequate rider. Fortunately for her, she'd never been assigned a protectee who wanted to go horseback riding.

Until now.

The old gelding she was paired with that afternoon was especially difficult to control. Lia spent the entire three-hour jaunt through the scenic mountains gripping the reins tightly and praying that she wouldn't get thrown off the horse. The tour guide, bringing up the rear beside her on the narrow trail, kept shaking his head in bewilderment and muttering apologetically, "I don't know *what's* gotten into him, miss. He's old, but he ain't never been this cantankerous before."

Her predicament didn't escape the notice of Magliore or Tiffany, who were riding alongside each other several paces ahead. Every time the sides of their legs brushed or a private smile passed between them, Lia's stomach knotted. She told herself she didn't care that Magliore and the other woman seemed to be hitting it off so well, but she knew better. She *did* care, and it bothered her to know that he could kiss her senseless one night, then cozy up to someone else the very next day.

Not that she could really blame him, Lia grudgingly admitted. He was a gorgeous, incredibly virile man who had been living in self-imposed exile for the last year. If he'd gone that long without having sex, as he'd implied over breakfast, who could blame him for seizing any opportunity to end his sexual drought? It was clear that Tiffany, with her provocative smiles and swinging hips, was only too willing to satisfy his every need.

Which was more than Lia could offer him.

At one point during the ride, Magliore glanced over his shoulder at her. Seeing her strained expression, and assuming her ornery horse was to blame, he asked, "Are you all right?"

Lia gave him a smile etched in steel. "Just peachy," she said tightly.

Tiffany looked back at her with a sympathetic little smile that was about as genuine as a three-dollar bill. "You poor thing. Not having much fun, are you?" Turning back to Magliore, she whispered laughingly, "Let's just hope she never has to whisk you away from danger while on horseback!"

As Lia glared at the other woman, she briefly fantasized about pulling out her pistol and firing a shot into the air, sending Tiffany and her horse plunging over the side of the mountain. But then she realized that the only bolting horse would probably be hers.

As if the afternoon excursion hadn't been trying enough, she now found herself holding up a wall at an informal gathering at the Laurel Lodge, where many social functions and formal dinners were held on the property.

That evening, at least thirty men and women milled around the room, their attire ranging from casual to elegant—jeans and khaki shorts blending with dark sport coats and beaded tops. Soft, muted music flowed through the area, barely audible above the din of laughter and conversation. Members of the dining staff bustled about with professional efficiency refilling drinks and offering scrumptious hors d'oeuvres from silver trays. A fire roared in the enormous brick fireplace and the chandeliers were dimmed, creating a cozy, relaxed atmosphere.

Nursing a club soda, Lia took in the entire scene from her inconspicuous position in a corner of the room. She'd spent most of the evening watching as Magliore, seated at a blackjack table with five others, quietly and methodically outmaneuvered the dealer. Tiffany stood just behind him with one manicured hand resting possessively on his shoulder. Her hair was swept into an elegant twist and she'd changed into a black summer sheath that clung to every voluptuous curve and displayed her long, shapely legs to advantage. Every time Magliore won a hand she leaned down, deliberately treating him to an eyeful of cleavage as she whispered something in his ear. Whatever she said to him usually elicited one of his slow, lazy smiles—a smile of such potent sensuality that any woman watching would envy Tiffany. It didn't help that Magliore looked devastatingly handsome in a black knit shirt that defined his broad, powerful chest and charcoal trousers that rode his long legs as if they it had been tailor-made for him. Even if it hadn't been Lia's job to watch him, she couldn't have taken her eyes off him.

And now, the sight of his dark head bent close to Tiffany's made her grip her glass so hard it was a wonder it didn't break. She wished she had something stronger than club soda, but she knew better than to drink in public when she was supposed to be on duty.

Not that anyone would notice. After four years of working on protection details, Lia had perfected the art of invisibility. She'd learned how and when to blend into the background without ever losing sight of the protectee, or any potential threats to him.

So when two well-dressed women wandered over to the refreshment table, two feet from where Lia stood, she shamelessly eavesdropped on their conversation without fear of detection.

"I just called home to wish my son good night," the bleached blonde was saying, "and I got into the biggest argument with my husband, Lucas."

"About what?"

"Every time I have to travel he finds a reason to pick a fight with me. This time it was the fact that I missed Connor's back-to-school night, for the first time in six years, mind you. I miss it *once* and suddenly my perfect track record is nullified." She huffed out a sigh of disgust.

Her companion, a tall black woman, shook her head sympathetically. "Men and their double standards. Look around this room. Do you think the wives of these army generals are sitting at home thinking of ways to punish their husbands for missing back-to-school nights, birthday parties and Little League games?"

"Of course not. They know the deal." Another deep sigh. "I know what Lucas's problem is. He's paranoid. He thinks that the only reason we're brought on these trips is to serve as sex toys for our lecherous bosses."

"Well…"

"Rhonda!" came the scandalized admonishment.

Rhonda chuckled unabashedly. "Oh, come on, Meredith. You have to admit that a lot of hooking up *does* go on during these trips. We both know of at least three women here who are sleeping with their bosses."

"We *suspect*," Meredith corrected. "We don't know for sure."

"Humph. Well, I *suspect* that we *will* know for sure before the night is over. All you have to do is look around the room to see who's pairing up with whom, and it's pretty obvious who's going to be sneaking out of whose cabin early tomorrow morning."

"Speaking of that, did you see the way Tiffany's been hanging all over that man at the blackjack table?"

Rhonda laughed. "It's kind of hard *not* to notice. She's so obvious about it. But can you really blame her? Look at him—he's hot!"

Meredith chuckled. "You definitely won't get any argument out of me. Who is he?"

"A visiting dignitary, Tiffany told me. From some teensy-weensy country in Africa."

"Which one?"

"Oh, shoot, I can't remember." Rhonda snorted. "If I could, you'd better believe I'd be packing up and moving there tomorrow!"

Meredith cackled. "I think Tiffany might beat you to it. She's been a permanent fixture at his side all day."

"I know. She's hoping they can get rid of his Secret Service bodyguard so they can go back to Tiffany's room and get down to business, if you know what I mean."

"I think I've got a pretty good idea," Meredith said with a lascivious grin that made Lia feel decidedly violent.

As the two women moved away, she didn't know whether to be relieved that Magliore's cover story seemed to be holding up, or annoyed that he and Tiffany were planning to give her the slip sometime that evening. Realistically, Lia knew she couldn't prevent him from taking a lover. As she'd told him yesterday, he was her protectee, not her prisoner. Hell, he could have an orgy with ten different women if he wanted, as long as Lia secured the premises beforehand.

God, she hated her job today.

A loud chorus of groans from the blackjack table reclaimed her attention. A small crowd had gathered to watch in amused disbelief as Magliore won another hand. As he raked in his chips, the distinguished-looking gentleman seated to his right clapped him affably on the shoulder and leaned over to whisper something that made Magliore roar with laughter.

Lia frowned, shaking her head. This wasn't exactly what she'd had in mind when she had told Magliore not to draw too much attention to himself. But she supposed she couldn't really complain. Truth be told, she'd rather have him engaged in a friendly game of blackjack with a bunch of other men than huddled in a dark, cozy corner with his little girlfriend.

No sooner had she completed the thought than she saw him rise from the table and take Tiffany's hand. Lia tensed, watching as the other players sent the smiling couple on their way with hearty calls of encouragement and wolf whistles.

Lia straightened from the wall, her narrowed gaze tracking Magliore and Tiffany as they started across the room. Toward the doorway.

Before she could take two steps to follow them, her path was blocked by a tall, barrel-chested man with clear blue eyes and steel-gray hair cropped military short in a crew cut. He wore an expensive dark blazer and neatly pressed trousers. Lia recognized him as one of the army generals who had arrived yesterday to attend the intelligence summit.

He smiled flirtatiously at Lia. "What's a beautiful young lady like yourself doing hiding in the corner?"

Lia could tell by his slightly slurred speech and flushed face that the general had had one too many drinks that evening.

She gave him a polite smile. "Good evening, sir. Having a good time?"

"Absolutely. After being holed up in meetings and strategy sessions all day, this little mixer is a welcome change of pace, know what I mean?"

"Of course," Lia said smoothly. Over the general's shoulder, she had a clear view of Magliore and Tiffany, who had paused near the doorway to converse with another couple.

"I must say," the general continued, running an appreciative gaze over Lia, "I've met plenty of Secret Service agents over the years, but I don't think I've ever come across one as fetching as you are. How long have you worked for the service, young lady?"

"Six years and counting," Lia murmured.

"Is that right?" He shifted closer, so close that his whiskey-scented breath now fanned her face. "It's good to know that the agency is not only open to hiring women as agents, but *beautiful* women to boot."

Lia gave him a wintry smile. "I'd like to believe that my qualifications had something to do with their hiring decision."

The general laughed loudly. "Of course, of course! I wouldn't dare suggest otherwise. I'm simply saying how refreshing it is to find a combination of beauty and brains in a Secret Service agent. Like I told you, the ones I've met had absolutely nothing going for them in the looks department."

Lia smothered an impatient sigh at the absurdity of the conversation. So this was how her evening would end, she thought. Fending off the sexual advances of a half-drunk letch, who also happened to be a four-star general. Great. What a fitting end to a day that had already been disastrous.

And it was about to get worse.

"Listen, darling," the general said, glancing around furtively as if to check for eavesdroppers, "I don't know what time your shift ends, but I'd be honored if you'd join me for a drink after this. I've got a real nice cabin all to myself. We'd have privacy to talk, get to know each other a little better—"

"No, thank you," Lia said coolly.

He blinked at her for a moment, then continued as if she hadn't spoken. "Mind you, I'm a happily married man. Been married to the same woman for thirty years, and damn proud of it. But there's nothing wrong with a man getting lonely and seeking a little companionship when he's on the road."

Lia gave him a level look. "With all due respect, sir, I'm not interested in providing companionship to you, or anyone else. Now if you will excuse me—"

As she tried to sidestep him his hand shot out, latching on to her wrist. His thoughts rushed to the surface of her brain, a volatile mix of lust and aggression.

Lia groaned inwardly, praying she wouldn't have to drop-kick the general in front of his peers and subordinates.

She met his leering stare, then glanced down pointedly at his hand. "Sir, I would advise you to—"

"Take your hand off her," a low, icy voice spoke from behind the general.

Lia's heart thudded as the general quickly dropped her hand and wheeled around to face Magliore, who had materialized out of thin air, it seemed. His expression was dark and menacing as he regarded the older man.

"Now see here—" the general blustered indignantly.

"General Bradshaw, is it?" At the man's tight nod, Magliore continued in chillingly soft tones, "Your secretary, Tiffany, has told me so much about you. What a wonderful boss you've been to her, so noble and upstanding, revered by all. She bragged about what a devoted family man you are, a pillar of the community. I told her you sounded too good to be true." He smiled, coldly mocking. "It appears that I was right."

The general's face turned an even brighter shade of red. Drawing himself up to his full height, he glared reproachfully at Lia. "Maybe it's *not* such a good idea for women to be Secret Service agents. No matter how many guns you may carry, you still need rescuing."

Lia bit the inside of her cheek to keep from saying something she might later regret. But as soon as the general had moved away, she turned angrily on Magliore. "What the *hell* do you think you're doing?" she hissed, acutely aware that they were being watched by several guests.

Magliore stared at her, incredulous. "*Me?* I'm not the one who was just trying to manhandle you."

"I didn't need you to intervene on my behalf. I can take care of myself!"

His jaw hardened, his eyes flashing with suppressed anger. "Pardon me for giving a damn what happens to you."

Lia opened her mouth to respond, then snapped it shut. They glared at each other across two feet of charged space.

"I'm ready to go." Magliore bit off his words.

"Are you sure?" Lia taunted, unable to resist. "I see your little girlfriend standing across the room with her arms crossed and her bottom lip poked out, looking like someone rained on her parade. Are you really sure you wanna leave her hanging like that? It may be hard to get back into her good graces later on when you sneak out in the middle of the night to go screw her."

Magliore's eyes narrowed on Lia's face, sharp and discerning.

Too late, Lia realized she'd said too much, revealed too much. She turned away abruptly. "You wanna go? Fine. Let's go."

They didn't exchange another word until they'd reached the cabin ten minutes later. Lia, still incensed by the general's parting words to her, stalked around the living room, snapping on lights while Magliore poured himself a shot of whiskey from the butler's pantry.

"For future reference," she said through gritted teeth, "the next time you get that classic male urge to charge in on your white horse and rescue the helpless damsel in distress, do me a favor. Just say no."

Magliore gulped down his drink, then gave a short, brittle laugh. "Please don't stand there and pretend this is about what happened with General Bradshaw."

"Of course it is!" Lia burst out, her temper flaring. "In case you still don't understand, Magliore, I am a *Secret Service agent,* a trained professional paid to protect others from danger. I am fully capable of getting myself out of uncomfortable situations. Especially situations in which the only real threat to me is a horny old man who's had too much to drink. The way you interfered tonight completely undermined my authority and made me look like a fool."

"I'm sorry!" Magliore exploded, his eyes blazing with fury. "Is that what you want me to say? I'm sorry, damn it. I'm sorry for offending or humiliating you. Believe me, that wasn't my intention. I watched him make his way over to you, and it put me on edge. And then I saw him grab you, and I just lost my head. Before I knew it I was marching across the room, ready to rip his damn head off. As far as I'm concerned," he snarled, "that bastard got off easy."

Lia stared at him, stunned into silence by what he'd just told her. The fact that he'd been watching her at any time during the evening, especially with Tiffany draped all over him, filled her with an incredible sense of satisfaction. And relief. She'd spent most of the day tortured by the sight of him and the other woman flirting with each other, tortured by mental images of them in bed together. Not once during the party had he glanced in her direction or given her any indication that he was even cognizant of her presence.

But he had been. And somehow that made up for everything she'd endured that day.

Giving her a sardonic look, Magliore splashed more whiskey into his glass and drank it in one swallow.

"Careful," Lia warned, half-seriously. "You don't want to end up an inebriated letch like General Bradshaw."

Magliore didn't so much as crack a smile.

Lia pushed out a long, deep breath. "All right. It's possible I overreacted a little."

He stared into his empty shot glass. "I know what you were upset about," he said softly, "and it had very little to do with the general, or what I said to him."

Lia swallowed with difficulty. No denial sprang to her lips.

Lifting his head, Magliore gave her a long, probing look that sent heat licking through her. When he spoke again, his voice was low and measured. "I've been trying to figure you out all day."

"Oh?" It was an effort to squeeze out the word, her lungs were so constricted.

He nodded, setting aside the glass. "You claim to regret kissing me," he murmured thoughtfully, "yet seeing me with another woman makes you so jealous you can hardly think straight. How do you explain that?"

Lia wanted to turn tail and run, get away from him as fast as possible. Instead she forced herself to remain standing in the middle of the living room, her chin angled in stubborn defiance. "I think you're putting words in my mouth."

"Am I?"

"*I* think so."

He came forward, a slow and predatory advance. "You think so, or you know so?" he said silkily.

Her heart beat wildly in her chest as he drew nearer. The air between them was charged with tension, almost suffocating in its intensity.

When he'd stopped in front of her, she stared up at him help-lessly. "What do you want from me?" she whispered.

He shook his head slowly. "Don't do that. Don't pretend you don't know what this is about."

"If you're still talking about what happened yesterday—"

A flicker of annoyance darkened his features. "Damn it, Lia," he growled. "You still can't even say it, can you? We *kissed*. We shared the most amazing *kiss* I've ever had in my life. Referring to it in abstract terms won't change what we did, or the fact that I want you so bad my body aches every time I just think about you."

Lia's breath snagged sharply in her throat, her belly quivered with arousal and her knees threatened to buckle. As she gazed into the searing intensity of Magliore's eyes, she had to fight the sensation of drowning.

She needed to escape. *Now.* Before it was too late.

She took a step backward. "I—I think we should call it a night. It's getting late."

"That's right, Lia. Run," Magliore taunted softly. "That's what you do best. Run."

Just like that, something snapped inside her. The agony of watching him with another woman, compounded by days of pent-up sexual frustration, finally pushed her over the edge, and she lashed out.

"Damn you!" she cried, placing her hand against the solid wall of his chest and shoving as hard as she could. "Do you think this is easy for me? Do you think I enjoy running from you? I'm a fighter. I've never run from anyone or anything in my life! Until now—until *you!*"

His eyes glittered in warning. "Lia—"

"No! This is what you've been waiting to hear, isn't it? That I want you just as much as you want me. That ever since we met, I've lain awake every night thinking about you, fantasizing about you, wishing we were two different people so I could make love to you. That every time I see you I just…I just—Oh, hell!"

Before Lia could stop herself, she cupped his face between her hands, leaned up and crushed her mouth to his, swallowing his sharp intake of breath. As his arms lifted and banded tightly around her waist, she traced the outline of his sensuous lips with the tip of her tongue, wondering how a man's mouth could be so soft, so temptingly lush. He tasted of whiskey and his own uniquely intoxicating flavor. She ran her tongue along the smooth edges of his teeth before boldly pushing her way inside. She plundered the silky heat of his mouth in slow, erotic sweeps that made him shudder. He wasn't alone in his arousal. Her flesh burned all over, her breasts throbbed, her loins ached. She wanted desperately to be naked with him, to feel his slick, powerful body mounted above hers. With a hoarse moan, she deepened the kiss, sucking greedily on his tongue until he made a sound deep in his throat, pure masculine hunger. Showing him no mercy, Lia poured all of her need, anger and stifled frustration into what became the most savage, bruising kiss she'd ever experienced.

By the time she wrenched herself free, she and Magliore were both gasping for air.

They stared at each other for several electrified moments.

As the fog of desire slowly cleared from her brain and sanity returned, Lia realized the enormity of what she'd just done. Without a word, she spun on her heel and bolted for the safety of her bedroom.

She didn't get very far.

Quick as a snake striking, Magliore reached out and captured her around the waist. Although she resisted, he was too strong for her, hauling her roughly into his arms. But instead of resuming the kiss, as she'd feared, he buried his face in her hair, holding her against him as he fought to control his ragged breathing.

"You're killing me, *chère*," he whispered hoarsely, his voice filled with raw torment. "I don't know how much more of this I can take."

Lia squeezed her eyes shut tightly, her face pressed against the solid warmth of his chest. She could feel his heart thudding beneath her cheek while her own slammed painfully against her rib cage. Her emotions were in turmoil. Every fiber of her being throbbed for him, ached for him. She wanted nothing more than to wrap her arms around his neck and pull his head down to hers for another earth-shattering kiss that would leave them both breathless and shaken. And she didn't want to stop there. She wanted to throw caution to the wind, forget the rest of the world and surrender to him—mind, body and soul.

She silently railed against the cruel hand of fate that had brought them together at this moment in time. Why couldn't they have met under different circumstances? Why couldn't they have met eight years ago during her previous trip to Muwaiti? She'd been younger, happier and carefree in a way she'd never been since then. Magliore would have been a young soldier in Seligny's army, unburdened by the demands of leading a revolution. They could have enjoyed a passionate island fling, and when it was time for her to leave, she would have taken her wonderful memories with her.

Assuming I would have wanted to leave.

Shaken by the unsettling thought, Lia drew a deep, shuddering breath and forced herself to step away, out of his arms. She didn't know whether to feel relieved or devastated when he made no attempt to detain her.

"Good night," she murmured.

He said nothing, and she didn't look at him, afraid to let him see the fear, the doubt, the yearning reflected in her eyes.

She had taken three steps toward her bedroom when he said in a low, husky voice, "I'm sorry."

Lia stopped, but did not turn around. "For what?"

"For putting you in this impossible position. For asking you to choose between duty and your own desires." He paused. "You're a good agent, Lia. A damn good one. I know how much your job means to you. I didn't fully understand before, but I do now."

Hearing the note of resignation in his voice, Lia slowly turned to face him. Her pulse was thudding. She moistened her lips with the tip of her tongue, unaccountably nervous. "Does this mean… Does this mean you're going to stop trying to seduce me?"

He held her gaze for a long, heated moment. "Is that what you really want?"

Yes. She heard the word in her mind, as clear as a bell, but for some inexplicable reason she couldn't bring herself to voice it aloud. She felt paralyzed, lungs locked, unable to inhale or exhale.

Watching her intently, Magliore's mouth curved in the barest hint of a smile. "That's what I thought," he murmured.

Lia swallowed. She felt like a small, cornered animal that had foolishly squandered an opportunity for escape and now found itself facing the bared fangs of its enemy.

She took a step backward. "Well, um, good night," she mumbled.

This time there was no mistaking the wolfish gleam in Magliore's eyes. "Good night, Lia," he said softly. "Sweet dreams."

An Important Message from the Publisher

Dear Reader,

Because you've chosen to read one of our fine novels, I'd like to say "thank you"! And, as a special way to say thank you, I'm offering to send you two more Kimani Romance novels and two surprise gifts – absolutely FREE! These books will keep it real with true-to-life African American characters that turn up the heat and sizzle with passion.

Please enjoy the free books and gifts with our compliments...

Linda Gill

Publisher, Kimani Press

Peel off Seal and Place Inside...

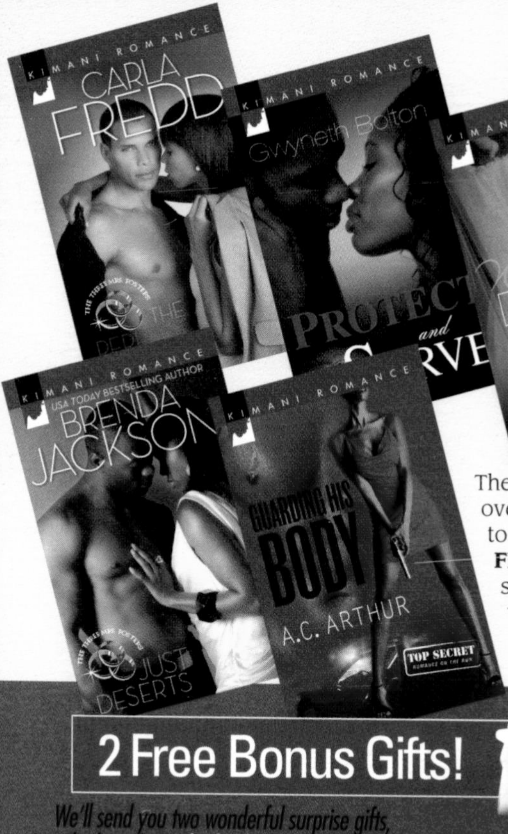

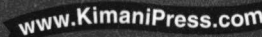

THE EDITOR'S "THANK YOU" FREE GIFTS INCLUDE:

▶ Two NEW Kimani™ Romance Novels

▶ Two exciting surprise gifts

YES! I have placed my Editor's "thank you" Free Gifts seal in the space provided at right. Please send me 2 FREE books, and my 2 FREE Mystery Gifts. I understand that I am under no obligation to purchase anything further, as explained on the back of this card.

PLACE
FREE GIFTS
SEAL
HERE

◀ **DETACH AND MAIL CARD TODAY!**

168 XDL ERR5   368 XDL ERSH

FIRST NAME	LAST NAME

ADDRESS

APT.#	CITY

STATE/PROV.	ZIP/POSTAL CODE

Thank You!

BUSINESS REPLY MAIL
FIRST-CLASS MAIL   PERMIT NO. 717   BUFFALO, NY

POSTAGE WILL BE PAID BY ADDRESSEE

THE READER SERVICE
3010 WALDEN AVE
PO BOX 1867
BUFFALO NY 14240-9952

NO POSTAGE
NECESSARY
IF MAILED
IN THE
UNITED STATES

Chapter 10

When Alexandre Biassou was ten years old, his mother was brutally murdered before his very eyes.

Her crime was adultery.

Her judge and executioner was her own husband.

He shot her three times in the face so that no one attending the funeral would remember the exquisitely beautiful woman she had been in life. Instead, she would be forever mourned as the hideously disfigured creature who had provoked the wrath of a monster.

Christophe Biassou never spent a day in prison for killing

his wife. Back then, the Muwaitian authorities did not look favorably upon adulterous women. Christophe was seen as the victim, the poor, trusting fool who'd been betrayed and humiliated by his whore of a wife. It was agreed that depriving him of his freedom, after the grievous injustice he'd already suffered, would be nothing short of a travesty.

And that was when his ten-year-old son learned that a man could commit any crime under the sun—even murder—and get away with it.

So when he grew up to become a politician, he thought nothing of engaging in bribery, extortion and embezzlement schemes—whatever it took to advance his political career and increase his personal wealth.

And when he set his sights on the Muwaitian presidency, and realized that Francois Seligny was the only obstacle standing in his way, Alexandre had no qualms about arranging his rival's assassination. As far as he was concerned, the ends justified the means.

Following in the footsteps of his father, Alexandre got away with murder.

That was the first time, but it certainly wouldn't be the last.

When his wife brazenly threatened to expose all his dirty secrets to a prominent British journalist who had contacted her, Alexandre saw to it that she "accidentally" fell overboard and drowned in the ocean while they were out sailing on their private yacht. No one dared question his story that he had been sleeping below decks when his wife, a notorious drunk, lost her footing and plunged to her death.

That was the only way Alexandre knew how to deal with people who posed a threat to him. He removed them from the equation—permanently.

It had been four days since Magliore's infuriating escape from Muwaiti, and Alexandre was still waiting to receive news of his whereabouts from his American co-conspirator. With each passing hour and day he grew more impatient, and anxious. Time was running out. Magliore must be found and killed soon if Alexandre were to have any chance at retaining his power—and his freedom.

The dire nature of his situation weighed heavily upon him, robbing him of sleep and making him lash out at anyone who had the misfortune of crossing his path, be it household servants or members of his administration.

Now, as Alexandre sat at a table in the palace courtyard playing chess with his ninety-year-old father, he found himself unable to concentrate. When Christophe Biassou captured his king and won the game, Alexandre scowled.

Christophe glared reproachfully at him, his obsidian-colored eyes as shrewd and piercing as they had ever been. He scolded his son for not paying attention. Glaring at him, Christophe tapped a gnarled finger against his temple. "Chess is a game of strategy. You cannot win if you do not have a strategy."

Alexandre's temper flared. "*Merde!* You think I do not know that? How many times have I sat in this same chair and beat you soundly at this game?"

There was a time he would have severed his own tongue before daring to speak to his father with such blatant disrespect. But that time had long ago passed. Christophe Biassou was no longer the larger-than-life figure of Alexandre's youth, the man with the thunderous voice, brutal fists and volatile temper, whose very footstep had struck fear and awe in the heart of his only child. The years had turned Christophe into a feeble, embittered old man who needed his son far more than Alexandre had ever needed him.

And Christophe knew it, too, whether or not he was too proud to admit it.

"I know what has been eating at you," Christophe observed as Alexandre began setting up the chessboard for a new match. This time he would *not* lose.

"You're worried that you will not find the rebel leader in

time," his father continued. "You're worried that you will go to prison."

Alexandre did not reply. He had never consulted his father about his political affairs. After all, Christophe was a coarse, uneducated man who had spent most of his life toiling in the sugarcane fields. He knew nothing about politics, guerrilla warfare, military strategy or what it took to run a country. It hadn't taken any brains or ingenuity on his part to get away with murdering his wife; he'd simply been the benefactor of a legal system that did not value women. His counsel on most matters could be of little use or interest to Alexandre.

But that never stopped him from offering his opinion, anyway.

He wagged his bony finger at Alexandre. "You should have gotten rid of that boy when you had the chance. Instead you allowed him to hang around for years and make a fool of you. You cannot be a strong, respected leader if you cannot silence your enemies."

Alexandre clenched his jaw so tightly it hurt. "Are you going to play or talk, old man?"

Christophe made a sound of disgust. "I do not want to play again. There is no challenge in it for me if you are not focused on the game."

"Fine." With an impatient snap of his fingers, Alexandre summoned his father's nurse, who had been seated on a bench nearby reading a romance novel.

"Escort my father to his room," Alexandre ordered the burly woman. "It's time for his nap."

"I'm not tired," Christophe grumbled to no avail as he was assisted from his chair and led away.

No sooner had Alexandre gotten rid of his irascible father than a servant appeared at his side. "*Pardonnez-moi,* your excellency," the youth said, bowing deferentially. "This just arrived for you."

"*Merci,*" Alexandre murmured, calmly accepting the large envelope. But as soon as the servant departed, he ripped it

open with trembling hands, his heart pounding with anticipation.

Inside the envelope was a small black-and-white photograph attached to a one-page dossier on Special Agent Lia
Charles, the woman who had led the Special Forces team responsible for Magliore's extraction. Alexandre lingered over
the photo for a moment, reluctantly admiring the beautiful
young American who'd thwarted his mercenaries that night in
the jungle. If only she'd been captured and brought to the
palace. He would have thoroughly enjoyed ravishing her,
hearing her screams of pain and terror, before he sliced her
throat.

Chuckling darkly at the thought, Alexandre scanned the
document, skimming over the agent's impressive credentials,
until he came upon what he was looking for.

There, in fine print at the bottom of the paper, was the name
and address of the mountain retreat where Magliore and the
woman were hiding out, along with detailed instructions on
how Alexandre's assassin would gain access to the secure government facility.

As Alexandre calmly returned the document to the
envelope, a slow, cunning smile spread across his face.

I'm coming for you, traitor. Ready or not.

Armand jolted upright in bed, heart slamming against his
ribs, a fine sheen of sweat clinging to his bare chest.

As he blinked in the gloomy darkness of his room, trying
to make sense of what had awakened him, a clap of thunder
sounded outside, followed seconds later by the steady patter
of rain against the rooftop.

Slowly he eased back against his pillows, scrubbing his
face with his hands.

He'd fallen asleep dreaming about Lia—edgy, tantalizing
images full of smoke and heat and pulsing steel drums, sultry
dark eyes, glistening brown skin and moist lips parted in

sensual invitation. The whisper of soft, husky laughter teased his senses, and the seductive exploration of her mouth and hands made him writhe with longing. And then suddenly the images changed, became darker, menacing. He was running. Out of breath. Someone was shouting at him, telling him that he was in danger and must save himself. Lia, he realized. But when he stopped and turned around, he saw his mother and two siblings, Henri and Felicite. They were all staring at him with such sorrow in their eyes that he took a step toward them, seeking to comfort them. But they shook their heads frantically and pointed toward the ground, and when Armand looked down, he saw that there was a wide chasm separating them. Felicite and his mother began to cry—terrible, keening wails that tore him apart. When he started toward them again, the earth opened wider and swallowed him, plunging him into a dark underworld of blood, violence and mayhem. He heard machine-gun fire, mortar blasts, tortured screams. And he heard Lia again, yelling at him to run, to leave her behind. But he couldn't. He *wouldn't.*

This time when he turned around to reach for her, he found himself staring into the cruelly smiling face of Alexandre Biassou.

That's when Armand woke with a violent start.

"Merde," he swore hoarsely under his breath.

Tossing aside the covers, he swung his legs over the side of the bed, then stood and padded barefoot to the adjoining bathroom, where he splashed cold water over his face. A shudder ran through him at the memory of the disturbing dream, which had seemed all too real.

Especially the sinister smile on Biassou's face.

Nightmares were nothing new to Armand. He'd had more than his fair share of them over the last two years, harrowing dreams in which he saw the lifeless faces of comrades he'd lost along the way and men he'd killed in battle.

But this dream had been different. More intense. Ominous. Even now, as he stood over the bathroom sink, staring at his shadowy reflection in the mirror, Armand couldn't shake a horrible sense of foreboding.

Trouble was on the way. He felt it down to the marrow of his bones.

Over the last four days he'd been so preoccupied with Lia, so obsessed with seducing her, that he'd allowed himself to be lulled into a false sense of security. A state of relaxed contentment. Every time he was with her, he found it startlingly easy to keep reality at bay. To push unsettling thoughts of home, corruption and danger to the far recesses of his mind. After two years of fighting and living in self-imposed exile, Armand knew he'd earned the right to relax a little. But it was a luxury he couldn't afford to indulge for very much longer.

If there was one thing being a soldier had taught him, it was to be on guard at all times.

And if there was one thing he'd learned from Alexandre Biassou, it was to never underestimate your enemy.

Biassou's failure to prevent Armand from leaving Muwaiti alive did not mean he had given up on stopping him from testifying at the hearing. Biassou had too much to lose to surrender now. He would pursue Armand to the ends of the earth to keep him from ruining his future. There was no doubt in Armand's mind that if Biassou discovered where he was hiding, he would do everything in his power to find a way to breach the tight security and get to Armand.

The dream had been a warning, he realized. His intuition was telling him to be on the lookout, to be vigilant, because Biassou was coming after him. Hunting him like an animal.

Armand frowned, his gut tightening at another possibility. Maybe Biassou was going after his family, not him. After all, Biassou knew how much Armand's mother and sister and brother meant to him. He'd successfully managed to sneak them out of the country without Biassou's knowledge. Maybe Biassou had learned of their new whereabouts and decided that the only way to get to Armand was to kidnap his family and use them as bait to lure him out of hiding. Once he had Armand in his clutches, he would kill all of them.

Armand shuddered, closing his eyes and bracing his palms on the smooth, cool surface of the bathroom counter. Suddenly he was struck by a fierce urge to see his mother and siblings again—an urge so strong he was tempted to march next door, drag Lia from her bed and demand that she take him to his family. He needed to make sure that they were safe and sound. He needed to hug them, and tell them how much he loved them.

And if something *was* going to happen to him, he needed one last chance to say goodbye.

But he knew that Lia would never go for it. She wouldn't even give him the exact location of the federal safe house where his family was being kept. For security reasons, she'd explained. Which was also why taking him to see his family or arranging a clandestine meeting at a neutral location, was out of the question. It was too risky, too dangerous.

Armand understood the rationale. God knows he had no desire to put his mother and siblings in any more danger than he already had. But as disturbing images from the dream replayed in his mind, he knew he had to find a way to get in touch with his family somehow. One way or another he had to convince Lia to help him.

With his mind made up, Armand left the bathroom and crawled back into bed.

Lying on his back with his hands clasped behind his head, he watched out his window as a bolt of lightning cut an electrified path across the sky.

He knew that sleep would elude him for a few more hours, if not for the rest of the night.

Chapter 11

Tuesday, September 9, 2008
0700 hours
Thurmont, Maryland
Day 5

When Lia emerged from her bedroom at seven o'clock the next morning, she found Magliore standing at the living-room window, one hand thrust into the pocket of his jeans as he stared out at the heavily falling rain. He appeared to be deep in thought, not even glancing over at her as she made her way to the kitchen.

"Good morning," she said, already thinking ahead to what the day would bring. With Armand Magliore, nothing was ever predictable. Which—under vastly different circumstances— was just what she'd always liked in a man. Unpredictability. Spontaneity. A daring sense of adventure. Magliore had those qualities in spades.

"That was quite a storm last night, wasn't it?" she remarked. "Woke me out of a deep sleep. What about you?"

Magliore barely spared her a glance. "Yeah," he murmured.

As Lia headed into the kitchen to make a pot of coffee, she wondered if his moodiness had anything to do with the way they'd parted last night. She'd kissed him as if her very life depended on it, then retreated like a coward—for the second night in a row. Yet when he'd asked her point-blank whether she wanted him to stop pursuing her, she hadn't been able to give him an answer.

Lia cringed at the memory. She wouldn't blame him one bit for thinking she was a total flake or, worse, a tease.

Stop it, she ordered herself with a stern shake of her head. *Just because the man seems unusually distant this morning doesn't mean it has anything to do with you. Get over yourself!*

While she waited for the coffee to percolate, she rummaged around in the well-stocked cabinets, finding unopened boxes of buttermilk pancake mix and instant grits. From the refrigerator she pulled out eggs, milk, bacon and butter.

When she poked her head around the kitchen doorway, she saw that Magliore had not moved from his position at the window.

"I thought we could have breakfast here," she told him. "You know, since it's raining so hard outside. I thought we could save ourselves a trip to the main lodge in this downpour."

And avoid having to see your girlfriend, Tiffany, she added silently.

Magliore glanced over his shoulder at her. "I don't mind walking in the rain."

"I do," Lia said, straight-faced. "All that humidity is hell on my hair."

He just stared at her, as if trying to decide whether or not to take her seriously.

Lia ruined the moment by grinning. "Just kidding. Honestly, Magliore, how shallow do you think I am?"

This, finally, brought a faint smile to his face. "I don't think you're shallow at all. But I know how you sisters are about your hair."

Her grin widened. "Well, with a job like mine, *this* sister can't be worrying too much about her hair."

Magliore's lazy gaze roamed across her ponytail. "Do you ever wear it down?"

"Sometimes. Depends on the occasion."

He was silent for a moment. "Would you wear it down if I asked you to?"

"Why would you ask me to?"

"Maybe I'd like to see what you look like with your hair down, loose around your shoulders."

There was nothing overtly sexual about his words, or the way he was looking at her, but Lia shivered just the same. It was that deep, smoky voice of his. Even the most innocent conversation could sound indecent with that voice.

She shrugged, glancing away from him for a moment. "I'll think about it. So are you okay with staying here for breakfast? You said yourself it was the best way for you to keep a low profile."

He arched a brow. "And now you agree with me?"

"I never disagreed."

"No," he murmured, watching her with a vaguely amused expression, "I guess you didn't. So if we stay here, who's making breakfast?"

"I am."

"But I thought you told me you don't cook?"

"I don't. But I found everything I need to make pancakes and instant grits. How hard can it be to whip up some eggs and read some instructions on the back of a box?"

An hour later, Lia had her answer.

Seated across the breakfast table from Magliore, she surveyed the unappetizing array of food on her plate. The scrambled eggs were brown, the grits were runny, the bacon was overcooked and the pancakes looked nothing like the fluffy, perfectly round flapjacks displayed on the box.

As she watched, Magliore lifted one from his plate and studied it, turning it this way and that as if it were a foreign organism beneath a microscope. "Most unusual thing I've ever seen," he murmured, his mouth twitching. "And yet somehow familiar…"

"Familiar?"

He nodded. Suddenly his face broke into a wide grin. "I know why. This one is shaped like Muwaiti!"

Lia stared at the pancake for a moment, then burst out laughing. He was right. It did bear an uncanny resemblance to the small Caribbean island!

"I'm touched," Magliore said, chuckling as he reached for the bottle of syrup. "You knew I was feeling homesick this morning, so you decided to make me a pancake in honor of my homeland."

"Right. That's *exactly* what I had in mind," Lia confirmed, wiping tears of laughter from her eyes. "I'm so glad you appreciate the gesture."

"Oh, most definitely. Just as I appreciate the time and effort you put into making, ah, breakfast this morning."

Lia grinned ruefully. "You might want to hold off on thanking me until after you've actually tasted the meal in question," she advised.

Magliore grinned, forking up some eggs. "Oh, I'm sure it can't be all that—" He froze, midchew. The look on his face could only be described as one of horrified disbelief.

Lia howled with laughter. "Don't say I didn't warn you!"

Magliore shook his head at her, his eyes dancing with mirth. Instead of grabbing the closest napkin and spitting out the eggs, he bravely swallowed the mouthful of food, then chased it down with several gulps of strong black coffee.

"You continue to amaze me, Lia Charles," he said with another shake of his head.

Lia chuckled. "I would say thank you, but somehow I don't think that was meant as a compliment."

He laughed. "An astute observation."

"I don't know where I went wrong," Lia complained, watching her soupy grits run like water through the tines of her fork. "I followed all the directions to the letter. And I had no way of knowing the eggs would stick to the bottom of the pan if I didn't spray it or use butter."

Magliore chuckled, pouring syrup over his lopsided stack of pancakes. "Don't beat yourself up. It was your first time. It always gets easier after that."

"Ha! You think I'm actually going to try this cooking experiment again? No way. I've learned my lesson."

"I'm really sorry to hear that."

"Why?" Lia said drolly. "You enjoy being forced to eat unpalatable food?"

He laughed. "How do you know it's unpalatable? You haven't even tasted anything yet."

She grinned wryly. "I don't need to. The look on your face after tasting the eggs said it all." She heaved a deep sigh. "I guess we should have gone to the main lodge for breakfast, after all. I was crazy to think my food could compete with those melt-in-your-mouth country biscuits and incredible omelets."

"Maybe not," Magliore agreed, winking at her, "but I couldn't ask for better company."

Lia warmed with pleasure at his words—which, she supposed, had been his intent. She gave him a grateful smile. "You're just saying that to make me feel better about my disastrous attempt at cooking."

"Did it work?"

"Not nearly as much as watching you eat those pancakes, God bless you."

"Actually, they're not that bad."

She brightened. "Really?"

"Really. Of course," he drawled, his mouth twitching with

suppressed humor, "after existing on a steady diet of MREs for the last year, *anything* tastes good to me."

Lia poked her tongue out at him, and he began laughing.

The entire situation was so comical that she soon joined him. When she picked up one of her own oddly-shaped pancakes and waved it at him, he threw back his head and roared with laughter, which only made *her* laugh harder.

When their laughter finally subsided, Lia reached for her glass of orange juice and took a long sip. She studied Magliore quietly for several moments.

"Is that why you were so subdued this morning?" she asked gently. "Because you were feeling homesick?"

He nodded, meeting her gaze. "I miss my family."

Her heart swelled with compassion. "I know this must be very hard for you, being apart from them like this."

Again he nodded. "I wish I could see them."

"You know that's not possible," Lia murmured. "It's too dangerous."

"I know. I know."

Hearing the frustration in his voice, Lia sought to reassure him. "Your mother and your siblings are safe."

"How do you know for sure?" Magliore impatiently demanded.

"Because the agents assigned to protect them are the best," Lia said firmly. "They check in every day with my supervisor, Nancy Janikowski, to give a status report. If something had happened, she would have called me immediately."

"Maybe not," Magliore said darkly. "Maybe she wouldn't want me to worry and get sidetracked. Your government wants me to testify at this hearing, no matter what. I wouldn't put it past your supervisor, or anyone else, to withhold information from me that could possibly hinder my cooperation."

Lia frowned. "That makes no sense whatsoever. First of all, if something happened to your mother and siblings, no one would be heartless enough to keep that from you just to avoid rocking the boat. It doesn't work that way. Secondly, if Biassou's mercenaries somehow got to your family, that would mean our position may have been compromised, as well, which means we would need to be moved to another location right away. From a logistical standpoint alone, Janikowski would *have* to fill us in on everything."

Magliore looked at her, a hint of mockery in the curve of his mouth. "Such faith you have in your government, *ma petite*."

Her chin angled in defense. "If I'm not mistaken," she said evenly, "you were the same way four years ago."

His expression darkened. "And so I was. For all the good it did me."

Before Lia could respond, he shoved back from the table and stood, pacing to the window. She watched as he stood with his arms folded across his chest, gazing out at the torrential downpour in brooding silence.

In helpless frustration she turned back to her meal. But even if there had been anything remotely appetizing on her plate, she'd already lost her appetite.

Taking a deep breath, she rose from the table and made her way over to Magliore. His back stiffened as she approached, tension radiating from every muscle in his body.

She stopped beside him. She wanted to reach out and touch him, offer him comfort, but she was afraid he'd pull away from her, and for some reason she didn't think she could handle that.

"I won't pretend to comprehend just how difficult this has been for you," she began softly. "I don't have any siblings, and I've never had to look after my parents. They've always had each other for that. You've been taking care of your family ever since you were fourteen, and suddenly you're expected to relinquish that responsibility to virtual strangers? That *can't* be easy for you. I understand that, believe me, I do. All I'm asking is for you to be patient. After the hearing you and your family will be together again, even if I have to take you to them myself. I promise you that."

An eternity seemed to pass before Magliore turned, fixing his penetrating eyes on her. "I just need to know that they're okay," he said quietly. "I know I agreed to these terms when I brokered the deal, and the last thing I want is to put their lives in any more danger than I already have. But if there's any way you can let me talk to them for a minute, or get a message to them somehow—"

Lia started shaking her head even before he finished speaking. "It's too risky."

"Please," he implored huskily. *"S'il vous plaît."*

Lia stared up at him, seeing the desperation, the urgency, the naked vulnerability in his eyes. As the seconds ticked past, she felt something crumble inside her. She recognized it as the last of her resistance.

She blew out a deep, resigned breath. "Actually, there is a way you can safely communicate with your family."

"How?"

"A videoconference." Lia glanced out the window at the driving sheets of rain spilling from the gray sky. "And the best part is, we don't even have to leave the cabin."

When Nanette Magliore sat down in front of a video monitor and saw her oldest son for the first time in weeks, tears of joy welled in her dark brown eyes. She was a petite, dark-skinned woman with salt-and-pepper hair worn in a soft natural that accentuated the smooth roundness of her face. She was flanked by her two children, Felicite and Henri, twenty-four-year-old fraternal twins who bore little resemblance to each other. While Henri appeared to be as tall and darkly handsome as his older brother, Felicite was petite like her mother and astonishingly curvaceous, with a coffee-and-cream complexion and an exotic blend of features. The only feature the twins shared was Armand's amber-colored eyes, but even in that they were different. While Henri's eyes were serious and intense, his sister's glowed with an irrepressible spirit that was infectious.

At the moment, all three members of the Magliore clan were staring at the video monitor with identical expressions of happiness and relief.

The moment they saw Armand, they all started speaking at once. But it was Nanette's thickly accented island lilt that broke through first. "Is that you, *mwen fis?*" she asked tearfully.

Magliore laughed, a sound of pure, unadulterated joy that touched Lia's heart. "Of course it's me, Maman. Who else were you expecting?"

His lighthearted quip was met with a rumble of appreciative laughter. "We could not believe it when they told us we would be seeing you today," Nanette said, beaming at her oldest son. "I told the agent in charge it would be cruel to tease us and get our hopes up for nothing."

"You should have seen Maman," Felicite interjected with a playful grin. "She threatened to knock that poor man upside his head with her *bous* if he was lying to us. And you know how heavy Maman's *bous* is!"

Everyone laughed. Even Lia, who stood to the far right of Magliore, out of the camera frame, chuckled at the thought of the petite woman assaulting a federal agent with her purse.

"They were not teasing you, Maman," Magliore said, smiling warmly as his deep voice took on the lazy, lilting cadence of Muwaitian patois. "I will be forever indebted to Special Agent Charles for arranging this special meeting."

"Is it safe?" Henri asked. "They told us it was too dangerous to see or speak to you at all."

Magliore nodded. "They are right, *mwen frè*. It is very dangerous. But the government has sophisticated technology to make this videoconference one-hundred-percent safe."

"How?" Henri inquired, his eyes alight with avid curiosity.

"Well, basically, the transmitting signal between our two locations is scrambled to keep any unauthorized individuals from tracing—" Seeing the glazed look that came over his mother's and sister's eyes, Magliore laughed. "Ah, never mind the technicalities. The point is, this is the safest way for us to communicate with one another. Now, how is everyone doing? *Tout bagay anfòm?* Are you being treated well?"

All three nodded vigorously. "They told us not to describe too much where we are staying," Nanette said, "but I can tell you that it is *very* nice. Very comfortable."

"Très bon," Magliore said approvingly.

Felicite groaned. "I think I've gained too much weight from all this good food they're feeding us."

Magliore smiled affectionately at his sister. "You look just fine to me, *'tite chatte.*"

Felicite grinned, blowing him a kiss. "And that is why *you* are my favorite brother," she cooed.

Henri laughed, reaching behind his mother to tug on one of Felicite's long, beautiful braids. "She's just mad at me because I told her to stop flirting with Agent Rollins. You would tell her the same thing if you could see the way she's been carrying on."

"Bah! You tell stories. Besides, it's not my fault he's so handsome," Felicite said, smiling coquettishly at someone off-camera, presumably Agent Rollins.

Lia hid a knowing chuckle behind her hand.

"Your sister, she likes America," Nanette informed Armand. "She's even thinking about staying here permanently."

Magliore raised a dubious brow. "Because of Agent Rollins?"

Felicite laughed. *"Non!* Of course not! Not that you couldn't tempt me into running away with you, *cher,"* she hastened to soothe the agent's wounded ego, flashing another demure smile at him. "I just want my brother to understand that I have other reasons for liking your country so much."

"She likes the president being a woman," Henri elaborated.

"She thinks all countries should be run by women. I told her she will feel differently when *you* become the next president of Muwaiti."

Magliore laughed, shaking his head. "Still campaigning for me, eh, little brother?"

Henri grinned unabashedly. "If I tell you often enough, maybe you will start taking the idea more seriously."

"Petèt," Magliore said softly. "Maybe."

Felicite's eyes widened with shock. *"Bigre! Tu es sérieux?"*

"I'm serious." He smiled at her, his eyes twinkling with mischief. "I will say anything to keep you from leaving home, *'tite chatte."*

"No one is leaving home," Nanette said with the decisive resolve of a true matriarch. "America has been good to us, yes, but Muwaiti is where we belong. Where we all belong," she added with a pointed look at her daughter.

"Sekonsa," Magliore said in agreement.

Inexplicably, Lia felt a knot tighten in her stomach. She refused to examine the cause.

"I miss all of you," Magliore said quietly to his family.

"We miss you, too," they chorused in heartfelt unison.

"I will be so glad when this is all over and we can be together again," Nanette added.

"Me, too, Maman." Magliore hesitated, then said humbly, "I'm sorry."

His mother and siblings exchanged confused glances. "Why are you sorry?" Felicite demanded indignantly.

"For putting all of you through this ordeal," Magliore said, his voice thick with suppressed emotion. "If I hadn't started this war with—"

He was interrupted by a barrage of vehement protests.

"Nonsans!" his mother cried. Leaning forward in her chair, she fixed her son with an intent, piercing gaze. "Listen to me, *mwen fis,* and listen good. You have nothing to be sorry for. *Anyen*—nothing! Before we left home, do you

know what our people were saying about you? They called you strong and brave. They said any man willing to sacrifice his own life for the good of his people deserves to be called a hero. That is what you are, *cher*. A hero. If your father was alive today, he would be as proud of you as we are." Her voice broke on the last word, and tears misted her eyes. "This is your legacy, Armand Jacques Magliore. To return to your countrymen the future that has been wrongfully stolen from them. Don't ever, *ever* apologize for fulfilling the destiny God has chosen for you."

By the time she'd finished speaking, Lia felt tears clogging the back of her throat. She was not the only one who'd been moved by Nanette Magliore's eloquent, powerful speech. Both Felicite and Henri had tears shimmering in their eyes as they stared at their older brother.

With his head slightly bowed and his hands clasped between his legs, Magliore sat without speaking for a few minutes, absorbing his mother's impassioned words. He seemed to be overcome with emotion, as well as an overwhelming sense of gratitude that rendered him temporarily speechless.

As Lia gazed upon him, she felt her heart expand in her chest, leaving her suddenly breathless and…frightened.

What on earth was happening to her?

Before she could answer her own panicked question, she heard Magliore draw a deep, ragged breath and slowly exhale. Lifting his head at last, he gazed at his family. "I love all of you," he said in an achingly husky voice. "*De tout mon coeur.* With all my heart. Whatever happens, don't ever forget that."

Hearing an eerie note of farewell in his voice, Felicite burst into tears.

Magliore looked anguished. "No, no, don't cry, *'tite chatte,*" he entreated his sister. "You know what your crying has always done to me."

Felicite turned and sobbed into her mother's shoulder. Tears rolled silently and mournfully down Nanette's face as she comforted her weeping daughter. Henri looked as helpless as his brother, who glanced over beseechingly at Lia.

She stepped forward, clearing her own constricted throat. "We should, uh, wrap this up soon."

Magliore nodded. He stood, walked over to the monitor and knelt down. With searing, focused intensity he stared into the sorrowful faces of each of his family members. "I have to go, but I want all of you to listen to me. Are you listening?"

They nodded dutifully, staring intently at him.

"When this is over," Magliore said with fierce conviction, "we're going to organize the biggest, most festive parade our town has ever seen. We're going to march through the streets with our fellow countrymen, rejoicing and proclaiming our freedom to the rest of the world. And then, when the celebration is over, we're going to roll up our sleeves and get to work rebuilding our homeland. We're going to make Muwaiti greater than it has ever been. Do you believe me?"

His mother and siblings nodded, their eyes bright with renewed hope and determination.

"We're going to get through this," Magliore continued with feeling. "But you have to remain strong and courageous. Not just for yourselves, but for me, as well. I need your strength, your courage, your love. That's what keeps me going. That's what has *always* kept me going." Slowly he lifted his hand to touch the screen. When Nanette, Henri and Felicite moved forward to press their hands against his in a touching show of solidarity, he smiled softly. "I will see you very soon."

When the call ended a few minutes later, Lia, still moved by the heartrending family reunion, began putting away the videoconferencing equipment.

Without warning Magliore reached for her arm, gently turning her toward him.

She stared up at him as he cradled her face between his hands. When she saw the sheen of tears glistening in his eyes, her heart swelled with an emotion so intense it took her breath away.

She closed her eyes as he leaned down and brushed his lips across hers in a brief, achingly tender kiss.

"Thank you," he whispered.

Lia nodded wordlessly, not trusting her voice.

She watched as he walked quietly to his room and closed the door behind him.

And then she just stood there, immobile, realizing that the greatest threat she faced was not losing her reputation or her job—or even her life.

It was losing her heart to Armand Jacques Magliore.

Chapter 12

Two hours later Armand stood in his bedroom doorway with his arms folded across his chest, a smile tugging at his mouth as he gazed across the living room at Lia. She was seated on the sofa with her legs crossed yoga-style, her notebook computer propped on her lap as she worked on what appeared to be a report. Just how much progress she was actually making remained to be seen, since she couldn't seem to keep her eyes open. As Armand watched, she would tap away furiously for a few minutes, but then, as her eyelids grew heavy, her fingers would still over the keyboard and she'd nod off.

This went on for about ten minutes before Armand, feeling mischievous, decided to have some fun with her. Ducking back into his room, he toed off his boots and socks, then crept soundlessly across the living room. When he reached the sofa where Lia was dozing quietly, he leaned down and whispered in her ear, "Wake up, sleeping beauty."

She jumped nearly five feet into the air.

Armand stepped back from the sofa with a shout of laughter. Lia whipped her head around and glared at him.

"I'm sorry," he gasped, clutching his stomach. "I couldn't resist."

Her eyes narrowed dangerously. "You are *so* lucky I realized it was you before I went for my gun."

This only made him laugh harder.

Shaking her head in disgust, Lia turned back to her laptop. "Your poor sister," she muttered. "I can only imagine the horrible pranks you must have played on her when you were growing up."

"Actually," Armand countered, wiping tears of mirth from the corners of his eyes, "Felicite was the prankster, and a damn good one, at that. She was so devious she hardly ever got caught. Just ask my brother. He was her favorite victim."

Lia grunted noncommittally.

Armand rounded the sofa to plunk down beside her. "What are you working on?" he asked, glancing over at her computer.

She hit a button and the screen went blank. "Just trying to catch up on some work."

Armand chuckled. "So secretive."

"Nature of the beast," she quipped, closing her laptop with a snap and leaning forward to set it down on the ottoman. She rolled her head in a counter-clockwise motion, then lifted her hand and rubbed the muscles at the back of her neck.

Without thinking Armand reached up, replacing her hand with his own. She tensed immediately.

"Relax," he murmured. "Let me help you out a little."

She hesitated, then gave a slight nod.

As his fingers began kneading the skin at her nape, he felt the tension slowly ebbing from her body. Her eyes drifted closed and her head fell forward limply, giving him greater access to her neck and shoulders. God, she felt incredible.

"Why didn't you lie down and take a nap?" Armand asked before his imagination began to wander. "You kept falling asleep out here."

"I know," Lia mumbled drowsily. "Rain always makes me sleepy."

Even as she spoke, thunder rumbled outside, right above the cabin. A strong gust of wind sent billowing curtains of rain lashing against the windows. The lights flickered.

"It hasn't let up all morning," Armand observed, gently working the knots out of her shoulders.

"It's not going to," Lia murmured. "It's supposed to be like this all day."

"Think the electricity will go out?"

She shook her head. "They've got backup generators. Why? Are you afraid of the dark?" she teased.

"Not exactly," Armand said with a low chuckle. He could think of far worse fates than being trapped alone in a dark cabin with the sexy, beautiful woman of his dreams. "Are *you* afraid of the dark?"

Lia smiled, her eyes still closed. "That's what candles are for. And I— *Ohh, that feels so good,*" she said on a soft, husky moan of pleasure.

Blood rushed straight to Armand's groin. *Damn,* he thought grimly. Maybe giving Lia a massage wasn't exactly the best way to avoid temptation, as he'd recently vowed to do.

After last night's harrowing dream, followed by the emotional meeting with his family that morning, Armand had decided it was time to revert to what he called "soldier mode." He'd spent the last two years in this state of mind, so focused on surviving and anticipating his enemy's next move that he learned to ignore the demands of his body for food, sleep, even sex. *Especially* sex. Of course, it was easier not to think about your neglected libido when you were stuck out in the middle of the jungle with a bunch of unwashed roughnecks, as he'd affectionately called his men.

Armand was so preoccupied by his thoughts that he didn't even realize his fingers had stilled on Lia's neck—except for his thumb, which idly stroked her silken skin—until she glanced back curiously at him.

He reluctantly dropped his hand, flashing a small smile. "There. That should do the trick."

"Mmm, thanks. That was wonderful." As she unfolded her long legs and rose from the sofa, his gaze was drawn to the way her gray jogging pants molded to the lush roundness of her bottom. As she arched her back, stretching her muscles with a contented purr, he felt another sharp jab of lust to his groin.

"I didn't realize how much tension I was carrying around in my body," Lia murmured.

I know the feeling, Armand mused, painfully aware of the straining at his zipper. He thought about Tiffany, who'd repeatedly pressed her voluptuous body against his and whispered things in his ear that would make a porn director blush. Armand had been nowhere near as turned on by her as he was now, watching Lia engage in something as innocent as stretching.

Maybe soldier mode could wait another day or two.

When she bent down to retrieve her laptop, her cotton pants stretched snug across her bottom. It took every ounce of willpower Armand possessed not to get up, grab her around the waist and grind his aching erection against her tight buttocks. He imagined her moaning softly and rolling her hips, slow and sensual, urging him closer—

"Since it appears that we're going to be trapped indoors all day," Lia said, interrupting his erotic fantasy as she knelt in front of the sofa, "I thought we could play cards or a few board games to help pass the time."

Or how about I carry you into my bedroom and make love to you long and hard into tomorrow morning?

Lia, who'd brushed against his arm as she removed the sofa cushion beside him, glanced up sharply, as if she'd read his mind. Thank God that was impossible.

"Did you say something?" she asked suspiciously.

Armand schooled his features into a blank mask. "No. I was going to say your suggestion sounds good—the games." He paused. "What are you looking for?"

"My thumb drive," she muttered irritably. "It came un-plugged from my laptop when you scared me earlier, and now I can't find it. Could you get up for a second so I can check under your cushion?"

Armand complied, then stood watching as she searched the sofa, then checked the floor underneath.

"Aha! Found it." When she popped up triumphantly, her face was eye-level with his crotch—where, as it turned out, he was still nursing a monster of an erection.

Armand saw the exact moment Lia noticed his predica-ment. Her eyes widened a fraction, her lips parted soundlessly and a deep flush spread across her cheekbones.

As he stood there, air stalled in his lungs, holding himself so rigid his muscles ached, she lifted her gaze slowly to his face. He was prepared to see embarrassment, censure, even disgust reflected in her expression.

He didn't expect to see desire. Raw, naked desire.

His heart began to bang hard against his rib cage, the rhythm echoing in a hot, heavy pulse between his legs.

"Lia—" His voice was rough, hoarse with arousal.

He should have kept his damn mouth shut.

Her sooty lashes fluttered, and she blinked as if she were emerging from a deep trance. Jerking her eyes away, she got to her feet and quickly stepped away from him.

An all too familiar wave of frustration swept through him.

She cleared her throat briskly. "I, uh, need to go put away my computer. W-we can pick a game to play when I get back."

As Armand watched her hurry from the room with her com-puter tucked beneath one arm, he thought, *I've got a sugges-tion for you, Lia. How about we play hide and seek? You hide, and I'll seek. And when I find you, I get to do whatever I want with you.*

When Lia returned to the living room several minutes later, Armand had built a fire, dimmed the lights on the high ceiling beams and draped a thick, knitted afghan across the back of the sofa, where he sat waiting for her. The scene was so cozy and inviting that Lia faltered for a moment, debating whether to proceed or run back to her room to hide out there for the rest of the day. Deciding that she'd done enough running over the past five days to last her a lifetime, she drew a deep, steadying breath and forced herself to continue moving forward.

"It's going to be a little hard to see the board game with the lights turned so low," she said, striving to make her voice sound as normal as possible. The *last* thing she wanted him to know was that the idea of being alone in a dimly lit room with him struck terror in her heart.

As he watched her walk toward him with a look of lazy masculine appreciation, Lia wondered what he saw when he looked at her. Surely he couldn't find her remotely appealing in her plain white T-shirt and gray sweatpants, with her hair scraped back into its usual ponytail and her face scrubbed clean of makeup. Yet *something* had definitely turned him on earlier. She'd seen the unmistakable proof of his arousal—seen it, and felt an answering hunger deep in the pit of her stomach. In a moment of sheer insanity she'd been tempted, so damn tempted, to reach up and unzip his jeans and take his thick, throbbing erection in her hand. Her mouth had literally watered at the tantalizing image.

"I thought we could watch a movie first," Magliore said as Lia reached the sofa. "If that's all right with you?"

"A movie? Um, yeah, sure." She supposed that was safe enough. They could sit next to each other like two strangers in a dark theater; for at least two hours, they wouldn't even have to talk or interact with each other.

"Let me see what kind of selection we have." She walked over to the pine entertainment center that was built into the brick wall. Beneath the big-screen television set were several rows of shelves containing a wide range of DVD movies, from old classics to current blockbusters in just about every genre—

action, animation, drama, suspense, horror, romance, westerns, comedy. There were even a few blaxploitation films, she noted with a soft chuckle.

"What are you in the mood for?" she asked.

Believe me, you don't want to know.

Lia froze, then snapped her head around to stare at Magliore. But instead of looking at her, he was gazing out the window at the falling rain, and he seemed not to have heard her question. Yet Lia could have *sworn* she'd heard his voice in her head, as clear as if he'd spoken the words aloud. The same thing had happened earlier, when she'd suggested playing cards or board games to pass the time. She was almost certain she'd intercepted his thoughts about making love instead. *Long and hard into tomorrow morning.* But that was impossible, Lia decided, giving herself a mental shake to dismiss the notion that she'd heard Magliore's voice in her head. She'd already determined that she couldn't read his mind. Especially not from across the room.

The more plausible explanation was that the thoughts she was hearing were a manifestation of her own feelings and desires. *She* wanted to make love to Magliore long and hard into tomorrow morning, and *she* was the one having a hard time choosing a movie, because what she was in the mood for couldn't be found on any of those shelves.

"Is there anything in particular you'd like to watch?" she tried again.

His gaze returned to her face. "It doesn't really matter to me. I can't remember the last time I even watched a movie—it's been so long. I'm sure whatever you pick will be fine."

Nodding, Lia turned back to the shelves and scanned the titles again. She automatically rejected movies about war, tyranny, corruption, political strife or civil unrest, not wanting to give him any painful reminders of what was happening in Muwaiti. For that same reason, she also bypassed movies with excessive violence, gore and killing, which pretty much eliminated most of the horror films. She wouldn't have minded watching a classic blaxploitation flick for old time's sake, but she didn't know whether Magliore would appreciate the humor or cultural references. Being black in America was different from being black in a Caribbean province largely governed and inhabited by blacks.

Damn it. Why was she making this so hard?

From across the room, Magliore chuckled softly. "Why are you making this so hard, *chère?*" he drawled, echoing her thoughts. "I'm not a film critic. I won't criticize whatever choice you make."

"I know that," Lia muttered.

"If I had known how difficult this would be for you," he said dryly, "I would have chosen the movie myself while you were in your room. But I know how strongly you American women feel about being able to make your own choices."

Lia scowled. "Very funny, Magliore. You know, I've had just about enough of you and your sexist remarks and—"

He laughed. "Just pick a damn movie, woman!"

Lia quickly selected a psychological thriller she'd wanted to see last year, then popped it into the DVD player and grabbed the remote control.

As she made her way back to the sofa, Magliore watched her, his eyes dancing.

"You didn't have to yell at me," she said with as much icy hauteur as she could muster, considering she wanted to laugh, too. She *had* been taking ridiculously long to make a selection.

"I'm sorry," Magliore said, looking anything but apologetic with that irreverent grin tugging at his lips.

"Yeah, right." As Lia sank down on the sofa beside him, she realized it hadn't even occurred to her to sit elsewhere. There was a perfectly comfortable love seat or a leather armchair she could have curled up on, but she hadn't.

So much for wanting to keep your distance.

"I shouldn't have yelled at you," Magliore said, trying very hard to sound remorseful. "How can I make it up to you?"

Lia gave him a sidelong look. "Well…since you asked, I always like to eat popcorn when I'm watching a movie."

"You want me to get you some popcorn?"

"Yes. There should be a box of microwave popcorn in one of those cabinets in the kitchen."

"All right. Consider it done. Anything else?"

"Hmm… How about a nice cold beer? In a glass."

Magliore nodded, rising from the sofa. "Popcorn and beer, coming right up."

Lia waited until he'd almost reached the kitchen before adding, "Oh, and could you bring me some marshmallows? For some reason I always crave something sweet after eating popcorn. Must be all that salt."

Magliore turned and stood in the doorway, staring at her with a look of mild exasperation. "Popcorn, beer and marshmallows," he said slowly, with exaggerated patience. "Will there be anything else, *mademoiselle?*"

"No, that should do it," Lia said cheerfully, smothering an impish grin.

"Are you absolutely sure?"

"Yep." When he'd disappeared inside the kitchen, Lia waited a beat, then called out, "I'll need a few napkins to wipe the butter off my fingers. And don't forget to pour the beer into a glass!"

She heard him mutter something in French that made her throw back her head with a shriek of laughter.

He emerged several minutes later, balancing a bowl of popcorn, two bottles of beer, an empty glass and a bag of miniature marshmallows on a wooden tray.

As Lia watched, still grinning, he set the tray on the ottoman, then with a smooth, gallant flourish proceeded to fill her glass.

"Here you go, *mademoiselle,*" he murmured.

"Thank you," Lia said, accepting the cold glass from his hand. "Has anyone ever told you that you'd make an excellent waiter?"

"Yes," he said wryly as he sat down. "When I was fifteen, I had a summer job as a bartender and waiter at one of the popular tourist restaurants in downtown Port le Duc."

Lia grinned, watching his grim expression. "Something tells me you didn't like it very much."

"Other than the long hours and having to deal with drunk, obnoxious tourists—the Americans were the worst—it wasn't all that bad. The owner liked me, so to compensate for the embarrassingly meager wages he paid, he used to let me sneak food home to my brother and sister. They loved the conch, salt-fish and *chictai*."

Lia groaned loudly. "Mmm, don't you dare talk about Muwaitian food. Not unless you can produce a plate filled with those foods right this very second."

Magliore smiled. "Believe me," he said, "if I could, I would."

Glaring balefully at him, Lia stuffed a handful of popcorn into her mouth and chewed, feeling sorely cheated.

He laughed and took a swig of his beer.

"So how long did you work at that restaurant?" Lia asked curiously, reaching for more popcorn. "Just one summer?"

He shook his head. "Two. That was about all I could handle of tourists."

Lia cast him a knowing grin. "I bet you got hit on all the time."

He smiled. "What makes you say that?"

She laughed, rolling her eyes. "Well, gee, let me think. Hmm. Could it be because you're ridiculously good-looking? I mean, I can just see you at fifteen, not yet a man, but still irresistible in cutoff shorts and T-shirts that showed off the muscle tone you'd developed from all that swimming. I bet those horny women used to flock to that restaurant just to ogle the hot, young island stud with the dreamy eyes and melting smile.

Come on," she teasingly cajoled. "Tell me they didn't slip you their hotel-room numbers and pinch your butt every time you turned around."

Magliore let out a choked laugh. "I was just a kid!"

When Lia twisted her lips and gave him a don't-insult-my-intelligence look, he chuckled. "A gentleman never kisses and tells."

Lia grinned. "Uh-huh. Just as I thought. You probably flirted right back and got those women all hot and bothered, thinking they were going to have a steamy island fling, like the heroine in *How Stella Got Her Groove Back*."

He flashed a wolfish grin. "What can I say? They tipped very generously."

"Oh, I bet they did." Chuckling, Lia reached for her glass and took a sip of beer, watching him over the rim. She could definitely see him working his magic on those poor tourists, even at the tender age of fifteen. The kind of raw animal magnetism Armand Magliore possessed was innate, instinctive, as natural to him as breathing. He'd been born to seduce women.

If she wasn't careful, she could easily become his next victim.

Shoving aside the unsettling thought, Lia asked, "Where'd you work after quitting your job at the restaurant?"

"I continued working in the tobacco fields," he answered, settling back against the sofa.

"Continued? You mean, you worked in the tobacco fields at the same time you were a waiter at the restaurant?"

"Not quite at the same time," he said with a small, teasing smile. "I couldn't be in two places at once."

Lia made a face at him. "You know what I meant."

He chuckled. "Yes, I know what you meant. And yes, I worked in the tobacco fields during the same time that I waited tables. On the days I wasn't scheduled to work at the restaurant, I reported to the fields."

"You were only a teenager," Lia said softly.

He nodded. "I was fourteen years old when I first started

working. It was shortly after my father died. My mother worked tirelessly as a seamstress, but it was difficult for her to support herself and three young children on her modest income. We needed more money, so I got a job."

"You got two jobs," Lia said softly, her throat constricting around a knot of emotion. She knew his background, knew he'd been looking after his mother and siblings since his father's death eighteen years ago. But she hadn't realized the full extent to which he'd assumed responsibility for his family's survival. He'd basically sacrificed his childhood in order to take care of them and provide for them. Was it any wonder his mother and siblings looked at him with such adoration, loyalty and unconditional trust in their eyes? He was their rock, the glue that held them together. They would be lost without him.

Magliore shook his head in response to her previous statement. "I didn't start working at the restaurant until the following summer."

"Well, what was your schedule like during the school year?" she prodded, hoping he wouldn't tire of her questions. She'd always been naturally inquisitive, but with Magliore, her curiosity took on a whole new level of intensity. She found herself wanting to know everything about him, wanting to understand every facet of who he was.

"I worked a few hours after school every day and on the weekends. But my education was always the first priority. My mother would have it no other way. If I wanted to miss a day of school in order to earn some extra money, she adamantly refused. She always told me that education was a powerful weapon against poverty, ignorance and hopelessness, and as long as she had breath in her body, her children would not squander their educational opportunities. Although she was a seamstress and my father was a tobacco farmer, Maman always believed God had greater things in store for me and my siblings."

"And she was right," Lia said quietly. "Here you are—a leader of men, a revolutionary. Poised to change the lives of over five million people because you were courageous enough to take a stand against a brutal dictator."

He said nothing for a moment, turning his head slightly to watch the flames leaping and dancing on the hearth. When he spoke again, his voice was remote and reflective. "When I joined the Muwaitian army at the age of seventeen, my only concerns were providing a better life for my family and being able to afford college. President Seligny's generous commissions made it possible for me to achieve those goals, but it was his vision for the country that enabled me to become the best soldier I could be." He paused, a muscle clenching in his jaw. "I never thought I would one day find myself in a position of trying to overthrow the government."

With a gentle smile, Lia said, "As a wise man once told me, 'Life can be that way sometimes. Unpredictable.'"

Recognizing his own words to her from a few days earlier, Magliore chuckled quietly as he turned to look at her. "A wise man, huh? I honestly don't know what pleases me more. The fact that you think I'm wise, or the fact that you called me ridiculously good-looking a few minutes ago."

Lia laughed. "Don't let it go to your head, Magliore. I was just stating the obvious. Try not to read too much into it."

He smiled, absently rolling the neck of his beer bottle between his fingers as he fell silent for a few minutes.

Lia considered starting the movie, but the truth was that she was enjoying their conversation. Tucked within the cozy confines of the mountain cabin, with a fire roaring in the hearth, thunder rumbling overhead and rain lashing the windows, she and Magliore could have been the only two people in the world. At that moment, she felt closer to him than any other man she'd ever known. It was a scary yet wonderful feeling.

Laying her head against the back of the sofa, Lia slanted a soft smile toward Magliore and said, "I like your family. I can tell how close the four of you are, how much you mean to one another."

He nodded slowly. "The death of my father brought us together in a way nothing else could have. We had to learn to depend on one another, or we never would have made it through the bad times. And there were plenty of those."

Her heart stirred with compassion. "I'm sorry about your father," she said quietly. "I know he was killed by an armed robber, who was then apprehended and shot by the police. I can only imagine how devastating that must have been for you and your family."

Magliore nodded. "It was. It was probably the most devastating day of our lives. He was a good man, and he meant everything to us. But we had to learn to go on without him, and as difficult as it was, we eventually had to learn to forgive the man who took his life."

Lia gazed at him, her heart swelling with pride and admiration. "Over the course of my career, I've spoken to many family members of murder victims. I've always been humbled and amazed by those who somehow found the strength to forgive the criminals who took away their loved ones. I honestly don't know if I could be that strong or magnanimous."

"It becomes a matter of self-preservation," Magliore said somberly. "You can either spend the rest of your life consumed by anger and hatred, or you can learn to forgive and seek closure. Thankfully, my family chose the latter."

"They're amazing people," Lia said warmly.

His mouth curved in a poignant smile. "I've always thought so."

Smiling companionably, Lia tucked her legs beneath her on the sofa. "Felicite is beautiful, and Henri looks just like you."

Magliore chuckled. "Everyone always says that about both of them. And once you get to know them, you realize that while they might be twins, they're as opposite as night and day."

Lia grinned. "I could already tell."

"Henri is analytical and reserved, while Felicite is free-spirited, emotional and impulsive. They're both headstrong, but while Henri likes to present clear, rational arguments to make his point, Felicite tends to become feisty and combative. If that fails, her backup strategy is to win you over by the sheer force of her charming personality, and she's not above using her feminine wiles to get what she wants."

"Poor Agent Rollins." Lia sighed heavily. *She* definitely knew what it was like to find herself at the mercy of a Magliore sibling. It was like swimming against a very powerful, dangerous current.

Magliore chuckled dryly. "Agent Rollins will be fine. If anyone can keep Felicite in line, Henri can. He's been doing it his entire life, though it hasn't been the easiest job in the world."

Lia smiled. "Is that why you call your sister *'tite chatte*— little cat? Because she's so feisty?"

Magliore grinned. "That, and because she used to bring home every stray cat she could find and beg my parents to let her keep them. They refused each time, but that didn't stop her from sneaking home a new stray every week. My father finally gave her an ultimatum—he could either feed and shelter *her,* or feed and shelter the damn cat that would replace her in the family. You can guess which choice she made."

Lia laughed. "Smart girl."

"Yep."

After another moment, Lia mused, "I always wanted a pet."

"Yeah?"

She nodded. "I used to beg my parents for a dog."

Magliore eyed her curiously. "Why didn't they let you have one? I always thought most American families had dogs."

"Well, since we moved around so much, my parents thought it would be too stressful to own a pet." She didn't add the part about animals having a particular aversion to her.

She didn't have to. Magliore brought it up. "I don't really see you owning a dog, anyway. Even now that you're an adult."

"Why?" Lia asked warily. "Because of my job?"

"That's one reason."

"What's another reason?"

He studied her thoughtfully for a moment. "Truth be told, you don't seem like much of an animal lover. You were extremely uncomfortable on that horse yesterday, and I think he picked up on that, which is why he was so difficult to manage. Horses are very sensitive animals."

"I know that," Lia snarled, incensed by the reminder of yesterday's humiliating horseback ride. It was bad enough that he and Tiffany had been all over each other the entire time. Now he had the nerve to disparage her riding skills? To lecture her about her failure to put the horse at ease? Talk about adding insult to injury!

Watching her eyes turn to angry slits, Magliore laughed. "Hey, I'm not saying you did anything wrong! I'm just making an observation."

"Oh, really? An observation based on what? The five seconds your eyes *weren't* plastered all over Tiffany's—"

He groaned in exasperation, throwing his hands up in the air. "*Merde!* Are we back to that again? Are you still jealous because I was paying more attention to that woman than you?"

Lia's nostrils flared. "I was not—"

His raucous bark of laughter cut her off. "And you're still denying it. God, woman, you are so stubborn!"

Lia ground her teeth, glaring mutinously at him. "All right, fine. Maybe I *was* a little annoyed by all the PDA that was going on—"

"PDA?"

"Public display of affection."

"Oh, right." His mouth twitched with suppressed humor. "Please continue."

Thrown off balance by the interruption, Lia opened and closed her mouth, struggling vainly to remember what had seemed so important a moment ago.

Magliore watched her, his eyes glimmering with amusement. "Let me help you out. You were in the middle of denying, for the second time, that you were seethingly jealous of Tiffany yesterday."

"What? *Seethingly* jealous of— Oh, forget it. Just forget it!" Lia jabbed a finger at him, her eyes narrowed in challenge. "You know what, Magliore? If you want to sleep with Tiffany, be my guest!"

"Really?" he drawled, his voice dripping with sarcasm. "Now all of a sudden I have your permission?"

"Absolutely. If you want, I'll even walk you over to her cabin right now. I'm sure she misses you and is wondering at this very minute where you are and why you haven't made an attempt to see her today. So here's your chance. Far be it from *me* to keep young lovers apart!"

Magliore stared at her in amused disbelief. "Let me get this straight. Just to prove that you *aren't* jealous of Tiffany, you're willing to get up right now and escort me to her cabin so that I can have sex with her?"

"That's right," Lia shot back without flinching. "I'm ready to go whenever you are."

"Are you?" He held her gaze, his voice deepening to a low, husky caress as he said, "So while I'm in there, holding Tiffany in my arms, stroking every inch of her body, kissing her mouth, her breasts, between her thighs… While I'm in there making love to her, where will you be?"

Lia swallowed. "R-right outside the room. In the living room."

"Are you sure?" he said silkily. "We'd probably be making *a lot* of noise. All that moaning and groaning and heavy breathing. You might want to wait out on the porch instead. But then again, Tiffany might be a screamer, so—"

Averting her gaze, Lia snatched the remote control from the ottoman and viciously stabbed the Play button. "Let's just watch the damn movie," she snapped.

Magliore chuckled deep in his throat. "That's what I thought," he said softly.

This time, Lia didn't argue.

Chapter 13

Twenty minutes into the movie, Lia realized she'd made a very bad choice.

It wasn't the mediocre acting, the slow pace or even the convoluted plot that led her to this conclusion.

It was the first love scene.

The film had been billed as a "taut cat-and-mouse thriller" between an ambitious federal agent and the sultry femme fatale art thief he'd been sent overseas to pursue and capture. The couple's first sexual encounter took place inside a locked vault at a Roman bank. The love scene was so blatantly sensual, so graphic, that Lia was tempted to get up and check the DVD case to see whether the movie was rated X instead of R.

As if it weren't torturous enough that she'd just been forced to visualize Magliore and Tiffany having sex while she waited outside the bedroom, now she had to sit here, less than a foot away from him, and watch a fictional couple thrust and gyrate their way through an explicit sexual encounter. She assiduously avoided looking at Magliore, keeping her eyes trained on the television screen.

As the actress's convincing cries and moans filled the silence of the living room, a slow, burning flush crept up Lia's neck and spread across her face. To conceal her embarrassment, she relaxed her features into a blank mask, as if she were watching nothing more stimulating than a documentary on the mating habits of insects.

Still, no documentary had ever made her so painfully aware of how long it had been since she'd had sex. Long enough that when the male lead rammed the woman against the wall and savagely took her from behind, Lia's nipples tightened and heat bloomed between her legs. Whatever she thought of the rest of the movie, she could not doubt the authenticity of the actors' passionate performance in *this* scene.

When Magliore leaned over, reaching inside the bowl of popcorn cradled in her lap, she nearly jumped out of her skin.

"Here, just take it," she snapped, shoving the bowl into his hands without meeting his gaze.

"Thank you."

She heard a trace of wicked amusement in his voice, even though she still refused to look at him. Her face had grown hotter and her hips suddenly felt restless; she actually had to control the urge to squirm on the sofa.

After what seemed an eternity, the steamy love scene finally ended. Only then did Lia hazard a surreptitious glance at Magliore. His hooded, speculative gaze held hers for a long, heated moment before she looked away, feeling breathless and undeniably aroused.

She didn't turn her head again until the movie was over and the credits were rolling.

When she looked over at Magliore, she was surprised, and a little relieved, to discover that he'd fallen asleep. His breathing was deep and even, one hand rested on his flat abdomen, and one long, jean-clad leg was propped on the ottoman.

Lia found herself staring at him, her eyes tracing the sculpted line of his thick black brows, the strong bridge of his nose, the new growth that darkened his rugged jaw, the sensuous curve of those full, masculine lips. His dense black lashes fanned out in perfect formation from his closed eyelids, tempting Lia to touch them to see if they felt as silky as they looked. She felt a pang of guilt when her gaze landed on the small scar above his right eye where she'd kicked him the night of his extraction. But it was *his* fault for attacking her in the first place, she told herself. And somehow the scar only managed to heighten his dark, dangerous appeal.

While sleep did not soften his features, she noted, he looked peaceful. Unguarded in a way he would never allow when he was awake.

She toyed with the idea of playing a prank on him—stuffing popcorn up his nose or pouring beer over his head—to repay him for the way he'd startled her awake earlier, but she couldn't bring herself to move. And she didn't want him to wake up. Not until she'd drank her fill of him, committed every last feature to memory. Because when this assignment was over, and he and his family returned to Muwaiti to begin their new lives, Lia knew she would never see him again. And that knowledge filled her with indescribable sorrow.

That's when she knew she was in love with him.

Against her better judgment, against her *will,* she had fallen in love with a protectee. She had fallen in love with Armand Magliore.

Lia knew there was no use denying it. She'd been courting this outcome for days. Every time she looked at him, touched him, saw him smile or heard him laugh, she felt herself falling harder. Listening to his stories about Muwaiti, and then watching his poignant interactions with his family that morning, had left her utterly captivated. Afterward, when he'd kissed her so tenderly and thanked her with tears shimmering in his eyes, Lia knew she was a goner.

She loved that he was strong and fearless, yet tender and vulnerable to his sister's tears. She loved that he could be brooding and intense one minute, lighthearted and playful the very next. She loved that he could bring her to her knees with one smoldering look, yet infuriate her enough to want to strangle him.

She loved him with a fierce protectiveness that made her want to shelter him from all hurt, harm and danger. She loved him with a blind desperation that left her feeling exposed and helpless and completely at his mercy. There was no precedence for these alien, terrifyingly wonderful feelings she was having. Nothing like this—nothing like *him*—had ever happened to her before.

Lia was so absorbed in her thoughts that she didn't notice Magliore stirring awake, his amber-colored eyes opening and focusing on her face.

By the time she realized he was staring at her, watching the revealing play of emotions across her face, it was too late.

Their gazes locked for an arrested moment.

Lia's heart pounded painfully in her chest. Afraid that he'd seen the truth reflected in her eyes, she jumped up from the sofa, prepared to do what she always did—run like hell.

Already anticipating her reaction, Magliore leaped to his feet and grabbed her, forestalling her retreat. Lia shivered as his arms banded tightly around her waist, imprisoning her against his body as he leaned down to whisper in her ear, "No more running."

All she could manage was a pathetic whimper.

Roughly he cupped her face, angled it upward and crushed his mouth to hers. He kissed her greedily, brutally, his tongue thrusting deep. She responded with a hungry desperation fueled by her recent discovery. She *loved* him. And right or wrong, she would have him. Right here, right now.

Breaking the kiss, he shoved his hands into the sides of her hair, loosening her ponytail and forcing her head back to expose her neck. She shivered, her insides clenching as his lips and tongue trailed a simmering path of nerves along her throat and collarbone, scraping his teeth along her sensitized flesh. He was pulling at her hair, hurting her, but somehow the pain only intensified the sweet, throbbing ache in her loins.

She reached down with trembling hands, grasping his T-shirt and tugging it over his shoulders and head. As she tossed it to the floor, her gaze was already devouring the sight of his bare chest. He had the body of a warrior who had seen his share of battles. Lean and powerful, hard and ridged with muscle. His deep-mahogany skin bore more than a few scars, which only enhanced his brutally male beauty.

No sooner had she removed his T-shirt than he reached for hers, his warm, calloused knuckles rasping her flesh as he impatiently stripped her of her shirt, then her black lace bra. Her legs quivered as she stood before him, her full, aching breasts bared to the smoldering intensity of his gaze.

"You're even more beautiful than I imagined," he whispered huskily.

Lia sucked in a sharp breath as he cupped her breasts in his hands. Lowering his head, he drew one erect nipple into the moist heat of his mouth. Her back arched, a ragged moan escaping her throat. He sucked first on one nipple, then the other, until she felt the exquisite pull of his mouth everywhere—in the pit of her stomach, between her trembling thighs. As if that weren't tormenting enough, he ground his hips provocatively against hers, stroking her against his rigid erection until her panties were soaked, and she felt dangerously close to climaxing.

Dropping to his haunches, he finished undressing her, peeling off her sweatpants and underwear with an economy of motion. For several moments he just stared, as if hypnotized, at the nest of black curls at the juncture of her thighs, which only made her wetter. Her breath stalled in her lungs. And then finally, with a low, guttural oath, he bent his head and pressed a hot, carnal kiss to her pulsing center. Lia sobbed in mindless ecstasy, her knees buckling beneath her. He caught her in his arms, surging to his feet.

Through the fog bank of desire clouding her brain, she realized that he was still wearing his jeans. She reached out, fumbling blindly with his zipper. Her hands shook as she yanked his jeans and dark briefs over his taut, powerful thighs and endless legs. His erection jutted toward her, long, thick and impossibly hard. Her loins ached, her *whole body* ached with the primal need to have him buried deep inside her. Their gazes locked as she curled her fingers around his throbbing penis and stroked him, making him swear hoarsely.

Too ravenous to wait any longer, he grasped her buttocks and lifted her into his arms. They both shuddered violently the moment their bodies collided. Lia closed her eyes and clung to him, her arms clasped around his neck, her legs wrapped tightly around his waist.

Lost to everything but the anticipation of finally having him inside her, she didn't realize he'd carried her halfway across the room until her back hit the smooth warmth of the pine wall.

With one savage thrust he entered her, burying himself to the hilt. Lia cried out wildly, clawing at the corded muscles of his back, her thighs quaking uncontrollably. She was already on the verge of an orgasm when suddenly he froze, stiffening against her.

She whimpered in protest, opening her eyes to stare up at him in panicked confusion. Why had he stopped? What was he waiting for?

His eyes were tightly closed, as if he was in agony. As if he, too, was already on the brink of losing control. "You feel so damn good," he uttered raggedly. "I don't... I can't..."

Lia rocked her hips desperately against him. "Please don't stop," she begged. "Please. Please. *Please.*"

She nearly sobbed with relief when he began moving inside her, plunging deep and retreating in a slow, blatantly erotic rhythm that threatened to send her over the edge. "You have no idea how long I've waited for this, *chère*," he groaned thickly. "A lifetime."

Lia would have made some sort of response, but she was beyond forming coherent speech. How was it possible she'd lived this long without experiencing this kind of pleasure? How had she survived?

Armand—for he was no longer Magliore—slanted his mouth over hers, seizing her lips in a kiss of such searing passion her head swam. As his mouth opened and closed over hers in hungry demand, their tongues mated feverishly. Heat encapsulated her entire body. A bead of perspiration pooled in the hollow at the base of her throat and trickled down. He chased it with his lips, making her shiver.

The rhythm of their lovemaking changed, from slow and sensual to fast and frenetic. Every nerve ending, every cell in her body clamored for release. As he drove into her, staring into her eyes, she didn't need to read his mind to understand what he was communicating to her. The message was clear—he didn't want her to ever forget that it was he at her center, moving through her core, possessing her body. There would be no room for doubt or confusion.

Lia knew she would never, *ever* forget. This moment, this man, would be permanently branded upon her memory, her very soul, long after he was out of her life.

Her nails raked his back as he pounded ruthlessly into her. She arched backward, pressing her sweaty body closer to his as she felt pressure building inside her, as intense as the storm raging outside.

Watching her face with a look of feral possession, he whispered huskily, "You belong to me now." She whimpered as he eased out of her with excruciating slowness, almost to the tip. "Do you know why?"

Lia thought she shook her head frantically, but she couldn't be sure.

"Let me show you."

He surged back inside her and she came. Violently.

As wave after wave of ecstasy crashed through her, she screamed his name loud enough to drown out the clap of thunder that suddenly shook the cabin.

With a powerful thrust and a triumphant shout, Armand joined her moments later, shuddering so deeply she nearly came again. She clung to him tightly, her body still reeling from the aftershocks of the most mind-blowing orgasm she'd ever had.

She didn't know how long they remained like that, their bodies locked together as they panted and trembled against each other.

It was only when the lights flickered, then went out completely, that she raised her head weakly from his shoulder and glanced around the dark cabin in dazed confusion.

Chuckling softly, Armand nibbled her bottom lip. "We must have knocked out the power, *chère*. Even the backup generators."

Lia blushed, even as a shaky laugh escaped. "I actually think you might be right."

"Don't sound so surprised," he said huskily, gazing into her eyes. "I always knew it would be this way between us. Explosive."

"Earth-shattering," she agreed, and they shared a lazy, intimate smile.

Realizing that his arms might be getting tired from holding her up against the wall, she reluctantly began disentangling herself. But Armand stopped her.

"Stay," he whispered against her mouth.

He didn't have to ask twice. She tightened her slippery thighs around his hips, hugging him closer, keeping their bodies joined.

They kissed, a long, deep, provocative kiss.

Drawing back, Lia rested her damp forehead against his with a breathless little sigh. She couldn't remember the last time, if ever, she'd felt so deliciously sated after sex. "It's been hours since we ate, er, breakfast. Are you hungry?"

"Yeah," Armand murmured, his penis hardening inside her once again, "but not for food."

Instantly aroused, Lia tightened her arms around his neck and clung to him as he strode purposefully toward his bedroom. They fell across the rumpled king-size bed, coming together in the center and wrapping around each other with the mindless craving of new lovers.

Four hours later, lying on his side with his head propped in his hand, Armand gazed down at Lia's sleeping face in the candlelit darkness of his bedroom. She lay snuggled against him with the covers pulled up to her chin, as trusting and peaceful as a child. Light and shadow played across her features, serenely beautiful in slumber. Her soft, lush lips were parted slightly, and every so often she made these adorable little sighing noises that brought a smile to his face. After hours of intense lovemaking, her thick, black hair was loose and disheveled, spread across the pillow the way he'd always envisioned in his fantasies.

But this was no fantasy, Armand reminded himself with a renewed sense of wonder. After eight long, torturous years of dreaming and fantasizing about her, Lia Charles was finally in his bed. He wasn't going to tempt fate by questioning his good fortune. All he knew was that he'd awakened from a nap earlier to find her watching him with an expression of such tender yearning it took his breath away. Even now, hours later, he was afraid to hope his eyes hadn't been deceiving him. He was afraid to believe he'd seen love—*love*—shining in her eyes as she stared at him.

It was too much to hope for. Her sudden reappearance in his life, when he thought he'd never see her again, had been miraculous enough. To have her love would make him the happiest, most grateful man on earth.

After carrying her into the bedroom hours earlier, he'd made love to her over and over again, unleashing years of pent-up need and desire, until she literally begged for mercy. Blowing hair out of her eyes, her body still trembling from an orgasm, she'd laughingly threatened to lock herself in her bedroom unless Armand promised to let her rest for *at least* an hour. He'd agreed, albeit reluctantly. He couldn't get enough of her, and it had nothing to do with his yearlong sexual drought. Lia would have made him insatiable even if he'd been bedding a different woman every night for the past ten years. Making love to her was like nothing he had ever experienced before. Just the sheer pleasure of hearing her scream his name as she climaxed surpassed his fantasies.

But it wasn't just about the explosive chemistry between them, the sheer intensity of their lovemaking. It was about the powerful connection they shared, both in and out of bed. Sometimes when he and Lia looked at each other, he had the uncanny sensation that they could see into each other's souls.

Armand chuckled quietly to himself. If his soldiers could see him now, they would hardly recognize the lovesick fool he had become. They knew him as a fearless fighter, a hardened renegade, a leader of men. Hardly the type to lay awake for hours romanticizing about soul mates. If they could see the silly grin on his face as he watched Lia sleeping in his arms, they would swear she had cast some sort of spell over him. And, in a way, they would be right. He had been in love with her ever since he saw her standing outside the town clinic that fateful afternoon. Only a sorceress could steal a man's heart without ever having to say a word.

Even now, when he should have been as exhausted as she was, he couldn't take his eyes off her. The sight of her curvaceous form outlined beneath the covers tempted him to strip away the blanket, bury his face between her thighs and feast on her luscious sweetness until she shuddered and came violently in his mouth. But a promise was a promise, so he kept his hands, and his tongue, to himself. He'd even let her sleep an extra thirty minutes. Why not? He was feeling generous.

Besides, if he could somehow convince her to return to Muwaiti with him and marry him, he'd have the rest of their lives to ravish her. Because there was no doubt in his mind that he wanted Lia to become his wife. Together they could help rebuild the land they both loved so much. He would never forget what she'd told him four days ago. *I felt like something was compelling me to stay, almost like I'd be leaving a part of myself behind if I left the island.*

Those words had sent chills up and down his spine, confirming his growing belief that he and Lia were destined for each other. She wouldn't have felt such a powerful connection to the island, *his* home, if they weren't meant to be together.

But Armand knew it would take more than prophetic words—even her own—to persuade Lia to return to Muwaiti with him. Her whole life was here, in America. Her parents, her friends, her job. Even if she were willing to leave her parents behind—which would be difficult, given how close they were—Armand knew she'd never agree to walk away from the Secret Service. She loved her job, and she'd made it abundantly clear to him that any man who forced her to choose between a relationship and her career would come out on the losing end.

Armand didn't like losing, especially when it came to losing the woman he wanted to spend the rest of eternity with.

He was so desperate to keep Lia in his life that he'd even fantasized about getting her pregnant. Surely she wouldn't walk away from him if she was carrying his child, he reasoned. And the idea of her having his baby, bringing *their* son or daughter into the world, filled him with unspeakable joy.

But it was a short-lived fantasy. When he apologized to her for not having any condoms, since he'd spent the past year living in the jungle, she'd laughed and assured him that she was on the pill, so they were at least protected from an unplanned pregnancy.

So much for *that* idea.

No, Armand thought as he gazed upon the sleeping woman

in his arms, he wouldn't have enjoyed trapping her into marriage, anyway. He wanted her, *badly,* but not at the expense of her happiness. Somehow he had to convince her that she couldn't live without him any more than he could live without her.

The way she'd looked at him earlier gave him hope. If Lia loved him, truly loved him, then she would see that they could have a beautiful future together in Muwaiti.

What about America? a voice pricked his conscience. *Why does she have to be the only one making all the sacrifices? Do I love her enough to sacrifice returning to my beloved home-land? If our love is real, does it really matter where we live, as long as we're together?*

As if Lia had channeled those thoughts into his mind, she suddenly stirred awake, stretching languorously beneath the covers. Her soft, purring moan sent a jolt of hunger speeding to his groin.

Those long, sooty lashes lifted and she peered up at him. "How long have I been asleep?"

Armand smiled. "About an hour and a half."

Her lips curved in a drowsy smile. "Thanks for giving me a little more time."

He chuckled softly. "I figured you would need it. I plan to keep you up very late tonight."

She groaned, but he could tell she was pleased. She enjoyed their lovemaking as much as he did. That was very promising.

As he stared at her she parted her lips, drawing his thumb into the silken heat of her mouth. Need ripped through him.

She watched through smoky, heavy-lidded eyes as he pulled the covers from her body. He slipped his hands between her knees and parted them. His fingers slid downward, massaging the smooth, sensitive skin of her inner thighs until her breathing quickened.

With a slow, sensual smile he moved down and pressed the tip of his tongue to her warm, moist opening. She let out a broken moan, her hips flying off the bed. His groin ached, hot need stabbing through him as the scent of her arousal filled his nostrils. She closed her eyes and threw back her head as he flicked his tongue against her throbbing sex, going a little deeper each time, swirling, teasing, torturing. When his teeth scraped the slick nub of her clitoris, her stomach muscles clenched and her thighs began to quiver uncontrollably. Cupping her bottom, he lifted her hips higher, sliding into her with his tongue, stroking deeper with a wild and increasing hunger. She writhed against him, her breathless gasps and moans filling the room.

Knowing that she was about to come, he pulled away abruptly and covered her trembling body with his own. She locked her long legs around his hips as he drove into her with a sharp, powerful thrust. She cried out, opening herself wider, inviting him even deeper. He began moving inside her, hard, fast strokes that made her pant and arch against him, matching his rhythm. He whispered erotic promises in French and she responded in kind, fueling his savage hunger. Their coupling was fierce, elemental, marked with the blind desperation of two lovers who knew the future was uncertain.

Armand rolled Lia on top of him so that she straddled him, knees planted wide on either side of his body. She sat back, sinking deeper onto his erection. She braced her hands on his shoulders, her hair falling in a wild curtain across her face. He groaned as she rocked her hips frantically, her breasts bouncing as he bucked under her, forcing himself deeper into her wet heat, so deep that she soon exploded with a loud, mewling cry, her inner muscles contracting violently around him.

She was still sobbing as he shifted positions, turning her over so that he could take her from behind. He held her close, his fingertips digging into her hips as he thrust high and deep inside her. Moaning with pleasure, she reached back and grabbed his butt so tightly he thought she'd leave permanent handprints. He drove into her repeatedly before finding his own release with a powerful shudder that shook his whole body and tore a hoarse shout from his throat. He didn't pull out of her until he'd emptied every last drop of his seed into her pulsing womb.

As the tremors gradually tapered off, he gathered her into his arms and drew the covers over their bodies. Closing his eyes, he tenderly brushed his lips across her temple and stroked her damp hair, as her breathing slowed to a steady deepness. This time he, too, fell asleep, lulled by the precious feel of her breath against his chest, comforted by the warmth of her body curled against his. Right where she belonged.

Chapter 14

Wednesday, September 10, 2008
0900 hours
Thurmont, Maryland
Day 6

The next morning, Lia didn't have much time to dwell on feelings of shame or regret for sleeping with Armand.

Shortly after they returned from having breakfast at the main lodge—she'd learned her lesson about trying to cook—she received a phone call from Nancy Janikowski's secretary, who informed Lia that an electrician was en route to the cabin to investigate the faulty wiring.

Lia asked curiously, "Where's Janikowski?"

"She's on a special this week," the secretary answered vaguely, using agency jargon for a special assignment.

Lia frowned. "She didn't tell me she'd be out of pocket for a few days."

"Well, she is. She'll be in touch with you when she gets back, Agent Charles."

As Lia thanked the woman and hung up the phone, she thought, *Something's not right.*

She couldn't put a finger on the reason for her sudden unease. The unpredictable nature of the job affected everyone in protective services, even those in management. It wasn't unusual for Janikowski, or any other supervisor, to have to drop everything in order to accompany an advance team to a hot location, which was any location where heightened security was needed—especially on the eve of the September 11 anniversary. In all likelihood, Janikowski was traveling with the president's protection detail, lending additional support during the chaotic election season. She probably hadn't had an opportunity to contact Lia before she had left to let her know she'd be out of the office for a few days.

That was the most logical explanation, Lia decided. Yet she couldn't shake the feeling that something was terribly amiss….

She was so lost in her thoughts that she didn't realize Armand had spoken to her until he reached out and gently touched her shoulder, startling her.

"Sorry," she murmured, flashing him an apologetic smile. "I got sidetracked. What did you say?"

His gaze roamed across her face. "I asked you if something was wrong. You've been frowning ever since you got off the phone. Is everything all right?"

Seeing the unasked question in his eyes, Lia hastened to reassure him. "Your family is fine, don't worry. That was my supervisor's secretary, letting me know that an electrician is coming out today to check the wiring."

Armand nodded, sitting forward on the sofa. "There's really no point though, is there? Aren't we leaving here on Friday to fly to New York for the UN hearing?"

"Yes, but it's better to be safe than sorry." She paused. "Which is why I want you to stay out of sight when the electrician gets here."

He frowned. "Stay out of sight?"

"Yes. Stay in your bedroom, and keep your door locked."

His frown deepened as he stared at her. "Are you anticipating trouble?" he asked quietly.

Lia let out a short, grim laugh. "I *always* anticipate trouble. It's my job to anticipate trouble."

Armand didn't smile. "And where will you be while I'm hiding in my room?"

"You're not hiding! You're staying out of sight until the electrician leaves. It's just a precaution."

"And where will *you* be?" Armand pressed.

"Out here with him, of course. To make sure he does whatever he's supposed to do before I sign off on the service ticket. Once he's gone, you can come back out, I promise." When Armand said nothing, she let out an exasperated laugh. "You act as if I'm sending you to your room as punishment!"

A small muscle pulsed at the base of his jaw. "I'd rather remain out here with you," he said in a low, steely voice.

"And I'd rather you didn't," Lia retorted. "So since *I'm* the one calling the shots around here—"

Armand rose abruptly from the sofa and paced over to the window, where he stood staring out at the clear, bright morning.

Lia watched him for several long moments, realizing that although she loved him deeply, there were many things she still didn't understand about him.

"Why can't you just let me do my job?" she asked, frustration edging her voice. "Why do I have to meet with opposition every time I ask you to do something?"

He glanced over his shoulder and met her accusing stare. His mouth curved in a crooked half smile. "You didn't really think that was going to change after yesterday, did you?"

Lia stared at him, then couldn't help but chuckle. "I don't know. Maybe I did. I should have known better. You are as stubborn as—"

"A mule. I know. I've heard." He smiled again, his eyes softening on her face. "If you really want me to stay out of sight while the electrician is here, I will. You obviously have your reasons."

"I do. I always do." She gave him a gentle, teasing smile. "But thank you for cooperating. It makes my job a whole lot easier when you do."

"Don't thank me just yet," he said, turning away from the window. "My cooperation is conditional."

Lia eyed him warily. "What are the conditions?"

He came toward her slowly, his hands tucked into the pockets of a pair of loose khaki trousers he wore better than a male runway model.

Her pulse quickened as he stopped in front of her. He reached out, tenderly brushing his knuckle across her cheek before taking her chin between his thumb and forefinger.

"I will agree to your request," he said huskily, "if you agree to mine."

Lia swallowed, ensnared by the intoxicating heat of his gaze. "That depends on what your request is."

He smiled, slow and sensual. "After the electrician leaves, I want you to slip into something more comfortable. We're going to pack a basket and have a picnic at the lake. I already know the spot—it's shaded by trees, so we can have all the privacy we want. After our picnic, we're going to come back here and soak in the hot tub for a while. By the time I carry you out, you're going to be so relaxed and ready for me to make love to you that your insides will be trembling. I'm going to build a cozy fire, lay you down on a thick blanket, then take my time caressing you, pleasuring you, tasting and exploring every beautiful inch of your body. I'm going to make love to you, Lia, until you don't know whether you're coming or going, until you can't even remember your own name. We'll stop long enough to enjoy a romantic candlelight dinner, and then we will return to the bedroom—or the kitchen, the living room, the deck or anywhere else you desire—to have each other for dessert. All…night…long." He brushed his thumb across her parted lips, gazing at her beneath his lashes. "How does that sound?"

Lia was speechless, lungs locked, unable to inhale or exhale. Her nipples had hardened, her clitoris was throbbing and her loins felt deliciously full.

"Lia?" His voice was a deep, velvety caress that snaked between her legs. "Do we have a deal?"

All she could manage was a trancelike nod, and he chuckled softly. "Good. I'm looking forward to it."

Not half as much as *she* was.

When the electrician arrived an hour later, Armand kept his word and retreated to his bedroom. Before letting the private contractor inside the cabin, Lia made him unzip his blue jumpsuit so she could pat him down for weapons. She checked his photo ID, called his employer to verify his credentials, then dialed another number to run his driver's license and the tags on his company-issue van. While she waited for the all clear, she studied the uniformed man, mentally cataloging every detail of his appearance. She'd already learned from his license that he was a thirty-four-year-old, Caucasian male, five-eleven and one hundred eighty pounds. Beneath his baggy jumpsuit he was trim and athletic, no stranger to a regular fitness regime. His blue eyes were flat and lacked warmth, though he smiled easily enough. He had no facial hair, no tattoos, the only identifying mark being a small raised scar just below his left ear. The scar intrigued her, so she asked him about it.

He reached up, touching his skin as if he'd forgotten the scar was there. He laughed grimly. "A souvenir from an old girlfriend. I made the mistake of letting her shave me—while she was mad at me. 'Course, I didn't know *that* until afterward."

Lia, who'd been trained to read eyes, to decipher the subtle nuances and vocal inflections that betrayed human emotion, couldn't doubt the veracity of his story. If he was lying, he was very good.

She grinned sympathetically. "Ouch. Live and learn, I guess."

He snorted. "You can say *that* again."

She listened into her cell phone another moment, then nodded and disconnected the call. "All clear, Mr. Westfield. Thanks for your patience."

"No problem. I understand. Call me Zach."

She gave him her most charming smile. "And you can call me Lia."

The flicker of interest she saw in his eyes gave her the opening she needed. As she stepped aside to let him enter the cabin, she asked, "Would you care for something to drink?"

"No, thanks." He swept a cursory glance around the cabin. "If you could just show me where the circuit-breaker box is located, I can get right to work."

Lia had no intention of turning her back on him, so she just smiled and said, "Keep going. You're heading in the right direction."

As he continued toward the rear of the cabin, he casually remarked, "I've never taken a service call out here before. This is a nice piece of property. The feds really know how to live it up."

Lia gave a low, indulgent laugh. "But of course. The only problem is that we're so far removed from civilization that things can get pretty dull. I'm always looking for ways to liven things up a little. Know what I mean?"

He glanced over his shoulder at her, and she could tell by his expression that he was trying to figure out whether she was too good to be true.

Lia smiled flirtatiously. "Turn right at the corner. The circuit-breaker box is located next to the laundry room."

As he opened the box and began his inspection, Lia made her move. Leaning close to him, she murmured, "So this is your first time out here, huh?"

"Yes, ma'am." He winked at her. "But I will definitely have to make sure it's not my last."

Lia chuckled throatily. "You do that," she purred, boldly and deliberately sliding her hand beneath his jumpsuit collar to touch the back of his neck. He tensed a little, but did not move away.

They didn't tell me the agent was so hot... Damn... Never been with a black woman before, but I'd definitely make an exception for her... Beautiful... Maybe when I take care of him I can get a piece of this action... No one said I couldn't do her before I kill her... I need to run out to the van and pretend to get my tools....

Keeping her sultry smile in place, Lia slowly withdrew her hand from his neck, chilled by the thoughts she had intercepted. Just as she'd suspected. This man wasn't an electrician. He was one of Alexandre Biassou's hired assassins.

Their location had been compromised.

Zach, or whatever his real name was, smiled easily at her. "I need to run out to the van and get my tools."

"All right," Lia said, her voice betraying nothing.

Before he had taken two steps, she pulled her 9mm and pointed the gun between his shoulder blades. "Don't move," she said, low and controlled.

He froze in his tracks.

"Put your hands in the air where I can see them. *Slowly.*"

As he moved to comply, her finger tightened reflexively on the trigger. She took a cautious step toward him. "Who are y—"

He spun quickly, knocking her gun hand to the side and up. The Glock spat a round into the ceiling, and wood and plaster dust rained down on them as they struggled for control of the weapon. From somewhere inside the cabin, Lia heard footsteps pounding on the floor, rushing in their direction. A heavy male fist slammed into her right cheek. As pain erupted inside her head she released the gun, and it clattered across the floor. Her assailant seized her viciously by the hair, one arm locking across her shoulders like a crowbar. Lia spun around in his arms, ramming her elbow into his solar plexus. He reared backward, clutching his throat. Before he could recover from the blow, she swung her right leg in a roundhouse kick that connected with his chest and sent him crashing into the wall. As he slumped to the floor, she went for her backup piece strapped to her ankle. Still gasping for air, he scrambled on his hands and knees, diving for the fallen Glock at the same time she drew a bead on his forehead.

"Freeze!" she shouted hoarsely.

In defiance, he raised the gun and took deadly aim. Lia fired, hitting him in the shoulder before he could squeeze the trigger. Half a second later, another shot blasted a hole through his chest. He let out a gurgled scream, then crumpled to the floor.

Stunned, Lia wheeled around in time to see Armand lowering his weapon, lethal fury burning in his eyes as he stared down at the fallen mercenary, then at her.

Swearing hoarsely, he tucked his gun into the waistband of his trousers, then cupped her face between his hands, his frantic gaze sweeping across her disheveled hair and bruised cheek. "Are you all right?" he demanded.

She nodded quickly, shaking off his hands as she turned and hurried over to the motionless body on the floor. Blood was oozing from the deep wounds in the man's shoulder and chest, and one leg was jerking spasmodically.

Lia holstered her weapon, then quickly knelt beside the body and pressed her finger to the carotid artery. She could barely detect a pulse.

"Damn it!" Acutely aware of Armand watching her, she bent close to the man's slack mouth, keeping her finger on his fading pulse.

"Who sent you?" she demanded urgently. "Who are you working for?"

Failed... Quick...silver... Don't...wanna die...

"Who are you working for?" Lia repeated, knowing she was running out of time. "How did you find us?"

Quick...silver... Don't... Quick...silver...

"What does that mean?" Lia shouted as blood bubbled from his mouth.

"What are you doing?" Armand asked. "He's not saying anything—he's dying."

"Yes, I can see that!"

No sooner had the words left her mouth than the mercenary's eyes rolled upward, his leg stopped moving and his head lolled limply to the side.

He was gone.

Lia pounded his chest in outraged frustration. "Damn it!"

Armand stepped forward, seizing her arm and pulling her roughly to her feet. "That's enough, Lia. He's dead."

"I know!" she exploded, whirling on him. "Why did you shoot him?"

Armand looked incredulous. "What the hell do you mean? He was going to kill you!"

"I needed him alive so that I could interrogate him! That's why I only shot him in the *shoulder.* You weren't supposed to kill him!"

Armand stared at her, then hauled her into his arms and held fast. "I almost lost you, damn it," he whispered fiercely into her hair. "I don't care about anything else. I almost lost you!"

Lia closed her eyes for a moment, allowing herself to absorb his strength, his comforting warmth, as the adrenaline slowly ebbed from her body. He was right. She'd nearly been killed. But that was the nature of her job, and she'd survived much worse. The sooner Armand got that through his thick head, the better off they'd both be.

Drawing a deep, steadying breath, she pulled out of his arms. When he reached out and gently touched her bruised cheek, she winced. He swore, his eyes simmering with leashed violence.

"I'm fine," Lia reassured him. Mustering a wan smile, she added, "Besides, there's nothing more you can do to him. You've already killed him."

Armand glanced down at the dead man, looking as if he wanted to unload a few more rounds into him. "I shouldn't have left you alone with him," he growled.

"Yes, you should have. He came here to kill you, and he might have succeeded if you had been too busy trying to rescue me. Which, by the way, is becoming a rather bad habit of yours." Lia started down the corridor, pulling her cell phone out of her back pocket and dialing Janikowski's cell number. Her call went straight to voice mail.

"Nancy, this is Lia. I know you're out of pocket for a few days, but I really need—" She stopped abruptly, struck by a sudden, awful suspicion that made her go cold all over. "I need to talk to you," she continued in carefully measured tones. "Please call me as soon as you can."

When she turned around, Armand was standing there, watching her with an unreadable expression. "You didn't tell her." It wasn't a question.

Lia shook her head. She crossed quickly to the living-room window and peered outside. Finding the road leading to the cabin empty, she signaled to Armand to step out onto the porch with her. She didn't speak until she'd checked the outdoor light fixtures, pine floorboards, a pair of Adirondack chairs, and the undersides of the wooden balustrade that ran the length of the wraparound porch.

Satisfied that there were no listening devices—at least out here—she turned to Armand and uttered the words she never thought she would hear in her lifetime. "I think there's a mole in the Secret Service."

Armand said nothing, his jaw tightening as he stared at her, waiting for her to continue.

Lia wished she didn't have to. "There are only a handful of people who know about your arrival in the United States to testify at the hearing. At least one of those individuals is work-ing with Alexandre Biassou. That man inside the cabin was sent here to kill you. He couldn't have known where you are, or gained access to this property, without the assistance of whoever hired him."

"So the question is," Armand said grimly, "who hired him?"

"I don't know," Lia muttered, her mind racing a mile a min-ute as she paced the length of the porch. "I wish to God I knew. I haven't been able to reach my supervisor. I was told she'd be out of the office this week."

"How convenient."

Lia didn't respond. The same thought had already occurred to her. "We have to get out of here," she said suddenly, stopping in front of Armand. "Whoever sent that man here probably planted listening devices inside the cabin. Which means he, or she, heard everything that just happened."

Including what happened between us yesterday, she thought with a sick feeling of shame and betrayal. The idea of one of her colleagues—someone she trusted—eavesdropping on her and Armand making love made her feel more violated than anything she could or would ever experience in her life.

But Lia had more pressing matters to worry about. Like get-ting Armand out of there safely and finding out who the damn traitor was.

"We have to get out of here," she repeated, more urgently this time. "We don't have time to sweep the cabin for bugs. I *know* we'd find them, so there's no point in even looking. When we go back inside, I want you to pack your things and be ready to leave in five minutes. Do you understand?"

"What about my family?" Armand demanded. "If Biassou found me, he may have found my family, as well!"

"Listen to me," Lia said, cupping his face in her hands, forcing him to meet her intent gaze. "I know you're worried about your mother and siblings. Truth be told, I am, too. But my first and foremost priority is to get you out of here alive. As soon as we reach a safe location, I will call Agent Rollins to make sure your family is okay, and I will warn him and the other agents to be even more vigilant than before."

Armand clenched his jaw, his nostrils flaring. "That's not good enough," he ground out. "I want to know for sure that they will be safe. I want them with me!"

"That's not possible. Not yet. Look, we have to get ourselves to safety before we can be of any use to your family. There are six agents assigned to their protection detail. Believe me when I tell you that your mother and siblings are better off staying where they are than going on the run with us. Now please," she said imploringly, gazing into his tormented eyes, "if ever there was a time I needed your cooperation, that would be now. Please trust my judgment, Armand. *Please.*"

He closed his eyes for a moment, leaning his forehead against hers. She could feel the tension radiating from his body, sensed his internal struggle. She held her breath, hoping he would make the right decision, praying he wouldn't make this situation more dangerous than it already was.

After a lengthy silence he raised his head and looked at her, his eyes glittering with steely resolve. He had reached a momentous decision.

"You're the boss," he said roughly. "Now let's go."

Chapter 15

A search of the mercenary's utility van revealed a large cache of weapons hidden beneath various tools and supplies that belonged to a legitimate electrician. The arsenal included rifles, handguns, submachine guns, live grenades, land mines and several rounds of ammunition.

"All this to assassinate one man," Armand muttered grimly as he surveyed the stockpile. "I don't know whether to be alarmed or flattered."

Lia gave him a bemused look as she grabbed two rifles and as many rounds of ammo as she could. "Be alarmed. That'll serve you better in this situation."

In addition to the weapons, they also found a spare jumpsuit, which Armand quickly put on over his clothing, with the bulletproof vest Lia had given him. The jumpsuit's sleeves and pant legs were a little too short, but no one would notice while he was seated behind the wheel. They had decided to make their getaway in the van instead of Lia's Secret Service vehicle, which could be tracked. They also agreed that Armand, disguised as the electrician, would drive the van since Lia would be recognized by the marine guard patrols as they left the property. Although she didn't suspect the military's involvement in the plot against Armand, she wasn't taking any chances.

She'd searched the interior of the van, hoping to find some clue into the mole's identity, but all she turned up was the phony work order attached to a clipboard. Although she knew that finding his cell phone would have been too good to be true, the mercenary had also been smart enough not to leave behind any notes with names, phone numbers or addresses scrawled on them.

They left the rural property without incident and headed onto a deserted stretch of highway that would eventually lead them to the interstate. When they were a safe distance from the retreat, Lia climbed from the back of the van to sit up front with Armand. It was noon. Warm, bright sunlight slanted through the windshield, baking the interior of the vehicle.

The steep, narrow road wound through the mountains in a seemingly endless series of hairpin turns that could prove deadly in a high-speed chase. Secret Service agents assigned to protection details received extensive training in defensive driving, therefore Lia was prepared to react if she and Armand suddenly found themselves being pursued by assassins. But first she had to get behind the wheel.

"First chance you get," she told Armand, "pull over on the shoulder so that I can drive."

He shook his head. "I'll drive."

She gave him an exasperated look. "Aren't you the same man who told me twenty minutes ago that *I'm* the boss?"

His mouth quirked. "You are."

"Then why are you arguing with me about driving?"

"Because you're a better marksman than me." When she gaped at him, he gave her an amused sidelong glance. "Don't look so shocked. I'm not too proud to admit that a woman can shoot slightly better than me."

Lia let out a choked laugh. "Gee, what a concession! *Slightly* better?"

He chuckled. "That night in the jungle, when the men in the jeep were pursuing us, my shot took out the front passenger. Yours took out the driver."

"So?"

Armand gave her a pointed look. "I was aiming for the driver."

"Oh." Lia grinned ruefully, keeping a watchful eye on the side-view mirror. "Well, you certainly had no problem with your aim today when you put a bullet in that man's heart."

"Damn straight," he growled. Lia got the impression he was more incensed with the mercenary for hitting her than for coming to the cabin to kill him.

"The point is," said Armand, "if we find ourselves being chased again, your shooting skills will be more useful to us if you're not the one driving."

Lia supposed she couldn't argue with his rationale. For once.

"How did you know he was lying back there?" Armand asked suddenly. "The mercenary. Did he say or do something that made you suspicious?"

"You could say that," Lia hedged.

"What was it?" Armand prodded. "What made you suspicious?"

"He had a scar below his left ear," she said, thinking fast. "He said an old girlfriend cut him while giving him a shave. He was lying."

"How did you know?"

"The scar looked like it had been made from the blade of a hunting knife, not a razor blade. I'm guessing he didn't expect me to know the difference. In his line of work, he probably gets into altercations all the time. That scar was a souvenir from someone else he once tangled with."

"Well, he won't be tangling with anyone anymore," Armand said darkly.

"No, he won't." Lia exhaled a long, weary breath. "I really wish I could have questioned him, though. We need to know who and what we're up against."

Armand frowned. "We already know who and what we're up against. Alexandre Biassou. A coldhearted, murdering bastard."

"Yes, but who is he working with here in the States? Who is his accomplice? That's what I was hoping to find out from the merc."

Armand's frown deepened. "Did you really think he would give up that kind of information? Those mercenaries are trained to withstand hours of interrogation. I've seen men like that endure the worst forms of torture without breaking a sweat. They know that whatever you put them through will pale in comparison to what their employer will do to them if they crack under pressure and talk. Biassou's punishments are notoriously gruesome."

"So I've heard," Lia said grimly.

Armand looked at her. "We did that man a favor by ending his miserable life, Lia. When Biassou learns of his failure, there will be hell to pay."

Suppressing a mild shudder, Lia closed her eyes for a moment. She could feel the onset of a migraine behind her eyelids, sharp pinpricks of pain that intensified with each blink. She didn't know whether the headache was a result of stress or the vicious left hook she'd taken from the mercenary. Probably a combination of both.

Watching as she lifted her hand and gingerly touched her swollen cheek, Armand said gruffly, "You should have put some ice on that. I brought a couple of steaks that were in the freezer. As soon as they thaw, I want you to put one on your face."

"I'll be fine," Lia grumbled, embarrassed by all the fuss he was making over her. "You know, this isn't the first time I've been punched in the face, or worse, and it won't be the last. Stop treating me like a girl."

Armand scowled, not in the least bit amused. "You're going to have one hell of a shiner in the morning."

"I think that's the least of my concerns right now," she muttered.

Armand looked as if he wanted to say more, then reconsidered. He lapsed into stony silence, a muscle working in his jaw.

"Hey," Lia said softly. When he glanced over at her, she gave him a small, conciliatory smile. "I don't mean to sound like an ingrate. Thanks for bringing the steaks. I'll put one on my cheek as soon as we get where we're going."

He nodded shortly. "Remind me again. Where are we going?"

"A place where we'll be safe. A place no one but my parents would think to look for me."

"How do you know the Secret Service won't find us? They must be searching for us by now."

Lia shook her head. "They have no way of tracking me. I left everything back at the cabin—the car, my cell phone, my radio. Everything traceable. And they have no reason to be searching for us just yet. Janikowski is the team leader and my liaison when I'm out in the field. Unless she hears from me that there's an emergency, she has no reason to sound the alarm. As for the mole, my gut instinct tells me that he—or she—is going to lie low for at least twenty-four hours before trying to contact me."

"Even though he knows what happened at the cabin?"

Lia nodded. "He would draw too much suspicion to himself if he suddenly rushed over there to investigate a shooting that hasn't even been reported. He would have to explain how he knew there was trouble, which means he would have to own up to planting the listening devices, which he's *not* going to do. No, he's going to lay low for a day and hope to God that the hired guns take care of us. Which is another reason he won't launch a search for us. He knows the mercs can't get to us as easily if we're in protective custody. He wants us to be out here, on our own. Vulnerable."

Armand studied her taut profile. "Since you dumped your cell phone, how will you know if he tries to make contact?"

"I'm going to buy a prepaid phone and check my voice mail messages. And then in the morning I'm going to call Janikowski to let her know our location was compromised. If I still can't reach her, I'll call the assistant director."

Armand frowned. "Either one of them could be the mole."

"I know," Lia murmured, turning her head to look out the side-view mirror. "I'm counting on it."

She saw a dark, nondescript sedan speeding toward them at the same time that Armand said, "Looks like we've got company."

As the dark sedan closed in on them, Armand could make out two men behind the tinted windows. The muzzle of an assault rifle was already emerging from the passenger window.

Armand stepped on the gas, and the van lurched forward just as gunfire erupted.

The first shot shattered the rear windshield, spraying glass everywhere. The second shot took out the driver's-side mirror.

Lia cocked her M16 and quickly belly-crawled into the backseat.

"Be careful!" Armand urged.

With one eye on the road, he watched through the rearview mirror as she huddled at the back door, pointed her rifle through the open window and fired on the mercenaries. The sedan swerved sharply as the passenger returned fire, bullets thudding into the van's metal doors.

"Be careful!" Armand shouted again.

"Keep your eyes on the road!" Lia yelled back.

Armand eased off the gas just enough to keep the van from going into a tailspin as he took a deadly curve. Behind them the sedan kept pace, relentless in pursuit.

More shots rang out. Armand lifted his eyes to the rearview mirror just in time to see Lia pick off the passenger, who'd leaned out the window to return fire. *Atta girl!*

"Damn it!" she screamed.

Armand whipped his head around, afraid she'd been shot. "What?" he demanded.

"It's an armored car! Bulletproof windows and padded tires that won't go flat!"

Even before Armand received that disturbing tidbit of information, he knew they were at a disadvantage. The armored vehicle was smaller and faster than their van. He wouldn't be able to outrun or outmaneuver it on the narrow, twisting road. He would have to outmuscle it instead.

The lone pursuer suddenly veered around the van and sped up alongside them. As he and Armand locked gazes, the mercenary pointed his Glock out the passenger window.

Armand shouted to Lia, "Brace yourself!"

He wrenched the steering wheel left, ramming the side of the van into the sedan. The deafening crunch of metal filled the air. The other car skidded across the deserted two-lane road.

Taking advantage of the temporary reprieve, Armand floored the accelerator. The van sprang toward eighty. Not good enough.

From the back window, Lia fired at the sedan as it recovered its tracks and began racing toward them again. The driver returned fire. *Pop, pop, pop!*

Lia ducked for cover as bullets sprayed the van.

In no time at all the mercenary caught up to them, roaring up beside Armand.

Gritting his teeth, Armand hit the brakes and went into a controlled skid. As the other car shot past them, he quickly righted the wheel and gunned the accelerator.

He barreled toward the sedan, which had stopped in the middle of the road, straddling both lanes at a cocky angle. As

Armand bore down on him, the driver suddenly swung into a one-hundred-and-eighty-degree turn. But he'd misjudged the time it would take the van to cover the distance. Armand hit him at full speed, using the van as a battering ram.

This time the sedan went into a wild spin, fishtailing off the road before coming to a sudden stop right at the edge of a steep slope.

After a few seconds the driver's door opened, but before the disoriented man could bail out of the doomed car, the front end pitched sharply forward. The sedan hung over the edge for a moment, then nosedived down the precipitous, rocky slope.

Armand was still gripping the steering wheel, trying to catch his breath, when Lia hopped back into the passenger seat.

She leaned over and gave him a quick, hard kiss on his mouth. "Nice driving. Now let's get the hell outta here!"

Chapter 16

That night, Lia and Armand ate dinner by a large campfire in the middle of the woods. It wasn't quite what Armand had in mind when he'd promised her a "romantic candlelight dinner," but after the harrowing day they'd had, he figured she'd give him a pass.

"How was your steak?" he asked with a lazy smile, watching as she licked her fingers, tossed her clean bone into the fire, then set aside her paper plate.

"Delicious," she pronounced with a deep sigh of satisfaction. "Best steak I've ever had. My compliments to the chef."

Armand chuckled dryly. "As I mentioned before, I've had a lot of practice roasting meat over campfires. Nothing to it."

She grinned at him. "You don't give yourself enough credit. The meat was tender and seasoned just right. If left to *me,* those steaks would have been nothing more than a charred mess."

Armand nodded. "Yeah, you're probably right."

"Hey!" Lia said indignantly, slapping him playfully on the shoulder.

Together they laughed, and it felt good. Really good. They'd had very little to laugh about over the past several hours.

After the close call on the highway, they'd ditched the bullet-riddled van in exchange for an old but serviceable sedan they bought at a used-car lot for two hundred dollars. By the time Lia had finished shamelessly flirting with the salesman, he'd been ready to hand over the keys for every vehicle on the lot. Armand empathized with the poor guy.

Back on the road, he and Lia had traveled for another two hours before reaching their new hideout, the site of an old underground bunker that had been used by Union soldiers during the Civil War. Located on a large tract of privately owned land in rural Virginia, the bunker did not belong to any historical society, Lia explained, but rather to an old friend of her father's. The owner, a retired widower who actually lived on the West Coast, had no intention of selling the land, which had been in his family for generations. Whenever he came to Virginia, he always invited Lia and her parents to join him for camping and fishing on the property. Because Lia had always been fascinated with the underground bunker, he'd laughingly given her a key to it should she ever need a "place to hide."

Little did he know that years later, finding herself on the run, she would seek refuge in the same bunker she'd once explored and played in.

Armand, who wasn't too keen on spending the night in a dank, dusty underground hole haunted by the ghosts of dead soldiers, would much rather sleep under the stars, as he'd often done back home. But if Lia insisted that they take shelter in the bunker, he'd keep his promise to cooperate. As long as they were together, it didn't really matter where he slept.

The summer night was thick and sultry, and a steady chorus of nocturnal creatures' humming filled the air. Ribbons of moonlight streamed through the canopy of pine and fir trees surrounding their campsite.

Before arriving at their new destination, they'd stopped

at a discount store and stocked up on food and camping supplies to get them through the next three days, if necessary. Lia had bought a prepaid phone and called to check up on Armand's family. He hadn't taken an easy breath until she had hung up and reported that his mother and siblings were doing just fine. When he had asked her why she was pouting, she had informed him that his mother was about to prepare *chictai* for Agent Rollins and the others. Even Armand had been jealous.

When Lia had checked her voice mail, there were no new messages. Just as she'd predicted.

Although she hadn't come out and said it, Armand knew how traumatized she was by the recent turn of events. She had devoted her life to the Secret Service. She'd sacrificed friendships, a love life, stability—hell, her own safety—in order to be the best agent she could be. To discover that someone within the agency had betrayed her trust, violated her privacy and was now trying to kill her had to be the most devastating thing she'd ever experienced in her life. Armand wanted to comfort her, hold her. Reassure her that everything would be all right.

Even if he didn't necessarily believe it.

"Do you want another beer?" Lia asked, interrupting his grim musings as she reached into the large cooler beside her.

He shook his head. "No, thanks. One is enough."

Absently he watched as Lia opened a bottle of water and took a healthy swig. She was sublimely beautiful, even with the darkening purple bruise on her right cheek. She had braided her hair into a neat, thick plait that hung between her shoulder blades. At some point she had changed into tan cargo pants and a white tank top that drew his gaze to her sleekly toned arms and the enticing fullness of her firm, round breasts. He remembered sucking her dark nipples, stroking and caressing her breasts as he drove inside her exquisite heat. He remembered the feel of her long, slippery legs locked around his waist, the scrape of her nails against his back, the wild thrusting of her hips.

If the threat of dying had not diminished his hunger for this woman, he knew nothing ever would.

"There's something I've been meaning to ask you," he blurted, reining in his imagination before he tackled her to the ground and mounted her with all the finesse of a caveman.

Lia glanced at him, and he wondered if he'd only imagined the wary look that crossed her face before she smiled inquisitively. "What is it?"

"You told me a few days ago that when you visited Muwaiti, you met an old Creole woman who reminded you of your grandmother. Does that mean you have Creole blood in your family?"

She nodded. "On my mother's side. She's from Louisiana. The Delahousses of Baton Rouge."

"Do you speak Creole?"

She shook her head regretfully. "My mother speaks very little herself. After she married my father, she moved away from home and sort of lost track of her family, her culture."

"That's too bad," Armand murmured.

"It is. When I was growing up, on the few occasions we actually visited Baton Rouge, I used to feel like such an outcast among my aunts and uncles and cousins, who teased me mercilessly for not speaking or understanding Creole." She grimaced at the memory. "For the longest time I blamed my mother, as well as my father, for alienating me from that part of my heritage. I swore, that if I ever got married, I would not do the same thing to my own children."

Armand gazed at her, inwardly smiling at the stubborn defiance that glittered in her dark eyes. "I would teach you Muwaitian Creole," he offered, "but I'm afraid it wouldn't help you much with your Louisiana relatives."

"And that's the really weird thing," Lia said, turning to him. "I actually understand more Muwaitian Creole than the Creole spoken by my mother's people! I understood just about everything you and your family were saying to one another yesterday. Isn't that amazing? I mean, considering that I was only in Muwaiti for two weeks—eight years ago, at that—I think it's pretty remarkable that I still remember the language."

Because you belong there, Armand thought. *With me.*

"That *is* pretty amazing," he said aloud. "But then you already told me that you've always been very proficient with languages. You speak French beautifully," he added, shivering at the memory of the erotic promises they'd whispered to each other as they made love. Damn, that was one of the *hottest* things he'd ever experienced.

Lia met his gaze, and the banked heat in her eyes told him she remembered, as well. Glancing away, she took another sip of her water. "Considering the large Creole population in Muwaiti, I always wondered why Creole isn't one of the official languages."

Armand scowled. "Because Alexandre Biassou believes in mass conformity, much like the French colonists who arrived on the island after the early African settlers. Biassou detests the Creole language. He's been known to refer to it as an uncouth, bastardized version of French, a dialect spoken only by the uncivilized and illiterate. It drives him crazy that there are different variations of Creole spoken throughout the country. He believes that in order for Muwaiti to compete on a global scale, we must all speak French, the language of the so-called noblemen who colonized and enslaved our ancestors."

Lia shook her head in disgust. "A dictator through and through," she pronounced with withering scorn. "It's rather hypocritical of Biassou to talk about competing globally when he has single-handedly destroyed the Muwaitian economy and damaged important free-trade agreements with so many countries. Furthermore, he has lowered workers' wages and—"

Seeing the way Armand was staring at her, and mistaking the cause, she broke off abruptly with a sheepish grin. "Er, sorry. Didn't mean to get carried away. I know I'm preaching to the choir."

"No, I wanted you to continue," Armand said huskily, his heart racing with excitement and something else, something he was afraid to identify. "Your passion was…inspiring."

Lia chuckled self-consciously. "Like I warned you before, there are certain issues I feel very strongly about. Greedy, corrupt presidents who take from the people they're supposed to be serving is one of my hot-button issues."

Armand smiled, still gazing intently at her. "My countrymen would be very fortunate to have such a strong, passionate advocate on their side."

"They already have one—you. And when you become president," Lia said with a sly smile, "you can reverse everything that horrible man has done over the last four years. And hey, you can even make Creole one of the official languages."

Armand shook his head. "I'm not running for president," he said, but his voice lacked the usual vehemence he expressed whenever his brother Henri broached this topic, which had been often.

"Why not?" Lia demanded. "Why wouldn't you consider running for president?"

He tossed a few chunks of wood onto the dying fire, watching as the flames leaped and danced to life. "I'm not a politician," he said simply.

"Who says you have to be?" she challenged. "If I'm not mistaken, the current Muwaitian president is a politician, and look how *that* turned out."

Armand's mouth twisted sardonically. "Good point."

Lia studied him thoughtfully for several moments. "I know I've only known you less than a week, but I think the people of Muwaiti would be very lucky to have you as their new president. Who better to lead the country into the future than the man who fought to get it back for them?"

Armand smiled a little. "That's very good. Maybe I could use that as a campaign slogan. I don't suppose you'd be interested in becoming my speechwriter?"

She chuckled. "I already have a job, but if you decide to use that as your slogan, I'll let you take the credit. How does that sound?"

His smile softened. "You've got a deal."

Inexplicably his throat felt tight, clogged with emotion. It had been a long day, he reminded himself. He was tired and edgy, and his nerves were frayed like hell. The raw emotion he suddenly felt was a delayed reaction to the harrowing events of the past eleven hours.

But deep down inside Armand knew it was much more than that. Time was running out. He had only a few more days to convince Lia to return to Muwaiti with him when this assignment was over. And even *that* depended on the outcome of the hearing. If Alexandre Biassou walked away a free man, Armand knew what he had to do, and nothing or no one—not even the woman he loved—would stop him. He knew that killing Biassou would put an end to his future, one way or another. But as far as Armand was concerned, a future under the continued dictatorship of Biassou was no future at all.

"Penny for your thoughts," Lia said, watching him quietly.

He managed a half smile. "They're worth more than that," he quipped. But her words had triggered a memory from earlier, an image that had been nagging at his conscience all day.

He looked at her. "There's something else I've been meaning to ask you about."

"What's that?"

"Back at the cabin, when you were leaning over the mercenary's body—" This time there was no mistaking the wary gleam that filled her dark eyes. She bit her bottom lip and glanced away.

Intrigued, Armand continued, "You were asking him who had sent him there. At one point you screamed, 'What does that mean?' as if you'd heard something. But he hadn't said anything. I know, because I was standing there the whole time.

Why did you ask him that? It was almost like…" He trailed off for a moment, searching for the right words, knowing he would sound crazy no matter what.

Finally he just blurted, "It was like you were trying to read his mind."

Lia was staring into the fire, not at him. So she didn't see the look of utter astonishment on his face when she said quietly, "I was."

Lia was as shocked as Armand to hear those two words leave her mouth. She hadn't planned on sharing her secret with him—ever.

Now it was too late.

In a low, carefully measured voice, Armand said, "Did I hear you correctly? Did you just tell me that you were trying to read that mercenary's mind?"

Lia hesitated, then nodded. "Yes."

"How?"

She drew a long, deep breath and took the final plunge. "I can read minds."

Armand said nothing for what seemed an eternity.

When Lia finally worked up the courage to look at him, she found him staring at her in stunned disbelief. And then suddenly a wide, knowing grin swept across his face. "That was good, *chère*. Very convincing. You almost had me going there."

Lia stared at him wordlessly.

As the silence stretched between them, his eyes narrowed on hers. "Wait a minute," he said slowly. "You weren't teasing me, were you?"

"No."

"You…you can *read minds*?"

Lia nodded. "That's how I knew the mercenary wasn't really an electrician. Yes, the lie he told about the scar made me suspicious of him, but I didn't know for sure until I actually read his mind. I'd patted him down before letting him inside the cabin, so he had to leave his weapons in the van. When he claimed he needed to go get his tools, that's when I stopped him."

"My God," Armand breathed, staring at her with a mixture of curiosity and fascination. "How long have you had this gift?"

"My whole life. I inherited it from my great-grandmother Genevieve, who was a voodoo priestess in Baton Rouge. She owned a storefront boutique back in the fifties, but because many whites weren't entirely comfortable patronizing a black-owned business, she had to come up with additional ways to make a living. So she told fortunes, read palms and tarot cards, practiced voodoo. Her ability to read minds proved to be lucrative for her and her family. Until the day she read a white customer's palm and realized that the woman was planning to harm her own child."

"What did she do?" Armand asked. "Your great-grandmother, I mean?"

"She begged her not to do it, but the woman got angry and claimed she didn't know what Grandma Genevieve was talking about. After she left the store, Grandma Genevieve didn't know what to do. She was a black woman living in the segregated South. If she warned others or went to the authorities with what she knew, they would call her crazy or throw *her* in jail for slandering a white woman. So she kept quiet, hoping she was mistaken, or hoping that the lady would change her mind about hurting her child. Two days later, the drowned body of a little white boy was found in the river. When the townspeople learned that the woman had gone to see my great-grandmother just days before she killed her son, and that Grandma Genevieve had done nothing to prevent it, they became enraged. They set her store on fire while she was trapped inside. She died in the blaze."

"Mon Dieu," Armand muttered grimly. "That's terrible."

Lia nodded in agreement. "My mother wasn't very proud

of that part of her family history. Which is why she and my father never told me about my great-grandmother. When they found out I had inherited Grandma Genevieve's mind-reading ability, they were shocked and devastated. I remember my mother crying and rocking me in her arms, saying it wasn't my fault, that it was a family curse that had skipped two generations. That's when I learned all about Grandma Genevieve, the voodoo priestess."

"How old were you when you found out you could read minds?" Armand asked, clearly riveted by her tale.

"I was five years old when I could actually articulate what was happening to me. Before that I didn't understand why I could hear other people's thoughts when I touched them."

"Wait. You have to be touching someone to read their mind?"

"Yes. That's how it works for me. I can't read minds without skin-to-skin physical contact." A sad little smile touched her mouth. "One day when I was five, my father picked me up and was carrying me to the car to take me to school. I looked into his eyes and asked him, 'Daddy, how did Mommy catch ovarian cancer?' He was so shocked he nearly dropped me!"

Armand said quietly, "Your mother had ovarian cancer?"

Lia nodded. "They had just found out the day before. They were waiting for the right opportunity to tell me. My father thought I must have overheard them discussing it in their bedroom. When he asked me if I'd been eavesdropping, I pointed to his head and told him, 'I heard it in here.' I think that was the first time I ever saw my daddy cry."

Armand reached over and gently touched her cheek. "I'm sorry," he murmured.

Lia captured his hand and held it between hers. "It's all right. Thankfully they caught the cancer in time. My mother has been cancer-free and healthy for over twenty years."

"That's wonderful," Armand said warmly.

Lia nodded, smiling. "Her only regret was that she couldn't have any more children. But after a while, she realized that having *one* psychic child was more than enough for her to handle."

Armand chuckled softly. "I'm sure." He looked down at their joined hands, and Lia didn't need her gift to know what he was thinking.

"You're wondering whether I can read your mind," she murmured.

He nodded, meeting her gaze. "Can you?"

She searched his face. "How would it make you feel if I could?"

"A little embarrassed, to be honest with you."

"Why?"

His lips quirked, and there was a decidedly sensual gleam in his eyes. "If you knew some of the thoughts I've been having about you, believe me, you'd think twice before coming anywhere near me."

Lia's belly quivered with arousal. She gave him a sultry smile. "How do you know I haven't been having rather explicit thoughts about *you?*"

He flashed a wolfish grin. "I sure as hell hope you have."

Lia laughed, gently tracing the lines in his warm, calloused palm.

He watched her for a moment. "Are you reading my palm?"

"Uh-huh. Do you know what I see?"

He shook his head, his eyes never leaving hers.

"I see you testifying at that hearing in five days, telling the world all the reasons why Alexandre Biassou deserves to spend the rest of his rotten life behind bars. I see those wise, compassionate members of the Security Council heeding your people's cry for justice and handing down the punishment Biassou so richly deserves—"

"Death," Armand growled.

Lia stopped, probing the feral intensity of his eyes. "If that's what the Security Council decides—"

His face hardened. "That's what he deserves. Nothing less."

A fine chill ran through Lia, despite the humid night. "Listen to me," she said, low and controlled. "You are *not* to take the law into your own hands. If that's what you're thinking of doing, put it out of your mind right now!"

A mocking gleam entered his eyes. "You mean, you don't know what I'm thinking?"

"No, I don't!"

He frowned. "What are you saying? You can't read my mind?"

"No, damn it. For whatever reason, I can't read your mind, Armand. It's never happened to me before, but I guess there's a first time for everything. You must have some sort of genetic anomaly that counteracts my psychic ability!"

"Really?" He blinked, then shook his head as if to clear it. "This is surreal. I can't believe we're actually having this conversation. I feel like we're on the set of a movie, where the two dueling superheroes suddenly realize they're the yin and yang to each other."

Lia was not amused. "Go ahead and make fun of me," she fumed, quickly gathering their trash. "That's the kind of reaction I expected from you anyway, which is why I've never told anyone but my parents!"

"Wait a minute!" Armand protested as she jumped to her feet. "I wasn't making fun of you."

Ignoring him, Lia marched over to the trash receptacle and dumped in their empty plates and bottles. Armand grabbed her before she could start toward the storm-cellar door that led down to the underground bunker.

"Look at me." He tipped her chin upward, forcing her to meet the glittering intensity of his gaze. "I was *not* making fun of you, Lia. I think you're the most wonderful, extraordinary woman I've ever met. I believed that before you told me about your special gift, and I believe it even more so now."

"You don't think I'm a freak?" Lia retorted.

Armand shook his head, tenderly stroking her cheek. "How could I ever think that about you? Do you have any idea how much you mean to me? I'm in love with you, Lia. I love you so damn much it kills me to think about going back to Muwaiti without you."

Lia's heart squeezed painfully. Tears rushed to her eyes, spilled down her cheeks. But before Armand could gather her into his arms, she stepped out of reach and pinned him with an unwavering stare.

"If you love me, then promise me you won't go after Biassou if he walks," she commanded, her voice husky with emotion. "Promise me."

Armand clenched his jaw, then shook his head slowly.

"Promise me."

His eyes went hard and flat. "I can't make that promise."

"Damn you!"

"Lia—"

"Are you crazy?" she screamed. "Do you have a death wish? Do you have *any* idea what will happen to you if you try to kill Biassou? If you succeed, you'll be sent to prison—or executed! And if you fail, God help you. Remember those gruesome punishments you were talking about earlier? The ones Biassou is notorious for? How much worse do you think it will be for *you* if you try to kill him? He will subject you to the worst, most excruciating torture you've ever imagined, and then he will smile in your face before killing you! Is that what you want? Are you trying to become a damn martyr?"

"What other choice do I have?" Armand exploded, his eyes flashing with fury. "I had that son of a bitch right where I wanted him—twice. But I was trying to be honorable and humane. Like my father, and like Francois Seligny. So I let Biassou go. *Twice,* damn it. And because I spared his worthless life, hundreds of innocent people have died. Do you think my act of mercy comforts me at night? Do you think I congratulate myself for taking the high road? No! So, yes, Lia, if the

Security Council fails to do what's right, I'm going after Biassou to finish what I started."

Lia stared at him, trembling with rage and despair. "I won't let you. For your own good I'm going to tell someone. I'm going to make sure you can't get anywhere near him."

"Don't bother," Armand sneered. "I got to him before, and I will get to him again. Believe that."

Chilled by the lethal promise in his eyes, Lia realized she was fighting a losing battle. Heaving an angry breath, she threw her hands up in the air.

"Fine," she snapped. "You want to get yourself killed? Be my damn guest. If that's how you want to repay me for repeatedly putting my ass on the line to save you, that's fine with me. You know what? Don't even come down to the bunker with me tonight. Sleep out here, out in the open. There's no point in me trying to protect you anymore if you're just going to run out and get yourself killed anyway!"

Armand descended upon her. She fought against him, swinging wildly and shoving at his chest, but he was too strong for her, pinning her arms between them, imprisoning her in his embrace until the fight gradually drained out of her and she melted in his arms with a muffled sob. He crushed her to him, kissing her fervently, running his hands over her hair and face, whispering tender endearments against her mouth.

With only a look passing between them, they turned and made their way down the concrete stairs into the dank, dusty cellar. Lia had lit scented candles earlier, hoping to dispel some of the gloom and the musty odor that permeated the air.

They undressed each other quickly, fingers tangling in their desperate haste. When they came together, flesh to flesh, it was in an explosion of heat and need. Wrapped in each other's arms, they sank to their knees on the soft pile of sleeping bags that covered the cement floor. He cradled her face between his hands, and her head went back as he kissed her throat, his teeth and tongue tormenting the sensitive flesh until a liquid rush flooded her loins.

She pushed him onto his back, then straddled his lower thighs. He propped himself on his elbows and watched as she brushed her wet, pulsing sex along his skin, back and forth, up and down, making him shudder. Their gazes locked as she leaned down and took his throbbing penis deep inside her mouth. He swore hoarsely, his eyes smoldering with desire as she sucked him, using her tongue in ways she'd never dreamed of doing to another man. She could feel the tension building in his body, hear his harsh breathing in the silence of the cellar.

And then suddenly he was gripping her hair, pulling back her head. His tiger eyes gleamed in the candlelit darkness, fierce with arousal. He sat up, and she quickly climbed onto his lap, wrapping her legs around his hips, locking her feet behind his broad back. He grasped her buttocks, lifting and sliding her onto his erection. Her breath hissed out of her, her back arching at the erotic invasion.

With her body molded perfectly to his, he began thrusting inside her, long, deep, penetrating strokes. She clung to his big shoulders, her fingertips digging into his muscles, her body on fire. He lowered his head, closing his full lips around one distended nipple. Lia moaned, waves of pleasure crashing through her. She reached down behind her, stroking his engorged testicles. He groaned and thrust harder, faster.

As she stared into his hard face, watching his focused intensity, she realized she had never felt closer, more connected to anyone than she did to this man. Whatever happened tomorrow, she would always love him, always long for him.

He gripped her tightly, driving rhythmically inside her. She clawed at his back, driven by a savage, blinding hunger that threatened to consume her. Moments later she came with a violent shudder, her head falling back on a soundless cry as the force of his own release filled her.

They made love long into the night, intensely, passionately, because the future was paved with danger and tomorrow was not promised. And when the end came for both of them in a final shattering climax, Lia buried her face against his chest and closed her eyes as silent, mournful tears rolled down her cheeks.

I love you. Please don't ever leave me.

Chapter 17

Thursday, September 11, 2008
0900 hours
Fredericksburg, Virginia
Day 7

The next morning after breakfast, Lia pulled out her prepaid cell phone and checked her voice mail.

Still no messages.

She disconnected and stared at the phone, frustration and dread coiling in her gut. The mole was waiting for her to make the first move.

Sooner or later, she'd have no choice.

Beside her in the car, Armand stared through the windshield, a solitary muscle leaping in his jaw. He'd been mostly silent throughout breakfast, his face preoccupied and stony. Even when Lia joked that the waiter was staring at her bruised cheek and probably blaming Armand for it, his answering smile was distracted. Now as they sat in the car, he seemed totally oblivious to her presence. Or so she thought until he suddenly spoke.

"How much do you know about the assassination plot?"

Startled, Lia looked at him. "The one involving Biassou?"

Armand nodded tightly.

"I don't know the details, if that's what you're asking. For assignments like these, protective agents are usually kept on a need-to-know basis. In this instance, *you* are all I need to know. However, based on the hush-hush nature of your extraction and delivery to the United States, I have to assume that Biassou was either plotting to assassinate the president, or the vice president."

Armand stared at her, vaguely amused. "You never even asked."

"I'm not supposed to. That's against protocol." She searched his face, her mouth curving ruefully. "Of course, now that I've broken just about every rule in the book, I might as well go all the way. President or vice president?"

"The president. Biassou despises Grace Fordham. He sees her as a serious threat to his regime. If she's reelected—"

Lia snorted. "That's a foregone conclusion. She's very popular in this country. She has a commanding double-digit lead over her Republican opponent in all the polls. Some are even calling the election a mere formality."

Armand nodded with a grim smile. "Of course, Biassou knows all this. Which is why he's trying to get rid of her now, before she's reelected. His presidency won't survive four more years of her aggressive campaign against him."

Lia turned in her seat to face him. "So how did you learn about the assassination plot?"

"Jean-Claude Baptiste, a disgruntled member of Biassou's party, came to me and told me everything. He even provided incontrovertible proof of the plot—tapes, audio recordings from secret meetings."

"He gave you copies?"

Armand nodded. "Biassou suspects, but doesn't know for sure that I have copies. After he killed Baptiste, he ransacked his house and confiscated everything. Whoever is working with him doesn't know about the copies, either. I suspect he, or she, planted the listening devices in our cabin hoping I would confide in you."

"Good thing I never asked," Lia muttered.

Armand smiled blandly. "I wouldn't have told you anyway."

"Why? Because you don't trust me?"

"No, because I don't want to endanger your life any more than it already is. Why do you always have to think the worst?"

"Force of habit. Anyway, why wait weeks until the hearing? Why not just present the evidence to the Security Council and arrest Biassou now?"

"Because no one knows I have the evidence. No one but President Fordham."

Lia frowned. "I don't understand."

"For the last two years, Fordham has been monitoring the situation in Muwaiti and working to build a case against Biassou. She's had several meetings with members of the United Nations Security Council to explore the possibility of bringing Biassou to trial for crimes against humanity. When I first contacted the Secret Service to alert them to the assassination plot, it took a while for my message to be screened, authenticated and routed through the proper channels. It was President Fordham herself who contacted me again. She said she'd been praying for that final piece, the linchpin in her case against Biassou. If I didn't know better, I would think she was happy that he was plotting to assassinate her. She said my testimony would give her the ammunition she needed to finally nail the bastard."

Lia let out a choked laugh. "She actually *said* that?"

Armand chuckled. "Verbatim. And when I told her about the evidence in my possession, I could have sworn she jumped out of her chair and danced around the Oval Office."

Lia laughed. "That wouldn't surprise me. I've met her several times over the years, even spent a weekend with her at Camp David when I was filling in for one of the members of her protection detail. She's quite a character—warm, charming and feisty as hell."

Armand smiled a little. "Anyway, we both agreed to keep the evidence concealed until the hearing. The information she filtered through the channels was that I *didn't* have the proof. Fordham knew that Biassou couldn't be acting alone, that he had to have a co-conspirator who was helping him plot her assassination, someone with top-secret clearance and someone who would have access to her itinerary. By waiting until the hearing, she was hoping to flush out the mole."

Lia's mind was reeling. "And has she? Has she learned the mole's identity?"

Armand stared at her. "That's what you and I have to find out," he said with quiet gravity. "I've been the bait. Now we just have to lure in the prey."

Lia held his gaze for a moment, then drew a long, deep breath and nodded. She knew what she had to do.

She dialed Janikowski's cell-phone number. Once again, she got her voice mail. It was as if Janikowski had simply disappeared off the face of the earth.

"Something's wrong," Lia muttered, disconnecting the call.

"She's still not answering?"

"No. And I don't think it's because she's in on this. I think something has happened to her."

Armand frowned. "Call the assistant director."

Lia was already dialing the number to Bill McManus's office. His secretary answered and patched her through almost immediately.

"Special Agent Charles," McManus greeted her congenially. "I was just about to call you."

Lia looked at Armand. "You were, sir?"

"Yes. Nancy asked me to pinch-hit for her while she's gone.

She had a family emergency and had to leave town suddenly. It was a private matter, from what I understand, so she instructed her secretary to let everyone know she was on a special assignment. Anyway, I've been making my rounds this morning, checking in with all her agents out in the field. You were next on my list."

"I see." Lia could hear the dying mercenary's voice in her head. *Quick...silver... Don't... Quick...silver...*

What had it meant? Was he thinking of a name? A place? A secret code?

"So how's everything going with Magliore?" McManus inquired, a friendly smile in his voice. "How's he adjusting to life outside of Muwaiti?"

"Oh, well, you know. As well as can be expected." The voice was growing louder in her head, a persistent buzz. *Failed... Quick...silver... Don't...wanna die...*

Closing her eyes, she reached up and rubbed her temple, which was suddenly throbbing.

On the other end, McManus shuffled a stack of papers. "Well, if you don't need anything—"

Lia blurted, "Actually, sir, there is something I need to tell you."

"Yes? What is it?"

She locked gazes with Armand. "Our location was compromised. I had to get Magliore somewhere safe."

"What?" McManus sounded genuinely shocked. "When did this happen, Agent Charles?"

"Yesterday, sir."

"Yesterday?" he echoed in disbelief. "And you're just now reporting—"

"Under the circumstances, sir, I felt I had no other choice." *Quick...silver... Quick...silver.*

"Fine," McManus snapped. "We'll discuss it when you come into the office. I'm dispatching a team to pick up you and Magliore. What is your location?"

Lia hesitated. She could imagine an angry flush suffusing McManus's face. She could see his thin lips pressed together, his gray eyes narrowed in the telltale manner that always warned others when he was not in a good mood. No, wait, Lia amended. Not gray…silver. His eyes were more silver. And something else… Another agent had once described him as having an unpredictable temperament. Calm and friendly one minute, volatile and abusive the next. Because the Secret Service used code names for presidents, first ladies, and other prominent individuals and locations, the agent had joked that if McManus ever had a code name, it would be Quicksilver.

Quicksilver.

Lia froze, the muscles in the back of her neck tightening. A clammy sensation settled over her skin.

"Special Agent Charles," McManus ground out tersely. "What is your location?"

Lia swallowed. "I'm sorry, sir. I can't tell you that."

"What?" he exploded. "Special Agent Charles, have you taken leave of your senses? Need I remind you that Armand Magliore is a key witness in an investigation that could have international ramifications? He is a Secret Service asset, not your damn boyfriend!"

"Interesting word choice," Lia said softly. "I never said anything about him being my boyfriend, sir. Where would you get that idea?"

On the other end, McManus swore loudly and viciously. "For the last time, Agent Charles, I am ordering you to—"

"Does the name Quicksilver mean anything to you?"

Dead silence.

And that was all the confirmation she needed.

"Listen," McManus said in a low, conciliatory tone, "let's discuss this when you get here. You've obviously had a very trying—"

"Goodbye, sir," Lia said coldly.

She ended the call and looked over at Armand. He was watching her with a quiet, sympathetic expression.

"I'm sorry," he murmured.

Lia shook her head, numb with shock. "Bill McManus was responsible for my promotion and transfer to protective services four years ago. Since then, he's been very supportive of my career growth and achievements." She stiffened, struck by a new realization. "He's the one who assigned me to protect you. He sent me on this mission fully expecting me to be killed alongside you. Like a lamb to the slaughter."

Armand nodded grimly. "So what do you want to do now?"

Lia's jaw hardened. "I want to make him pay for what he's done."

"Then I think it's time we reached out to someone who can make that happen."

Their gazes held. They spoke at the same time: "President Fordham."

Chapter 18

Armand bent over the bathroom sink and splashed cold water over his face and into his eyes, which felt gritty after several days of sleep deprivation. Reaching for a paper towel, he patted his face dry, careful not to drip water onto his well-tailored charcoal suit. Lia had whistled appreciatively when she had come to his hotel room that morning to check up on him. "President Fordham has impeccable taste," she'd declared when Armand had told her where the suit came from.

Armand had gazed into her eyes as she had fixed his tie,

teasing his clumsy handiwork. "Hey, I haven't worn a suit in years," he'd retorted with a grin. "Knotting a tie wasn't exactly a skill I needed to survive in the jungle."

She'd laughingly agreed, and as he had held still for her, his mind had been filled with an image of her, cheeks glowing with health and happiness, belly swollen with their first child, smiling at him as she arranged his tie before he left for work. The image was so vivid, so powerful, that a wave of longing had swept through him, making his chest tighten painfully.

At that moment Lia had met his gaze, her smile fading when she saw the raw, naked yearning on his face. An unnamed emotion had filled her eyes before she had glanced away and straightened his collar, murmuring, "You're good to go," before turning and quietly leaving the room.

It was the last time they'd been alone together this morning.

When they arrived at the United Nations headquarters for the hearing, Lia disappeared with a team of other Secret Service agents to secure the building, leaving Armand in the custody of two senior agents from the president's protection detail. At Grace Fordham's insistence, the two men had pretty much replaced Lia once she and Armand had become guests at the White House. Although the elegant accommodations, sumptuous meals and gracious hospitality were unrivaled, Armand had found himself missing the rustic mountain cabin, even the underground bunker in the woods, where he and Lia had been completely alone, cut off from the rest of the world. In stark contrast, the White House mansion had been a constant beehive of activity, and there had *always* been other people around—stewards, staff, Secret Service agents. After having Lia all to himself for nearly a week, Armand had considered himself lucky if they were left alone for more than five minutes. Even their leisurely stroll through the picturesque Rose Garden had been observed by curious onlookers.

It wasn't the way he'd hoped to spend his final days in America with her.

President Fordham had assured him that, barring any unforeseen circumstances at the hearing, he and his family would be able to return to Muwaiti within a week.

Which meant he had a week to convince Lia to return home with him and marry him—a daunting task further complicated by their lack of privacy. On the few occasions when they were alone, Lia had assiduously avoided talking about their relationship, or the future.

He'd told her that he loved her, but so far, she hadn't reciprocated. So he had decided it was time to lay it all on the line. It was time to tell her the whole truth, that he'd been in love with her for the past eight years, ever since he had first laid eyes on her outside that clinic. Surely she couldn't turn him away after hearing a confession like that, he reasoned.

He hoped.

If Armand hadn't been so preoccupied with thoughts of Lia, he might have heard the dull thud of two bodies hitting the floor outside the men's restroom. He might have looked up faster when the door suddenly opened and a dark shape stepped inside the room.

By the time he switched off the tap water and turned his head, Alexandre Biassou stood less than ten feet away.

And he was pointing a silenced pistol right at him.

Armand's mouth went dry. *So this is how it will end,* he thought grimly. Gunned down by his worst enemy in a Manhattan restroom. It shouldn't have surprised him. Hadn't he always known, on some unconscious level, that his own life would end in bloodshed, just as his father and his mentor had died violently?

Slowly, deliberately, he wadded up the used paper towel and dropped it into the trash receptacle built into the counter.

"So we meet again, *diable,*" he murmured, his voice edged with dark humor.

Biassou's cold, black eyes gleamed with malicious satisfaction. "Did you think this was over?" he demanded in deep, thickly accented tones. "Did you think you had won?"

"I have," Armand said with unerring calm. "At this very moment, the members of the Security Council are listening to audio recordings in which you describe how you intended to assassinate the president of the United States. Bill McManus, your co-conspirator, has already been taken into federal custody and has confessed to everything, including the murder of Nancy Janikowski, who had the misfortune of stumbling upon your assassination plot and confronting him. All of your dirty little secrets have been exposed. This hearing is nothing more than a formality. Your fate has been sealed."

"You insolent little fool!" Biassou spat, a vein throbbing in his temple. "I could have given you anything you wanted. Wealth, prestige, property, an abundance of beautiful women at your disposal. I could have made you prime minister—second-in-command."

Armand let out a harsh laugh. "I thought I made it perfectly clear to you before that my soul is not for sale, *diable*. I want nothing to do with you or your corrupt regime."

Biassou smiled, a slow, sinister smile Armand recognized from his nightmare. "If my fate has been sealed," the dictator said, raising his gun to eye level, "so has yours."

A sudden commotion down the hallway made him hesitate for a split second, his head cocked at a listening angle.

Quick as a thought, Armand dove to the tiled floor just as Biassou fired at him. The blast was muffled by the silencer, but the bullet that grazed Armand's left shoulder was very real.

Ignoring the hot stab of pain, he raised his pant leg, seized the small knife strapped to his ankle and hurled it at his adversary. The knife shot through the air and hit Biassou squarely in the chest.

His eyes bulged in shock, then slowly lowered to the pearl-handled knife protruding from his body. Recognizing Francois Seligny's weapon, he coughed and then began to laugh, a dark, menacing rumble that sent chills down Armand's spine and made him wish he could have snuck one of his guns into the building.

Biassou looked up, his malevolent gaze locking with Armand's. "I appreciate your sense of poetic justice, Magliore," he rasped. "Killing me with the blade of your slain mentor. Perhaps the three of us will meet again in hell."

He raised his pistol and Armand calmly closed his eyes, bracing for death, thinking of Lia and what would never be.

The next sound he heard was the bathroom door crashing against the wall and the blast of a single gunshot. He opened his eyes in time to see Alexandre Biassou pitch forward like a felled tree, a bullet hole punched neatly through the center of his forehead. His body landed on the floor with a heavy thud and did not move again.

Lia stood in the doorway gripping a 9mm, her nostrils flared, her dark eyes simmering with controlled rage. When her gaze landed on Armand sprawled a few feet away, wounded but very much alive, tears of relief sprang to her eyes. She holstered her weapon and hurried to his side as a flurry of agents rushed in after her, shouting and barking commands into radios and earpieces.

Kneeling on the floor beside Armand, Lia gathered him into her arms with such stunning force she knocked the air from his lungs. "Oh, my God," she whispered fiercely. "You gave me the scare of my life, damn it!"

Armand tried to laugh, but the sound was strangled, muffled against her fragrant bosom. He could have stayed there forever.

"How the hell did this happen?" another agent demanded, leaning over the dead body of Alexandre Biassou.

Lia answered in angry, staccato tones, "He hired someone to create a diversion in the lobby, and while everyone was distracted, he killed the guards assigned to him and came after Magliore. He had a silencer for the gun he took. The two agents posted outside the restroom probably never even saw him coming. He should have been handcuffed, damn it!"

She drew back from Armand, running one hand over his face, checking his wounded shoulder with the other.

"It's just a flesh wound," he reassured her, pulling himself into a sitting position as pain lanced through his side. "I can hardly even feel it," he lied.

But Lia was already removing his suit jacket and ripping off his shirt to assess the damage. He mustered a sheepish grin for the agents who hovered nearby, watching him with concerned expressions.

"You all right, Mr. Magliore?"

Armand nodded, gazing dreamily at Lia. His beautiful avenging angel. "I'm fine, gentlemen. Just fine."

One week later
Washington, D.C.

Lia sat on a downtown park bench, watching as passersby strolled across the manicured green lawn, sharing carefree laughs that made her envious. Although the afternoon sky was overcast, matching her somber mood, she wore a pair of dark sunglasses to reduce the risk of being recognized.

News of the "deadly showdown at the UN," as the media had dubbed it, had sent shockwaves around the world. One week later, the conspiracy plot involving Alexandre Biassou, President Fordham, the Secret Service and the Muwaitian rebel leader and whistleblower remained the lead story of every news broadcast and newspaper around the globe. Lia, who had hoped to fly beneath the radar, was stunned to wake up one morning and find her photo splashed across the front page of the *Washington Post*. She began receiving so many calls from reporters that she changed her phone number. When the new number was somehow leaked to the press, she unplugged her phone altogether.

Even if she weren't bound by protocol not to speak to the media, Lia had no desire to rehash what had happened when *she* was still struggling to cope with everything.

According to his deposition, Bill McManus had met Alexandre Biassou two years before, when he had accompanied the U.S. secretary of state on a peacekeeping mission to

Muwaiti. Although the peace talks had broken down, Biassou had sensed that he had an ally in the assistant director, who, as it had turned out, was opposed to a female president from the beginning. The two men had begun secretly corresponding, and it wasn't long before the assassination plot was hatched. To ensure that the trail would never lead back to him, McManus had stipulated that his name, identity and the specific nature of his involvement be withheld from members of Biassou's faction. Biassou was simply to tell his men that he had a powerful American informant, nothing more.

McManus had been so determined to cover his own tracks that he had murdered Nancy Janikowski, whom he had known and worked with for years, when she unwittingly intercepted a communiqué from Biassou. He'd shot her in cold blood, then buried her body in the woods and fabricated the story about a family emergency.

Lia blinked back tears, reliving the sight of her former supervisor lying in a coffin at the funeral, her dark hair neatly combed over the gaping bullet wound in her temple. The likelihood that McManus would be convicted of treason did little to assuage the grief and anger Lia felt. The weight of Janikowski's death, on top of everything else that had transpired over the past two weeks, pressed down on her like an anvil. She wondered if she would ever recover from the shock, the pain of betrayal, the senseless loss of a good friend and colleague.

Only time would tell.

She didn't turn her head as Armand walked up the path and joined her on the park bench, deliberately sitting on the opposite end.

"Thanks for agreeing to meet me out here," he said ruefully. "I know it's probably not a good idea to be seen in public together, but it seemed like the only way to finally get some privacy. Your apartment is crawling with reporters, and even a public park seems more private than the White House."

Lia smiled softly. "You don't have to thank me for coming.

You didn't think I would let you leave without saying good-bye, did you?"

Armand stared down at his hands clasped between his legs. "I was hoping you wouldn't say goodbye at all," he said in a low voice.

Lia's heart contracted. She kept her eyes trained ahead. "How's your family doing? Are they enjoying their stay at the White House?"

"For the first few days. Now that the novelty is wearing off, they're eager to return home and be reunited with their friends. I am, too."

Once again Lia felt that painful squeezing in her chest. Forcing herself to ignore it, she said, "That's understandable. How's your shoulder?"

"Good as new. How's your heart?"

She started, caught off guard by the question. She swallowed. "I—I don't know what you mean."

"Don't you?"

Lia said nothing.

"Take these off," Armand murmured, reaching across the bench to remove her sunglasses. "I can't see your eyes. And you look like a Secret Service agent."

"I *am* a Secret Service agent," Lia said, quietly emphatic. *And I always will be.* She let the unspoken words hang between them.

Armand held her gaze for a long, charged moment.

She was the first to look away. "What time does your flight leave tonight?" she asked, although she already knew the answer, had been agonizing over the date and time of his departure for days now.

"Eight," he replied.

She nodded, her throat tightening.

"Am I the only one," he said huskily, "who thought we had something special, a rare, powerful connection?"

Lia closed her eyes. "Of course not," she whispered.

"Then why do you refuse to discuss our future together?"

"What kind of future can we have, Armand?" she cried, opening her eyes and staring at him. "We live thousands of miles apart from each other."

"It doesn't have to stay that way!"

"Who's going to make the sacrifice?" she challenged. "Who's going to leave behind everything they know to make this work?"

His piercing amber eyes drilled into hers. "I love you, Lia. I want to marry you. I want you to return to Muwaiti with me. Help me rebuild my country. Help me restore my people's faith and trust in the government. Help me fulfill whatever destiny God has chosen for me. For *us*."

Lia stared at him, her heart beating savagely against her rib cage. It was tempting, so very tempting, to accept his offer. She loved him like no other. But what he was asking of her, *demanding* of her, was too much.

"Damn it, Armand!" she exploded. "You're forcing me to choose between your life and mine. My mother had to make the same choice, and it's not fair."

His expression turned fierce. "Are your parents happy? Have they not been happily married for over thirty years?"

"That's not the point!"

"Then what *is* the point?" he snapped.

"The point is that I love my job, and I worked too damn hard to get where I am just to walk away. The fact that you can't understand that is problematic in and of itself."

"What I can't understand," Armand growled through clenched teeth, "is how you can remain so loyal to an organization that abused and betrayed your trust."

Lia's eyes narrowed sharply on his face. "Don't you dare try to use what happened as leverage. The Secret Service did not abuse and betray my trust—Bill McManus did. There's a big differ—"

"I love you, damn it. I love you!"

She wavered, hot tears filling her eyes. "I know—"

"No, you don't understand." Moving closer, Armand grabbed her face between his hands. The searing intensity of his gaze made her tremble. "This wasn't an overnight thing for me. I've loved you for eight years, Lia. *Eight* years."

She frowned. "I don't understand."

"I saw you that day, outside the clinic in Port le Duc. I was passing by, on my way to another military base, and I saw you! You were making the children laugh so they wouldn't be afraid of the vaccination needles, and I thought you were the most beautiful, bewitching woman I had ever seen. I went back the next day, but you had already left the island." His voice softened, deepening with emotion. "I never forgot you, Lia. I dreamed about you for years, wondering if I would ever see you again. In a strange way, dreaming about you helped me get through those dark, endless days and nights of fighting. You know how soldiers carry around photographs of their wives and girlfriends, their newborn babies? Well, I carried a picture of you in my mind, in my heart. You gave me something to hope for, something to believe in, even though I knew I would probably never see you again. And then, suddenly, you were there."

Incredulous, Lia traced his features with her eyes. She couldn't believe what she was hearing. "Why did you wait this long to tell me?" she whispered, her throat constricted.

He shook his head. "I don't know. It wasn't a conscious decision. When I saw you that night in the jungle, I was so shocked that you were actually there, I could hardly speak. After that night there just never seemed to be the right time to tell you. After a while I was afraid I might scare you off by coming across as an obsessed weirdo."

Lia chuckled softly. "I wouldn't have thought that about you."

"I wasn't taking any chances." His eyes probed hers. "Anyway, would it have made a difference if I'd told you earlier?

Would we be having a different conversation right now if you'd known how long I've been in love with you?"

Averting her gaze, Lia pushed out a long, shaky breath. "I…I don't even know what to say. What you've just shared with me… I'm humbled beyond words."

"I don't want your humility, Lia." His voice was strained.

She turned back to him, realizing she'd unintentionally hurt him. "I love you. After everything we've been through, you *must* know that. I love you so much. When I realized that Biassou was missing, and I couldn't reach anyone on the radio, I was so scared. My God, I've never been so scared in my life! I—I thought I might be too late. I thought he'd already killed you, and it…it tore me apart!"

"Don't think about it," Armand murmured soothingly. "It's over now. You got there in time, and you saved me, sweetheart. Let's put all that behind us and look ahead to the future. Come home with me, Lia. Be my wife."

Her heart thudded hard in her throat as he stared into her eyes, ensnaring her, compelling her, bending her to his will as easily as he had seduced her.

She forced herself to break eye contact. She couldn't breathe, couldn't *think* straight when he was looking at her like that. "Why can't we reach some sort of compromise? Maybe we could—"

"I can't leave Muwaiti." His tone was flat. Final.

Lia looked at him. "But *I* have to leave my family, my job, my home," she said bitterly. "Is that it?"

He just stared at her, awaiting her decision.

Her insides began to tremble. "I—I need more time. I can't just make a life-altering decision like this on a spur of the moment."

"How much time do you need?"

"I don't know!"

After a lengthy silence, Armand rose to his feet. When he spoke, his voice was cool and detached. "I think you've already made your decision. Goodbye, Lia."

She stared up at him, stunned and angry that he could close the door between them so neatly. As if he were merely adjourning a business meeting that had not gone according to plan. She half expected him to reach out and politely shake her hand.

Her chin lifted proudly. "Goodbye, Armand." How she got those words out past the tightness in her throat was beyond her.

He inclined his head, then turned and walked away.

Lia sat there, watching as he climbed into the nondescript town car that would take him back to the White House. Back to the airport.

Out of her life.

This time for good.

Chapter 19

Six months later
Early March

Somehow she made it through the bleak days and weeks and months that followed. She returned to work after taking just a week off and was informed that she'd been transferred to the president's protection detail—a request made by Grace Fordham herself. Two weeks later Lia received another honor, the Presidential Award of Valor, for the courage and resourcefulness she had demonstrated in protecting Armand Magliore. With her parents, friends and colleagues beaming proudly and cheering her on, Lia had accepted the prestigious award, smiling through her heartache and despair.

It had been several weeks before the media maelstrom resulting from the thwarted assassination plot died down, and the November election once again had dominated the news. As expected, Grace Fordham had defeated her Republican opponent to become reelected, but it was the outcome of another election that soon captured the world's attention. In January Armand Magliore had been elected president of Muwaiti by an overwhelming majority, the largest landslide victory in the country's political history. Lia had watched, with tears in her eyes and her chest bursting with pride, as he addressed a jubilant crowd of supporters, thousands of whom had traveled from around the country to usher in their new leader. She had been riveted by the sight of liberated Muwaitians cheering, waving banners and chanting Armand's name with tears of joy streaming down their faces. By the time he had finished his rousing speech, in which he thanked his fellow countrymen for their resilience under Alexandre Biassou and exhorted them to help him rebuild their great nation, Lia was weeping, as well.

When Grace Fordham had traveled to Muwaiti to personally congratulate the new president and to discuss a long-overdue alliance between their two countries, Lia had known it was too soon for her to face Armand again. Fordham had granted her request to forgo the trip, demonstrating the kind of compassion and sensitivity one could only expect from another woman. It was for that same reason that Fordham, upon her return, hadn't told Lia that Armand was rumored to be engaged to Nathalie Seligny, the daughter of former President Francois Seligny. Nathalie, who had returned to Muwaiti after the election, had reportedly accompanied Armand to various social and political functions. When Lia found out—courtesy of a newspaper article titled Muwaitian President Courts Potential First Lady—she'd been devastated.

That was what had finally pushed her over the edge. She took a leave of absence from work and retreated to the comforting warmth and familiarity of her childhood home in Arlington, Virginia.

One Saturday morning in early March, she and her parents were seated in the living room, watching television and debating whether to spend the day working in the garden or catching a matinee and having an early dinner. They had just voted on the latter when the news anchor suddenly announced, "And now, as promised, we bring you our exclusive interview with Muwaiti's newly elected president, Armand Magliore."

Lia froze.

Her mother shot a warning look at her father, who cleared his throat and reached for the remote control on the coffee table.

"No!" Lia cried. "Don't turn it off."

"But, baby—"

"I want to watch it."

Stephen Charles sat back against the sofa, shrugging at his wife as if to say, *What else could I do?*

Lia's pulse thudded as Armand's darkly handsome image filled the television screen. He was dressed in a simple yet tasteful charcoal suit that reminded her of the one he'd worn to the UN hearing. She remembered teasing him as she had re-knotted his tie, then looking into his eyes and seeing the love and desperate yearning she felt mirrored in his gaze. She'd run from him that morning, afraid to face her innermost desires, afraid to wish for something that could never be.

And now, as she greedily drank in the sight of him, she wondered for the umpteenth time whether she'd made the right decision by letting him walk out of her life.

The sound of his deep, magnetic voice filled the living room, washing over her, into her. He was describing his vision for Muwaiti, a true democracy where every citizen, regardless of economic status, could achieve their greatest potential and provide for their families with the full support of their government. The gushing reporter proceeded to rattle off a list of his accomplishments, all the more impressive given the short time he'd been in office.

Unlike his predecessor, Armand had established a cabinet filled with smart, progressive men and women who valued integrity as much as he did and who weren't afraid to disagree with him. He had brokered important treaties with neighboring governments and was working cooperatively with the international community to lift trade sanctions on the exportation of Muwaitian goods and resources. In an effort to revitalize tourism, he had launched a global ad campaign in which he and fellow Muwaitians appeared in a number of television spots surrounded by the lush, tropical beauty of their island. Working with his advisors, Armand had already developed an economic-stimulus package that would resuscitate the economy, drastically reduce unemployment and poverty and increase wages for all workers, including the farmers and merchants who were the backbone of the country's labor force. He successfully overhauled the military, instituting a new-and-improved organizational structure and cleaning house from top to bottom. Those who had gone into hiding after Biassou's death were captured, tried and convicted of their crimes—and no one celebrated this more than the farmers and merchants who had been regularly terrorized by the lawless soldiers.

The news interview was interspersed with footage of Armand as he took the reporter on walking tours of burned-down schools, businesses and neighborhoods—casualties of Biassou's reign of terror and violence. Armand outlined his plans to rebuild the damaged properties and develop new, affordable housing communities once the economy was stabilized. Lia's heart ached at images of him swinging small children into the air, hugging old grandmothers, digging ditches alongside day laborers, laughing and conversing with his reunited freedom fighters. He was their native son, and seeing him on the streets and in the villages, moving freely among his people, made Lia realize like never before that he could never belong anywhere but Muwaiti.

The interview was nearly over when the reporter broached the subject Lia had been dreading. "Is there any truth to the rumors that your marriage to Nathalie Seligny is imminent?"

Armand chuckled softly, and Lia found herself holding her breath, her stomach clenching as she awaited his response.

"Come on," the smiling reporter cajoled. "You *have* to know that everyone is dying to find out whether the world's most eligible bachelor will soon be off the market. Come on, Mr. President, you can give us a little hint. If you want, you can even convey a special message to her while millions of viewers are watching."

Lia could feel her parents' concerned gazes on her. Her father had leaned forward, preparing to grab the remote control and switch the channel if Armand so much as uttered an affectionate word to Nathalie Seligny.

Just when Lia thought she couldn't take the suspense anymore, Armand lifted his eyes to the camera and said with quiet sincerity, "My fighting spirit, my hopes and dreams, will always belong to my beloved countrymen. But my heart has been stolen by the extraordinary woman who saved my life more often than I probably deserved. I never truly thanked her, so if by some miracle she's watching this program, I want her to know how much I appreciate everything she did for me. I wouldn't be here without her."

Lia was half crying and half laughing as she jumped up from the sofa, her heart bursting with sheer joy and relief. "I have to go," she whispered fiercely. "I have to go to him!"

Her parents traded meaningful glances.

"We know, baby," Helene Charles said with a soft, intuitive smile, moisture shimmering in her own eyes as she gazed at her daughter. "We know."

It was just after one o'clock the following afternoon when Lia arrived in the capital city of Port le Duc. The international airport was small but modern, bustling with tourists toting luggage and cameras. The ad campaign apparently had worked.

As Lia walked through the busy terminal, listening to the musical cadence of accents wafting around her, she felt an incredible sense of homecoming.

This was where she belonged.

She'd known it the very first time she visited Muwaiti. She knew it now.

She stepped out into the sunny, humid afternoon and quickly surveyed the row of taxicabs and airport shuttles lining the curb. She went with the first driver who approached her, his teeth flashing white against his shiny dark skin as he beamed a welcoming smile at her.

"You look familiar, *mademoiselle,*" he said, his eyes meeting hers in the rearview mirror. "Where you headed to?"

When Lia told him her destination, his face split into a wide grin. "I think President Magliore will be very happy to see you."

Not as happy as I'll be to see him, Lia thought with mounting anticipation.

As the taxi cruised through the narrow streets of the bustling port city, she took in the colorful sights and sounds as if it were her first visit to the island. She saw whitewashed buildings flanked by swaying palm trees, sidewalk vendors hawking their wares to tourists, and locals gathered in front of shops and restaurants. She saw exotic masks and costumes, wooden figurines and beaded necklaces on display in storefront windows, and she could hear the pulsing rhythm of steel drums interspersed with the sounds of traffic. The city was gearing up for the Carnival of Port le Duc, the national parade that drew thousands of revelers annually. In a week the island would be engulfed by lively music, elaborate floats and nonstop festivities. Already Lia could feel a difference in the air, in the way people moved, an electric energy and vitality that had been missing during her trip to Muwaiti last year. She knew the changed atmosphere had as much to do with the country's new leader as the upcoming Carnival celebration.

They left the main thoroughfare and headed down a two-lane highway that hugged steep cliffs overlooking a breathtaking expanse of turquoise ocean. Before long the presidential palace rolled into view, a large estate set against a stunning

backdrop of mountains. Nestled by tall palms and painstak-
ingly trimmed bushes that exploded in vibrant profusions of
bougainvillea, and featuring steep French windows and
columned porticos, the white mansion did not seem austere and
uninviting nor excessively lavish. It exuded an air of gracious
hospitality that lulled visitors into forgetting that the head of
state resided here.

And suddenly Lia realized why. "This isn't the palace that
Alexandre Biassou built," she said aloud.

The cabdriver smiled at her in the rearview mirror. "*Oui.*
You are correct. This is the original presidential palace, home
to every leader we had before the tyrant. President Magliore
did not want to reside in Biassou's fortress. He considered
tearing it down, but then he decided to turn it into an orphan-
age. Now many of the children don't even want to leave." He
laughed.

Lia smiled, warming with pleasure at Armand's generosity.
A moment later her smile disappeared as they drove past an
unmanned security booth and continued up a long cobblestone
driveway. They passed acres of manicured green lawn and a
stone fountain at the center of the property before coming to
a stop at the bottom of a wide, steep staircase.

Lia climbed out of the taxi before the driver could get out and
open her door. Her stomach was knotted in a vicious tangle of
nerves. She didn't know what she was going to say or do when
she saw Armand. She'd just have to let her heart do the talking.

As the driver removed her suitcase from the trunk, a man
she presumed to be the butler emerged from the house and
quickly descended the steps. "The president is not expecting
any guests today," he said imperiously. "What is the nature of
your visit to the palace, *mademoiselle?*"

Before Lia could respond, the cabdriver laughed and said,
"*Look* at her, mon. Do you not recognize her?"

The butler squinted at Lia for several moments. As recog-
nition slowly dawned, his eyes widened in surprise. He bowed

deferentially and began apologizing. "Forgive me, *mademoiselle,* I did not know you were coming to Muwaiti. This is such an honor. No one told me to expect—"

"*Lia?*"

Lia lifted her gaze to the house—and froze. There, standing in the open doorway and staring at her in stunned disbelief, was Armand. Raw emotion swept through her body with such force it brought tears to her eyes and rooted her to the spot.

He stepped from the doorway and started down the steps, his eyes never leaving hers. He looked so good, and decidedly *un*-presidential, in a black Bob Marley T-shirt and dark jeans that rode low on his hips. President or not, he would always be a renegade. And that was one of the many things she loved about him.

He came to a stop before her, his expression incredulous as he gazed down at her. "What are you doing here?" he whispered hoarsely.

"I…" She had dreamed about him nearly every night for the last six months, and now that he stood less than a foot away from her, words failed her.

Armand just kept staring at her, as if he thought blinking or looking away would cause her to disappear.

They barely noticed as the butler discreetly paid the driver, tipping him generously. It was only when Lia heard the taxi door opening that she broke eye contact with Armand long enough to smile and wave at the friendly cabbie. "*Merci beaucoup,*" she told him.

He tipped his head, grinning broadly. "Enjoy your stay, *mademoiselle.* May it be a long one!"

A silent look passed between Lia and Armand. He gently took her hand, then leaned down and retrieved her suitcase, ignoring the butler's protest. Together they ascended the stairs, their gazes locked on each other.

A small crowd of servants and aides awaited them inside the sweeping elegance of the entrance hall. They were staring at Lia with identical expressions of awed curiosity. Suddenly she felt shy, self-conscious.

Armand handed her suitcase to the butler, then announced, "Everyone, I would like you to meet Miss Lia Charles, from America." His eyes met hers. "She will be staying with us for a very, very long time."

Lia's heart soared.

A loud round of applause filled the room, and as the household staff members bowed and welcomed her with radiant smiles, Lia blinked back tears.

No sooner had the crowd dispersed than she threw her arms around Armand, crushing her mouth to his, kissing him with a blind, hungry desperation she had suppressed for too long. He clutched her tightly to him, his lips ravaging hers, his hands rushing up and down her back.

"I was a fool to let you walk out of my life," she said in a choked whisper against his mouth. "I've been so miserable without you these past six months—so dead inside. I'm so sorry for hurting you!"

He shook his head, brushing tender kisses across her face. "I shouldn't have pressured you like that. I should have given you more time to decide what you wanted."

"But I already *knew* what I wanted," Lia said tearfully. "I wanted *you,* but I was too stubborn and afraid to admit it, and I almost lost you."

Grasping her head in his hands, Armand pressed a hard kiss to her mouth and said huskily, "You could never lose me. I love you. I never stopped."

"I know," she said with a wobbly smile. "I saw the interview on television. What you said at the end— I've never been so relieved in my life!"

He stared at her in wonder. "I've loved you for eight years. Did you think I would get over you in six months?"

"I don't know." She lowered her gaze uncertainly. "When I heard about you and Nathalie Seligny—"

"Look at me." Armand coaxed her chin upward, his eyes tunneling into hers. "Nathalie and I are just friends. That is all we will ever be. You're the only woman for me, Lia. You've ruined me for all others."

A huge, silly grin spread across her face. "You really have a way with words, Armand Magliore. Or should I call you Mr. President? Or Your Excellency? Or would you prefer Your Royal Highness?"

He laughed and she smiled, her voice gentling. "I'm so proud of you, Armand. You did it. You became president of Muwaiti. I was so ecstatic when I heard!"

"You inspired me," he said quietly. "That night at the bunker, when you were speaking with such passion, such conviction, about the problems plaguing Muwaiti. It really struck a chord in me, made me realize like never before what needed to be done."

Pleasure shimmered through her at his words. "Thank you for saying that. But I can't take all the credit. As I recall, it was your brother, Henri, who urged you to run for president long before I did."

Armand grinned sheepishly. "Which is another reason why I made him my chief of staff. Maybe, just maybe, I should start taking his advice more often."

"Maybe." Lia grinned. "Felicite is going to make a wonderful ambassador. She has the perfect personality for it, and I know she'll represent Muwaiti well wherever she goes. That is, if her overprotective big brother lets her go anywhere."

Armand chuckled. "She's a resident ambassador, which means she will reside here at home. But there will be plenty of opportunities for her to travel abroad. I want to repair our diplomatic relations in the international community. Felicite will help me do that."

Lia smiled, laying her hand against his cheek. "You're going to do so many wonderful things for this country—even more than you already have."

Armand caught her hand and brought it to his mouth, pressing an openmouthed kiss to the center of her palm that made her belly quiver. Holding her gaze, he said, "There's still much work to be done. I've surrounded myself with the best people, but I'm still missing the most important piece. I need *you* by my side, Lia. I need you to help me lead my countrymen—*our* countrymen—into the glorious future I promised them. Will you do that?"

Her heart bursting with elation, Lia threw her arms around his neck and kissed him so hungrily there could be no doubt in his mind what her answer was. But just in case it was still unclear, she smiled into his eyes and said, "If you're asking me to be your first lady, the answer is *yes*."

Whooping with delight, Armand lifted her into his arms and swung her around. Lia laughed, wondering if it was possible to be so thoroughly, deliriously happy.

Setting her down gently, his eyes glittering with excitement, Armand began making plans. "You're going to sit right beside me on the float during next week's Carnival kickoff parade. I'm going to introduce you to the people of Muwaiti as their soon-to-be first lady."

His excitement was contagious. Lia smiled at him, even as tears of joy blurred her vision. "How soon are we talking about?"

"Very soon. I can't wait much longer. And I already know the place, this beautiful old cathedral that overlooks the ocean. It holds almost a thousand, which *still* won't be enough for the number of people who'll want to attend our wedding. If you'd like, we can go look at it tomorrow."

"I'd like that very much."

"We can tell my family tonight over dinner. They're going to be thrilled. They know, better than anyone, how badly I've missed you." He grinned. "At one point they even considered flying to America to convince you to change your mind about me."

Lia smiled warmly. "You have a wonderful family. I look forward to getting to know them better."

"They're going to love you, Lia."

"I hope so." She hesitated, biting her bottom lip. "Uh, about the whole mind-reading gift…"

He chuckled softly. "Don't worry, *ma petite*. It will be our little secret."

Lia grinned ruefully. "It's just that I wouldn't want them to feel weird around me. I realize it's hard enough getting to know new in-laws without having to worry about them being able to read your mind. Especially if you're thinking something like, 'What the hell does he see in *her?*'"

Armand laughed. "I don't think you'd ever have to worry about that, but I understand what you're saying." Sobering after a moment, he searched her face. "No regrets about moving away from your parents? Leaving your job?"

Lia gazed at him. "The only regret I would have is not spending the rest of my life with you."

He took her hand, splaying her fingers across his heart. She didn't have to read his mind to know what he was telling her. *I love you.*

"I love you, too," she mouthed back, and he smiled.

"As for my parents," she continued, "they've already told me that they plan to visit us on a regular basis. I believe their exact words were, 'Just try to get rid of us.' And as for my job…well, something tells me I will be *very* busy as first lady of Muwaiti. And who knows? Maybe one day I'll open my own international security consulting firm. I've always had that in mind as a possible second career after retiring from the Secret Service. And speaking of security," she said, giving Armand a stern look, "we need to discuss *your* security plan around here. I was rather alarmed when I arrived this afternoon and saw that no one was manning the security booth."

Armand chuckled, shaking his head at her. "How'd I know you would have a problem with that?"

She arched a brow, awaiting his explanation.

He sighed in resignation. "Today is Sunday. I like to give the guards the weekends off to spend time with their families. And I've never particularly cared for leaders who live in ivory towers and hide behind fortresses. I want to be accessible to my people."

"I know that, darling. And I understand, believe me, I do. But you have to be practical. You're president of one of the largest countries in the Caribbean. I know that the people of Muwaiti adore you and would never want to hurt you, but, as I've always told you, it's better to be safe than sorry. No one would begrudge you having round-the-clock security here at the palace. When it comes to your safety, I'd rather not take any unnecessary risks."

He shook his head, a poignant smile playing about his lips as he looked down at her. "Always my protector, my guardian angel."

She touched his face. "I almost lost you once. I never want to go through that again."

Armand held her eyes for a long moment, then sighed. "All right. We can carve out some time tomorrow to review my security detail."

"Thank you." Lia gave him a teasing smile. "So you *are* trainable."

He smiled softly, stroking a hand over her hair. "Only for you." He ran an appreciative gaze over her, taking in her short, breezy skirt and strappy high-heeled sandals. "God, you look incredible. I've never seen you in a skirt and heels before. And your hair is down, just the way I like it."

"I know," Lia said demurely. "I did it just for you. And sometime tonight, when everyone else has gone to sleep, I'm going to sneak into your bedroom suite and do everything I've dreamed of doing to you for the last six months."

Armand groaned, his eyes darkening with desire as he sank his fingers into her hair and tipped her head back. "Don't tempt me, woman," he growled, nuzzling her throat. "If you knew how badly I've wanted to carry you upstairs and make love to you ever since you arrived, you wouldn't tease me like that."

Lia smiled, shivering at his touch and the deep, seductive

timbre of his voice that sent heat curling through her blood. She'd never stood a chance of resisting this man. She'd been thoroughly seduced—mind, body and soul.

"Armand?"

"Yes, sweetheart?"

"Thank you for holding on all those years. Thank you for waiting."

He lifted his head and looked at her. All the adoration in his heart was evident in his intense gaze. "You were more than worth the wait," he said huskily.

Their lips met in a deep, searing kiss that left them both trembling in anticipation of the night ahead, and the many nights to come.

As they drew apart, Armand gave her a tender smile and held out his arm to her. "Come. Let me give you a tour of your new home."

Lia's eyes misted as she stared at him. *Home,* she silently marveled. *With Armand.* She could hardly believe it. After a lifetime of feeling lonely and alienated from others because of her psychic gift, she had finally found love and unconditional acceptance in someone other than her parents. She had found someone with whom she could share her triumphs and fears, her hopes and her dreams. Someone who would cherish her, nurture her, protect her as fiercely as she would him. She had found someone to share her life with.

As far as she was concerned, *that* was the only gift she would ever need.

Smiling into his eyes, she slipped her arm through his, and together they started off, walking into their new life as one.

All work and no play…

SUITE
Temptation

Acclaimed Author
ANITA
BUNKLEY

When Riana Cole kissed Andre Preaux goodbye to conquer
the San Antonio business world, Andre had given up without
a fight. Now, years later, they are reunited, and memories
of delicious passion come flooding back. Andre is
determined to get her back, but this time he's negotiating
for one thing only—her heart.

"Anita Bunkley's descriptive winter scenery, likable,
well-written characters and engaging story make
Suite Embrace very entertaining."
—*Romantic Times BOOKreviews*

Available the first week of September wherever books are sold.

KIMANI
ROMANCE™

Where there's smoke, there's fire!

Make it
Hot

Gwyneth Bolton

Brooding injured firefighter Joel Hightower's only hope
to save his career is sassy physical therapist Samantha
Dash. But as the sizzling attraction between them
intensifies, Samantha must decide whether a future with
surly Joel is worth the threat to her career.

The Hightowers
**Four brothers on a mission
to protect, serve and love.**

Available the first week of September wherever books are sold.

KIMANI™
ROMANCE

www.kimanipress.com   KPGB0830908

For All We Know

NATIONAL BESTSELLING AUTHOR
SANDRA KITT

Michaela Landry's quiet summer of
house-sitting takes a dramatic turn when
she finds a runaway teen and brings him
to the nearest hospital. There she meets
Cooper Smith Townsend, a local pastor
whose calm demeanor and dedication are
as attractive as his rugged good looks.
Now their biggest challenge will be to trust
that a passion neither planned for is strong
enough to overcome any obstacle.

*Coming the first week of September 2008,
wherever books are sold.*

ARABESQUE®

www.kimanipress.com   KPSKI040908

Was he still attracted to her?

No. She was letting her imagination run away with her. They'd spent hours upon hours together over the past fifteen years. Devin didn't want anything other than her friendship. If he did, he'd had aeons to express it.

She'd forced herself to forget how his kisses had scared the life out of her a long time ago.

Sure, there were moments—when he opened a door for her or innocently touched her the way a friend might—she had a flash of feeling for him. But the moments always passed.

Devin didn't really do "serious" when it came to his personal life. He never had. And now he was too absorbed in launching his company to give much thought to any woman.

Especially a crazy, screwed-up woman like Carey, pregnant with his cousin's baby.

Dear Reader,

I fell in love with my husband the traditional way: we met on a college campus, went on a bunch of dates, got married and became best friends along the way. The idea of two people being best friends first and then falling in love has always intrigued me. How do two people who know each other so well cross the line to become more than just friends? It seems so...romantic.

For Carey Langford and Devin Colyer, the feelings were there all along—the two just had to be challenged in the right way for those feelings to come out. Challenging them became the hardest part of writing their story.

The easy thing would have been for them to address the attraction years ago. The human thing, however, is to deny, ignore and fight until it's seemingly too late. For Devin, it takes believing there's no possible way he can ever have Carey to realize just how much he needs her.

Not realizing the depth of our feelings until we suffer a loss or face the threat of a loss is all too common in real life. Luckily, I write in a genre that always has a happy ending, and it isn't too late for Devin and Carey.

I hope you enjoy their journey to overcome their *Unexpected Complication*. Please visit me online at www.amyknupp.com or e-mail me at amyknupp@amyknupp.com to let me know what you think of Devin and Carey's story. I'd love to hear from you!

Sincerely,

Amy Knupp

UNEXPECTED
COMPLICATION
Amy Knupp

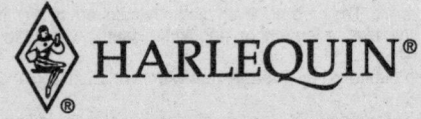

TORONTO • NEW YORK • LONDON
AMSTERDAM • PARIS • SYDNEY • HAMBURG
STOCKHOLM • ATHENS • TOKYO • MILAN • MADRID
PRAGUE • WARSAW • BUDAPEST • AUCKLAND

ISBN 0-373-71342-8

UNEXPECTED COMPLICATION

Copyright © 2006 by Amy Knupp.

www.eHarlequin.com

Printed in U.S.A.

To Justin, for listening to my plot problems at midnight,
for insisting I can do it when I don't think I can and
for being my best friend no matter what.

To Sharon, for challenging me to open the file
that very first time...and every day since.

To Anjana, for helping me become a better
storyteller by making me think—hard.

To Jan and Allison, for the priceless give-and-take, and to
Karin, Edie, Michelle and Liz, for the daily butt-kicking.

To my mom and dad, for always believing in me.
And to Carol and Larry, for cheering me on.

To the Des Moines girls—Kristin, Anna, Amy, Karen,
Becky and Mel—for telling me I'd succeed from the
time I came out of the writing closet.

To Victoria Curran, for the endless hours and effort
to make this a much better story and for seeing there was
something there in the first place.

Heartfelt thanks to all of you.

CHAPTER ONE

THERE WAS nothing dignified about peeing on a stick.

Not exactly what Carey Langford had imagined thinking at this particular milestone in her life. But there it was, the depressing truth.

The foolish, idealistic part of her had always imagined this moment of truth to be a little more...romantic, for starters. Not so lonely. Maybe filled with jittery excitement and a strong, loving man pacing outside the bathroom, anxiously waiting to learn if "Daddy" would become his new handle.

Instead, she was alone, her gut as well as her body twisted like a pretzel, dreading the appearance of a double line.

One hundred and twenty seconds had never lasted so long.

She sat on the edge of the drab green bathtub, elbows on her knees, and covered her eyes with her hands as if hiding behind her hair would make the whole matter disappear.

Carey checked her watch and stood. Her heart pounded as she crossed to the counter. Still not looking at the results, she picked the test stick up with shaking hands, said a short prayer and looked.

There were two lines.

She swore out loud, a single word that hardly seemed adequate to describe her circumstances.

Apparently no higher powers were listening to her prayers tonight.

Now what?

There were two other tests—she'd bought a three-pack. She'd use them as soon as she could to be sure the first one was right. But she knew the odds of getting a false positive—almost nil. Opening a drawer, she tossed the extras inside.

She shoved the stick with the two lines back into the wrapper and carried it to the kitchen trash, stuffing it in. In an effort to have the last say, she pulled the trash bag out, tied it shut and marched out to the banged-up metal garbage can in the garage. Ceremoniously, she dropped the bag in and slammed the lid down.

As if that would get rid of her problem.

The cool dampness characteristic of Iowa in late April made her shiver, and she hurried back to the house. The dramatic blues and violets of twilight, her favorite time of day, barely filtered through her consciousness. She let the door bang shut behind her.

Carey fell into the kitchen chair closest to the door. Somehow she'd managed to go from relatively carefree independence to the sobering prospect of parenthood in mere weeks.

She'd never run into something she hadn't felt she could handle, but right now a human-sized vise seemed to close in on her.

The phone rang, but she didn't move to answer it. She wasn't in the mood to talk to anyone. The machine on the kitchen counter picked up and she listened to her own cheerful voice state that she wasn't home.

"Carey, where are you? I just got back in town. Thought I'd stop by tonight if you were there. Guess not. I'll talk to you later."

Devin Colyer, one of her two best friends. Splendid timing for him to want to catch up. She hadn't had a chance to spend much more than an hour at a bar or five minutes on the phone with him for ages. His life had been hectic lately because of the computer security business he was launching.

She wasn't up for a visit from him tonight. Her ex-boyfriend was Devin's cousin and not his favorite person. Devin wouldn't take the news that she was pregnant with Jerod's baby well at all. When they'd first started dating, Devin had tried to tell her Jerod wasn't right for her. She didn't like to take the chance of him reminding her he'd told her so.

She'd just started to get over the anger and pain since she and Jerod had broken up a month ago. Granted, they'd only actually been together four months. But she'd known him for years, had practically idolized him since high school. That was a long time to build someone up.

That she'd been so stupid still smarted. How could she, cautious and jaded thanks to her mom's history with men, have been so blind as to think Jerod was the long-term type, the family type? He'd been seeing other women the entire time they'd been together. The truth hit her right in the face. Where men were concerned, Carey's judgment was completely unreliable.

Over the years, her mom had been used, dumped, snowed over, you name it. But at least she'd been happily married and very much in love when she'd wound up pregnant. So much for striving to be wiser.

Without thinking, Carey stood and grabbed the faded mustard-colored wall phone and dialed Monica Garrett, her friend since the first day of kindergarten.

But just before the phone could ring, she disconnected the call.

Damn.

Monica was the last person she could turn to with this. She and her husband had been trying to get pregnant for almost the entire year they'd been married. Carey's news would be like acid on the wound.

She slammed the receiver down, upset on Monica's behalf as well as her own. Still holding on to the outdated phone, she took a deep breath, closing her eyes.

All right. She was on her own with her numbing news. Might as well get used to it.

She shuffled to the living room, hitting the kitchen light on the way, plunging the house into darkness. Blessed darkness.

Grabbing an old fuzzy blanket from the couch, she settled into an ancient recliner on the far side of the room to ponder the irony of her life.

There wasn't a whole lot she could do, other than run out and tell Jerod the oh-so-happy news. She shook her head. He'd made it clear he had no interest in settling down.

She rubbed her belly, trying to imagine how it would feel to have a huge bump there, filled with a tiny being who would depend on her for everything. *Everything.* It was almost too much to grasp.

There were options, of course. Ending the pregnancy. Finding someone to adopt her child—but that was just it. It was *her* child already.

Carey adored babies. She'd always wanted kids eventually—lots of them. The thing was, though, she'd always wanted a husband to go with the kids. She knew from experience that growing up without a dad was difficult.

Her head throbbed as the truth set in—she'd be raising this child by herself. Huddling down deeper into the thick blanket, she let the tears fall.

She had no idea how much time had passed when the sobs finally subsided. Gradually, her thoughts calmed to one at a time instead of the painful barrage.

One thing she was certain about. She absolutely would not let her child grow up in a home without love or security.

A steady, heavy rain had started to fall at some

point. After a long while, she heard sturdy footsteps on the walkway outside her front door.

The knock fifteen feet away from her recliner startled her. She didn't move, barely breathed, willing the visitor to go away. At the second knock she glared at the door.

She heard keys jangle, and before she could process what was happening, the door opened.

"Carey?"

Devin stepped into the dark living room. She wished she hadn't given him the spare key. Her heart thudded so loudly she expected him to hear it, and she pulled the blanket up a little higher. He apparently didn't spot her sitting across the room, but she could see him in the glow from the streetlight through the doorway.

He was drenched. His dirty-blond hair hung limply to his collar. She watched a drop of water make its way down the slight bump in his nose. He blinked a few times, as if to adjust to the darkness.

"Carey?" he hollered. "You home?"

Taking a few steps into the hallway, he glanced toward her bedroom, his back to her. He flipped the light on, and Carey squinted against the brightness. He still didn't see her.

"What do you want, Dev?"

He whipped around, finally spotting her. Mopping his face with his upper arm, he stopped in the middle of the room.

"What the hell are you doing?" he asked, hands on his hips, hair dripping onto his shoulders.

"What does it look like I'm doing?"

"Why didn't you answer me?"

"Why did you let yourself in?"

"Your car's in the driveway. I figured you were here."

"I'm here."

If she'd been in a better mood, she would've laughed at the contrast they made. Devin was dripping wet, yet instead of looking like a drowned dog, he looked good—from his soaked Swim Naked T-shirt to his ratty tennis shoes. Carey, who was warm and mostly dry, could probably scare a small child with her tangled hair and puffy red eyes.

"So?" he said.

"I really want to be alone, Devin."

"I've been out of town for two weeks and that's all you can say?" His voice was teasing.

She grasped the arms of the recliner, willing herself not to snap. "Please, just go."

Turning, he headed toward the hall bathroom. "Be right back. I need to dry off. If you'll hear me out, I'll leave soon."

He acted as though he found her huddling in the dark every day.

When he returned, rubbing the back of his neck with a towel, he lowered himself to the couch. "When was the last time you talked to your friend in the IT department of that local textbook publisher?"

Carey wanted to scream—or maybe cry again. She was suffering and he wanted to talk about a possible client for his start-up company. Sometimes she admired his insane drive to make it a success, but not right now.

"It's been awhile," she told him. "A few weeks."

"I'm ready to get rolling, and I need some business. The publishing company would be a big boost if I could land it. Can you talk to him again, warn him I'll be calling and get me his contact info?"

"Devin, did it not occur to you that I'm having a crisis?"

He stopped drying himself and looked at her as if he hadn't seen her before. "What's wrong?" His eyebrows lowered. "This isn't…tell me this isn't Jerod related."

"It isn't Jerod related."

"Liar."

Carey shrugged.

"Thought you got rid of him."

"I did." *So to speak.*

Carey's stomach rolled, and a sheen of sweat broke out on her forehead. She threw the blanket to the floor and tore to the bathroom. Made it to the toilet just in time. She threw up until her throat was on fire and tears blurred her vision.

At some point, Devin bent down behind her and gently pulled her long hair out of the way. When her stomach finished rebelling, she held on to the cool, damp sides of the toilet bowl to steady herself.

"You okay?" he asked, touching her back lightly.

She nodded and squeezed her eyes shut. She sensed rather than saw him sit on the edge of the tub a couple of feet away.

"What's wrong, Carey? You never get sick."

Standing to lean over the sink, she shook her head weakly. This wasn't even morning sickness as far as she could tell; it'd come out of nowhere. It was stress, pure and simple. Her stomach was a pit of turbulence.

She splashed cold water over her face, not caring that it soaked her hair, too. Straightening, she grabbed a towel, focused on the linoleum floor.

"I'm pregnant."

CHAPTER TWO

"YOU'RE *what?*" Devin couldn't have heard right.

"You heard me." Carey was barely audible.

Ho...ly...shit. She was dead serious. He lowered his gaze as if there'd be visible evidence of a child growing in her abdomen.

She closed the toilet lid, sat on top of it and pulled her knees up, hugging them.

Devin stood, feeling the blow of her revelation as vividly as if a round of bullets had pierced his gut. For a split second, he wondered if he'd have to take a turn at puking. He sucked in air slowly and tried to calm himself, to no avail. He leaned against the bathroom counter, flattening his palms against the cool tile.

"It's Jerod's?"

She nodded once.

Carey was pregnant with his cousin's baby. His leech of a cousin who'd never deserved her in the first place.

Devin clamped his jaws together to keep from saying the hurtful things that popped into his head. As he hiked himself onto the counter, he felt numbed, disconnected and more than a little disturbed, as if he were witnessing a train wreck. "What the hell happened?"

Carey lifted her head from her hands, her eyebrows raised. "What do you mean, 'what happened?'"

He shook his head, too rattled to speak. The question was pointless anyway. Seconds ticked by while he struggled to digest the news. "Forgive me," he growled. "I'm a little bowled over."

"Yeah, well, you and me both." She walked past him out of the cramped room. "Don't you have somewhere else to be?"

He heard her bedroom door shut, but he didn't follow her.

Pregnant? It was too much to wrap his mind around.

How could she have been so careless? So clueless to fall for his self-absorbed cousin? Once again, he cursed the rotten coincidence of Carey running into Jerod several months ago on one of her photo assignments. She'd always had a thing for Jerod, even knowing how Devin felt about the guy. Devin had never really expressed how deep his dislike went, mostly because he knew it was irrational and steeped in jealousy. Not something he was proud of. Now he wished he'd said more.

When Carey had rattled on about her first date with his cousin, Devin had comforted himself, secure in the belief Jerod would blow it miserably within the first two weeks.

Obviously, he'd been wrong.

He rammed his knuckles into the tile, fantasizing about doing the same to Jerod's face. "Dammit!"

What Jerod had seen in her was obvious. Carey collected male attention like an eight-track tape player collected dust. She was a walking contradiction. She looked doll-like, innocent, with long lashes and creamy skin. Yet she was sexy as hell at the same time. Model-long legs, silky blond hair and deep, sapphire-blue eyes a man could ache to see cloud over in lust.

There was no question in his mind about a man wanting *her*. Devin had for as long as he'd known her—or almost. The exception was the short period when he'd thought Lisa somebody—he couldn't even remember her name anymore—had more to offer and he'd walked away from Carey to chase her. He'd regretted that ever since, and had never dared mention how he felt to Carey. He'd had his chance and ruined it.

What tripped Devin up was that *she* had gotten so carried away with such an egotistical bore.

Carey was one of the least practical people he knew. Her tendency to do things on a whim made him cringe. She'd gone out with her share of assholes, but she didn't usually stick with them for more than a couple of dates. Normally she was wary of men, which she claimed was because of her mom. Why she couldn't have been wary around Jerod was beyond Devin.

Rage propelled him off the counter and out of the

bathroom. He wanted her to show him how this whole thing made sense. Better yet, to tell him it was a cruel joke.

Devin tapped on her bedroom door but, as he'd expected, she didn't answer. Opening it a crack, he peered in. The only light came from the lamp on her nightstand, if it could be called that. It was like a lava lamp made from an antique gum ball machine. Blue globs floated where gum balls should have been. The bubbling light was just bright enough for him to see Carey lying in bed, facing him, stroking a cat curled against her.

"Can I come in?" he asked, his voice tightly controlled.

"Why not?" She sounded resigned.

He lowered himself to the foot of her girly double bed, inches from her feet. The fluffy, disgruntled feline his movement bounced from the cocoon between Carey's thighs and stomach let out a yowl, and Devin scowled at the animal before turning his attention to its owner.

"Why, Carey?"

"Why what?" She kept her hand protectively on the cat's back.

"Why anything? Why Jerod? Why didn't you use something?" His voice grew louder with each question.

Carey sprang upright. "We did use something. Give me some credit, would you?"

He couldn't muster sympathy for her bad luck. Not when she'd played the odds with Mr. Smooth. Not when the urge to punch something pulsed through him. "Does he know yet?"

She lay back on the pillow and stared straight ahead. "No. I'll tell him…sometime. I haven't figured it out yet."

"That should be interesting."

She whipped her head toward him. "Why do you say that?"

"What's not interesting about telling the man of your dreams you're carrying his child?" He couldn't stifle his sarcasm, even though he knew he was being a jerk.

"He's not the—" She stopped abruptly, shaking her head. "Devin, I don't need this. I'm upset enough without you railing at me about how stupid I am."

Devin bit down on a smart-ass response. He wasn't in the right mind-set to try to help her, couldn't seem to extinguish his anger. His own overreaction ticked him off even more.

He lay back on the bed, stretching out along the white footboard. A lead weight settled at the bottom of his gut.

Eyes closed, his mind jumped to an image of Carey and Jerod making a happy family with their baby. Nauseating. Maddening. And completely wrong. They could never make it work.

The mattress shifted slightly and his eyes popped

open to find a different mangy animal hovering inches above his face, staring him down. "Get lost, cat."

"Come here, Snicket," Carey said in a sickening, syrupy voice to the long-haired fuzz ball. "I suppose you think this is just what I deserve." She directed the last to Devin in a tone that held no hint of sweetness.

He bolted upright. "Hell, no. I think it's exactly what you don't deserve and it could've been avoided."

"So it's my fault? Is that what you're saying?"

"No, that's not what I'm saying. And before you put more words in my mouth, it's not his fault either. But you were playing with fire, Carey. What'd you expect?"

Damn! He wasn't sure where this cruel streak was coming from. All he knew was that he had the over-whelming urge to verbally attack. Her. Jerod. Anyone within earshot.

He ran his hand down his face, wishing he could take everything back. "Carey, I'm sorry. You need sup-port and here I am being a bastard."

The scowl on her face signaled her total agreement with his assessment. Devin gritted his teeth. He needed to finish this conversation without another flash of anger.

"So…you think you'll keep the baby?"

Surprise registered on Carey's face. "Yeah." She gave him a single, determined nod. "I'm having the baby." Her answer didn't shock him. Carey had never been one to shy away from consequences. He just hoped she wasn't dumb enough to take the man with the baby. He hated for her to be alone raising a kid, but he hated even more to think she could saddle herself with a man who would never measure up.

"What if Jerod feels differently?"

Carey sprung off the bed, sending both cats darting from the room. "Dammit, Devin, I don't care! I'm having this baby."

This time, his comment had been innocent. He hadn't been trying to make her mad; he'd genuinely wondered if she'd considered the possibility.

If he couldn't make her feel any better, he could at least stop making things worse. "I should leave, Carey. I'm not helping you at all."

She leaned against the doorjamb, her eyes penetrating his. "That'd probably be best."

Devin stood to go, pausing next to her. He felt the urge to say something right, to help her somehow, but he didn't know what.

Moments later, he stepped back into the rain. He breathed in the smell of wet earth, wishing the weather could dampen his animosity as he lumbered down the stairs. From the looks of the water running along the deserted street, it'd been pouring the entire time he'd been inside. He let the drops beat down on him, heedless. With each step, Carey's reality hammered at him.

Pregnant.

Jerod's kid.

Reaching his truck, he hopped in, flung the gear

shift in Reverse and gunned backward down the driveway almost before he could fasten his seat belt.

He hit the speed dial for Monica, hoping she could come over and hold Carey's hand or…something. She needed someone who could comfort her—someone who could handle her news a hell of a lot better than he had.

No answer. Damn. He'd failed Carey completely, and now thanks to his insensitivity—or was it oversensitivity?—she was alone.

He shut the phone and sped past the turn to his house, unable to stand the thought of going home.

Damn it all. Carey was in a huge fix, no matter how Jerod reacted. If he told her to get lost, she was on her own with a baby. If he married her, she was doubly screwed, stuck with a baby *and* an asshole. Frankly, he doubted Jerod would want marriage, but then what did he know?

He'd always considered himself to be the exact opposite of his cousin, but maybe he and Jerod were more alike than he'd thought. They'd both let Carey down.

Devin still had moments when he regretted like hell allowing his teenage hormones to take over. He and Carey had gravitated to each other ever since Monica had introduced them. When Monica used to flit off to her nightly family dinner, Devin and Carey would hit the fast-food drive-through and pick up a movie. One night, their closeness had led to tentative kisses.

They'd spent all of a month as more than friends, but Carey had always drawn the line at anything more than kissing.

Devin, being a normal, lust-driven teenaged boy and faced with Lisa what's-her-name, the new girl who oozed sexiness, had gently told Carey they were better as just friends.

Carey had seemed as relieved as she was pissed off. She hadn't given him the time of day for a good two weeks, which was as long as it took for Lisa to give Devin a taste of what he wanted and then dump him.

The only thing Devin had over Jerod was that he'd let go of Carey before picking up with someone else. Big goddamn deal. Not only had he treated Carey badly and incurred her brother's eternal wrath, it was probably the single largest screwup of his thirty years.

And now Jerod had a claim on Carey far deeper than the friendship Devin had with her. He closed his eyes in an attempt to block the urge to smash something.

The whole damn city closed in on him. He needed space and air…and a hold on his blasted emotions, which were raging like a confused adolescent.

He jammed his foot down on the accelerator, giving little thought to the rain, which had slowed to a steady cadence on the windshield. His truck fishtailed, and belatedly he realized he was going too fast.

CHAPTER THREE

THE PHONE JOLTED Carey out of a restless slumber, and she glanced at the clock. Ten till three. In the morning. Who in the…?

"Hello?" She was instantly alert.

"It's me."

Devin. What did he want…to rant about Jerod some more?

"Look, I'm sorry about earlier, Carey. I was a jerk."

"No argument here. But you could've waited till morning to apologize."

She'd put him out of her mind shortly after he'd left. She had every right to be angry with him, but frankly, compared to being pregnant, Devin's idiocy was small potatoes.

"I know you're not in the mood to help me, but I could use a lift from the hospital. I wrecked the truck."

She sat up straight, concerned despite her raw feelings. "A wreck? Are you okay? What happened?"

"I'm okay, just bruised some ribs. The truck's not so good though. Not that I could drive anyway, as much pain meds as they pumped in me."

"I'll be there in a few minutes." Vengeance wasn't her strong suit.

She asked which hospital before hanging up, then turned on the light to search for some clothes. She threw on old jeans and a black T-shirt, her favorite hooded sweatshirt and comfy sneaker-style mules. She paused in the bathroom to check in the mirror. Not much she could do about the death-warmed-over look, but she ran a brush through her hair and pulled it up with a band.

Fifteen minutes later, she pulled her yellow Volkswagen Beetle into the parking lot closest to the ER entrance. She hurried to the door, which was lit brightly enough for a blind man to see from a mile away. The sound of trickling water was everywhere, now that the heavy rain had finally subsided. The chill, damp air made her shiver, and she longed to put her worn-out body back in the warmth of her bed.

Devin sat on a cushioned bench against a brick wall across from the doorway.

For once he didn't look so hot. His face was uncharacteristically pale, and his eyes drooped. His hair was a shaggy mess. But he was otherwise intact. Carey couldn't deny her relief. Just because he was an idiot didn't mean she wanted him wrapped around a tree or laid up in a hospital bed.

"Hey," he said as she approached, weariness—and probably pain medicine—making his voice lower, huskier than usual.

"You look like hell. Let's go."

"Have to sign out first. They want to know I'm not driving. I need to get a prescription filled on the way home, too." Carefully, he got to his feet and pointed to a small, dark-haired woman on the other side of a large window.

They took care of the paperwork and walked out to the car in silence. After she unlocked the doors, Devin moved the passenger seat all the way back, and then gingerly lowered himself in. "I wish you'd get a real car."

"You should be worshipping this little car. It's saving your butt right now."

He exhaled slowly, as if in pain, and looked at her. "Yeah. You're right."

Carey started the car and pulled out. "What happened, Devin?"

He tried to take a deep breath, then grimaced. "Got up close and personal with a large oak tree."

"You ran into a tree?" She couldn't help it—she chuckled. "The guy who lectured me on birth control ran his truck into a tree?"

"Yeah, well."

"Was anyone else involved?"

"Just me and the tree. And the truck. I'd bet money it's totaled."

She glanced sideways at him. Devin was no speed-limit stickler, but he wasn't reckless, either. That was *her* role. She wondered what the real story was. "Good thing you've got money to put on it."

"Not as much as you'd like to think," he muttered.

Carey frowned and decided to ignore the comment. "Where'd you meet up with this tree?"

"Outside of town, couple of miles from Grand."

"What were you doing way out there?"

She felt his glare even as she kept her gaze on the road. "Driving." His tone dissuaded her from asking more questions.

After driving through the all-night pharmacy for pain pills, Carey detoured into a fast-food drive-through and ordered enough to feed a family of four.

A few minutes later, she pulled into Devin's driveway. "Home, sweet bachelor pad," she said.

The two-story house was a showcase of the latest domestic technology. He'd built it a couple of years ago after selling the house he'd inherited from his parents, and while he didn't give much thought to the decor, gadgets were his pride and joy. In addition to all the electronics inside, he had an inground pool set in a backyard paradise. Carey loved to tease him about his testosterone-driven dream home.

She didn't actually know how much money Devin had, but she knew his parents had been fairly flush when they'd been killed in that car accident. She suspected Devin had plenty to live on, despite his desperation to make his company a success.

They went through his front door and down the hallway past the formal living room to the kitchen, which was more lived-in, with a sloppily folded newspaper on the bar and a few dirty coffee mugs in the sink. Carey and Monica had helped him choose the custom off-white cabinets and brown-and-black granite counter-top. Not to mention the floor tile—a neutral taupe—and the stainless-steel fixtures. There was more space in this room than Devin could use in a decade—his cooking skills were as lacking as Carey's—but it looked like a gourmet kitchen, mostly thanks to Monica's expertise.

"When can you take a pain pill?" Carey asked as she set the hefty bag of food on the kitchen bar.

Devin glanced at the clock on the range. "Half an hour." He turned on the small light over the sink, took two glasses out of the cupboard. "Drink?" He longed for a beer but figured it wouldn't sit well on top of the pain-killers.

"Sure. H2O on the rocks, please."

He filled the glasses from the dispenser on the freezer door and made his way to the bar where she sat. Sliding onto one of the raised stools was agony.

"Why don't you go to bed?" she asked.

"I want some fries." He stared at her expectantly. "I assume with all you ordered you're planning on sharing. Besides, I need to stay up for that pill."

She nodded sympathetically. "I'll wait with you. Wasn't getting much sleep anyway." She opened the bag, handed him an order of French fries and spread the rest of the food—a double cheeseburger, a box of chicken nuggets and another large fries—in front of her.

Devin chuckled, shaking his head at her obvious appetite.

Examining her face, he noticed her eyes were red, with deep shadows under them. Her hair hung limply in a ponytail, and her clothes were wrinkled. She looked exhausted. Understandably. He vowed not to make her feel bad again. "Stress will do that." He reached for the saltshaker on the counter and dumped some on his fries.

"Devin," she said between bites, "we need to talk about my situation."

His taste for French fries suddenly disappeared. He finished chewing what had become rubbery and tasteless, then forced it down and took a long gulp of water.

He could do this. He could sit here and listen to whatever she had to say about Lover Boy, and he could refrain from spouting off with the wrong thing again. He'd do it if he had to bite his tongue off.

"What about it?" he asked warily.

"I know you don't care for Jerod."

He nodded once, thinking what an understatement that was.

"I don't know what's going to happen, but..." Carey paused and swallowed hard. "It would really help if you'd keep your opinion to yourself." Her voice squeaked out the end of the sentence.

Devin ran his fingers through his hair, frustrated again with the lack of control he'd shown earlier. "I know, I know. I'm sorry. Really." He grabbed the empty food bag and absently crushed it into a tight wad. "Did you talk to him yet?"

She turned her head, eyes brimming with moisture. "No way." A single tear slid down her cheek. "I'm dreading it."

Sympathy tugged at him, squeezed his chest till it hurt. He stroked his thumb across her cheek to wipe the tear away, wishing he knew what to do to make her feel better.

"Carey." He patted her leg awkwardly. "It'll work out."

She shook her head adamantly.

"It will. Somehow it will." As he watched her wipe her eyes with a napkin, he realized he wanted that for her as much as she did. As long as it didn't involve marrying Jerod.

Carey let out an indelicate sniffle. Tears streamed down her face.

"Damn." He was disgusted at himself for causing her tears. "I'm trying to help, Care, not make you cry."

She covered her face and sank forward to lean her elbows on the counter. Devin propped his arms on the edge, too, and tried to conceive of what she must be going through, what must be running through her head. He imagined preparing for parenthood, caring for a baby day and night, committing to that child's well-being for the rest of his life. Hell, no. Couldn't do it. Couldn't begin to fathom it. Just trying made him antsy.

Helplessness was not a feeling he tolerated well. He jerked to his feet and winced as pain shot through him.

Once he recovered, he reached for her shoulders and rubbed them. Leaning forward, he whispered, "It'll be okay, Care." Without thinking, he brushed a kiss on the side of her head.

He massaged her shoulders and neck until she stopped crying, enjoying touching her far too much. This wasn't the time. There would never be a time for it.

Carey uncovered her eyes and straightened, and Devin instinctively backed off. He picked up his glass, popped open the pill bottle and swallowed a capsule with a swig. Then he took the glass to the sink.

Carey grabbed another napkin and blew her nose. "It doesn't feel like it'll be okay."

He couldn't stay across the room from her for long. He felt drawn to her, needed somehow to reassure her.

Leaning on the counter next to her, he propped his weight on an elbow and shifted until the stabbing pain in his ribs lessened. He let out a slow breath. "What if he wants to get back together, get hitched?" He strived for a casualness he didn't feel.

Carey took her sweet time to reply, and with every second, Devin's muscles tensed more. Finally she shook her head slowly.

"He won't. He made it crystal clear he can't stand the thought of being with one woman, much less a woman and a needy baby."

f...

his

image...

"I c...

"Oh,...

or somet...

Devin...

guess was...

of what Dev...

deeper and fu...

about what he...

"Really. I am. But…" He backed...

cabinets, gripping the counter...

know you've got it in you to...

"Thanks," Her voice...

He needed to put...

almost morning...

to crash...

free. Thi...

ach...

34

...mad as hell

She shrugged... false nonchalance. "I saw what I wanted to see, I guess."

What she'd wanted to see was a devoted man who loved her. And then she'd caught him with—and all over—another woman.

He wanted to put his arms around her, draw her close, feel her body against his. He wanted her to feel safe.

No. You can't touch her.

Touching Carey was torture. And damn if it wasn't heaven, too.

Words would have to do.

"I'm sorry you have to go through this, Carey."

She raised her eyebrows, challenged him.

up against the
    ... with both hands. "I
    ... be a great mom."
    ... was hoarse, tired.
    ... some distance between them. "It's
    ... We both need to sleep," he said. "Feel
    ... in the spare bedroom."
    ... nk I will. I'm so tired the backs of my eyeballs
    ..."

He led her slowly up the stairs. At the doorway to the guest room, he flipped on the light to make sure the bed was made up for company. Seeing that it was, he forced the image of the blankets wrapping around Carey's body from his mind. "'Night."

"Good night."

In his own bedroom, he changed into some boxers, flipped on the television out of habit and crawled carefully into bed. Ignoring the TV, he stared at the ceiling, trying to get Carey and her predicament out of his mind.

His attraction to her was no big deal. It hadn't been for some time. Most days it was just there in the background. Not an issue. He and every man worth his spit considered her easy on the eyes—a fantasy girl. He no longer lay awake at night pining away for her. He'd gotten over that long ago.

Or so he'd thought.

Now was not the time for hormones to strike. The thing was, though, it wasn't just physical. It couldn't be, not with Carey. Not after all these years.

In all the time they'd been friends, he'd never seen her as vulnerable as she was tonight. Never felt such a pull to take on her problems with her.

Tonight, it was painfully clear that he wanted Carey more than he thought.

Shit…what if he loved her?

Why else would he act like such a lunatic ever since hearing she was pregnant with Jerod's kid? God damn. He'd picked a fine time to fall in love. He didn't *do* love. Not now, not later.

It didn't matter one iota what he felt or what he wanted, though. There was no way in hell he would get any more involved with the woman who carried Jerod Mauriello's child. Even if she was his best friend. Even if he loved her. He'd just have to get over these crazy-ass feelings. Immediately.

CHAPTER FOUR

AN INCESSANT, annoying noise blared into Carey's dream. An emergency. A fire alarm.

The doorbell.

Opening one eye, she glanced at the clock on her nightstand. Eleven twenty-seven. Sunlight. She struggled to remember what day it was and why she wasn't up yet.

Oh, yeah. Devin. She'd left his house shortly after dawn to come home and she'd been sleeping ever since. Funny, she still felt as if she'd been dragged down a gravel road by a bus.

The doorbell echoed through the house again. Throwing the covers off, Carey grumbled as she hauled her butt out of bed.

She yanked on yoga pants under the oversized T-shirt she'd slept in and padded down the hallway to open the door. It was Monica, the feisty brunette she'd shared every detail of her life with for twenty-some years. The one she hadn't been able to face last night. The very one she still didn't want to confide in.

"Hey," Monica said, raising her brows.

Her clothes, as usual, looked as though she'd raided the petite rack of an expensive New York boutique. From the sleeveless shirt that wrapped around her middle to the cropped pants with a large tropical print—perfect on Monica's short frame but they'd look like a Hawaiian vacation gone bad on Carey's long legs.

"Is it Saturday morning?" Carey asked. Had she forgotten plans or something?

Monica nodded with a half grin. "Did I wake you up?"

Carey stepped back to let her friend in, feeling like a traitor. "Can't you ever wear crappy sweats and an old T-shirt?" Carey closed the door. "Don't answer that, Mo."

Monica laughed.

Carey had to break the news right away. She'd couldn't pretend nothing was wrong. The problem was figuring out how.

"Don't take this the wrong way, but you don't look so good," Monica told her.

"Thanks. Rough night. Didn't get much sleep."

Monica chuckled, apparently thinking Carey'd had too much fun.

They dropped onto opposite ends of the sagging sofa, and Carey turned sideways, her bare feet on the faded gold cushion between them. How to tell her friend?

"Carey? What's going on?"

She couldn't look at Monica. "I have no idea how

to say this…" She closed her eyes. "I found out last night I'm pregnant."

Silence ensued, and finally she dared a glance at Monica. Her friend's eyes were wide and her jaw dropped. "You're pregnant? With Jerod's baby?"

Carey nodded slowly. "I'm so, so sorry, Monica. I know how hard you and Kyle are trying to have a baby—"

"Stop it. You're…" She paused to study Carey's face. Her shoulders slumped. "You're not thrilled."

"I'm not thrilled for my own sake. I'm pissed as hell for yours."

"Oh, God, Carey. Don't worry about me. What are you going to do?"

Carey fiddled with the hem of her T-shirt. "I don't know, really, beyond having the kid."

"Does Jerod know?"

"Not yet. That's my project for the day, I guess."

"You sound like you're on your way to a funeral."

"It'll be awkward, to say the least. I haven't spoken to him since we broke up and here I am with this." Carey leaned forward and ran her hands through her tangled hair.

"When are you going to tell Devin? He'll flip."

"Consider him flipped. He walked in not long after I took the test last night."

"Oh, no. Did he give you a hard time?"

"Pretty much. And then he wrecked his truck."

"What? Is he okay?"

Carey filled her in on the rest of the details.

"Why didn't you call me?" Monica demanded. "Oh, I wasn't home. Did you try?"

Carey shook her head. "It was the middle of the night. What could you have done? He just needed a ride."

"I mean about the pregnancy."

Carey didn't want to tell her she'd decided against it. "I wanted to be alone. I was in shock, trying to absorb it."

Monica nodded and neither of them spoke for a while.

"What'd you come over for this morning?" Carey finally asked. Drop-by visits from Monica had been rare since she'd gotten married.

"Oh…nothing much."

"Baloney. Tell me."

Monica was obviously sizing her up.

"What?" Carey insisted. "You had a reason. What was it?"

Monica's brief smile turned into a grimace. She exhaled loudly as she leaned her weight on the arm of the sofa. "I came over to whine to you that another month just passed and no baby. My period showed up."

"Shit." Carey closed her eyes, nearly crushed by her sense of guilt. "I'm sor—"

"Stop it! Carey, if you apologize one more time, I'll hurt you. I'm okay. Really. I'd be lying if I said it didn't sting a little bit, but I'm behind you on this. Completely."

"How could you be okay when I waltz into your world and tell you I have exactly what you've been trying to get for months?"

"I have a strong hunch you didn't run out and get knocked up to spite me."

"Well, when you put it that way…" Carey stood. "Fate is one cruel SOB."

"You got that right." Monica rose, then brushed her hair behind her ears. "Once you get over the shock, you're going to be so excited, Care. Really."

"I don't know. I doubt I'll ever get past scared as hell."

"You will. And maybe if we're really lucky, I'll be pregnant soon and we can go through this together."

Tears flooded Carey's eyes.

"Oh, no. Don't tell me, the mood swings are already starting," Monica joked. "God help us all."

"You're insane, Mo. Go home to your sexy husband. Make a baby."

She walked Monica to the door and they hugged.

"Don't worry about me," Monica whispered. She smiled, but her expression was sad. She turned and went down the three concrete stairs to the walkway.

As her friend of twenty-four years walked toward her black Miata, Carey could only imagine the pain she must be causing her.

CAREY CHANGED her clothes yet again. She lacked experience in what-to-wear-to-tell-your-ex-you're-carrying-his-baby situations. She'd never seen it covered in any of the fashion magazines.

At first she'd gone for casual and safe, then a little dressier, back to casual, and now she pulled on some slim-fitting khaki pants and a carnation-pink sweater with a deep, cleavage-revealing V-neck over a lace-trimmed tank. She finished it off with her favorite pink heels. Pulling her hair back at her nape, she hoped she looked appealing and confident, not scared spitless.

"What can he do to me?" she asked Snicket, short for Persnickety, the pure white Persian who acted as Carey's shadow. "It's not like I got pregnant on purpose."

He could kick her out. He could raise his voice. He could even ask her to marry him, but Carey had a hard time imagining that. At any rate, she knew she could handle whatever he doled out. It was the not knowing that was turning her into a basket case.

The cat, who'd perched on Carey's dresser as she worked on her hair, ambled closer and rubbed his chin on Carey's hand.

"Someone said petting a cat lowers a person's blood pressure." She stroked the cat's soft, bony back. "Maybe I should throw you in my purse and take you with me, huh?"

The feline lifted his nose and hopped from the dresser to the bed to curl up on Carey's pillow.

"Okay, I'll take that to mean I'm on my own." It seemed *alone* was becoming a recurring theme in her life. Too bad she wasn't good at alone.

Carey glanced in the mirror one last time. "This is as good as it's going to get today." The dark circles under her eyes still popped out, despite extra concealer. No surprise, after the night she'd had.

Grabbing her purse, she left the house. It was only a matter of time before she confirmed exactly where she stood.

A gust of wind caught the storm door and blew it wide open. The sky had darkened considerably since she'd seen Monica off. Heavy clouds hung low to the west, casting an eeriness over the neighborhood. A storm was brewing.

Twenty minutes later, she pulled into the visitors' parking lot in front of Jerod's condo, a high-rise building by Des Moines standards. The first few times she'd been here, the plush lobby had impressed her. Now she barely noticed it.

She rode the elevator to the ninth floor and found herself standing in front of his door far too soon. Gathering her confidence, she knocked. She hadn't warned him she was coming, preferring to take a chance on whether he'd be in or not. Calling him would have raised his suspicions and given him time to prepare for her. It was better to have the element of surprise on her side.

Her palms were sweaty. When she heard footsteps, she wished she'd thought about what she was going to say.

Before she could blink, there he was, looking as

though he expected visitors or had plans. But of course, he would. Socializing was a big part of his life. He'd told her a dozen times, schmoozing was a vital part of his career as the owner of the television station he'd inherited from his aunt and uncle, Devin's parents.

Dressed in crisp jeans, a white shirt and spotless brown leather shoes, he made Carey glad she'd opted for something a little dressier than her usual Saturday attire. His almost-black hair was the only part of him that showed any sign of dishevelment, but that was the norm. His hair always fell as it pleased and was the bane of his existence.

His well-proportioned face fell almost immediately. Wariness filled his hazel eyes.

"Carey."

No warmth in that greeting. In fact, she detected a distinct chill in the air.

"Come in," he said.

Better than a door slammed in her face. She followed him into the entryway.

"Hi, Jerod."

"What are you doing here?" he asked as he closed the door behind them.

"We need to talk. Could I sit down?"

His brow furrowed as he studied her for a beat, then he seemed to snap to attention, as if he'd remembered his manners. "Sure, sure." He gestured toward the living room. "I'm surprised to see you."

Not nearly as surprised as he'd be to hear her news.

"Have a seat," he said politely as they entered the spotless room. There was no sign whatsoever of the man who'd behaved as though she walked on water mere weeks ago.

Carey settled on the white leather love seat. Nothing had changed since she'd last been here—the furniture still looked virtually unused, the entertainment magazines on the cherry coffee table were spread in a perfect fan, and there wasn't a speck of dust anywhere, thanks to a twice-weekly cleaning service. Carey much preferred the comfortable den down the hall.

But comfort wasn't her objective this afternoon.

"How have you been?" he asked as he lowered himself onto the matching white sofa. The civility came automatically—it was ingrained in Jerod to be gracious to visitors. But still…his tone was cool, and his smile didn't quite ring genuine.

"Fine," she answered, distracted. "Um, Jerod. I… have some news."

He stiffened, waiting.

"Um, well…" She swallowed hard. *Great start.* "I'm…pregnant."

There. She held her breath and watched for his reaction. The start of an understanding nod. Widening eyes as realization began to sink in. The rise and fall of his Adam's apple as he tried to swallow. "Oh." Then it was his turn, she saw, to watch her closely, gauge her intentions.

Just as she'd thought. He'd confirmed what she'd already decided. Jerod wasn't father material. Or husband material. He also wasn't offering to be either one, she noticed.

"Okay," he said, rising and wandering toward the tall window on the opposite side of the room.

His back to her, he gazed out at the dramatic sky in silence.

Carey settled against a cushion to give him time to absorb the shock. The moment was surreal, far, far removed from the good times they'd shared—the good times she'd mistaken for meaningful times. They were almost like strangers.

Minutes ticked by and, at last, he turned to face her, resting his hands on the windowsill behind him. "What do you want me to do?"

"Do? Um, I'm not sure how to answer that." She narrowed her eyes.

"Do you want money? Me to marry you?" His tone was so matter-of-fact, she couldn't tell how he felt. No interest. No hostility. Nothing.

"Would you?" She had to ask.

"I…" He pinched the bridge of his nose. "I don't know, Carey. I guess I'm a little stunned here. Do you know how this happened?"

"Remember the night of the party at Andrew Ingram's house? Afterward when we went to your place?"

"Vaguely."

"We were…up most of the night…" She couldn't help blushing. "You mentioned there might've been a problem with the condom."

He nodded slowly. "I have some recollection of that."

Carey shrugged. "That's my guess. The timing's right. Almost eight weeks ago. But really, it doesn't matter. What matters is what's coming."

"I don't suppose you'd be open to ending the pregnancy?"

"No. I can't." She fought to keep her annoyance in check. "I won't."

"So you're going to have it."

It hadn't really been a question as much as a statement.

"Do you really want to get married, Carey?" She heard uncharacteristic doubt in the question.

She hesitated, a dozen thoughts running through her mind. "Actually, no. Stop sweating. You're off the hook, at least on that."

His relief was obvious. He crossed the room and sat next to her on the sofa, suddenly not quite as standoffish. "I can give you a little money each month…" He sounded removed from the situation, as if he were negotiating a contract for the station or something. No, not even that…he'd show a lot more enthusiasm if his career were involved.

It rubbed Carey the wrong way.

Apathy wasn't what Carey wanted. At all. And it wasn't what she'd subject her baby to. If he wasn't in it because he wanted to be, then she didn't want him in it at all. This child was not going to grow up feeling like nothing more than a burden.

She stood. "You know what, Jerod? Thank you for offering. I think you're probably trying your best to do what's right." She paused, blowing stray strands of hair from her face. "I don't want your money. We'll be absolutely fine on our own."

He rose, too, and looked at her as though she were crazy. "Carey, you can barely get by on your paycheck as it is."

She hadn't been angry before, but this statement insulted her. "I do just fine, thank you. Nowhere close to your way of living, but I can survive. And I will."

Jerod looked at her vacantly for several seconds, then finally shrugged. "Do it your way."

"Goodbye, Jerod."

She walked to the door and instead of feeling sad, as she'd expected, she was relieved. She knew where she stood.

Minutes later, she hopped into the Bug for cover as large drops of rain began to pelt the pavement. Behind the wheel, she sucked in stifling, humid air. Her hands were shaking.

She pulled out into traffic. The giant question that had loomed over her for the past eighteen hours was answered. Now she could focus on the myriad other considerations of becoming a single mom. She swallowed her trepidation.

Without thought, she headed toward Monica's part of town…then stopped herself. She refused to talk to her about this pregnancy any more than she could help.

Devin wasn't an option, either. Understanding wasn't his strong suit lately. He'd only offer I-told-you-he's-a-jerk and other useless feedback.

In spite of her relief, she felt lonely. Going home to an empty house would depress her. Her mom's house…no. She wasn't up for that scene yet. Her brother and sometimes-roommate Trent was in Alaska for who knew how long.

She was completely alone.

Carey had never liked being alone. She supposed she'd have to get used to it, since late nights out and smoke-filled bars would become a thing of her past, especially while she carried this baby in her womb. And she'd be alone with a newborn soon. She didn't figure the little one would be the best conversationalist.

Carey steered aimlessly around town in the rain, her stereo blaring. She tried like the devil to ignore the uneasiness in her stomach, the fear that seemed to hover just behind her, like a silent stalker intent on following her home.

"Dammit, I can do this. Without Jerod's money."

There, she finally addressed the fear foremost on her mind—her impulsive rejection of his financial help.

Could she live without child support? Was that fair to the baby?

Things would be tight, but they'd make it work. She *could* do this without a man's support—*somehow*.

CHAPTER FIVE

By WEDNESDAY afternoon, reality had had plenty of time to set in. Carey had turned her situation over and over in her mind and had come to a few conclusions.

One, she needed more income.

Two, she couldn't fly all over the country as a freelance photographer once the baby came, and would probably have to cut down on travel even before the birth.

Three, she needed either to find more local gigs or get a part-time job somewhere.

Four, this would be challenging, but she was up for it. She *could* do it. The details of how just hadn't come to her yet.

The doorbell rang, yanking her from her thoughts. She got up from the kitchen table to answer it.

Carey's odd work hours often allowed her to be at home in the middle of the day, just like the stay-at-home moms and the otherwise unemployed. She'd learned long ago that if someone knocked on the door between the hours of nine and five, odds were it'd be either a religious zealot here to save her soul or a college kid bursting with a sales pitch for more magazine subscriptions than she could read in a lifetime.

She opened the door to find the last person she expected—her mother.

She'd avoided her mom all week and had yet to tell her she was pregnant.

On more than one occasion, Carey had lectured her mom on not rushing to bed with a man. It was plain to see Carey had done exactly that—rushed to bed with a man she didn't know as well as she thought. She wasn't in the mood to eat crow just now.

"Hey, Mom, what are you doing here? Aren't you supposed to be working?"

Her mom sighed woefully. "I took off early. Mind if I come in?"

The rims of her mom's eyes were red, her mascara slightly smeared. Carey had a feeling she knew what was wrong. She backed up and opened the door wider to let her in. "Have a seat. Want something to drink?"

"I could use a hard one."

"Mom. You don't drink."

"Special day." Her mom collapsed on the sofa.

"You seriously want something with alcohol in it?"

As much as her mother combed the bars for single fifty-something men, she didn't succumb to the "vices" inherent in the bar-hopping lifestyle. She avoided drinking and smoking and rarely swore. Taking the wrong man home was her special exception.

"Sure. What do you have?"

Not much, as it turned out. "Maybe a beer, and I think I could scrounge up a rum and Coke."

"Can you make it taste like Coke?"

"I could give you a straight Coke."

"I'll try it with a little rum."

The irony that ruled Carey's life lately struck again. She mixed her mom an unheard-of drink while she herself couldn't have a sip. She wondered what on earth could have Penny Langford Stringer in such a state. Man trouble was typical and didn't usually call for a stiff drink.

Returning to the living room, Carey handed her mom the cocktail and looked her over for a clue. She wore her usual work attire—a long, billowing blue-and-yellow skirt that hid never-ending legs a twenty-year-old would envy, a plain white blouse with a conservative V-neck and strappy heels. Her unnaturally blond hair curled sedately under below her ears as usual.

At fifty-two, her mom was still a knockout, which was why she had no problem luring men home. In all fairness, Carey suspected sex wasn't her mom's ultimate goal. A husband was. She just didn't seem to know of any other way to snag one.

"Tell me, Mom. What happened?" Carey sat on the sofa next to her.

"Bad day all around. Had it out with my boss, which is one reason I left early."

"Was…he okay with that?"

Her mom shrugged. "He won't fire me, if that's what you're worried about."

"Okay. So what's the other reason you left early?"

"Harold broke up with me on my lunch hour."

"Another one bites the dust," Carey muttered.

Her mom, however, had perfect hearing and a dash of nosiness to go with it. "Why? Are you and Jerod not still together?"

"Actually, no. We broke up a month ago. But I did the breaking up, and it wasn't on his lunch hour. What was Harold's problem?"

Her mom had been dating the guy for several weeks, which was longer than a lot of them lasted. Carey had met him once, and he seemed to have left his personality at home that day. But she was accustomed to not caring for the men her mother entertained.

"Turns out he's married."

Carey's jaw dropped. She reached to squeeze her mom's arm in sympathy. She'd developed a certain immunity to her mother's love woes over the years, but this one shocked her. Mr. Anti-Personality had a wife? And he was crafty enough to hide it? "That really sucks. Did you have any clue?"

Her mom shook her head. "There were lots of times he couldn't see me, but he's an accountant. It was tax season." She took several gulps of the rum and Coke, making a bitter face when she finished. "I'm tired, Carey. So tired."

She suspected her mom referred to more than a lack

of sleep. "Don't take this the wrong way, but why don't you rest for a bit? Take some time out from the dating scene?"

Her mom looked sad. "No. I'm not going to give up. I know there's someone out there, someone as wonderful as your father was. I'm going to find that man."

"You can find him later. Give yourself a break."

"You don't understand."

"No, I don't. I never have." Carey stood, her ire building, both at her mom for putting herself through this and at the men who kept treating her like dirt. Crossing her arms, she paced to the other side of the room. "You've been married four times, Mom. Dad was the only good guy. You've gone out with half a bajillion men in between." She stopped and perched on the arm of the love seat opposite the sofa. "Why do you do this? Don't you think it's possible to be happier on your own?"

Her mom's eyes widened. "You don't get it, do you?" A hint of anger underlined her words.

It was enough to set Carey off. "No, Mom. I don't. What is so attractive to you about getting your heart stomped on every other month? Why do you insist on doing it? Don't you like yourself more than that?"

Her mother stood, and though they were the same height, at this moment, Penny Langford Stringer definitely seemed mightier. "You're young, Carey. I try to remember that. Yet at your age, I had two kids and a settled life."

"Settled until Dad died. Then you were alone again and couldn't be happy."

Tears appeared in her mom's eyes, and Carey felt an ounce of remorse for the blunt comment. But it was true. Her mom had never once been happy when she didn't have a man in her life. And she was rarely happy for long when she did.

"My marriage to your dad was the best thing that ever happened to me. We loved each other so much…" She took a deep breath and started again. "I can only hope you'll understand how it feels one day, Carey. I hope you can find it. I hope *I* can find it again."

"Don't hold your breath for me. I'm not looking."

Her mom shook her head, speechless. She set her drink down on the end table and walked to the door. "I don't have it in me to argue with you, too." She reached for the doorknob, then turned back. "It's worth looking for, worth fighting for, Carey." She paused, clearly overcome by emotion. "What I wouldn't give for both you and I to be able to find the kind of love I had with your father…."

She opened the door and walked out without another word.

Carey's heart went out to her mom, in spite of the harsh tone of their conversation. She'd been searching for so long, and didn't seem to grasp that what she'd had years ago she'd been lucky as hell to find once.

Carey sighed. Broken heart or not, she was worse off than her mom this time.

Pushing the unsettling thought away, she headed to the bathroom for a shower. Devin's birthday party for his grandpa started in two hours and she and Monica had promised they'd be there early to help.

"YOU GUYS want screwdrivers like the geezers? Or beer?" Carey asked the other two. She'd appointed herself the bar wench for the night. Devin was relieved for the assistance, as entertaining was miles outside of his comfort zone. He'd pushed any feelings he had for Carey out of his mind so that he could enjoy the evening.

"Beer's fine," Monica said.

"I've got it." Devin headed for the fridge, which was much fuller than usual. "Just don't let *them* hear you call them geezers."

Fresh air wafted in through the open kitchen window, carrying the aroma of newly mown grass and a chorus of laughter from the group on the deck. Devin's grandpa and his three self-described old-coot friends lounged around the outdoor table, along with Kyle, Monica's husband.

His grandpa turned eighty-five today, and Devin had wanted to do something special for him.

Gramps was in his element. He didn't get to see his friends much anymore since he couldn't drive and refused to move into the city closer to Devin. All four old guys had spent the evening so far trying to one-up each other flirting with Carey and Monica. The women were good sports and gave it right back to the octogenarians.

Devin had to look closely to recognize Gramps wasn't feeling as great as he let on. He was in good spirits, but he hadn't moved from his spot on the deck since he'd arrived. Completely out of character for a man who'd always been active. And he hadn't turned his oxygen supply off once, which was telling. And disturbing. Gramps was the kind of man who would never ask for help, who hated lugging a little tank around with him to be able to breathe. He loathed needing help at all.

Devin was still coming to grips with his grandpa's recently discovered heart condition, too.

He set one of the beers on the counter in front of Monica, who was chopping vegetables for salsa. "Thanks, Dev." She smiled and took a drink, then pushed her dark brown hair behind her ears. "So, Carey, did you tell Jerod yet?"

Devin's pulse rate kicked up a notch. Carey glanced at Monica, dread in her expression, as if she hadn't wanted the topic to come up. But how could she expect that they wouldn't talk about her pregnancy or the jerk who'd knocked her up? It was tough to ignore that her whole life had changed in the course of a few days.

"Yeah. Saturday."

"And you didn't tell me about it yet? It's been almost a week," Monica pointed out.

"I know. I haven't been in the mood to talk about it."

"You better not be tiptoeing around for my sake."

Carey whipped her head toward Monica. "Don't flatter yourself." She forced a laugh. "I've had a lot to figure out."

"So what did he say?"

Devin waited for the answer as eagerly as Monica, although he didn't want to think about why it mattered to him so much.

Carey was annoyingly silent as she poured orange juice into the glasses in front of her. When she'd filled all four of them, she set the carton down. "He wasn't excited."

Monica held her knife in the air above the jalapeño pepper she'd been cutting, staring at Carey. "And?"

"And…he asked me what I wanted him to do. He asked if I wanted to get married."

Devin's heart stopped. Surely she didn't….

"What'd you tell him?" Monica demanded.

"No." Finally she looked up at them. "Come on, guys, what'd you expect?"

Neither answered.

"After watching my mom settle for the wrong men all these years, did you think I'd hook up with him just because I'm pregnant?" She turned back to the concoctions on the counter.

"And don't say it," Carey continued, pointing the bottle of vodka at Devin. "I don't want to hear how you told me so again."

Devin set his beer on the counter and raised both

hands in surrender. "I didn't even say much while you were dating him. I think I showed admirable control."

Her only reply was to glare at him.

He rubbed his thumb and forefinger over his eyes to massage away the headache that had taken root hours ago. "I said I was sorry for the other night."

"What, exactly, happened the other night?" Monica asked, chopping rhythmically again.

"I was a jerk."

"He was a jerk," Carey announced at the exact same time, which made them all laugh.

"At least we have that straight," Monica said.

"I overreacted. But it still burns me up that you're the one whose life is affected till the end of time."

"Which way do you want it, Devin? Do you want him to marry me and play daddy or do you want him out of my life?"

He couldn't answer that, because honestly, both options made his blood boil. "What I want doesn't matter a damn bit. So what else did you two decide?"

Carey carried the glasses over to the refrigerator to fill them with ice. Taking her time to drop exactly four cubes in each one, she seemed not to have heard the question. She rummaged through one of Devin's lower cupboards and stood up holding a seldom-used baking pan. One by one, she placed the drinks on the make-shift tray.

"*We* didn't decide anything." She opened the fridge and grabbed a beer, popped the lid off and set it on the tray as well. "He offered to give me child support. I turned him down." Carey took the tray and set it on the counter next to Monica, who was now stirring her creation. "Which reminds me, I need the name of a good doctor."

"What do you mean you turned him down?" Devin interrupted.

"I don't want his money."

He moved beside her. "You're letting him off the hook?"

"Yes." Carey gritted her teeth for a moment, then turned back to Monica. "Would you recommend the doctor you go to?"

Devin stifled a smile. Selfish lout that he was, a large part of him was glad she'd given Jerod the boot, his money and all. This was one example of Carey's impulsive nature he could actually stand behind, although he suspected he shouldn't. He should try to talk her into taking the bastard's money for the baby's sake…and hers. He absently shoved tortilla chips in his mouth.

"Dr. Estes is good. Not bad looking either," Monica said.

"You think I should go to a male doctor?"

Monica shrugged. "Why not? He's seen girls naked before. It's all clinical to him."

"A good-looking OB/GYN? I don't know if I could have a good-looking man down there doing *that*."

"He's really easy to talk to," Monica said.

"Talk? I'd prefer if he just checked and ran."

Monica laughed. "Yeah, until you have some mysterious vaginal itching and you're begging him to give you something for it."

"Hey, I'm eating here," Devin complained. The manly bunch on the deck was looking more and more appealing.

"You people die or what?" Kyle's voice boomed at the back door. "The men are hungry. Got something I can take out to appease them?"

Monica stirred the salsa once more, then picked up the full chip-and-dip serving bowl she'd brought along. "At your service." She shot her husband a flirty look and followed him outside, leaving Devin and Carey by themselves.

"So. Are you sure it's best to let Jerod off the hook?" That was the best he could do to convince her to change her mind. Weak, he knew.

"His heart wasn't in the offer, Devin. I don't want this baby ever to feel like just an obligation, and that's exactly what she'd be to Jerod."

"Makes sense to me."

She stopped in the middle of taking a tray of chicken wings out of the oven and stared at him. "It does?"

"Yep. A monthly check from him would be nice, but that makes everything a little harder."

"Such as?"

"Custody. Visitation. Rights. All that stuff."

Carey ignored the food in the oven. "I don't think he wants any of those." He saw fear in her face. "Do you? Do you think he'd try to get the baby?"

He grabbed the hot pad from her and took the pan out. Closing the oven, he said, "I don't know, Carey. I wouldn't think so, but you should protect yourself from him."

"Great."

"What?"

"You just opened up a whole new batch of worries for me to lose sleep over."

"Happy to help." He'd missed out on many hours of sleep himself over the past week, thinking about her.

She stood there chewing on her thumb, lost in thought. "I'll talk to Kyle and see what he knows. He can set me up with a good lawyer."

"Good idea," he said as he transferred the wings to a platter. "I'm afraid to ask…do you have a backup plan for all the baby expenses?"

"I'll…figure it out. I'll need to work more. I hope I can find some new sources for work around here. I won't be able to travel much."

Devin hesitated, watching her. "This won't save you financially, but I do have something to run by you."

Carey gave him her full attention. "What's up?"

"I need someone to help me with all my marketing materials for CMT. A few photos and some desktop publishing. I thought you'd be perfect." CMT Computer Security was his baby. He hoped she knew he didn't trust just anyone with it.

"If the price is right, of course I'm up for it," she said loftily.

He chuckled. "I'll pay you fairly."

"You've got yourself a deal." Carey offered her hand.

He took it, shook on the agreement, then released it.

"Hey!" came a gravelly voice through the kitchen window. "Service! What's an old man gotta do for a drink around here?"

Devin picked up the platter of chicken and headed around the bar. "Come to the office on Monday and we can talk details."

Carey picked up her camera from the counter and slung it around her neck, then grabbed her makeshift tray of drinks and followed him out on the deck.

CHAPTER SIX

"YOU GOT the prettiest waitresses this side of the Atlantic," Gus hollered as they made their way out onto the deck. "You don't hold a candle to 'em, Devin, my boy."

Gus looked Carey up and down as she approached, and Devin shook his head, grinning. What a lot of love-starved widowers.

Gus was right though. Monica was impeccably dressed as usual. And Carey…she wore an orange-flowered sundress with skimpy straps and a snug fit. Any man in his right mind would agree she looked spectacular.

Carey nudged Gus as she placed a glass in front of him. "One screwdriver, just how you like it, easy on the OJ." She moved around the oval table, placing glasses in front of Albert, whose crispy, tanned skin looked as though he'd spent every day of his eighty-odd years baking in the sun, and Jones, the quietest of them, whose first name was still a mystery to Devin. She circled to Gramps. "And a virgin screwdriver for the birthday boy."

Gramps grumbled good-naturedly. "Damn medications. I believe you mean OJ straight up, Miss Carey."

"And here I thought men liked virgins," she said to a round of approving hoots as she placed the single beer in front of Kyle, who held Monica tucked against his side.

Carey walked back around the table with her camera, "Dev, lean down by your grandpa."

When he did, she shot several pictures of the two, smiling. She kept clicking away, even after they'd stopped posing.

Devin sat in the deck chair to his grandpa's left, thankful the pain in his ribs had eased up in the last week. "You can't give the bartender a hard time, Gramps. She's the only one we've got."

"And the only one without a drink," Gramps said. "Someone get that girl a refreshment."

Devin held his breath, wondering if Carey would confess to her condition.

"Don't you worry about me. You didn't see what I downed in the kitchen," Carey said, sitting on the bench to the old man's right.

The men were in rare form tonight, cracking more one-liners than a room full of politicians up for reelection.

"How's that company of yours coming along?" Gramps asked Devin after a few minutes had passed.

Devin took a swig of beer. "Not bad. Starting slower than I'd hoped, but I'll get there."

"You take your time and do it right, you'll be okay."

Devin nodded, knowing he was right, but feeling unsettled and impatient anyway. "I just need a couple of big contracts to reassure me right now."

"I've still got some contacts. Why don't I call them up, put in a good word for you?"

Gramps had been successful in business himself, and Devin valued all the input he offered. He'd offered plenty along the way, as Devin took classes and planned for his company. Gramps had been his one-man cheering squad from the moment Devin had gotten serious about doing something practical with his interest in computers. However, the one thing Devin didn't want was for his business to ride on the coattails of Gramps's accomplishments. He wanted to build his own success. Needed to. Gramps's charity wouldn't prove a thing.

"I'd rather not do it based on your merit," Devin said. "But thanks for the offer."

Gramps didn't answer, just tapped his gnarled fingers on the table.

"I've got my first year's budget set," Devin told him, noticing Carey leaned in to listen to their conversation instead of continuing the repartee with the others. "My goal is to show a profit by month thirteen."

Gramps narrowed his eyes. "You think that's going to be feasible?"

"It'll be tough, but the way I have it on paper, it could happen. I'll make it happen."

"Slow down. Take your time. They're dead, son. You can't prove a thing to your parents."

"Maybe I just need to prove it to myself," Devin said half-heartedly.

The need to show the world his parents had been wrong about him drove him like a crazed man. He needed to prove that their antisocial, apathetic son who spent his time "puttering" with computers had it in him to build something just as important as their TV station.

Devin could tell by Gramps's raised eyebrows he didn't buy it for a second. So be it. Actually, there was more than just himself and his parents in the equation. There was Gramps, too.

Devin thought of Gramps as a father figure, the man who'd taught him anything good he knew. It was because of the old man's faith in him that Devin had the chance to pursue the company of his dreams in the first place. It humbled Devin how much his grandpa had already done for him, most notably the large donation of capital for the start-up. He couldn't wait for the day when he could show Gramps he'd done it, that he'd taken the old man's investment and his belief in him and made it into a company he hoped would sustain him for the rest of his life.

While Devin's parents had had no confidence in him, Gramps had. And for that leap of faith, Devin had gone so far as to name the company CMT after him, Carl Martin Thaylor.

"I worry about you, Devin."

"Don't. I'm fine."

Gramps steepled his fingers in front of him. "Your whole life is about this company of yours. Believe me, I learned the hard way there are more important things than work."

"I've waited far too long for this chance. I'm not going to blow it."

"I'm saying you shouldn't blow off everything else." Gramps removed his glasses and busied himself cleaning the lenses with a corner of his shirt. "It's been over a month since I last saw you."

So that's what was bugging the birthday boy. Devin swigged down some beer. Damn. He hadn't expected a guilt trip from his grandpa. It was true, he hadn't taken the old man out to dinner for a while. Until recently, he'd made a point of doing that on a weekly basis. But he'd thought Gramps understood. His grandpa was the only one intimately familiar with the reason for Devin's tunnel vision. No one else could begin to conceive of how Devin's parents' death five years ago—or rather, the message they'd sent with their will—had affected him.

Devin hid his frustration, still determined to make this a special night. "Name a night next week."

His grandpa smiled. "I'm easy, son. Whatever night suits you."

"Wednesday then."

Gramps nodded, then turned his attention to the

back door of the house. Devin followed his line of sight, instantly enraged.

"Happy birthday, Grandpa." Jerod's grating voice momentarily caused a lull in the noisy celebration.

The old guys filled the lapse in conversation pretty quickly, but Devin barely noticed. His cousin walked out onto the deck, completely overdressed in suit pants, a dress shirt and an ugly tie.

"What the hell is he doing here?" Devin asked under his breath.

"You said invite who I want. I invited all my grand-kids."

Any of the other grandkids would've been fine. Hell, Devin would love to see Landon or even Jerod's sisters. But welcoming Jerod into his home was a hell of a lot to ask.

Devin glanced at Carey, who shrugged and gave a what-the-hell look, but he could tell she was just as thrown off to see her ex.

"Is there a problem?" Gramps asked him. "I hoped you could ignore your differences for a couple of hours on my birthday. He's family, something I don't have much of left."

The old man rose slowly, checked to make sure his oxygen tank fanny pack was attached to him, and saun-tered toward the new arrival.

Devin followed, waiting behind Gramps as he hugged Jerod. After a brief exchange, Gramps returned to his chair again, inviting Jerod to join the group.

"Didn't realize you were coming," Devin said to him, trying to hide his animosity from the other guests.

"Wouldn't miss it." Jerod smiled as if he had no clue he wasn't welcome.

He'd always acted that way, as if he couldn't figure out why Devin hated him.

"You can stay as long as you leave Carey alone." He said it too quietly for anyone else to hear.

Jerod shot a passing glance his way, then walked off, leaving Devin with the urge to beat the hell out of him.

Heading back toward the table, Devin adopted a nonchalance he didn't feel. He met Carey's eyes and it was obvious she wasn't comfortable.

"Sorry," he mouthed to her as he sat down.

She nodded briefly and tried to smile.

Monica hopped up and took Jerod's drink order, then disappeared into the kitchen.

Jerod stared at Carey, at the opposite end of the table from him, but she didn't glance at him once. Good for her. If he harassed her at all, he'd answer to Devin.

As the evening wore on, Devin had never been so grateful for the banter and loud laughter around the table. The constant noise made it almost possible to forget his cousin was present. Carey was clearly aware of him, though, as she seemed to go out of her way to laugh loudly and frequently.

Finally, Carey whispered she was going to bring out

the cake. She slipped inside unnoticed, just as Jones told a dirty joke.

Carey closed the door behind her and breathed out a long sigh. She prayed Jerod didn't try to talk to her. They had nothing to talk about.

She took the cake from the fridge and moved it to the bar, then searched through the plastic grocery bag for candles and matches. She finally dug out a wax number eight and a number five and plunked them into the frosting.

When the door opened, she assumed it was Monica coming inside to help. It wasn't.

Jerod glided in with a concerned expression. He *should* be concerned—that Devin would follow him.

"I have to take the cake outside," Carey said before he could speak.

"Carey, please. Can you give me two minutes?"

She waited for him to get it over with.

"I'm still a little blown away by your news the other night."

She nodded impatiently.

"Have you been to a doctor?"

"Not yet. But there's no mistake, Jerod. I tested three times."

He stuck a hand into the pocket of his suit pants as he watched her. "I thought I'd give you another chance to accept some cash."

He looked so pleased with himself, smug.

"No thanks, Jerod."

"If you turn it down now, don't come begging for help later."

"I don't intend to." She bit down on her irritation. "I'd rather we didn't get tangled up in finances and obligations. Ever."

He shrugged dismissively. "You're a stubborn woman, Carey."

"Yes." She nodded her head. "I am."

His head bobbed up and down slowly several times, as he shrewdly assessed her. "Never let it be said that I didn't try to help."

"You've done your duty. Now I have to take the cake out."

She felt strangely apathetic toward him as she grabbed the matches and slid her arms under the box.

She forced a smile on her face and rejoined the party, leaving Jerod to exult by himself.

As she took her seat next to Devin again, he asked, "Is Jerod inside?"

"He came in to see if I'd changed my mind about child support."

"Did you?"

"What do you think?"

"I think you're a hardheaded woman."

"You're right. He made sure I was aware he'd tried to help. It's as if he's trying to protect himself."

"Dammit. I didn't see him sneak inside or I would've interrupted."

"It's okay, Dev. I can handle him."

He took the book of matches from her and lit both the candles. Then the group sang a painful version of "Happy Birthday." Gramps managed to blow both candles out without help, although it was obvious to Carey it was a struggle. She hoped Devin didn't notice. He worried about his grandpa too much already.

"Where'd Jerod go?" Gramps asked, surveying the group.

"I'm sure he'll be out soon enough," Devin said.

Carey couldn't understand what he muttered under his breath, but she could tell it wasn't friendly. She had to admit his protectiveness toward her where Jerod was concerned touched her—more than a little.

She seemed to be the only one who noticed when, several minutes later, Devin sneaked back inside.

CHAPTER SEVEN

DEVIN CLOSED the door to the noisy bunch on the deck and listened for Jerod. He heard something in the front living room and strode in that direction.

"What the hell were you thinking showing up here tonight?" Devin said when he spotted Jerod checking out his DVD collection.

"Thought I'd wish the old man a happy birthday."

"You're making Carey uncomfortable."

"I didn't know she'd be here, but even if I had, my relationship with her is none of your business."

"You screw around with one of my best friends and damn right it's my business."

"Get off your high horse, man. All I did was date her."

"And knock her up."

Jerod narrowed his eyes. "She told you?"

"Hell, yes, she told me."

"She had an equal part in that, you know."

"Okay." Devin nodded once. "I'll give you that. She had a serious lapse in judgment the whole time she went out with you." He stalked closer.

Jerod rammed his fingers through his thick hair. "Look, I offered to help. She doesn't want my money. She should get rid of it, but she won't. She's made her decision, man."

And he'd washed his hands of the whole problem.

"She's much better off without you, but I hate that you get off scot-free."

"Why does my involvement with Carey make you so mad? It doesn't have anything to do with you."

It was a good goddamn question.

A smug look appeared on Jerod's face. "You want her for yourself, don't you?" He shook his head and grinned as if he were the smartest man since Einstein. "You can't stand that I slept with her."

"Get out of my house. *Now!*"

Jerod shrugged and sauntered out the front door just as Devin was on the verge of kicking the crap out of him.

Devin ran his hand down his face, shaking with fury and wondering what the hell had happened to his common sense. Jerod had baited him and he'd leapt at the bait.

He leaned on the arm of the overstuffed chair by the front door, unable to face the party in the backyard just yet.

The bitch of it all was that Jerod was right. Devin couldn't handle that his cousin had slept with Carey. He *did* want her for himself. And this goddamn realization that he loved her had come a few weeks too late, because now there was no way in hell he and Carey could be together. Not when Jerod had had her first. Sure as hell not when she was carrying Jerod's child. It didn't matter whether he loved her or not. There was no way he could *not* think about his cousin's claim on her. No way he could ever step in and raise Jerod's baby.

In a frustrated rage he kicked the big beige ottoman across the room. Swearing like a street kid, he strode to the kitchen and grabbed another beer from the fridge. He chugged down a good half of it and tried to can the ugliness he felt.

He set the bottle down and, leaning over the sink, splashed ice-cold water on his face. After drying off with a paper towel, he returned to the living room and sank into the overstuffed chair.

He heard the back door open and close and stifled a groan. He wished everyone had left already so he didn't have to act as if nothing was wrong.

Carey stepped into the doorway between the kitchen and living room and spotted Devin. She took a few steps into the room.

His eyes were bluer than usual, matching the shirt he wore. His hair was mussed, as if he'd run his hands through it repeatedly. In the low light, his scowl looked dangerous…

"What are you doing in here? Where's Jerod?"

"Gone."

"Why?"

"I made him leave." His voice was flat.

She noticed the upturned ottoman apprehensively. "Were there…problems?"

"Hell, yes. That's why I made him leave."

"How'd this get turned upside down?" she asked as she bent to right the footstool. Pulling it to where he sat, she perched on it just in front of his legs, facing him.

Devin sank his head back into the massive cushion and looked at her through half-closed eyes. Carey could tell by his agitated state that Jerod had really gotten to him. She was dying to know what had elicited such a strong reaction.

She rested her hands on his knees. "You really don't like him, do you?"

He laughed, but it rang hollow. "No. I really don't like him. Can't stand the son of a bitch." He said it with such vehemence, Carey was taken aback.

She tilted her head slightly. "I knew you didn't like him, but you've never acted like he was that big a deal."

Devin didn't say anything, just slumped there with his eyes closed.

"What's the story, Devin?"

"I don't want to talk about him."

She considered beating him on the chest until he talked but opted for a more peaceful method—for now. "What started the whole problem between you two? I'm missing something."

He pulled back in the chair to sit up straighter, away from her. Then he ran his hands over his face. "I really don't like talking about it."

"I want to know. Come on, Dev. Why do you hate him?"

He exhaled, obviously frustrated she wouldn't let it go. But she wasn't about to ignore it. His reaction to Jerod tonight was far worse than any mutterings of dislike she'd heard from him before.

"It'll sound stupid," he said quietly.

She shrugged. "When it comes to Jerod, I think I've got you beat on 'stupid.'"

He hesitated, then finally opened up. "Ever since we were little kids, he's tried to force his way into my family. His mom deserted his family. His dad worked two jobs to support the five kids. They rented an old, deteriorating house about a mile and a half from ours, but in a very different neighborhood."

"Crummy part of town?"

He nodded.

Carey knew how nice the house Devin had grown up in was—she'd been there enough. There was no question the Colyers had been well off. "How crummy?"

"The city demolished the entire neighborhood several years back because there was nothing worth saving. A strip mall sits in its place."

Carey couldn't hide her surprise. She'd never met any of Jerod's immediate family, either in high school or in the past few months as Jerod's girlfriend. She'd never had a hint he'd grown up destitute. As the owner of a local television station, there wasn't an ounce of poor left in him.

"He used to walk over to our house every day and hang out from the time he was maybe seven. I would have been three or four years old."

He looked so troubled she wanted to touch him again but didn't dare after he'd jerked his legs away.

"He was only interested in my parents. Barely gave me a second glance."

She parked her elbow on her leg and supported her chin with her hand. "I don't understand."

"I didn't either for a long time. All I knew was that he got a hell of a lot more attention from them than I did. They loved him. He pestered them with questions about the TV station from the beginning. Begged them to take him on tours, let him play on the news set."

"Did they?"

"Of course. They were ecstatic to have a boy in the house who spoke their language."

"While you were hiding in your room taking apart electronics." She couldn't count the times she'd found him with a computer case or a radio or something else opened up as if to perform surgery.

He nodded grimly. "I was the guy who wasted his life on computer games. They didn't know me, never even tried to know me. I wasn't Mr. Outgoing so they wrote me off early. Not so with Jerod. By the time I met you, he was practically a full-time employee at the station." He stood and paced.

"I never knew. I met him at your house once or twice, but then I hardly ever saw him. I had no idea he was with your parents more than you were."

"Jerod's the son they always wanted, and he played it for all he was worth."

"What happened to his family?"

"They're still around. His dad lives here in town on the east side. Three of his four sisters are married, scattered around the country. I think the other one took off, too, but I don't remember where. Family's never been a big thing for any of us."

Carey had known that about Devin. It was a big part of what had drawn them together as friends in the first place.

She could only imagine how Devin had felt to have his cousin step in and build a lasting relationship with the parents who'd shunned him. Carey's own mother had merely been too busy and too focused on finding the second love of her life. There hadn't been anyone who had "stolen" her mom from her.

His hatred of Jerod was starting to make sense now. "How come you've never told me any of this before? Especially when I was seeing him?"

"Would it have made any difference?"

"I don't know. It might have. I always just figured your dislike of him was a guy thing. He's well off, well known around town, good looking, a little conceited…"

Devin shook his head. "It's been ingrained since I was a kid. My parents continually chose him over me." He inhaled sharply, then released the breath. "There. I told you. I've basically been jealous of him since before I knew what jealous meant. What's that say about me?"

Carey stood and forced eye contact. "It says you were a normal kid who needed his parents."

Arms crossed, he stared her down, defiance etched into his features. "It goes beyond that. I no longer need them, but I still can't stand *him*. To this day, he still pushes my buttons."

She was confused. She hadn't been aware that Devin and Jerod had any regular contact before tonight. "How does he do that?"

He continued to stare at her with such intensity she shivered. "You, Carey."

"Me?" She tilted her head. "I'm a button?" That made no sense whatsoever, but her heart pounded anyway.

The back door opened and Devin snapped to attention. He reached the kitchen just as Gramps hollered for him. Carey followed, completely befuddled.

"Time for this old boy to get home and hit the sack, son," Gramps said.

Devin glanced at his watch and nodded. "Nine-fifteen. Pretty late for an eighty-five-year-old."

"Damn straight. What have you two been doing holed up in here?"

"Sorry about that. Carey and I had something to discuss."

"No need to apologize. I've been catching up with the boys." His eyes twinkled.

"How are they doing out there?" Devin asked, motioning toward the door.

"See for yourself. I need to switch tanks and see if Gus is ready to go." He stopped short, then, clearly confused. "Where's Jerod?"

"He had to leave. Said to tell you good-night."

"Was he okay?"

"Is Jerod ever okay?"

Devin wandered outside to give the old guys some guff before they took off. They all stood in a bunch between the door and the table, jawing with Monica and Kyle. Carey came out right after him and stacked plates and trash, taking them into the house.

"You still okay to take the birthday boy home?" Devin asked Gus.

"Hell, yeah."

"How many of those girl drinks did you down?"

Gus raised his head and looked him over through the lower part of his bifocals. "You show me a girl who can take vodka straight and I'll show you the girl of my dreams, boy."

Devin motioned to Monica and Carey, who'd just come back outside. "Take your choice, old man." He grinned.

"I'll take one of each then." He winked at the

women. "'Spose you think I'm too juiced up to get behind the wheel."

"Just making sure."

"I had one o' them cocktails, sir. Hours ago." He saluted.

Devin saluted back as Gus went inside.

"Monica, thanks for the help. Or should I say thanks for taking over?"

"You bet. They all loved it. Especially your grandpa."

Kyle shook Devin's hand. "She's right. That's one happy man tonight. You certainly did right by him."

"I hope so." He apparently hadn't done well in the recent past. He had no idea how to fix it though. There were barely enough hours in the day as it was.

He'd take Gramps to dinner Wednesday as he'd promised, and he'd tell him exactly where he stood. He loved the old man, but his company currently required all of his time. As a former businessman, Gramps would understand if Devin could only make it once or twice a month.

AT 2:47 A.M., Carey rolled over for the umpteenth time, smacking her pillow down, as if her inability to sleep was the pillow's fault. Then in exasperation, she sat up and let out a stream of obscenities directed at Devin. Unfortunately, he was at home in his own bed, probably sleeping peacefully, and couldn't hear a word she said.

What the hell had he meant earlier tonight? Jerod pushed his buttons with *her?* She'd wanted to confront him and find out what that was all about before she left, but he'd shooed everyone out the door as soon as his grandpa had taken off with Gus.

The look on his face when he'd said it haunted her. His eyes had been intense; she'd never seen them like that before, full of so much emotion. Even now, remembering that look brought about a tingling awareness.

Maybe he was being the protective best friend who was ticked off that Jerod had screwed her over. Actually, she knew that was part of it, but she couldn't help wondering if he meant something more. If he felt something more. He'd felt an attraction once, albeit briefly. His feelings apparently hadn't been overpowering enough to fight off the wiles of Lisa Palmer. He'd walked away from Carey without hesitation. Since then he'd never shown a hint of anything more than friendship.

Carey lay back down and pulled all the blankets up to her chin. She was making too much out of an ambiguous comment. A mountain out of a molehill, her mother would say.

Closing her eyes, she pictured a procession of fuzzy sheep jumping over a fence and counted them. She made it to seventeen before losing interest and going back to Devin's words.

So what if he did mean something more, something like jealousy? He'd admitted he'd always been jealous of Jerod, and then two minutes later had brought her name into the mix. Maybe Devin was trying to say he still had feelings that went beyond friendly.

Her eyes opened wide in the dark room as every inch of her body warmed. *Was* he still attracted to her? Why was her body reacting this way after all this time?

No. She had a hard time believing he felt anything deeper than friendship. They'd spent hours upon hours together over the past fifteen years. They knew each other well—too well.

She was letting her imagination run away with her. Devin didn't want anything other than her friendship. If he did, he'd had aeons to express it.

She'd forced herself to get over him, to forget how his kisses had scared the life out of her, a long time ago.

Sure, there were moments when he opened a door for her or innocently touched her the way a friend might, and she had a flash of feeling for him. But then the moment of weakness passed.

Devin didn't really do serious when it came to women. He never had. He dated plenty, but Carey couldn't name a single one who'd lasted more than a few weeks, even before his parents died and he'd become so focused and overscheduled. Now he was too into attaining his goals to give much thought to a woman.

Especially a crazy, screwed-up woman like Carey who was pregnant with his cousin's baby.

She hopped out of bed and stormed to the living room where she'd tried to distract herself after the party. She had a future to figure out. There was a load of things to plan, from income to day care. With concerns like that, who had time to daydream about a man who might or might not have feelings for her he didn't want to discuss?

She stretched out on the floor and vowed to put him out of her mind for good. Or at least for the rest of the night.

CHAPTER EIGHT

LATE MONDAY afternoon, Carey trotted down the stairs to Devin's basement office, relieved he'd turned the air conditioner on. She pulled her T-shirt away from her chest in a fanning motion. The temperature outside had hit the mid-eighties, which was rare for Iowa in early May. "Hello?" she called out.

"Hey!" Monica, who had recently started working as Devin's assistant, spun her chair around to face Carey. "What are you doing here?"

"Looking for a dinner companion. Got plans?"

Monica smiled regretfully.

"What am I saying…the husband, of course," Carey said. "I hope Devin's an easier catch than you. I need to talk to him anyway."

"I heard my name," Devin said from his corner office, the only one that had actual walls. The rest of the room was divided by low partitions into four workstations. Monica occupied the one right outside Devin's, and the others were for future expansion, Devin had explained. The wall that separated his office from the others was mostly solid except for a large floor-to-ceiling window that allowed him to see the entire basement from his chair.

"Have fun with him," Monica said, raising her eyebrows. "He's been moody all afternoon."

"Men are not moody." Devin came out of his hideaway and stretched. "Men are grumps. Women are moody."

"Pig." Monica smiled. "I'm ready to take off. Anything else I need to finish first?"

"Go on. See you in the morning."

"See you. Let me know when you go to Dr. Estes, Carey."

Monica's desk was spotless, with the papers stacked neatly in labeled metal trays. She shut her computer down and grabbed her oversized purse, which Carey joked could double as a beach bag for a family of four, then waved as she headed out the door.

"So," Devin said, looking Carey over. "Thought you'd be by earlier today to talk about the project."

"We didn't set a time, did we?"

"No. I just assumed you'd show up during business hours."

"Business hours? I barely know what business hours are. If you want me here at a certain time, say so." She returned his scrutiny, making a point of inspecting him from head to toe. "What's the occasion? You're all spiffed up." She struggled to ignore the way looking at him jump-started her pulse. It was that damn comment Friday…it'd put her imagination into overdrive.

He wore khakis that fit…nicely, and a black polo shirt. He looked much calmer than he had when she'd left his house Friday night.

"I'm working. I dress nicely sometimes."

She glanced down at her own sloppy wardrobe of capri jeans and a plain mint-green T-shirt. "I might not have dressed nicely, but at least I shaved," she said, glancing at his stubble.

"Clean-shaven is overrated," he grumbled. He strode back into his office and Carey followed.

"Does dinner come with this interview?" she asked.

He chuckled. "I don't need to interview you. I know all your quirks already. You're a great photographer in spite of them."

"Thanks, I think."

"I'll buy dinner, but there's a catch."

Carey groaned. "What, master?"

"We eat it on the boat. Gramps says I work too much."

"He's right."

Devin had a sleek, overpriced fishing boat he'd spent most of last summer on. He'd taken Carey on a few zips around the lake as well. Even though it was a cramped fishing boat, complete with geeky removable raised seats at each end, the thing could move.

"I can handle a boat ride."

"Actually, I was going to drop a line for a bit." He stacked papers in three piles on his desk as he spoke. "I'll finish this stuff up when I get home."

Carey collapsed into Devin's chair and propped a foot up on the desk. She made a face. "You know I don't fish."

He grabbed her legs at the calves and set her feet on the floor. "Come on, it'll be relaxing. We'll talk about the project, eat some subs, get some fresh air."

"All of that's fine. It's the fish and worms I could do without."

"Free dinner. Besides, you haven't ridden in my new Excursion yet. Let's go."

She rolled her eyes, wondering what the big deal was about riding in a new vehicle, but he didn't see it because he'd already shot out the door. Carey jumped up to follow him. Dinner had her hooked. Besides, maybe they could continue their conversation from last Friday. If not, she could at least hit Devin up for help with the business idea she'd gotten in the middle of the sleepless night.

After Devin changed into jeans and a gray, long-sleeved T-shirt, loaning Carey a sweatshirt for when the sun got low and the temperature dropped, they went out to the garage. With Carey's guidance, Devin backed the SUV up to the boat trailer, which took up half of his garage. On the way out of town, they picked up subs.

He pulled into the parking lot at the marina twenty minutes later. There were only a few vehicles, most of them gas-guzzlers attached to empty trailers. Beyond the lot, the calm water glistened in the late-afternoon sun.

After a few minutes, the boat was in the water tied to the dock, and Devin parked the SUV and the trailer. His tension from the day began melting away.

The air smelled of spring and humidity, which in his mind meant fishing.

While he was getting the cooler of drinks from the back, Carey eased down from the passenger seat, mumbling something about how impractical his new vehicle was. Devin led the way onto the dock, calmed by the gentle sound of water lapping against the boats. It never failed—whenever he set foot on the docks, the rest of the world faded away. It'd been far too long since his last visit.

He set the cooler on the deck of his boat and climbed in over the driver's seat. Once he'd helped Carey in, their eyes met, and he dropped her hand, squeezing by her to the driver's seat. But he was unable to avoid brushing against her in the limited floor space of the two-seater.

She cleared her throat and stuck her hands in her back pockets. "What do you want me to do?"

"Take a load off, pregnant lady. I'll handle everything."

She set her purse on the floor and sat on the only other seat, which was still noticeably close to him. He intended to park himself on the lone pedestal seat at the front as soon as they got settled.

Her eyes focused on him as he unlocked the storage compartment where he stowed his tackle box. He wished he'd had time to stop and get some live bait, but the sun still set earlier than he liked. He wanted as much time as he could get on the water. Fishing jaunts would be rare this summer as he busted his butt to get CMT off the ground.

"You know, for someone who complains about my little car so much, you could really use some extra leg room in this thing," Carey said, trying to prop her feet up on the panel in front of her. Her legs were too long, and her knees were rammed up her nose. "So tell me about the marketing stuff. What do you need me to do?"

He listed several ideas he'd had. He wanted two or three different brochures, each targeting a different segment of the local market. Carey said it would be easy, which didn't surprise him. He had no problem trusting her artistic abilities.

"Think you can get the brochures done in two weeks or so?"

He started the motor, and Carey leaned closer so they could talk above the noise.

"Should be able to. You'll supply the text you want?"

"Yep."

"Then yes. Shouldn't be a problem. So can I drive?" She gestured toward the controls.

"Do I look crazy?"

She made a show of looking him over. "Crazy enough to contract me. Please?"

"Have you ever driven a boat?"

"Whose boat would I have driven?"

"No, Carey, you can't drive."

"Come on, it's easy. It can't be much different from a car."

"I wouldn't let you drive my car either," he said, laughing.

She crossed her arms and pretended to pout, her lower lip catching Devin's attention. The wrong kind of attention. He turned his focus back to the controls.

They were out of the cove now, away from the marina, and he opened it up. He stood so that the wind whipped through his hair as they tore around the lake. Carey shrieked and laughed, and he could tell she loved it as much as he did.

There were few other boats around to get in their way, so they spent a good fifteen minutes at full throttle, skimming over the surface. Carey knelt on her seat in order to get the full effect of the wind.

He glanced at her out of the corner of his eye, loving to see her happy. Her blond hair flew behind her. She was totally into the moment.

Devin slowed when he neared his favorite spot, a quiet cove surrounded by tall trees on the shore opposite the marina. Several dead trunks jutted out of the water close to the edge. When he killed the engine, the chatter of birds in the woods drifted out to them. He leaned into the seat for a moment, taking in the peace, breathing in the fresh air.

Standing, he leaned forward to get his gear out of the rod box. "Want a rod?"

"Devin. I don't fish."

He grinned. "Someday I'll get you to try it." He climbed onto the deck and set up the pedestal seat, then sat and started tying on a lure.

"Yeah, sure you will."

He cast the line out the front of the boat.

As silence descended over them, Carey turned sideways in her seat and stretched her legs out to the driver's side. She wished he'd spent his money on a speedboat with room for about six people. Propping her elbow on the back cushion, she leaned on her hand and watched Devin work his supposed magic with the slimy creatures of the lake.

She was itching to ask him what he'd meant when he said Jerod pushed his buttons with her, but staring at his back as he fished, this didn't seem the most opportune time. Instead, she decided to tackle the easier of two conversations. "I had an idea over the weekend. I wanted to see what you think of it."

Devin swiveled his chair. "What kind of idea?" he asked warily.

"Don't worry, it's nothing that involves you. Well, not too much."

Leaning forward, she propped her elbows on her knees. If he laughed, she'd either feel like a fool or throw him overboard. Or both. "I've been thinking a lot about my future. You know, after the baby's born. As I said before, I won't be able to travel much for work anymore."

"Probably not."

"So I'm thinking about starting my own business." The words came out of her mouth in a rush.

Devin's eyes widened as he turned fully toward her, dragging the fishing pole with him. "What kind of business?"

"The kind I know. Photography." She wove her fingers together to stop from picking at the seam of her pants.

"What kind? Studio? Weddings?"

"Yes." She smiled. "Both. I'd probably start with weddings since I can't afford a studio yet. I'd also want to keep freelancing whenever I could get local gigs. I don't want to lose my contacts."

He reeled in in silence for several seconds until his lure finally came to the water's surface. He brought it the rest of the way in. She waited for him to say it was crazy, that she could never handle it along with a newborn baby or even a pregnancy.

"I think it's a hell of an idea."

Her heart sped up. "You do? You don't think I'll bomb?" She hopped up, had nowhere to pace, and tucked herself back on the seat, kneeling. Unable to contain her nervous energy.

"Carey, you're damn good at what you do."

"Yeah, but what I do is take pictures. Numbers are not my friend."

"You can learn that stuff."

"I, um, actually was hoping you'd help me get started."

Devin laughed and her hope crumbled momentarily.

"Do away with the meek, timid act, and hell, yes, I'll help you."

"Yes!" She jumped up again and threw a fist into the air.

His approval and agreement to help locked everything into place. With Devin behind her, she felt a lot better about her chances. She knew without a doubt she could handle the photography, but the technical details of running a business scared her. She didn't want to screw anything up.

She climbed onto the deck and threw her arms around Devin from behind.

"What are you doing?" he asked, holding his pole away from her.

She laughed. Leaning close, she kissed his cheek. "Thanks, Dev." Before she pulled away, she got a whiff of him—masculine, with hints of spice and soap. The alluring scent caught her off guard. She took in a close-up view of his stubble-roughened cheek, then his lips.

Backing off, she felt a bit dazed. She shook her head and grinned as she made her way back to her seat.

Her reaction meant nothing. She was just excited about the prospect of going into business. And touched that he believed in her enough to stand behind her.

Out of nowhere, tears filled her eyes. Feeling like an overemotional idiot, she tried to wipe them away, but Devin didn't miss them.

"You're crying?" He smirked. "You're a head case."

"Hormones," was all she could spit out around the sudden lump in her throat.

Unfortunately, those very hormones that were raging out of control not only made her cry at inappropriate times, they also seemed to give her inappropriate thoughts about Devin.

They spent the next couple of hours on the water mostly without speaking, which suited Carey fine. She loved the peace, the gentle rocking of the boat and the chance to covertly watch Devin. At one point, she dragged out a small notepad she carried in her purse and jotted down ideas for names of her new business-to-be.

As the sun dropped toward the horizon, Devin finally packed it in. She'd watched him reel in two good-sized fish plus a small one he'd thrown back. The keepers were stowed away in the place one stowed fish—whatever he'd called it—so Monica could fry them. Neither he nor Carey could do them justice in the kitchen. Monica could, and she usually froze the catch until she had enough to cook for all of them.

After placing his fishing rod in the storage panel with more care than he'd probably give a newborn baby, Devin stepped down to the floor. Grinning wickedly, Carey jumped over to the driver's seat before he could sit.

"What are you doing?" He looked at her in confusion.

"Driving."

"Oh, no, you aren't."

"Why not?"

"Do you know how much this thing cost me?" He pretended to sound outraged, but the grin on his face told a different story.

"This old thing?"

He closed the foot of space between them, hovering over her.

"How could I wreck your boat, Dev? Come on, show a little faith." She laughed as he grabbed her wrists to try to steer her back to the other seat.

"I don't want to know the answer to that question. I'm sure you could wreck it somehow."

He pulled gently by the arms. Carey let out a howl of surprise as he lifted her right out of the seat until she stood.

"Bully."

They were both laughing now, and Devin put his hands on her hips to switch places with her in the small floor space. As their bodies touched, they froze and their laughter died. Carey's heart raced like a jackrabbit on speed.

Devin's eyes darted to her lips for an instant, almost too fast to see, but she'd noticed. Her breath felt as though it was hung up on something in her throat and she swallowed. The whole of her focus became his face. She imagined running her fingers over the stubble, along his jaw, to the back of his neck to pull him closer....

Clearly, she was losing it.

"Devin," she said in a husky near whisper. "What did you mean when you said Jerod pushes your buttons with *me*?"

He held her gaze for a beat, then snapped to attention as her words sank in. He adopted a business-as-usual distance that quashed the heat pounding through her.

"Nothing. Let's not go there."

"I want to go there. I want to know what you meant."

He turned and lowered himself to the driver's seat in a single movement. She still stood, ready to do battle, her hand on her hip. Devin shook his head but didn't meet her eyes.

"I shouldn't have said it," he said. "It's...irrelevant."

She narrowed her eyes, puzzled. Irrelevant? Either he'd said more than he wanted to Friday and was embarrassed about it, or...he hadn't meant a damn thing by it.

"We need to go before it gets too dark. The lighting by the marina sucks."

In other words, she was dismissed. Deflated, she sat down, her mind spinning. Damn him.

He started the engine. Then he looked at her and

smiled, as if nothing at all out of the ordinary had happened.

Fine. If he didn't want to think about it, then neither would she. It meant nothing. It was just an offhand comment. Unfortunately, there was nothing offhand—or imagined—about the sparks that had passed between them just minutes before.

ON THE DRIVE home, the silence between them was suffocating. It'd taken longer than Devin had hoped to get the boat on the trailer and out of the water, and he and Carey had snapped at each other a couple of times.

He stole a glance at her across the darkness in the front seat. Her head was angled more toward the passenger window than the windshield. He couldn't see her expression, but she snapped at a stick of gum in a telling agitated rhythm.

How had it turned into this? He'd tried to avoid thinking about how he felt because loving Carey was a dead end. Now there was tension between them when the comfortable banter failed, like out on the boat. They'd gotten carried away in some damn hypnotic moment and now they weren't even speaking. He'd been a split second from kissing her when she'd opened her mouth about his half-cocked slipup Friday. Just in time.

Admitting how he felt about her would be pointless. What good would saying the words do when he couldn't act on them? His feelings were strong—and growing, dammit—but they couldn't stand up to the harsh truth that she was pregnant with his cousin's baby. Her reality was something Devin absolutely could not live with.

CHAPTER NINE

A FEW DAYS later, Carey let herself into Devin's house as he'd told her to do and went downstairs to the office. They'd arranged to shoot Devin's picture for the brochure today so she could get to work on the rest of it.

She was apprehensive about seeing him. Just enough to make her palms sweat.

After the scene on the boat, she wasn't sure how to act. Normal would be best, but that seemed impossible.

"Hello," she called at the bottom of the stairs. Monica wasn't at her desk, but Carey could see Devin at his.

When she got to the doorway, she saw that Monica sat across from him. "Am I interrupting?"

"Hey, there you are," Monica said, smiling as she stood. "We're done."

Carey finally looked at Devin for a brief, telling moment. He felt awkward, too.

Monica paused next to her in the doorway, glancing between the two, her brow furrowed.

"Hi," Carey said unnecessarily. "Photos today."

"Yeah," Monica said. "I knew there had to be a good reason for the tie."

"I figure we're billing me as CEO on the brochure so I might as well try to look like one," Devin said, tightening the tie and standing to put on a sports jacket. "Or at least not like some geeky computer guy who's shut in the basement all the time."

Carey smiled. He'd shaved, and of course she couldn't take in that detail without thinking about more intimate things than shooting his picture. Like running her fingers over his skin, kissing him.

She lowered her camera bag and set it on the chair Monica had vacated. "We're doing a shot of you first, right?"

He nodded.

"I also want to do a couple others…some abstract shots of computers just to use in the design."

"Sounds good to me. Where do you want me?"

In the bedroom.

She turned away from him under the guise of searching out a good location, unable to completely stifle a grin. "We'll do a few different shots. One at your desk. One over there against that wall; maybe we'll move the plant closer. Let's start with those. But first I need to grab a drink of water, if you don't mind."

"Help yourself."

Devin watched her walk away, appreciating the view more than he should but not giving a damn at this moment. When she disappeared up the stairs, he crossed to his desk and made notes to himself on something Monica and he had discussed before Carey came in. He started straightening his office since she'd suggested a picture at his desk. Not that it was terribly cluttered, but he wanted it to look respectable.

An old Go-Go's song burst out from nowhere, surprising him, until he remembered that was Carey's cell phone ring. He glanced out to see if she'd returned yet but saw no sign of her. He followed the sound to her bag and unzipped the side pocket. Lucky guess, he thought, as he pulled out the phone and hit the talk button.

"Hello?"

"Uh, I was trying to get hold of Carey Langford?" The male voice struck a familiar chord.

"Jerod? What the hell are you doing calling her?"

"What the hell are you doing answering her phone?"

At that moment, the phone was whisked away from his hand from behind. He turned to see Carey glaring at him.

She took the call and walked out of his office, shutting his door as she went. But he kept an eye on her out the window.

Scowling, he collapsed into his chair. Was she still in regular contact with the bastard? What the hell did they have to discuss?

Carey hung up and knocked on the door.

"Come in." Devin sounded grumpy.

"Don't start," she said as she entered.

"I didn't."

"Yet."

"How often do you talk to him?"

"Why does it matter?"

He shoved his hands in his pockets and ignored the question.

"Devin, why does it matter?" She was sick to death of tiptoeing around whatever it was they were tiptoeing around.

"What are you going to do if that baby comes along and three months later, oh, suddenly Jerod decides he likes the child and deserves to split custody with you?"

"He won't." She said it with conviction, especially after the conversation she'd just had with Jerod. "What would *he* do with a baby?"

"I'd rather not find out," Devin said a little more calmly. "What'd he want?"

"Nothing important." She wasn't about to tell Devin he'd practically begged her to end the pregnancy. Jerod was doing everything he could to get rid of what he considered a problem.

"Let's get this over with." She attached the wide angle to the digital camera, which had cost as much as several months of car payments, then swung the strap over her neck.

"Start with the other pictures," Devin said. "I'm not in the mood to smile."

She wasn't particularly, either. She wished Devin

would shut up about Jerod and Jerod would leave her alone. It was her business, dammit. Her business alone.

THAT EVENING, Devin drove out to Gramps's house, which was an hour away in the middle of seemingly endless cornfields. The farmhouse had always been a refuge when he was growing up, but tonight, he couldn't help feeling a little resentful. He had an early appointment tomorrow with a potential client, and he'd be up half the night finishing preparations. All because Gramps thought Devin was neglecting him.

At twenty after six, they sat on opposite sides of a shabby, vinyl booth at the Finer Diner. It was the only restaurant in the unincorporated burg closest to Gramps. Surprisingly, the place served better-than-average home-style food. Not long ago, Devin and Gramps had been regulars.

The old place had been open for as long as Devin could remember, though it had changed names several times over the years. None of the new owners had ever redecorated that he knew of.

Booths lined each side of the small dining room, and a long scarred counter stretched across the back, butting up to the kitchen. Four more tables were scattered in the middle of the room. None of the upholstery matched—some seats were a faded pink, others were slate-blue, apple-green and mustard-yellow. The white floor was vinyl and Devin would bet it was as old as the building, judging by the cracks and missing tiles.

The walls were mostly windows, so anyone walking down the main drag could easily check out the diners inside. Tonight, there were only two other occupied tables. Devin and his grandpa had chosen the one farthest from the street, near the kitchen.

After finishing his country-fried steak, mashed potatoes and green beans, Devin shoved his plate away and stuck his wadded-up napkin on top. He'd bided his time, waiting to bring up the subject that'd eaten at him all week. Finally, two more families walked in, and the noise level was such that they could talk without the cook overhearing every word Devin said.

"I'm sorry you feel like I've been neglecting you lately."

Gramps met his eyes for a beat. "Business can be tough to put aside."

"That's just it. I don't want to put it aside. I *can't* put it aside."

The old man chewed on a hunk of meat for what seemed like forever. He nodded once, acknowledging the claim, and Devin watched the food slide down his bony throat. Gramps wiped his mouth with his napkin. "A few evenings off now and then won't kill you or the company."

"You're supposed to be the guy who understands. Has it been so long since you were in business you don't remember what it's like?"

Gramps had jabbed another bite of meat, but he put

his fork down without eating it and looked directly at Devin. "I remember all too well, son."

Devin sighed in frustration. Gramps had been his supporter, his cheerleader, from the moment Devin's idea for CMT had germinated. It'd been after his parents' accident, a few weeks after their will had been settled. A time so painful, yet also eye-opening to Devin.

Of course his parents had favored Jerod in their will, leaving him their stakes in the television station and most of their money. Just as he'd always known— they had no faith in him, their good-for-nothing son.

After weeks of consuming anger, Devin had had a life-changing realization. His parents had been right. He'd had no ambitions for his future. Resentful and rebellious, he'd refused to go to college, taking dead-end jobs to drive his parents over the edge. But he'd been screwing himself instead of them.

He'd been sure about one thing—he wanted to make his living in computers, the very thing his parents had said he'd been wasting his life on. Devin had used his inheritance to enroll in college, getting an undergraduate degree as well as an MBA in five years.

And now Gramps seemed to be saying that everything he'd been working so hard for meant very little.

"What's going on? You know how important this is to me. Why are you giving me this guilt trip now, just as I'm getting started?"

Gramps shoved his half-eaten plate of food toward

the middle of the table and wiped his mouth with his napkin. He paused, gazing off at nothing. "Sometimes over the years, old people learn a few things here and there."

Devin sat back impatiently, ready for Gramps to get to the point.

"The thing I learned was that work isn't everything."

"For me, right now, it is."

"I know you think that."

"Damn right, I do. What the hell else do I have?"

"You're young, Devin. Bright. Ambitious. That's all good. But you still need to figure out the importance of people. Without people, the job won't mean a damn thing in the long run."

"I know people are important. Or at least you are. Don't give much of a damn for most of the rest of them." Carey's face flashed through his mind but he pushed the image aside.

"I'd hoped you'd be wiser than I was. But I've watched for five years. The closer you got to graduating, the more single-minded you became. In the six months since you started CMT, I've seen you less and less. If I thought it was just me you were shutting out, I wouldn't worry so much."

"No need to worry."

His grandpa ignored him. "I've made a lot of mistakes in my lifetime. Putting my job ahead of the people who were important to me was the biggest."

Devin shook his head. It was ridiculous that Gramps

considered himself a failure where his family was concerned. He was the single person who had actually acted like family to Devin. "I have a hard time believing that."

The lone waitress whizzed by and dropped off the bill and the toothpick Gramps always insisted on. She remembered how to get a good tip. A toothpick and a butterscotch candy for the old guy.

A shadow of emotion darkened Gramps's eyes. He stuck the end of the toothpick into his mouth and rolled it to the side so he could speak. "Did you ever stop to think maybe it was your parents instead of you? That they were the ones with a problem?"

"I know they had problems."

"Then why are you so bound and determined to prove them wrong?"

Devin shrugged. He didn't understand what his parents had to do with anything. "It motivates me."

"There's nothing wrong with motivation, but you're getting tunnel vision. Slow down a bit. If it takes you a year and a half instead of a year to show a profit, what's the difference?"

"Six months."

Gramps chuckled, which rubbed Devin the wrong way.

"Look, I appreciate everything you've done for me more than you know. But I have my reasons for the aggressive goals I set. It's my company. My life, for that matter."

"Sit back and take some advice for once, would

you?" Gramps voice was too loud and Devin looked around to see who was paying attention. The people at the two closest tables turned away when he made eye contact with them.

"Say what you want to say," Devin said firmly but quietly.

Gramps switched the toothpick to the other side of his mouth, then pulled it out and threw it on his plate. He leaned forward, his jaw working. "What I want to say isn't easy. It's not something I've ever talked about."

Devin leaned forward, intrigued in spite of himself. Gramps was so serious, almost morose.

"I told you I screwed up a bunch. You may not believe me but there's proof."

"Such as?"

"My children. Specifically, my daughters. Somehow, I didn't do as badly with Jonathon." Jonathon was Devin's uncle, his mother's oldest sibling, who lived in Louisiana. "But look at your mom. She died not knowing a damn thing about how important a family should be. I don't know if she realized how much I loved her. And I know you don't have a clue how much she loved you—"

"If that was love, I'd hate to see apathy."

Gramps continued as if Devin hadn't spoken. "She never grasped that people are what make our lives worthwhile. Not jobs or anything else."

"I suppose not."

"Why do you think she was that way? What the hell

screwed her up so bad she couldn't see something that should be obvious?"

"Ambition?"

"To hell with ambition. Someone had to teach her that ambition was so blasted important in the first place."

Devin absently dragged the plain glass saltshaker closer and turned it slowly in his hands. He had no idea where Gramps was going with this.

"We learn from example, son. From our family. She learned all that from yours truly."

Devin met his grandpa's eyes now and saw more than concern in them. Guilt. Regret.

"And your aunt Linda. Where the hell is she? She didn't even have the guts to stick around for her family when things got tough. Think she read that in a book somewhere?" He shook his head. "You get things from your parents, even when they don't mean to teach you."

Linda was Jerod's mom, and Devin couldn't argue she'd been a mess. No one had seen or heard from her since she'd walked out years and years ago.

"But I don't have kids. I'm not going to have kids. There's no one for me to screw up."

"Just yourself." Gramps stared pointedly at Devin. "You're not getting all of what I'm saying."

"So say it."

"Regret sucks, as you kids would say. That took me sixty-some years to figure out. When I retired, my career was history, and what did I have? Not too damn much. Money, sure. But the *people* were missing because I'd been missing from their lives for all those years.

"My wife had learned to live without me. My kids had not only started their own adult lives, they'd learned it all wrong from me. You'll notice they didn't make haste to come visit their mother and me. It took me a couple years of twiddling my thumbs and feeling sorry for myself before I realized it was my fault."

Devin lost the urge to fight as he watched his grandfather. The twinkle so often in Gramps's eyes had disappeared.

"Even if you don't have kids one day, you'll be much more content with yourself if you give everything you've got to your relationships."

"That's a hell of a lot to say to get me to come out for dinner more often." Devin's attempt at levity fell flat.

"I'm just a small part of it, Devin." Gramps raised his shaggy white brows. "I want you to have a fulfilling life. Take your grandpa out for dinner. Make peace with your cousin. Find yourself a girl and settle down. You'll be much happier in the end."

The plea in Gramps's eyes struck Devin with the force of a two-by-four to the head. There was no way Devin could pretend to miss the message. It was as good as an order.

The first suggestion he might be able to handle. The other two, not a chance in hell.

"I'll give it some thought," he said noncommittally.

Gramps nodded. "See that you do."

CHAPTER TEN

CAREY PARKED halfway up her driveway, hopped out and unloaded the trunk. By the time she got to the side door, she realized she'd left her keys in the ignition.

As she swore to herself, the door to the house whipped open from the inside and she nearly stumbled backward in surprise.

"Trent Langford, I'm going to kill you!" She thought her face might split in half from her huge grin. Very carefully, she set the grocery bags on the kitchen table, then ran into her brother's arms. They held on to each other for several seconds. "You almost scared the pee out of me!"

He beamed at her. "Look at you," he said, shaking his head. "Sight for sore eyes."

She could say the same. She took in the details of his appearance, not quite able to believe she was seeing him in the flesh. His dark hair was a good two or three inches longer than usual, shagging down into his eyes and hanging well past the collar of his worn plaid flannel shirt in back. Shadows rimmed his blue eyes, as if he hadn't slept for a week. She couldn't help hugging him again.

"What are you doing here?" she asked.

"Such a warm welcome back to my own house." He dropped his arms and stepped back to get a better look at her. "I just came home for a while."

She eyed him warily. Home had never been a huge consideration for either of them. They both preferred to roam the country, find adventure while making just enough money to support the habit. "I can't believe you're here. Are you home for good, Wilderness Man?"

"I'm home for now," he said. "Get in here and talk to me. What's with all the crap in the bags?" He gestured toward the paper sacks on the table.

"It's called groceries. Long overdue."

He pulled her toward the living room, but Carey's stomach had a different idea. "I need to eat first. You hungry?"

"I could eat," he said. "As long as you're not cooking." She stuck her tongue out at him.

"For your information, I start a cooking class next week." She'd decided that learning to cook would be more economical than eating out every night for the rest of her life, especially once she was paying for two.

Trent looked at her in disbelief as he sat at the kitchen table. "Now I need a beer."

She laughed. "Sorry. I didn't buy any."

He stared at her. "Let me get this straight. You're learning how to cook *and* you're out of beer. That's scary as hell. And believe me, it takes a lot to scare a wilderness man."

Carey smiled as she started unloading, setting a couple of TV dinners on the counter.

If he thought *those* were major changes, wait till he knew the pregnant part of the story.

She didn't relish telling him that nugget of news. There was no doubt in her mind he wouldn't be happy about the prospect of becoming an uncle. No matter how well-meaning he was, Trent was old-fashioned. Not to mention as overprotective of his little sister as a mama bear. It was sure to be an ugly scene.

She poured him a tall glass of lemonade from the carton she'd just bought. "So you finally got tired of the great outdoors, huh?"

"Just needed a break." He took a long drink, avoiding her eyes. "I'll pay you for half of the groceries."

So he would be here for a while—at least long enough to share a grocery bill. She waited for him to say more, but he didn't.

"What'd you need a break from? The nasty smell of salmon?" She put one of the dinners into the microwave and started it.

"Nah, the fishing was perfect."

She noticed he still hadn't answered her question and decided she'd pry later. Let him get his bearings first. She wanted to hold on to her secret for a while longer; let him keep his. If he had one.

He caught sight of the book on running a business

Carey had left on the table. "What's this?" he asked, picking it up.

She could say it was Devin's. He and Monica were the only ones who knew of her plans so far, and it still made her squirm to put herself out there by announcing her ambitious intentions. No, she was being foolish. Trent would get behind her idea.

Carey leaned against the counter and crossed her legs at the ankles while the TV dinner cooked, trying to come across as nonchalant. "I'm starting my own business."

"You're what?" Trent set his glass down hard. "What kind of business?"

"Photography, of course. What else would I do?"

He watched her pointedly. "What's going on with you? Seems like that's a pretty big change. It'll tie you down, and I've never known you to like being tied down."

She couldn't tell him that's exactly what she needed. Couldn't explain that a baby wouldn't fit in on a cross-country photo assignment. "I know what I'm getting into. I'm ready for it. I'll still freelance, too."

Trent stared at her as if she'd gone off the deep end. Carey almost laughed, but she knew how it must look to him—as if an alien had possessed her. The intense scrutiny made her feel jumpy.

She prayed he didn't notice the changes in her body,

which Monica had assured her were invisible to everyone else.

"Trust me, Trent. It's something I want to do."

"What kind of photography business are we talking?"

"I'll start with weddings until I can figure out what to do about a studio. I'd like to do both eventually, but I can't afford to rent a place yet."

"You've really thought this out?"

She smiled, unable to contain her enthusiasm. "Yep. I'm just getting organized, but Devin's going to help me with the business end of it."

Trent frowned. "What does he know about it?"

"He just started *his* own company. CMT Computer Security."

Trent sat back and crossed his legs. He stretched his arms behind his head. "You trust Colyer with your business, Carey?"

So much for avoiding sensitive topics. "Of course I do."

The microwave beeped, and she was relieved for the distraction. She shouldn't have brought up Devin's name. He and Trent had never gotten along.

"Let's not argue about Devin today. I want to hear all about your life in Alaska. Spill it."

She placed the cardboard platter of food in front of him and sat down in the chair next to his. Her appetite had disappeared, probably because she wasn't telling him her biggest news. She'd have to break it to him sometime, and soon. But not today.

Now that he was home, it would be harder to avoid the whole telling-her-family-she-was-pregnant-and-alone debacle. She leaned back and focused on her brother's response.

DEVIN HEARD muffled footsteps on the stairs and strained to see out his office window to the hallway. Monica had mentioned Carey would be by after her doctor's appointment this afternoon.

He couldn't deny the lust he felt when Carey rounded the corner. It was automatic, involuntary. Unwanted.

Optimism and good humor emanated from her, from the bounce in her step to her easy smile.

He couldn't help smiling back and meaning it. It, too, was a natural response. Seeing her made him feel good.

And he had no business feeling that way. Just looking at the clothes she wore was a reminder. A white shirt that hung lower than the cropped, belly-revealing ones he was used to seeing on her.

Ever since he'd realized he might be in love with her, pretending she was just another friend was getting more and more difficult. Something deeper pulsed under the surface, and no matter how hard he tried, he couldn't ignore it. His emotions had gone out of control. To say it made him uneasy would be a gross understatement.

He picked up the phone and got busy.

After hanging up a few minutes later, he entered the appointment he'd just made, thanks to Carey for the contact, in his PDA. He couldn't help overhearing Monica and Carey on the other side of his office wall.

"Tell me all about the appointment," Monica said. "Don't you dare hold back because you think I might get jealous."

"I couldn't hold back if I wanted to. I heard the baby's heartbeat," Carey said excitedly. "It was amazing!"

"I wish I could've been there. I'd love to hear your little one. Besides, if I go with you, I'll know what to do when it's my turn."

Devin was vaguely aware Monica and Kyle had decided to start popping out kids. Damn unfair that Carey had beat them to it—unfair to both women.

Listening to Carey, he couldn't discern any lingering regrets. He had to give her credit. A lot of it. In her place, he wasn't sure he'd have the grace to let go of the anger and self-pity so easily. Good for her. She'd figured out how to move on and leave the negative circumstances behind.

"I'd love to have you come to the ultrasound with me, if it really wouldn't bother you."

"Are you serious? You'd let me do that?"

"Let you?" Carey laughed. "Going to those appointments alone sucks. Everyone else there has a man beside them. I'd love some company."

Devin ground his teeth and tried to tune out the conversation. It was so wrong for her to have to handle everything alone.

"When is it?" Monica asked.

Carey named a date and time a few weeks away.

Several seconds later, Monica replied, apparently having checked her calendar. "Shoot! I'll be in Colorado with Kyle that week."

"Ah, that's right." Carey's obvious disappointment affected Devin. "That's okay. I'll do just fine. And I'll get pictures to show you."

Feeling like a heel for listening in on their conversation, Devin emerged from his office. Monica was leaning back in her chair, legs crossed, and Carey had perched on Monica's desk.

"What's up, boss?" Monica said.

"I've got two new appointments. Finally got back with Simmons and also spoke with Tim Falstead."

"Oh, you got in with him," Carey said. Falstead ran a local publishing company, and Carey had done a few photo assignments for them in the past. "That's great. I know you'd love to land Lexington Publications."

Love to land them was putting it mildly. Lexington could move CMT into the black. It was the ideal company, the type Devin wanted to foster a long-term relationship with. "Falstead seems like a decent guy. Open-minded."

"Dev, do you have a minute?" Carey asked.

He glanced at his watch. It was close to five, but he had hours of work to do. Lucky for him, he also had hours with nothing to do *but* work. "Sure."

She hopped off the desk and preceded him to his office.

He shut the door on his way in, doubting she needed privacy but newly aware of how well sounds carried.

Carey raised her brows, then shrugged. "Since you closed that, do you think Monica's really okay?"

"About?"

"Me having a baby."

"You think she's jealous?"

"No…well, yes…" She looked thoughtful. "I just asked her to go to my ultrasound with me and maybe I shouldn't have. She seemed okay, but… Oh, never mind. Just being paranoid and hormonal."

"Carey…"

She met his gaze.

"I…" He what? He moved closer and leaned on his desk, not really knowing what he wanted to say. "I overheard part of your conversation. I wish I could help somehow."

She bit on the knuckle of her index finger thoughtfully, then raised her chin so she met his gaze head-on. "You could go to the ultrasound with me."

Oh, no. He couldn't. It was way too intimate a proposition. Besides, it was easier for him to deny the baby's existence for now. Soon enough, he'd be bombarded with it every time he looked at Carey.

Before he could utter a word, she closed her eyes, just for an instant, as if she regretted the words. "No," she said. "You don't want to do that."

Precisely, he thought. But he still didn't speak.

She stood and paced to the window behind him, looking out over the pool, which had just been prepped for the season. "I'm a big girl."

When he turned to look at her, she smiled confidently and he wanted to believe it.

"Soon to get bigger." His barb was a cowardly way out, but he couldn't bring himself to offer to go with her.

She walked back to the chair, thumping his head on the way by, and he chuckled uneasily. Why did he feel like such a jerk?

"What I really wanted to talk about, for one thing, was my company. I know I'm supposed to fill out a gob of paperwork for the government types, but I don't know what or where to get it."

Ah, this was a hell of a lot easier than going to her doctor's appointment. "Be glad to help."

For the next several minutes, he rattled off everything he'd gone through since finishing his MBA to get CMT up and running. Carey jotted down notes in a spiral notebook she'd brought with her. She asked several questions, and when he answered them all, she stood.

"Secondly, here's a proof of your brochures. First draft. Feel free to mark them up if you want changes."

She handed him the color printouts, which he looked over for a few seconds. "Wow. Nice job. I'll read them over tonight."

"Monica's waiting for me. Thanks for the help on the paperwork." She hurried around the desk and kissed his forehead.

Devin couldn't put the impending ultrasound out of his mind. He set the proofs on his desk and leaned back in his chair. As she walked away, he was once again bombarded by conflicting emotions. But he'd be damned if it was his responsibility to play daddy. Or husband. Or anything else besides just a friend.

But was it a friend's job to step in and hold her hand during her ultrasound? He didn't know the answer.

What he did know was that becoming more involved in her pregnancy wasn't wise. Not when just the sight of her revved his pulse.

Even if he did want to be a good friend to her, it'd be impossible for him to sit and look at Mauriello's baby inside her. He couldn't stand to think about it, let alone actually see it.

It wasn't Carey's fault, or the baby's. But he'd be hard-pressed even to visit Carey after the birth of the baby. That was no way to treat a friend. But he sure as hell didn't know what to do about it.

CAREY FOLLOWED Monica out of Devin's house. They'd planned a shopping trip so Monica could stock up on new clothes for the season—one of the benefits of having a successful lawyer for a husband.

"Okay if we drive separately?" Monica asked. "Then you don't have to bring me all the way back here afterward."

"Fine with me." Carey had to admit, going home was more fun now that Trent was back. It beat the heck out of an empty house.

She slid into the driver's seat, tossed the notes from Devin on the passenger seat and started the car, waiting for Monica to get in her own vehicle.

She'd meant what she said to Devin—she *would* be fine on her own. This baby was her sole responsibility, so she'd better get used to it.

She smiled. A little one grew inside her. She had to admit, she was beginning to get excited about becoming a mom. Freaked out, too, sure. She wasn't certain how she'd handle having someone dependent on her at all times. This baby would have to become her life.

Last night she'd even browsed online for nursery patterns and furniture. Not so long ago, she'd given Devin a hard time for spending his life at home in front of the computer. Now here she was staying in, surfing.

The phone in her purse rang out "Our Lips Are Sealed," and she reached down to dig it out. Her mother. And much more upbeat than when she'd walked out of Carey's so convinced they were both doomed to a life of unhappiness unless they each found their Mr. Rights.

"What's up, Mom?" Monica waved at her, and she backed out of Devin's and drove toward the new mall.

"I'm so glad I caught you," her mom nearly gushed. "I've got the best news!"

Carey didn't get overly excited. She'd heard this opening before. "What happened?"

"I've met a man."

Carey rolled her eyes. "Already? So soon after..." She couldn't remember the last one's name.

"I'm over Harold. He was a player. All he wanted was something short-term and sexual—behind his wife's back."

"Eww, Mom." She cringed at the thought. "So this new guy is looking for a soul mate, huh?" Carey wasn't sure if it was a good thing or a bad thing that her mother never recognized sarcasm when she heard it.

"He's...well, he's super, Carey. Different."

"Different how?"

"He seems like such a strong man. Levelheaded. Very attractive."

Carey ran through all the men her mom had hooked up with over the years, trying to remember a single one she would call levelheaded. There were none. She wasn't sure she'd heard her mom even use the term before. *Interesting.* "When and where did you meet him?"

"We met at the grocery store. Picking out strawberries."

"The grocery store? Mom, that's out of a sitcom."

Her mother giggled. "Two days ago. We've gone out the past two nights and talked the evening away."

"What's he do?"

She heard commotion in the background on her mother's end.

"I have to go, Carey. My boss is back early from his meeting. Can I stop by later?"

"Sure, Mom…"

Crap. Trent hadn't called their mother yet to say he was home. He'd asked for a few days of peace, and she'd just messed that up. "Actually, Trent just got home, so come on over."

"My son is home from Alaska?"

"Yep. I know he was going to call you as soon as he caught up on sleep." No need to mention he'd already been home for days.

"Well, then, double the reason to stop by. I can't wait to see him. I have a couple of errands to run after I grab a bite, so it'll be at least an hour. See you then."

The line went dead, and Carey dialed home to warn her brother. She wasn't sure which she dreaded more—hearing Trent's reaction or listening to her mother get her hopes up yet one more time that she'd met the perfect man.

THE SHOPPING TRIP with Monica was depressing. Carey had only gained four pounds so far, but her old size didn't fit. She either had to buy the next size up or go to a maternity store. Since her mom and brother didn't even know she was expecting yet, maternity clothes didn't seem like a good plan.

Instead, she'd bought nothing. Good on the budget, she supposed. She'd just continue to leave her pants unbuttoned until her stomach forced the issue.

Dropping onto the couch next to Trent, she held her hand over her abdomen to reassure herself said unbuttoned pants wouldn't pop open more.

"Who's the hottie?" she asked, looking over his shoulder at the photo he held. He'd finally developed his film from Alaska.

They were looking at the photos to pass the time while they waited for their mother. Trent hadn't been too upset about Carey's slip. She'd bet he felt guilty for not calling right away.

He handed her the picture, seemingly disinterested. "No one important. Just a woman."

The woman in question was an outdoorsy-looking brunette who was not in the least bit hesitant about touching nasty, slimy fish.

Carey stared pointedly at Trent, trying to pressure him into saying more. His gruff tone told her it wasn't "just a woman." He ignored her, fiddling with the remaining photographs, which confirmed her suspicions.

"What's her name?"

He looked up at her as if surprised she was still fixated on the woman. "Erin," he finally said.

"Erin," she repeated. "How well do you know Erin?"

"Well enough."

Oh, the joy of trying to communicate with a man who believed stringing three or more sentences together was better left to preachers and lawyers.

A knock on the front door had him jumping up to answer it. She laughed. Only the threat of having to tell all could make him look forward to a visit from their mother.

"Mom," he said, trying hard to sound thrilled to see her. He reached down and pulled her into a loose hug.

"How long did you think you could hide out here without calling me, young man?" Her tone was lighthearted. She walked past him and dropped wearily into the recliner.

"Have a seat," Trent said with a sarcastic grin.

"Why didn't you call me?"

"Hadn't had a chance yet," Trent told her. "Sorry, Mom. Things have been crazy. Been trying to get settled in."

"Trent's going to get a job," Carey said.

"Oh, really? You must be staying around for a while then."

Instead of answering, her dear brother turned the spotlight on Carey. "Did you know that Carey here is starting her own business?" The coward was using her to avoid having to disclose his plans. She glowered at him.

"Are you, now? Why do my own children keep secrets from me?"

Uh-oh, Carey thought. *They're both going to flip when they learn the extent of my secrets.*

"What kind of company? Why? I want to hear all about it," her mom continued.

"I thought you were here to tell us about Mr. Wonderful," Carey said, smiling, crossing her hidden fingers that the distraction attempt would be successful. The whys of her new venture were damn hard to explain without spilling all.

Trent shot a pained look at Carey and she shrugged smugly.

"Ah, yes. He *is* wonderful. His name is Phillip Weisbrenner. Widowed years ago. He's in construction, but very articulate and intelligent." Their mom let out a dreamy sigh.

"Okay, that's all we need to know," Trent said, only half joking.

She carried on about the man for several more minutes. "You'll get to meet him soon," she promised. "Now, back to you, Carey. Tell me what you're up to."

Carey took a fortifying breath. It was one thing to tell Devin about her dream business, but for some reason it was even harder telling her mom. She wouldn't laugh at her, just as Trent hadn't, but neither of them would understand how important it was to her. Of course, they couldn't grasp the significance until she told them about the baby.

Swallowing around a lump in her throat, she guessed it was time for the truth to come out.

Carey stood and paced. She paused at the front entryway. The heavy wood door was ajar and she peered out of the storm door, seeing nothing. She recited the information on her business, answering questions about where she'd find customers, whether she needed to buy any new equipment, where she hoped eventually to hold studio sessions. Then her mom hit her with the question she'd been dreading.

"What brought this on, Carey? You've never indicated you were tired of jet-setting around on freelance jobs. It seems awfully sudden."

"It's always been in the back of my mind."

Carey ran her fingers over the door handle. It'd be nice to open it and run away, but the time had come to be honest.

"Why now?"

"Maybe you'll understand better," Carey began quietly, "when I tell you I'm pregnant."

CHAPTER ELEVEN

DEAD SILENCE.

Carey turned to see both her brother and her mother staring at her.

"I'm going to assume you wouldn't bullshit about that," Trent finally said.

"I wouldn't bullshit about that."

"What the—" He stood, walked to the door and looked outside, too, as if he might spot an explanation out there hanging from the tree branches. "You're pregnant."

"Yes," she said unnecessarily.

Her mother was oddly silent, but Carey didn't have time to wonder about it before Trent started hammering at her.

"Who's the guy?" he demanded, hands on his hips.

"No one worth naming. He's no longer in the picture."

"Oh, you'll name him. He's not going to get away with this."

"It takes two to tango."

"And it takes two to bring up a kid the right way as well."

"Trent," her mom cautioned. "Calm down."

"I'm afraid that's not going to happen," Carey said to her brother. "I'll be raising the child by myself."

"It *has* to happen. You can't do it alone, Care." His voice was gentle now, but his words grated.

"Thanks for the vote of confidence." She crossed her arms in front of her chest.

"Don't take it personally," her mom said. "It's damn hard to raise a kid by yourself."

Carey threw her a curious glance, then Trent jumped back in.

"There's a reason it takes *two* to make a baby," Trent explained, "and that's because a kid needs two parents."

Tears filled Carey's eyes and she took a steadying breath. "Look, that logic is nice on paper. Very mathematical. But this baby is stuck with only one parent. The father thing is *not* an option."

"It's not a time for you to be stubborn."

"Stubborn? You think this is me being stubborn?"

"Then what the hell is it?"

She walked to the couch and sat down. "I don't love the baby's father. He doesn't want to be in the baby's life and he doesn't love me, either. I should never have gotten physically involved with him." She rubbed her hands over her eyes. "It was a huge mistake."

"Someone needs to make the asshole pay."

She whipped her head in her brother's direction. "Trent, you aren't listening to me. I *do not want* the father of my child in our lives. I don't want you to hunt him down and hurt him. He's not a criminal who needs to do his time."

"You're being selfish, Carey. What kind of kid are you going to bring up with no father?"

"Probably someone a lot like you and me."

"Is that really what you want?" His eyes pierced a gaping hole in her.

Elbows on her knees, she leaned forward, wishing she could hide. He'd hit on her biggest doubt. Growing up without their dad around had profoundly affected them both. Her mom hadn't had a choice…her husband had been taken away far too early by a disease with no cure when Carey was five and Trent was eight years old.

Did Carey have the right to choose that for her child? Could her baby truly be content and well-adjusted with just one parent?

She'd convinced herself she could be a better single mother than her own mom had been, but why should she believe that? She'd already proven she was just as foolish as her mother where men were concerned.

So what was she supposed to do? Jerod was out of the picture no matter what. She wondered how huge an injustice she might be doing the baby. It wasn't right that a child should have to pay with a lifetime of unhappiness just because of a mistake his or her mother made.

Sadness overwhelmed Carey. It would never work with Jerod, but could she make it work on her own?

"Lots of luck. You're going to need it," Trent said coldly. He glared at her before striding into the kitchen.

She jumped to her feet with the thought of going after him and beating the crap out of him.

"Let him go," her mother said. "He's just angry right now."

Carey fell back onto the couch. She felt sick to her stomach, and it had nothing to do with the growing baby, everything to do with Trent's final statement and the fears he'd replanted.

"Carey."

Carey didn't look up, even when she felt the couch next to her sink under her mother's weight.

"I'm sure you're going through a rough time." Tentatively, her mom touched Carey's knee. "I know what it's like to be a single parent. It's the hardest damn thing in the world."

If this was supposed to be a pep talk, it wasn't working.

"But I think you're doing the right thing if the father's no good."

Carey met her mother's eyes, shocked. Had she heard her right? Was she being…supportive of being without a man?

"When your dad died, well, I cried for two years. But then I tried to find a man I could love, one who'd be a good father. Because I knew I wasn't doing the best job by myself. Looking back, it might have been better if I'd just focused on being a mom."

Carey was taken aback. Her mother had never admitted any doubts about whether she'd handled parenthood well.

"I don't want to screw up this baby's life," Carey said in a quiet, unwavering voice.

"Your family will help you."

"Yeah, I can see Trent will trip over himself to come to my rescue."

"He's mad for you, not at you. He loves you, Carey. I've always been a little jealous of how close you two are. You two seem to have found the family bond I've always wanted."

She read the pain and regret in her mom's eyes.

"I'll help you with the baby if I can. You might think I've been a bad mother, but I do want my kids to have a good life. And my grandkids."

Carey stared at the woman, hesitant, tears filling her eyes again. She did not want to bawl in front of her mom. She took a deep breath. "We'll see how it goes."

Her mother patted Carey's arm. "I'll leave you alone."

After her mom saw herself out the front door, Trent came back into the living room. He'd been in the kitchen and probably had heard the entire conversation.

"You really think having Mom help out will take the place of a father for your kid?" His tone conveyed his anger even though he kept his voice down.

"Give me a break, Trent. I don't think anything of the sort. But at least she offered."

He stormed out the door, jumped into his truck and took off.

The tears that had threatened minutes earlier let loose. Trent's lack of confidence in her stung like lemon juice on a paper cut. He was one of the few people whose opinion mattered to her.

FORTY-FIVE MINUTES later, after getting the tears out and washing up, Carey waited for Devin to answer his door. She'd left the house so she wouldn't be there when Trent returned.

She knew Devin was home because his SUV was next to his boat in the open garage, but she'd already rung the doorbell twice. As she dug through her purse for his spare key, he appeared in front of her wearing only jeans. She couldn't help noticing in detail the muscles that sculpted his chest.

"About time," she said lightly, but when she looked up at his face, her tone turned serious. "What's wrong?"

His eyes were a stormy, steely gray, his jaw set. "Not sure." He motioned her inside. "Just got off the phone with Gramps."

"Is he okay?"

"I don't know. He seemed to be having trouble getting air. Sounded weak."

"Did you ask him if he felt all right?" she asked quickly.

"He said he was fine." He blew out a loud anxious breath. "He always says he's fine."

Devin paced away from her, staring at nothing. She followed taking him by the arm.

"Let's go," she said. "We need to check on him."

He nodded and disappeared upstairs, returning moments later wearing a shirt and shoes.

As they walked through the kitchen out to the garage, he muttered, "I'm not riding for an hour in the Bug."

"Yeah, well, my Bug is bigger than your boat."

But she backed her beloved car into the street to park it so they could take the Excursion. When she opened his car's door, loud, thrashing music assaulted her. She was usually all for noise, but this made her head ache. She gave Devin a questioning look as she climbed in.

Once they were out of town, she turned the volume down. "That racket will give the baby nightmares for sure."

He didn't move, and she wasn't certain he'd heard her. It was a solid two or three minutes before he finally spoke. "I suppose you want some classical crap?"

"There has to be a happy medium somewhere." Flipping the station to some nondescript jazz, she waited for him to comment.

"You don't buy that Bach makes babies smarter, huh?"

She smiled. An inane topic. "It'll take a lot more than violins and pianos to raise a genius."

He tapped her leg gently. "You've got smart genes when you use them." He grinned, which was the only thing that prevented her from socking him.

"Gramps is going to be ticked off that we're checking up on him. What if he's okay?" he asked solemnly.

"Then he's okay. And we know. That's a good thing."

"You don't know Gramps well. He hates being fussed over."

"We won't fuss. We'll think up an excuse to be there. Say we wanted to get out of the city or something."

Devin chuckled. "You think he wouldn't see through that?"

"You want to turn around and go home?"

He shook his head, his smile fading. "I need to check on him. I have a bad feeling in my gut." He turned the radio off. "You sure you don't mind?"

"I'm sure." They were already several miles down the highway anyway.

"Why'd you drop by in the first place?" he asked.

"Trent and I had an argument."

"Ah, good ol' Trent. What's the Marlboro Man's problem now?"

She couldn't suppress a grin, even though the tension between Devin and her brother drove her nuts. "I told him and my mom I'm pregnant."

Devin grimaced. "Double whammy, huh?"

"My mom wasn't bad, believe it or not. She offered to help with the baby."

Devin looked at her, puzzled, then returned his focus to the road. "Let me guess. Trent doesn't like the prospect of being an uncle."

"You could say that. He told me I need the baby's father to bring the child up right."

"I hope you told him that's a load of bullshit."

"I tried."

"What do you mean you tried?" He shook his head. "If anyone besides Trent gives you static, you have no problem setting them straight. Why do you roll over when he's around?"

"I don't roll over. He's my brother. We're close."

"Close, my ass. He mother hens you to death."

"He's my big brother, Dev. He grew up taking care of me while my mother was on the endless man hunt."

She didn't know why they bothered with this argument. "I'd really hate it if the two of you could get along," she said dryly.

"He's too damn protective of you. Like he's the only one concerned about your welfare."

Carey stared at him. "Are you concerned about my welfare?"

He ignored her.

"Trent means well." Carey pulled her legs up under her on the huge seat and stared straight ahead.

"Then what's the problem?"

She hesitated. "What if I *can't* do this alone?"

She sensed Devin looking at her.

"Carey."

There was a hint of tenderness in his voice. He squeezed her hand lightly. Their eyes locked for a moment, and then he returned his attention to the road. Her skin felt strangely tingly where he'd touched her.

"What?" she finally asked.

He hesitated. "I don't know. I was about to tell you to stop being so doubtful, remind you you'd gotten past that insecurity. But…" He shook his head as he trailed off.

"But?"

"What the hell do I know? I can't imagine what it's like to be pregnant and single. Shit, Care, I can't imagine being a father, single or not. Who am I to try to help you?"

His admission filled her with warmth. Made her feel better than all the pep talks in the world. She closed her eyes and leaned her head against the headrest. She still didn't have a clue how she'd get through this, but for now, Devin's understanding gave her the illusion of peace.

They rode in silence for several minutes. The sun was sinking, casting a golden glow over them. The smooth sound of the engine and the intangible connection she felt with Devin nearly soothed Carey into sleep.

"Have you thought about where you'll live after the baby's born?" Devin asked, jolting her awake.

The truth was she hadn't given it a single thought. It was easy to forget the house was Trent's since he'd spent so little time there until lately. "Probably the same place."

"With Trent?" There was disbelief in his voice.

"When he's there, which isn't often."

Devin bit down on the words he wanted to say. She couldn't be serious. Carey needed to get away from her brother. She claimed Trent meant well, and maybe he did, but still…he babied Carey, became too involved in her life. He still thought Devin was out to hurt her.

Chances were Trent would eventually stay home for good. And Devin suspected the guy got off on trying to run Carey's life.

"I need to settle down, Dev."

"Yeah, you do. You need your own place. Have you ever had your own place?"

Devin already knew she'd never lived independently.

She turned her head toward the passenger window and didn't respond.

As he turned off the highway toward his grandpa's house, his general mood went from piss-poor to scraping the cellar floor. Off the top of his head, he was worried that Carey was on the verge of making yet another flip decision she'd live to regret, that her brother would add to her stress level and that CMT might fail.

But that all took a backseat to Gramps and the possibility something was seriously wrong. He needed to do better by the old man before it was too late.

CHAPTER TWELVE

DEVIN PULLED into the long gravel driveway at dusk. Large oaks towered over the yard of his grandpa's stately old home and protected the sprawling front porch from the elements. The expansive, one-story house constantly required maintenance, which usually kept Devin busy on summer weekends. He never used to mind. But he'd been so busy with CMT this year, the old place already looked a little worse for wear.

He drove just beyond the house and parked in front of the solitary garage. He and Carey jumped down from the truck.

Letting himself in the back door, he hollered out, "Gramps?"

The old man ambled toward them from the living room, his oxygen hose trailing behind. Devin felt a rush of relief at the sight of him upright.

"Didn't I just get off the phone with you?"

Gramps's face was colorless, but his smile was genuine. Devin sized him up for any other signs of poor health. He seemed a little more bent than before. Devin wouldn't get used to seeing him as an old man in poor health anytime soon.

"You doing okay?" Devin asked.

"Doing dandy." He shuffled toward the kitchen. "Just on my way for my bedtime OJ."

"Straight up, right?" Carey teased.

"You got it, Miss Carey." He shook his finger at her affectionately.

Gramps made his way farther into the kitchen.

"He's pale," Devin whispered to Carey.

She nodded and put a finger to her lips to quiet him.

"How are you tonight, Miss Carey?" Gramps asked. His voice was less than robust.

"Not too bad for having to put up with your grandson for almost an hour in the car."

Gramps chuckled and looked at her appreciatively. "I like her, Devin. Did I tell you that before?"

"You told me."

Gramps had taken a shining to Carey the first time Devin had brought her out to meet him years ago. Their relationship made Devin happy, even though they always joined forces against him.

"You two lovebirds shouldn't have come all the way out here. Surely you've got better things to do. What're you doing—checking up on the old man?"

"We aren't lovebirds, Gramps."

"Maybe you should be. She's pretty and puts up with you. Now tell me why you're here."

Devin decided to be honest; his grandpa would see

through him if he wasn't. "It sounded like you weren't breathing too well when we talked on the phone."

"You caught me in the middle of my workout session."

"Ah," Devin said doubtfully. "And what kind of a workout would that be?"

"You never know what old men do for exercise. Tennis, golf, a little racquetball…"

"Yeah, sure. When did you buy a PlayStation?"

"A what?"

Devin smiled and shook his head. "Never mind."

"Well, you drove all this way, you might as well sit down and play some gin."

"You sure you're up for that? It's getting pretty late."

"I may be old and tired, but I can still gin you kids under the table. You up for cards, Miss Carey?"

"Sure am."

They sat at the kitchen table playing gin and drinking orange juice. Devin had set out to win big but was losing regularly. He enjoyed himself anyway. As long as he was with Gramps, he could relax a little. If anything with his health cropped up, God forbid, Devin would be there to get help.

After an hour or so, Gramps was tired out. "I hate to be rude to my uninvited guests, but it's time for me to hit the hay. This old boy's got a big day tomorrow." He saluted and stood.

"What's going on tomorrow?" Carey asked.

"Dragging my bones out of bed." He winked at her.

"Mind if we stick around awhile?" Devin said. "Might as well enjoy the country air while we're here." *And make sure you're going to be okay.*

"Suit yourselves. Sorry I can't join you. You probably want to be alone anyway." His heavy white eyebrows shot up a couple times suggestively.

They said good-night, and Devin watched out of the corner of his eye as Gramps shuffled out of the room.

"He said he's okay," Carey said, catching the concern he couldn't hide.

"I told you, he always says that. His color is off."

"He did look kind of gray," she admitted. "What do we do?"

"Let's go try to enjoy the evening like we told him we would. I'll check on him before we go."

The grass in the huge backyard had been recently cut, and his grandmother's flower bed was a fragrant wash of colors he could barely make out in the dark. The teenager who lived down the county road tended the yard, and Devin wondered if he should pay the kid a bit extra himself to check on Gramps.

At the back of the lot, near where the manicured lawn turned into a knee-high cornfield, they made their way to Devin's favorite spot: a large hammock hung between two giant elm trees.

He eased himself into it and motioned for Carey to lie opposite him, with her feet toward his head. Stretching out on his back, he gazed into the maze of leaves silhouetted above.

"You sure this thing can hold two?" she asked, frowning. "And a half?"

"I've never tried sharing it, but yeah, I'm sure." He glanced toward her middle. "And I don't think that qualifies as a half yet. I can hardly tell you're pregnant." Thank God. He wasn't looking forward to the day when Carey presented a visual reminder his cousin had slept with her. Although maybe it would keep his libido in check.

She steadied the hammock with her hands first, then backed up slowly until she was sitting. They swung back and forth, and she held on for dear life.

"Lie down and relax."

The emotions of the past few hours had exhausted him. He was ready to vegetate and escape from his thoughts. And yes, enjoy Carey's company. She'd been exactly what he'd needed tonight.

Her light hair stood out in the darkness, and he could see her studying his face. Finally, she stretched her legs out and settled in, lying on her side, turned toward him. Her face was next to his, inches away.

His heart pounded with awareness, destroying the peacefulness of the moment.

Her body fell into his, and her sweet scent enveloped him. Unwelcome desire surged through his veins, and he realized he'd been wrong to think he could relax with her at his side.

Her eyes were closed, as if she was unaware of the effect she had on him. As if she trusted him completely.

Trusting him at this exact moment was not particularly wise.

On one level, lying so close to Carey felt natural. They knew each other well, had been in each other's lives almost forever. He was well acquainted with her annoying habits and she with his. He knew secrets she kept from the rest of the world. He could even vaguely recall what it'd been like to kiss her in ninth grade.

But she was no longer an inexperienced teenager. Her nearness sent his pulse skyrocketing in anticipation and nervousness, like she was completely new to him. Like he was an adolescent on his first date.

A haze of lust had settled over him the second her body pressed into his. He could think of nothing but exploring every inch of Carey, her soft curves, her smooth flesh. He ached to hold her.

But he would never fit into this ready-made family.

He wanted to forget all the ramifications and kiss her till she screamed for mercy—here, now, with no thought to the future.

His arms were crossed over his abdomen, and it took every ounce of restraint he could summon not to touch her. He was relieved her eyes were closed, because his desire was hard to miss. Shifting minutely, he didn't want to disturb her but he needed relief from the confinement of his jeans.

He focused intently on the leaves above as they fluttered in the breeze. He sucked in a deep breath. Listened to the low droning of a bullfrog from the pond across the field. The only other sound was Carey's soft, steady breathing. Damn the woman. She'd fallen asleep practically on top of him.

CAREY WOKE UP to discover her arm draped across Devin's chest. Instantly, her entire body was alert.

He was asleep. His solid chest rose and fell beneath her hand, and she could feel his heart beat. She had a close-up view of the stubble on his face. What would happen if she touched it? What would he do if she climbed on top of him? If she kissed his slightly parted lips? If she...

She squeezed her eyes shut.

Forcing her concentration to anything other than the man who lay next to her, she tuned into the sounds of the late-spring night.

Crickets filled the darkness with their familiar, lulling melody. The breeze had chilled since they'd come outside, but Devin's body and the heat from the baby kept her plenty warm enough. Her wandering thoughts had nearly caused her to break out in a sweat.

She became aware of an intense need to pee. The baby couldn't be bigger than a grapefruit, but she would swear a watermelon was bearing down on her bladder most of the time.

It was one thing to wake up four times a night and stumble ten feet to the toilet, but it was quite another to have to unravel herself from Devin and an unstable net, tear across a yard the size of a football field and barge into a kind old man's house in the middle of the night. Her body would have to wait.

What would it be like if Devin was hers? If she could feel those arms around her whenever she needed them? Touch him when she felt the urge, kiss him, pull his clothes off, love him? Be loved by him?

Making love with him would be magical, she somehow knew that implicitly. She knew him better than just about anyone, but to discover him intimately, to see his face in the middle of passion, to hear his husky voice whisper as he moved over her....

Dammit. Bathroom. *Now.*

The question was how to get off the hammock gracefully?

Forget gracefully, just how was she supposed to do this?

There was no way she could swing her legs forward—Devin was in the way. She tried to turn over onto her stomach, but she couldn't get enough of a grip on anything to raise herself. Rolling on her back toward the edge, she finally swung her feet to the ground and pushed herself clumsily to a standing position. Somewhere along the line she'd miscalculated though, because the hammock didn't right itself once she was off. Instead, Devin rolled off and hit the ground.

A string of obscenities flew out of his mouth, his voice groggy from sleep, but his temper very much awake. She tried hard not to smile.

"I'm really sorry, Dev. I have to pee."

He glared up at her, and she pursed her lips on a laugh.

"*Really* have to pee." She sprinted toward the house, chuckling with every step. He'd have to wait to scream at her.

As she washed her hands in the bathroom, still amused by the look on Devin's face, she heard a strange noise coming from somewhere in the house. She dried her hands quickly, then followed the sound toward the bedrooms.

CHAPTER THIRTEEN

IT DIDN'T take long to figure out the noise was Devin's grandpa having some kind of coughing fit. She'd never been in any of the bedrooms before, but she had no trouble finding his, and she stood outside the closed door, unsure of whether to barge in on the old man.

"Gramps?"

Even if he wanted to answer, he didn't stop coughing long enough. Concern propelled her through the door. Light from the hallway illuminated the room enough that she could see him in bed. He was half sitting up, leaning on his elbow, coughing so hard she thought he might pop a vein. Having no idea what else to do, she helped him sit upright. The coughing slowed a bit, but he still couldn't talk.

"Are you okay?" she asked. *Stupid question.*

But he nodded, continuing to hack.

She grabbed a glass of lukewarm water from his nightstand and offered it to him, but he shook his head.

At that moment, Devin rushed in. "What's going on?"

"I heard him coughing from the bathroom."

The Harlequin Reader Service® — Here's how it works:

Accepting your 2 free books and mystery gift places you under no obligation to buy anything. You may keep the books and gift and return the shipping statement marked "cancel." If you do not cancel, about a month later we'll send you 6 additional books and bill you just $4.69 each in the U.S., or $5.24 each in Canada, plus 25¢ shipping & handling per book and applicable taxes if any.* That's the complete price and – compared to cover prices of $5.50 each in the U.S., and $6.50 each in Canada – it's quite a bargain! You may cancel at any time, but if you choose to continue, every month we'll send you 6 more books which you may either purchase at the discount price or return to us and cancel your subscription.

*Terms and prices subject to change without notice. Sales tax applicable in N.Y. Canadian residents will be charged applicable provincial taxes and GST.

OFFICIAL OPINION POLL

ANSWER 3 QUESTIONS AND WE'LL SEND YOU
2 FREE BOOKS AND A FREE GIFT!

0074823 ‖█‖█▐‖‖ ‖█‖▐‖ ‖▐‖‖   FREE GIFT CLAIM # 3953

YOUR OPINION COUNTS!

Please check TRUE or FALSE below to express your opinion about the following statements:

Q1 Do you believe in "true love"?

"TRUE LOVE HAPPENS ONLY ONCE IN A LIFETIME."
○ TRUE
○ FALSE

Q2 Do you think marriage has any value in today's world?

"YOU CAN BE TOTALLY COMMITTED TO SOMEONE WITHOUT BEING MARRIED."
○ TRUE
○ FALSE

Q3 What kind of books do you enjoy?

"A GREAT NOVEL MUST HAVE A HAPPY ENDING."
○ TRUE
○ FALSE

YES, I have scratched the area below.

Please send me the 2 **FREE BOOKS** and **FREE GIFT** for which I qualify. I understand I am under no obligation to purchase any books, as explained on the back of this card.

DETACH AND MAIL CARD TODAY!

336 HDL EFWK   135 HDL EFU9

FIRST NAME   LAST NAME

(HTF-SR-04/06)

ADDRESS

APT.#   CITY

STATE/ PROV.   ZIP/ POSTAL CODE

www.eHarlequin.com

She stood and gladly let Devin take over, hoping he knew how to handle it.

Apparently he didn't, because she could see in the dim light he looked as panicked as she felt. He patted his grandpa's back and asked him if he wanted a drink, to which the old man shook his head again.

"Should I call an ambulance?" he asked.

Another shake of the head.

"What do I do?" Devin's voice had risen.

Gramps lifted his index finger, signaling Devin to wait.

After a couple more long minutes, his coughing slowed, even if he was obviously still short of breath. He turned up the setting on his oxygen tank.

"I'm going to call your doctor," Devin told him.

"No." *Sputter. Wheeze.* "Happens…" *hack* "…sometimes."

"This has happened before?"

His grandpa cleared his throat loudly and leaned back against the headboard, exhausted.

"I'm taking you to the doctor tomorrow," Devin said. "Unless you need to go tonight."

Gramps shook his head. "It's okay. I just need…a couple of pillows."

"That didn't sound okay, Gramps."

"Sorry you had to witness it."

"Sorry, hell. We're going in tomorrow. No arguments."

His grandpa slumped against the pillow Devin propped behind him.

"Where are some extra pillows?" Carey asked.

He coughed again, but not as violently. "Living room."

She rushed off to find them. As she approached the bedroom again, she heard them bickering about whether or not he needed medical attention. They paused when she appeared with the pillows, and Devin pulled his grandpa away from the headboard to squeeze them behind him.

"Anything else I can do?" Carey asked, wanting to escape the tension in the room now that Devin's grandpa was over the spell.

"Not unless you can knock some sense into him," Devin muttered.

"I'll wait in the living room then," she said, uncomfortable. "Holler if you need something."

She settled into a lumpy, worn cushion on one of a pair of ancient love seats, trying to calm herself.

After about five minutes, Devin emerged from the hallway. "He's asleep."

"He must have worn himself out. What now?"

"I'm not leaving him alone." He collapsed on the other love seat. "You can take my truck and go if you want."

"And how would you get him to the doctor in the morning?"

He appeared to consider the options.

"I'll stay, too, Dev. I'm too tired to drive home anyway."

"That's fine." He crossed his legs and ran his hand through his hair. "We'll have to sleep on the bunks."

"Bunks?"

"There's only one spare usable bedroom. The others are used as an office and for storage."

She squashed the tremor of desire that pulsed deep in her middle.

They'd spent the night at each other's houses plenty of times. But they'd always slept in separate rooms. And she hadn't been ensconced in endless daydreams about him.

"Come on. I'll show you," he said, standing.

When she got up, he touched the small of her back, causing her to jump in surprise.

"It's the room my cousin Landon and I used to share during the summer. Not very big, but it'll do." He led her past his grandfather's room to a small room at the end of the hallway. It was decorated in a nautical theme suitable for young boys.

"Gramps would invite all of the cousins out during the summer from the time I was about ten. Started after he retired." Devin looked thoughtful for a moment. "Jerod was always too busy working at the station, and his younger sisters camped out with sleeping bags in the living room. Landon and I used to play pirate ship on these beds," he said. "We argued over who got to be the lookout guy on the top deck."

"No argument here. You get the top deck. I'll have to pee every hour or so."

He grinned. "That's a charming little thing I didn't know about you."

"It's the baby," she said. "It uses my bladder as a trampoline."

Besides the bunk beds directly in front of her, Carey saw a couple of black beanbag chairs stacked in the corner, a chest of drawers and a chair. Paintings of ships covered the dark blue pinstriped wallpaper.

Devin threw her a white shirt from one of the drawers. "It's old but it should cover you."

Pajamas. Great idea. She held up the T-shirt and wondered just how much of her it would hide. Not enough, considering her chest took up a lot more room than it used to, and the bulge in her middle, although everyone else called it small, looked to her as though she'd swallowed a hot air balloon.

"I hate people," she read from the shirt. "Speaking of charming…"

"My preteen rebel-without-a-clue stage. I usually only wore it around the house, if that makes you feel any better."

"Much." She stifled a yawn. "I'm beat. I think I'll hit the sack."

"I'll join you." He stopped in his tracks. "I mean I'll go to bed, too. In the top bunk."

There was an awkward silence for a few seconds

before he motioned toward a closed door. "Bathroom's there. Towels should be under the sink."

When she went in and shut the door, Devin whipped his clothes off and pulled on an ugly pair of plaid boxers he'd left in the dresser long ago. He climbed up to the top bunk just before Carey came back out. He'd turned the light off, but the one in the bathroom still shone into the room enough so when he looked down he could see her clearly.

Big mistake.

The T-shirt was too small and too thin, leaving nothing to the imagination. His pulse quickened and he grew hard. Again.

She carried her clothes she'd worn to the chair next to the door, bending to set them down, and he was graced with a scintillating glimpse of skimpy white satin panties.

Only Carey could make white seem sinfully enticing.

He rolled away from her and stifled a moan.

"Ready for lights out?" she asked.

Shit, was he. "Yep," he croaked.

He heard her soft footsteps head back to the bathroom, and then the room was dark. How the hell was he supposed to sleep with his pulse going ninety miles an hour and a hard-on that wouldn't quit?

He listened to her toss and turn for a while, trying his damnedest not to picture that luscious body moving under the blankets. Finally, she was still.

"Dev?"

"Yeah?"

"You're really worried about him, aren't you?"

The subject of his grandpa cooled him a bit. "Yeah."

"You're not worrying about the business thing, are you?"

"The business thing?"

"Turning a profit while Gramps is still around to appreciate it. Are you afraid that's not going to happen?"

He took awhile to answer. "It's there in the back of my head, but—"

If he lost Gramps, he'd be completely on his own.

"You're lucky to have him," she said quietly.

He nodded, a lump in his throat. Here he was, having a hard time fitting in one night a week for the man. He had to try harder.

Devin dreaded bad news from the doctor tomorrow. The coughing fit tonight had scared the hell out of him. Devin had felt like a helpless idiot standing there. He'd been on the verge of yanking out his cell phone and dialing 911.

"Do you think his problem tonight was related to the heart stuff?" Carey asked.

"I'd rather not talk about it. I can hardly hear you, anyway."

"So come down here and talk for a while. I can't sleep."

"I'm not coming down there."

"I don't mean in my bed. Get the chair. We used to talk into the early morning all the time. We haven't done that for ages."

Back then, they'd been able to discuss their dates, banter about the weaknesses of the other gender, generally give each other a hard time. Easygoing, laid-back sessions.

Now things had changed, if only in his mind.

"I'm tired, Care. And I need to call the doctor early."

She didn't respond. The minutes stretched out, and he found himself listening for any move she made, for even breathing to signal she was asleep.

As worn out as he was, he was wide awake.

She let out a deep sigh.

Hell.

He climbed off the end of the bed and grabbed one of the old beanbag chairs he and Landon had used in countless beanbag wars. Throwing it onto the floor next to Carey's bed, he plopped into it, resigned and fully aware he was asking for trouble. "What do you want to talk about?"

She chuckled. "That tired, huh?"

"It's impossible to sleep with all the racket you make."

"I've hardly moved a muscle. Are you still twitching from not sitting in your office, working late tonight?"

"Why do you say that?"

"It's all you do anymore, with the exception of the one fishing night."

"I like my work."

"You're obsessed with your work. Wonder why that is."

He didn't answer, hoping she'd get the clue and change the subject.

"Gramps seems to think it's because of your parents, deceased as they may be."

"Nooo," he moaned. "I don't want to play this game."

"What game?"

"Carey Langford, amateur shrink."

She laughed, and the sultry sound had his pulse racing once again. "Come on. It's my favorite."

He considered the upside of a fifth of whiskey. Too bad he hated the stuff.

"Your parents did a number on you," she said.

"Doesn't take a psychology degree to figure that one out."

"Good thing, since I don't have one."

She was quiet for a while and Devin was relieved she'd dropped it. Talking about his parents was a waste of time.

"What happened when they died?" she asked suddenly.

He rolled his head back on the beanbag. "What do you mean, what happened?"

"Something happened. It was shortly after that when you hatched your whole plan to go to school and start a business."

It was a good thing she was appealing in every other way because right now Carey's insistent yammering had the same effect as an annoying gnat that wouldn't stay out of his face.

"What happened was they left almost everything to Jerod and told me I had no future." He hoped to shock her and end the conversation quickly.

"You…you're kidding me, Devin."

He scoffed. "Wish I was."

"You never said anything…"

He hesitated. "Not something I'm proud of."

"I knew their death messed you up for a while but I never imagined it was anything like this."

He'd avoided Carey and Monica as much as possible after his parents' accident for a reason. He didn't want their sympathy. It only made it worse.

"I'm over it. It was a good thing in the end."

"A good thing?"

"Once I got over being ticked off, it opened my eyes. Got me motivated."

He heard her roll toward him and saw her blond hair fall across her shoulder in the dimness. "I hope I never do anything that awful to my child."

Her words brought the present rushing back. It was easy for him to forget she was pregnant, especially in the dark when he couldn't see the bump in her middle. The baby was probably on her mind all the time. "You won't, Care," he said in little more than a whisper. "You'll be a good mother."

She didn't speak immediately. When she finally did, her tone was serious. "Thanks for saying that. A vote of confidence from you means a lot."

His chest tightened, and his need resurfaced. Except

that it wasn't just physical. He needed to get away from her and the things she made him feel.

"Going to check on Gramps," he said as he rose from the beanbag chair. "Then sleep."

"G'night, Dev," she said, turning toward the wall.

He crept out of the room to temporary safety.

CHAPTER FOURTEEN

An hour later, Devin was back in the top bunk, grinding his teeth in frustration.

Gramps had been fine, sound asleep, though he couldn't really call it peaceful since there was a faint rasp to his breathing. Devin had reassured himself the oxygen supply was up high enough, then slipped out of the room. Back to the torture chamber.

Sleeping in the same room as Carey was the dumbest idea he'd had in a long while. He lay there and listened to her soft, even breathing. Imagined her chest rising and falling with each breath. Drove himself completely goddamn nuts with longing for the woman less than four feet away yet totally out of his reach.

Devin sat up. Between lust for the woman below and distress for the man down the hall, sleep wasn't going to come anytime soon. He climbed down the end of the bunk as quietly as he could and went out to the kitchen.

Carey awoke with a start to movement close by. She rose on her elbows and gradually realized where she was and who was making the noise. Devin. The bedroom door eased shut, and she heard his footsteps recede.

Sitting up, she rubbed her face. Once she'd closed her eyes, she'd crashed hard, in spite of the strange surroundings, Devin's proximity and Gramps's health. Being pregnant could wear a girl out.

Devin was fretting about his grandpa, she'd bet. With good reason. The scene earlier had certainly spooked her. No way could they have left the old guy alone after that. Her heart went out to Devin and what he must be going through. She slipped out of the low bed and went in search of him.

She found him sitting on the kitchen counter, elbows propped on his thighs. A bulb above the stove provided the inadequate light, no stronger than a nightlight, just enough to relieve the darkness.

"Hey," she said in a hushed voice.

He looked up, startled. "Hey."

She moved closer, taking in the plaid boxers and his naked chest, her heartbeat picking up speed. He made quite an arousing picture there in the dim light, rumpled and intense.

"He's okay now, Devin."

She reached for his hand. Eyes down, he squeezed her fingers and pulled her a few inches closer.

"I don't think he's okay."

She couldn't deny she was concerned as well, just as she couldn't throw empty reassurances at him.

"You'll take him in tomorrow and find out what's going on. The doctors will help him."

He nodded, seemingly lost in his thoughts. She wished she could say something to ease his worry.

Devin sucked in a deep breath. "I don't want to lose him."

Carey's chest constricted in sympathy. Sadness was etched in every inch of his face. She couldn't resist putting her arms around his neck and pulling him to her. His hands touched her waist, then his arms wound around her. Neither of them let go.

"Don't you dare count him out yet. He's not going to take it lying down."

She felt him nod.

"I know. I'm just shaken up by that spell. And he says that's not the first."

Carey didn't know what else to say, so she just held on. He didn't seem to mind, in fact, didn't budge at all. After several minutes, he slid off the counter, squeezing his large frame between her and the cabinets. Being this close to him gave her a certain thrill she didn't dare examine right now.

He drew her farther into his body. When she felt his unmistakable hardness pressing into her lower abdomen, a spark ignited and shot straight to her core. Her blood thrummed in her ears. She moaned, her mouth a whisper away from his ear.

His hands slowly caressed her back and she wanted

to melt into him. Having his arms around her made her feel safe and cared for, as she'd never been before.

He pulled his head away to look into her eyes, then leaned his forehead against hers. His breathing was rough, which only added to the heat building between her legs.

"Carey?" His voice was a gruff whisper.

"Hmm?"

"What would you do if I kissed you?"

She moved her head back a couple inches so she could gauge the look on his face. His desire burned into her. Her throat went dry and she lifted her mouth to his, tentatively, in reply.

Their lips touched so lightly it was like a whisper between them, but every nerve in her body was instantly on edge. She pressed her mouth more firmly to his and ran her hands along the base of his neck, through his hair, urging him closer.

"I like that answer," he said when they paused for air.

He kissed her again, slipping his hands under the thin T-shirt to rest just at the top of her underwear. Her skin seemed to burn under his touch… She longed to have his hands all over her.

He plunged his tongue between her lips, teasing, tantalizing. Carey urged him closer, running her hands over his immense shoulders. Being wrapped securely in his arms felt so natural, she wanted to burrow into him forever.

Their tongues met, and the erotic softness of his mouth was in stark contrast with the rest of his solid body. A couple of days' growth felt rough on her chin, and she held in a smile. She'd teased him so many times about his inability to shave every day. It would be difficult to taunt him about it without remembering how it felt on her skin, without recalling the sensation of his body pressed against hers.

The earthy masculinity of his taste and scent assaulted her senses. She opened her eyes, needing to assure herself this was indeed the man she knew so well. The sight of him engrossed in kissing her flooded her insides with raw need. He was no longer the skinny fourteen-year-old who'd kissed her senseless so long ago. There was nothing skinny or boyish about him anymore.

He explored her with his tongue, his breath shaky, his fervor barely under control. His desire fanned the flames inside her higher yet. His hands lowered and grasped her rear. He groaned. He ran his mouth along her jawline to just below her ear. "You feel so good, Care."

Carey knew she should slow things down before they got out of hand, but she couldn't get enough of him. When his hands trailed up toward her breasts, she zeroed in on his touch. He rubbed his fingers over one breast, then teased her nipple. Arching closer, she lost herself in the sensations his hands evoked.

Moments later, he lifted the T-shirt over her head

and dropped it to the floor. He dragged her to his chest, and the feeling of skin on skin made her catch her breath. The realization that she wanted even more of this man, wanted him naked, stretching over her, pounding into her, stopped her short.

"Devin."

The sound he made in reply was a cross between a sigh and an unrecognizable word.

"We have to stop."

"What's wrong?"

She pulled away enough to gain eye contact. "I'm almost completely naked in the middle of your grandpa's kitchen."

He gazed down at her body, then looked beyond her at the surroundings. "The middle is actually over there, about where the table is. Want to try it out?"

She laughed, tempted as hell to take him up on the offer. "I can just imagine Gramps's reaction when he comes out for a drink."

"So let's take it back to the bedroom."

She shook her head, despite the thrill still zipping along every nerve in her body. She wasn't thinking entirely straight. "We can't."

He stared at her for a long moment. His grin disappeared and his eyes became more serious with each tick of the suddenly deafening clock on the kitchen wall. He bent and picked up her shirt. Turning it the right way, he slid it back over her head and pulled it down to her waist, which for some reason moved her.

Devin would be the catch of a lifetime—if she were in the position to be looking.

He pulled her close and just hugged her—seemed to need the contact as much as she did. But touching was dangerous when both their bodies were so keyed up. After a few blissful seconds, she stepped away.

Devin drank in the sight of her. Her cheeks were flushed, lips slightly swollen, and her nipples protruded from his T-shirt, making her perfect breasts impossible to miss. It'd be a long while before he got the feel of them out of his mind.

He hoped his pulse would calm down in another day or two as well.

He reached behind him and flipped the light above the stove off. "Sleep," he said hoarsely. "Let's go."

Devin couldn't see a thing so he felt his way toward Carey, who hadn't moved. He took her hand and moved slowly down the hallway. Letting go of her when they reached the bunk beds was the hardest thing to do.

He tugged her so that she faced him and pressed a brief kiss to her lips. "Good night, Carey."

"'Night. Sleep well."

He half chuckled, knowing sleep would be a futile effort.

There was no doubt about it—he really did love her.

THE NEXT MORNING, Devin dropped Carey off at his place to pick up her car. Gramps had ridden in with them to see the doctor, complaining the whole way. Carey was relieved to get out of the backseat of the Excursion to be alone for a few minutes. She'd spent the car ride staring at the back of Devin's head, wondering what went through his mind about last night.

There had been no clue this morning that anything had happened between them just hours before. When she'd woken up a bit after seven, Devin had already dressed and left the room. She'd found him nagging his grandpa to get ready. She'd never had a chance to be alone with Devin. Not that she'd know what to say if she had.

Devin incited an ache deep within her. It went beyond the physical desire that could have so easily burned out of control last night.

She unlocked the Bug and climbed in, her cheeks burning as she remembered her body's reaction to him.

She cared about him. A lot. How could she not? They'd been friends forever. Ever since she'd found out she was pregnant and her usual active social life had come to a halt, he'd been the person she'd spent the most time with. Monica, too, to some extent, but she always had Kyle to go home to. There was no denying she and Devin had become closer in the past couple of months.

The kisses last night…well. The kisses took everything ten notches higher. There was serious chemistry between them. Devin stirred yearnings she hadn't felt for years—not since the last time he'd kissed her.

She turned down the street to her house—Trent's

house—forcing Devin from her mind and summoning the determination to get along better with her brother today.

She couldn't blame Trent for flipping out about the pregnancy. If he'd taken the news any better, she'd probably figure he didn't care about her.

Fights between them had been rare over the years; she wasn't used to it. Usually it was them against the world. Or against their mother, at the very least.

Pulling into the driveway, she noticed Trent's Ram in the single garage, so she backed into the street to park. It was weird sharing the house again. She normally loved having a roommate, but not one she fought with. Not one who could provoke her self-doubt in two minutes flat.

She entered through the kitchen, where Trent sat at the table, clutching a mug of coffee, the newspaper spread in front of him.

"Morning," she said.

"Where have you been?" he asked, narrowing his eyes.

"Nice to see you, too. Have you always been this much of a pain in the ass and I just didn't notice?"

He set the mug down. "Sorry."

"What's going on with you, Trent?"

He looked sharply at her. "Nothing. Why?"

"You seem on edge since you've been home."

"I'm not on edge. I think asking where you were all night is a legitimate question, especially considering your condition. So where were you?"

She grabbed a banana off the counter and pulled out the chair across from him. "I was with Devin. At his grandpa's house."

"Carey…" His tone of voice and his expression held a warning. "What the hell are you doing with him?"

"He's my friend, Trent. We spend a lot of time together."

"Including sleepovers?" He shoved his chair back angrily as he stood, then went to the dishwasher and started unloading it. "It's no wonder you got pregnant."

Her hand stopped halfway to her mouth and she stared at him in disbelief. "I don't believe you just said that," she said icily and stomped off to her bedroom.

Sure, she could've told him exactly why she and Devin had stayed all night in the country, but she didn't want to. Why should she have to explain herself? That her brother automatically assumed she and Devin were sleeping together ticked her off. Even if a part of her wished they could have done just that.

She needed to get out of the house before she punched his lights out. After taking a shower, she went to the kitchen to feed the cats. She could hear Trent rattling around in the basement.

Snicket sauntered up to her and rubbed against her leg, then ditched the affectionate act as soon as his bowl was full.

Carey was filling the large water dish just as Trent came up the stairs. She glared at him.

"We aren't getting started on the right foot, are we?" he asked.

"We?"

"We need to get some things straight if we're going to be roommates."

"What do you mean? How long are you staying?"

"If I find a good job, I'm not leaving," he answered. "I'm done traveling for a while."

She processed the information, waiting for him to apologize for being a jerk yet again.

"Carey, stay away from Devin. He's not good enough for you."

"Not good enough? How is it that I can get over him breaking up with me but you can't? That was high school. He and I have been friends for years since."

"Friends?"

"Friends."

"When you stay out with a man all night, it doesn't look like 'friends.'"

"Who the hell is watching me besides you?"

"The neighbors can see when you come home."

"So? I doubt they care."

"You'll give Mrs. Higsby a heart attack with that kind of carelessness. Give the old woman a break."

Mrs. Higsby was the dear woman who fed the cats whenever Carey had gone out of town on assignment. Carey knew her well...a lot better than Trent did, thanks to his long absence. He had some nerve to insinuate Carey's lifestyle would shock her.

She gave him what she hoped was an acidic look. "Somehow I've managed to live on my own for the past ten months."

"Yeah, and look what happened." Instead of anger, she saw concern in his face as he glanced toward her abdomen, but that didn't quell her temper.

"I...made...one...mistake," she said through clenched teeth. "In case you haven't noticed, I'm almost thirty. I make my own decisions, whether you're in Alaska or the next room."

She set the bowl on the floor. "Oh, and if it makes you feel any better, the possibilities of me getting knocked up again are zero. As far as I know, you can only have one baby at a time." So he thought she'd slept with Devin? Fine.

She slammed out of the house, shaking with anger. She had nowhere to go, but she sure wasn't staying there. So much for getting along.

It had never been like this before with Trent. They'd argued more in the past week than they had their whole lives. He wasn't acting like himself. Something was up, and it went beyond her pregnancy. She was dying to know what. But that would require them to get through an entire conversation without arguing, and so far that'd been a bust.

Maybe she should have explained about Devin's grandpa, but why couldn't he give her the benefit of the doubt?

Furthermore, why would it be any of his business

if she *did* sleep with Devin? The idea wasn't as crazy as it had once seemed. The bothersome dreams that had made her toss and turn last night were evidence of that.

Her brother was acting…bizarrely. He'd always been concerned, but he'd never been an asshole about it.

Regardless of what his problem was, she saw no sense in staying around and bearing the brunt of his permanent rotten mood. Devin was right. It was time to find a new home. She had enough stress without a self-righteous, temperamental brother criticizing her every move. Once she moved out, she'd sleep wherever she damn well pleased, whenever she felt like it.

She visualized Devin sitting on the counter last night wearing nothing but boxers….

Scratch that.

She'd busy herself preparing for parenthood. She'd stay at home knitting baby booties if she had to. Anything to avoid temptation.

She had just turned down said temptation's street hoping to find Monica in the office when her cell phone rang. It was Devin.

"Where are you?" he asked in a rush.

"In your driveway. What's going on?"

"I called your house and your asshole brother damn near hung up on me. They're admitting Gramps."

"To the hospital?" She killed the engine.

Devin grumbled an affirmative. "He's got extra fluid

around his lungs, so they kept him until they can get it down. Might be released as soon as tomorrow, depending." Fatigue and worry came through the phone loud and clear.

She struggled to find comforting words. "He'll be okay," she finally said, feeling helpless. "He's in the best place."

"I know." His voice cracked, and then she heard him take a slow breath. "As soon as he's settled, I have to run to a meeting. Did you say you're going to talk to Monica now?"

"I'm walking in as we speak. Want to talk to her yourself?"

"No. Just tell her to hold down the fort and I'm going to follow up with that guy who called yesterday, then run back here for a bit."

"Slow down, Dev. You know she'll handle everything here. Just do what you need to. Try not to worry about your grandpa."

"Lucky for me, I won't have time to worry," he said, attempting a lightness Carey knew he didn't feel.

She hoped to hell the old man's ticker held out. Devin would be devastated if it didn't.

CAREY TOOK her sweet time walking into the fancy restaurant to meet her mom for Sunday brunch. Her mom's reaction last week had been far too understanding and easy. Surely she wanted to meet Carey to tell her how she *really* felt. Quite frankly, Carey didn't care if her mother wasn't happy about her situation. There was nothing she could do to change it.

When she peeked around a large bank of greenery near the hostess to see if her mother had arrived yet, she saw her waving from the back corner. Appearing friendly and enthusiastic. Not like someone who was about to read her the riot act. Strange, indeed.

"Sweetie, I'm so glad to see you," her mom said, standing and brushing crumbs off her classy beige jacket before grasping Carey's hands. Genuine warmth radiated from her eyes.

Carey forced a smile. "Hi, Mom."

"You look so good. A lot of women get sickly looking when they're expecting, but not you. You're glowing, honey."

Oh, God. Glowing? She wasn't sure what to say.

Carey sat down uneasily. She could count on one hand the times they'd eaten together, just the two of them, in a restaurant. There was a reason for that. They had nothing in common.

"How's the new guy?" she asked, awkwardly.

"He's perfect," her mom gushed, leaning forward.

Carey noticed that her mother was wearing opal earrings and a necklace she'd never seen before and wondered if they were a gift from this perfect man.

"I'd love to have you and Trent meet him." She rattled off a date two weeks away. "Why don't you two come for dinner? We'll be out of town next weekend or I'd invite you then."

"I'll check with Trent and let you know. Where are you going?"

"There's a bed-and-breakfast out in the country. We're going for a romantic weekend." A blush colored her mom's cheeks.

"Sounds…nice." Carey didn't want any more details.

They went through the buffet line and returned to their table with heaping plates. Their conversation was a lot easier than Carey had imagined, as her mom asked dozens of questions about the pregnancy. She also shared bits of her own two pregnancies and labors when Carey asked. Carey was more than a little interested in hearing her mother's experiences and even asking her for advice. First time for everything.

After their plates were emptied and cleared away, her mom pushed a gift bag across the table toward her.

"What's this?" Carey asked, eyeing her nervously.

"A pregnancy gift, of course." Her mom's grin widened and she motioned for Carey to open it.

Carey was taken aback and confused. She tried to hide by digging into the layers of pink and blue tissue paper. She pulled out something book-shaped and hard. "You didn't have to get me anything, Mom."

"Of course I did! My first grandbaby is on the way. This is special."

Their eyes met and for just an instant, an understanding passed between them, a common bond.

Unwrapping the object, Carey wondered if her mom had taken to smoking crack for breakfast. Carey knew how to handle it when her mother blew her off, but this…?

"A journal of my pregnancy," Carey read. The art-work of stars and the moon cradling a small bundle of baby tugged at Carey's emotions, and tears sprang to her eyes. She glanced up and caught the strangest expression on her mother's face—something akin to pride. "Thanks, Mom."

Her mom pulled a smaller journal from her purse. She held it across the table, her hand shaking just a bit. "I kept this diary while I was pregnant with you. I don't know if it'll interest you, but you're welcome to take it and read through it."

"Really? You kept a diary when you were expecting me?"

"It was one of the two most important times in my life, Carey. I wanted to remember every bit of it forever."

Touched more than she wanted to admit, Carey flipped her mom's journal open and read an entry about how exciting it was to feel the baby moving.

This was the single most thoughtful thing her mother had ever done for her. "Thank you. I'll read every page. And I'll do my best to record everything in my own journal. What a great idea."

"Carrying a baby is such an important job—and a privilege. Enjoy this time, Carey, even though I know the circumstances weren't your first choice."

Carey merely nodded, mostly because her throat was swelling shut with emotion.

CHAPTER FIFTEEN

A WEEK LATER, Devin heaved himself onto the kitchen counter of the studio apartment Carey was considering renting. He felt better than he had all week. Gramps had finally been released the day before, and Devin had taken him home and spent the night there, despite the old man's fussing about not needing a babysitter. Things were looking up for both him and his grandpa.

Not so for Carey, judging by his surroundings. From his vantage point, he could easily see the entire place without turning his head.

"What do you think?" Carey asked Monica.

Her smile seemed forced. She was trying too hard to like the apartment.

"It's…small," Monica said. "Not bad, but tiny. You really couldn't find anything bigger?"

"Not on this side of town. I'd rather be cramped in a safe place than sprawled out in an apartment with bars on the windows and triple locks on the door."

The thought of Carey living unsafe or uncomfortable didn't sit right. He'd been the one to coax her to move, to find a small place for her and the baby, but a glorified closet wasn't what he'd had in mind.

"What are you going to do when the baby sleeps?" he asked. For the first time, he could actually see her pregnancy from a distance.

She wrinkled her brow, staring at the space. "Guess I'd have to be really quiet."

"I don't know, Care," Monica said. "It might feel like a prison. Besides, you're used to more space, even without another person to accommodate. That baby will grow and need a place to play."

Carey's shoulders drooped. She shuffled toward the half wall separating the bedroom from the rest of the studio space and leaned over it, resting her elbows on top. "I don't know what else to do." Her discouragement stirred his desire to help her.

Monica joined Carey, leaning her back against the half wall. "Are you sure you can't squeeze any more out of your income for rent? Even fifty dollars?"

Carey shook her head. "You guys wouldn't believe the figuring I did. I've never made a budget in my life, but I calculated down to the last hypothetical penny— everything from gasoline to diapers. I don't have a guaranteed monthly income, but I tried to be realistic. There's no room for anything extra. If I have to buy a box of cold medicine it'll throw the whole thing off."

Devin hopped down from the counter. Without

thinking, he started massaging Carey's tight shoulders. He felt the charge between them from the first instant of contact. She leaned her head back and moaned softly, and the sound sent his pulse flying.

Concentrating on the feel of each tense muscle under his fingers, he endeavored to loosen every knot, to dissipate every last hint of stress. Her pleasure became his mission.

For a short time, he let himself forget Monica was standing beside them, even though she and Carey continued to discuss every tiring detail of Carey's budget. After he'd worked over most of her shoulders, Carey turned to meet his gaze and he knew she, too, felt the pull between them.

Just then Monica's cell phone erupted into an annoying melody, and she dug it out of her pocket and answered it, ending the blasted noise.

Carey looked down, as if she'd been caught stealing the last cookie.

Monica walked outside to take the call.

Carey looked unsure of herself.

"You're not just moving out because I said you needed to, are you?"

She laughed. "Have I ever done anything just because you said I needed to?"

The tension between them seemed to dissipate as they fell back into familiar bantering.

He shook his head. "Just wanted to be sure."

"Trent interrogated me when I got home after we

stayed at your grandpa's. You'd think he was my dad, not my brother."

Devin didn't say anything, since what ran through his mind wasn't particularly kind.

"We haven't gotten along since he's been home," she said. "If I stay there, we'll be enemies in no time. I don't want that."

She paced to the window and back, her hands on her hips. Then she began another thorough inspection of every cupboard and corner.

Monica came back in, muttering about some woman who couldn't make up her mind for anything.

"Problems?" Devin asked her.

"Just your average indecisive mother-in-law," she said. "She's trying to decide what to buy Kyle for his birthday. Apparently she didn't like any of the suggestions I gave her yesterday." She looked at Carey. "What'd you decide?"

Devin's pager vibrated, and he quickly checked it. "One of my servers is having serious problems. I need to go follow up."

"So much for a day off, huh?" Monica said.

Carey followed him to the door. "Dev, thanks for coming with us." Her voice was quiet, as if she didn't want Monica to hear.

"You bet." He kissed her quickly on the forehead and jogged off.

"Ooo-kay, Langford, out with it," Monica said as Carey closed the door.

"Out with what?"

"Give it up. You know exactly what I'm talking about."

"And that would be…?"

Crap. Monica must have sensed things weren't normal between her and Devin.

"There was enough chemistry between you two to blow up a lab."

Carey raised her eyebrows. "That much, huh?"

"That much and more. Spill it. What did I miss?"

"Let's go. I'm not ready to sign a lease here," Carey said, grabbing her purse.

"Good. It's too small."

They were silent until they were in the car and Carey was backing out of the parking space.

"Are you two…?" Monica left the question hanging.

"No." They weren't sleeping together, screwing around, whatever.

"You're not having sex?" She said it as though it was difficult to believe.

Carey shook her head.

"Then what are you doing?"

Carey shrugged, whether because she didn't know how to answer or because she enjoyed teasing Monica, she wasn't sure.

"What torture method do I need to use to get details?"

Carey chuckled. "What details do you want, specifically?"

"I want to know what's going on! Quit teasing me, and tell me what the heck you and Devin are doing."

Carey didn't speak as she sped around a corner, amused when Monica clung to the door.

"You're trying to kill me *before* you tell me, I see. Usually it's the other way around."

"Girlfriend, if I had half a clue, I'd fill you in."

Monica stared at her, and Carey shrugged again, keeping her eyes on the road. She'd never had trouble confiding about men to Monica, but she honestly didn't know what to say. *I have a horrible crush on the friend who I have absolutely no romantic future with?*

"You're attracted to him."

"Yeah."

"When did this start?"

"Years ago."

Monica laughed. "Have you kissed him? I mean recently—since puberty."

Carey nodded.

"Details!"

Carey had to smile. "Our dear friend Devin still knows how to kiss."

"So it was good, huh?"

Carey resisted the urge to overdramatize the situation. "Yeah. Unfortunately."

"Why unfortunately?"

It was obvious, wasn't it? "There's no way we could have a future. I'm pregnant."

"So?"

"*So?* Monica, are you nuts? The baby isn't Devin's, remember? It's his cousin's. Slight problem there. Besides, even if the baby issue didn't exist, there's a huge chance I would screw things up with him. Again."

Carey pulled up behind Monica's car in front of Trent's house. To think she used to consider it *her* house.

"You can't compare a relationship with Devin now to your fling years ago. You guys were kids. Besides, it was more of a mutual-attraction, messing-around thing, right?"

"Whatever it was, I didn't hold his interest. With a baby on the way, not only am I less likely to hold his interest, but the stakes are so much higher now. I can't take the chance. I have to concentrate on what my child needs."

"Having a kid will bring about some sacrifices, that's for sure," Monica said. "But moms need to be happy, too."

"That's just it," Carey said emphatically, slapping the steering wheel. "I'm not sure I equate a relationship with being happy. They've always been just one more thing to worry about."

"You're just scared. We're all scared."

"Maybe so, but now's not the time to figure it out. I'm going to bring this baby up by myself. I'll be there for her—or him. I won't be out chasing men."

"Does Devin know you feel this way?"

"We don't talk about it."

"Maybe you should."

"No way. That'd be admitting there's something there."

"Judging by what I saw back there, there's no denying there's something going on."

Carey pulled her key from the ignition. "Let me live in my world of oblivion, please. I have enough problems as it is." She opened the door and got out, signaling the end of the conversation.

"Thanks for going with me to check that place out," she said as they stood next to Monica's Miata. "You guys are probably right. Something not so open would be better so the baby can sleep in peace."

"I'll keep my eyes open. The good thing is you're not on a tight schedule to find something."

Carey rubbed her abdomen. "Tell my belly that."

"You look great. I can hardly tell you're pregnant."

"My jeans have a different story to tell." She walked toward the house. "Talk to you soon. Thanks again."

"You bet," Monica said. As Carey reached the front steps, Monica called out, "You can only deny something for so long!"

Carey rolled her eyes as her friend laughed, lowering herself into the sports car.

She could argue with Monica. As a matter of fact,

Carey liked to think she was very good at ignoring certain things when she needed to. And her growing attraction to Devin definitely fell under the "needed to" category.

CHAPTER SIXTEEN

CAREY TRIED to read a parenting magazine while waiting for her name to be called. God knew she needed all the mothering advice she could get. But she couldn't concentrate. The anticipation of seeing her baby was so great, sitting still was impossible. Her crossed leg seemed to be bobbing of its own accord.

She'd looked forward to this moment for weeks, since the last appointment when the doctor had ordered the ultrasound to check the growth of the baby. Carey was smaller than Dr. Estes thought she should be—not by much, but enough to give him an excuse to take a closer look. He'd assured her the chances of a problem were slim, otherwise he would have done an ultrasound on the spot. She'd taken his words at face value. Until last night.

Sleep had been elusive as she'd imagined all the things that could be wrong. She'd even gone online and researched it, freaking herself out more. She'd made a mental note never to look for information on potential medical problems online again. Way too much scary stuff out there.

She slammed the magazine shut and tossed it onto the table beside her. Checking her watch yet again, she realized she'd only been waiting for fifteen minutes. Seemed like an eternity. She uncrossed her legs. The bouncing was beginning to annoy her.

The waiting room was full of pregnant women. She made a game out of trying to guess how far along each one was. It was hard to ignore that there was only one other woman who didn't have a man sitting next to her. Carey tried not to feel lonely, but when she watched the easy interaction of the couple nearest her, clearly in love and excited about starting a family, her heart ached.

Unable to sit still any longer, she jumped up and paced to the watercooler. Remembering how much liquid she'd already taken in—doctor's orders—she changed direction and ended up at a breast-feeding information display. She picked up a book and became engrossed in the potential problems of nursing a newborn. So much for it being a natural process.

She flipped through the pages until full-color photos showing proper nursing positions caught her attention. Positions? What the...? Didn't you just put the baby by the breast and it drank milk? Her confidence sagged, to say the least.

"Well, my greatest fear of being accosted by a bunch of breasts at the girly doctor's office has finally been realized."

Devin? She set the book down and turned, a torrent

of emotions crashing down on her. "Wh-what are you doing here?" He was the last person she'd expected to see...not that she'd expected anyone she knew.

His rugged face inched its way into a grin that melted her insides. His voice was a loud whisper. "The itching problem, you know."

Carey laughed nervously. "I have stuff for that," she whispered back. "Seriously, why are you here?"

"Why do you think I'm here?"

"I thought...we talked...I told you I didn't need you to come."

So maybe she'd lied, because she was ecstatic to see him. Having Devin here comforted her more than she'd ever guessed possible.

"This is a big deal," he said. "You shouldn't be alone."

Looking over his shoulder, she noticed they'd caught the attention of several patients. She pulled him down beside her into a seat, not letting go of his forearm. She needed the contact. "I'm so nervous I could pee."

He chuckled, seeming a little ill at ease.

"Actually that'd probably be from the gazillion gallons of water the doctor told me to drink. But still... I could hardly sleep last night."

"This is right up your alley, like a video of the baby, isn't it? What are you worried about?"

"What am I not worried about would be easier. What if they find something wrong?"

He rested his hand on hers. "They won't."

She couldn't force herself to let go of his arm, even when he moved his hand away. She was still unable to believe he'd walked in.

He'd *known* she needed him. It warmed her down to her toes. He'd remembered. And he'd taken time out to be here—for her. The guy who didn't even take time out for himself.

She'd truly thought she didn't need him to come with her. Thought she could handle the excitement—and terror—all by her lonesome. She'd also believed she'd been doing an okay job of it...until he walked in the door. Then it had struck her that she wanted nothing more than to have him by her side, to hold his hand as she saw her baby.

She removed her fingers from his forearm and entwined them in his, not thinking twice about the intimate gesture. Content, she leaned her head on his shoulder and closed her eyes.

She would have drifted off had it not been for her bladder feeling like a ketchup packet being stomped on by a two-hundred-pound man.

When they called her name, her pulse pounded. She jerked her head off Devin's shoulder and looked at him. "Let's go," he said softly, squeezing her hand.

Her chest tightened.

Devin followed Carey back into a maze of hallways and small exam rooms. She was in some kind of state—excited or nervous—he wasn't quite sure what. She did seem happy to see him though, which was a relief. The only thing he was sure of was that Carey shouldn't be alone.

The nurse showed them into a room equipped with a big machine. Carey hoisted herself onto the table, and the nurse motioned toward a chair for Devin. She asked Carey a couple of questions and noted the answers on a form, then told them the tech would be in shortly.

"She better hope so, otherwise she'll have a puddle to wipe up," Carey muttered after the nurse had left.

He chuckled but didn't say anything because his uneasiness had just tripled in intensity. He knew next to nothing about ultrasounds. What if Carey had to undress? Something he hadn't even considered as he'd weighed the pros and cons of showing up. Probably not a big deal if the man sitting at her feet was her husband and had seen the promised land a thousand times. But for a guy who was just along for the ride—okay, for a guy who was along for the ride and also happened to fantasize about that promised land from time to time—watching Carey get naked with an audience could prove to be an uncomfortable situation. He sure wouldn't sit there unfazed. Yeah, seeing every last succulent inch of her would be quite the experience…in other circumstances. Here, it would be nothing but awkward as hell.

A middle-aged woman in a white jacket walked in, smiling at them both. She greeted Carey by name after skimming the form in her hand and introduced herself. Then she turned to him.

"And are you—"

"He's a friend of mine," Carey broke in.

He didn't want to be her husband or the baby's father, but her haste to dispel the misconception smarted.

Carey lay back, and the tech told her to raise her shirt and lower her pants. He panicked until he realized she didn't mean all the way. Carey moved them enough for the woman to have full access to her slightly rounded belly. Devin forced himself to exhale.

Her skin looked soft, smooth, with no sign of the marks his mother had always grumbled about as if he were to blame. Nope, definitely nothing to complain about concerning the expanse of flesh in front of him. Unfortunately. He didn't want to like what he saw.

The tech produced a tube of something and sloshed it onto Carey's belly, rubbing it around. After dimming the lights, she picked up a wand and scooted closer to the machine.

"Do we want to know the sex of this baby?"

Carey glanced at Devin as if she wanted his input. He was caught completely off guard. Hadn't she thought about this before now? "You have to decide," he told her. Carey was the expert at spontaneous decisions.

She thought for a minute and smiled. "Yes. I want to know."

Without taking her eyes from the monitor, which

now showed a big white blur, she found Devin's hand and held on to it. Tightly.

The tech listed body parts she supposedly saw on the screen, but you couldn't prove it by him. He still saw a blob of static. He glanced at Carey to see if she was having any better luck, but judging by her concentrated expression, she wasn't.

"I...don't see anything but snow," she finally said.

The tech smiled at her. "Sorry, I was checking certain parts, getting some measurements. I'll slow down and point things out to you now." She moved the wand on Carey's belly and the view on the screen changed slightly. "Here we go. Here's the head. Nose...eyes... lips." With each word, she pointed things out, and suddenly Devin could see a face.

The face of his cousin's baby. Oh, there wasn't enough detail to see any resemblance, but Devin was fixated on it.

Carey's hand clutched him even harder. "There's my baby!" Her eyes lit up. She was radiant.

The father's absence had no bearing on this magical moment. At least not for her. For him, the thought of Jerod was distracting. Annoying. Devin should be glad he could be here to share this moment with Carey, but instead, he was stuck on the baby's paternity.

He held on to Carey's hand and concentrated on staying calm and appearing unbothered. He was here to support her and had to drop his stupid hang-up with the facts. Or at least hide it.

He'd never been one to expect fairness from life, but he couldn't help questioning why things had turned out as they did. Why Jerod? It could as easily have been him.

He wondered what it would be like if…

No. It *wasn't* his child. Carey *wasn't* his girlfriend. Even if he was foolish enough to love her, he knew… He didn't have it in him to bring up another man's child. Especially not Jerod Mauriello's.

"Here's the heart," the tech said.

Devin focused on Carey instead of the monitor, telling himself her face was much more interesting than a screen of hard-to-decipher images.

He could read her love for her unborn child as clearly as if she'd written it out for him and drawn pictures. There was no doubt in his mind she'd be the best mom the kid could have. She'd make up for the absence on the paternal side. He hoped the child someday realized how lucky he or she was.

"You still want to know what flavor you've got in there?" the tech asked.

Carey nodded, and Devin couldn't help peeking, even though it was all gibberish to him. There were no sex organs anywhere to be seen on the monitor.

"Looks like a girl."

A wordless sound of joy came from Carey, and tears formed in her eyes. He'd suspected she'd wanted a girl but had never asked. Bringing up the topic of the baby was something he didn't do.

After they'd selected some screen shots to print out, the ultrasound was over and they were led back to the waiting room, whereupon Carey darted to the restroom.

"Pee sample," she explained, when she returned. "Really hard to accomplish when you've got it coming out your ears. Come to the rest of the appointment with me?" she asked him as they crossed the lobby toward empty chairs.

"There's more?" He stifled a groan.

"I see the doctor next. Normal monthly stuff."

She sat, but he hesitated. "I think I better head back to the office." In truth, he'd had enough of dwelling on the baby's paternity.

She frowned but didn't say anything.

"I'm sorry, Carey, it's just that…" What? He wasn't dumb enough to tell her how he really felt about the baby. That'd be enough to kill their friendship. He left the sentence hanging.

"It's okay. Go ahead." She forced a grin, but it didn't quite ring true. "Thanks for coming to the ultrasound. That was the important part."

He tried to smile, but the lobby suddenly felt stifling, as though all the oxygen had been sucked out. He had to get out of there. "See you later," he choked out.

He felt like a shitty friend.

"THE BABY looks great," Dr. Estes said almost thirty minutes later as he looked over the information from the ultrasound. "Measurements checked out, all the parts are there."

"No growth problems," Carey said to reassure herself.

"None." He measured her belly as he spoke. "And you're catching up, too. You need to eat and gain weight this month. You still look small, but that's probably because of your long frame."

She breathed a sigh of relief. Seeing the baby had done wonders, but hearing the healthy report from the doctor finally put her mind at ease.

"Sounds good, too," he said, holding the Doppler to her lower abdomen as they listened to the whoosh-whoosh of the baby's sturdy heart.

Once again, she was awed by the sound.

"You, on the other hand, have me a little concerned," the doctor continued, putting the Doppler away.

Carey sat up, looking questioningly at him.

"Your blood pressure is up. Not to an alarming level, but we need to watch it."

She frowned, unsure of what to say.

"How's your stress level?"

That made Carey laugh. "Stress level? A bit elevated."

"What's going on?" He sat on the little swivel stool and made eye contact, giving Carey the impression he really did care and wasn't just trying to get to his next patient.

"Normal pregnancy things," she said, determined not to sound whiney. "Worrying about the baby, worrying about being a single mom, worrying about a place to live."

Dr. Estes chuckled softly. "Those aren't exactly run-of-the-mill worries. Sounds like you have a lot on your plate."

Carey grinned. "Is that a politically correct way to say my life is a mess?"

"I didn't say that," he said. "A place to live, huh? What are you looking for?"

She briefly explained how none of the twenty-plus places she'd looked at were suitable.

He sat back pensively. "Maybe we could work out something to help each other. My wife and I both have ridiculous schedules. We've thrown around the idea of renting out our garage apartment. We'd both feel better having someone on the property a little more regularly."

Carey felt a spark of hope, but then she realized he was probably talking more money than she had. It was a doctor's house, after all. The garage was probably bigger than Trent's entire house and yard put together.

"I have two cats," she said.

"Are they litter-box trained?"

She nodded.

"Shouldn't be a problem. The apartment has two bedrooms, a kitchen, small living area and bathroom. It's the size of a three-car garage."

"How much do you want for rent?" she asked, preferring to get to the heart of the matter before she got too excited.

"How much can you afford to pay?"

Without hesitating, she gave him the figure she'd come up with in her budget.

"That sounds okay to me," he said. "I'll talk to my wife and call you if you want."

"Where is it?" she asked, unable to believe her low budget hadn't scared him off.

"On the west side. Very edge of town." He explained exactly how to get there. It was a neighborhood she could only dream of living in—the kind anyone would want their child to grow up in.

"Where can I reach you once I've talked to my better half?"

She scribbled down her home and cell numbers on the back of the prescription tablet he handed her. "You'll let me know either way?" she asked, trying to contain her excitement.

"Of course. Within the next day or two."

She was ready to sign a lease on the spot, sight unseen. How bad could it be? It was in a great neighborhood, and it had actual rooms. Not half walls, but rooms. Please let this work out, she thought. If she was stuck with the crummy studio apartment, Devin would never let her hear the end of it, and she would likely go stark raving mad.

"Regardless of whether you decide you like our

place, I hope you find something soon. You can't put so much stress on yourself," the doctor said. "I want you back in two weeks, and we'll check your blood pressure again."

He listed symptoms of preeclampsia—his fancy word for high blood pressure—to watch for in the meantime, none of which she'd yet experienced. So much for leaving with a sense of relief. Seemed like there was always more to worry about, and she figured that would quadruple when the baby made its entry into the world. This motherhood thing was really starting to scare her.

CHAPTER SEVENTEEN

CAREY LET HERSELF into the house, hoping Trent wasn't home. The garage door was closed, which was a good sign. She wasn't in the mood for another argument. The day had been too emotional already.

After her appointment, she'd treated herself to sin in the form of a banana split with nuts and extra whipped cream for lunch. Seeing her baby, even if it was just on a screen, was cause for a mini-celebration.

When she'd finished the calorie fest, she'd rushed off to photograph a cow giving birth on a farm just outside of town for a children's magazine. She'd done work for them in the past and they paid well. A little cow blood was no big deal for a paycheck. She just hoped her own labor was more private.

For being such a special day, it had seemed to go downhill after Devin had left. The high blood pressure had her a bit spooked, even though it was probably just the worries she'd tormented herself with all night. Of course, she'd watch for the symptoms Dr. Estes had warned her of, but really, she felt okay. She would know if anything started to go wrong.

She dropped her camera bag by the door and took her purse with her to the kitchen table. Collapsing in a chair, she took out the ultrasound pictures she'd already looked at fifty times or so.

My little girl. She couldn't be more thrilled, not only at the gender news but at her daughter's bill of health. She couldn't bear to think about what she'd do if her baby had problems of some kind. She blew a kiss at one of the tiny black-and-white images, slipped one back into her purse and kept the rest out. She'd find a cute pastel-colored frame for the one of the baby's face.

The doorbell rang and she glanced at her watch. It was almost seven o'clock. Too late for a door-to-door, and she wasn't expecting anyone. She dragged herself up.

Devin stood on the front steps, hands in the front pockets of his jeans, his head cocked to the side. "Hi. Can I come in?"

"Of course." She still held the ultrasound pictures in her hand. "I was just admiring her," she said, holding them up.

He nodded as he entered but didn't really appear to hear what she'd said. Looking beyond her, he seemed to search for her brother.

"He's gone," she said.

"Carey." His mood was too serious. He didn't even move toward sitting down.

"What's going on, Devin?"

He cleared his throat. "I'm sorry I bailed on you today—"

"Devin, I said it was okay. I meant it." She really did. Once she'd seen the baby on the monitor and got the news there were no gaping problems, her fear had faded.

It was *her* baby. *Her* excitement. *Her* spectacular moment. Not his.

Hers and hers alone.

And she was okay with that. She'd just temporarily forgotten it in the midst of extreme relief and excitement.

Devin looked as though he wanted to say something else as he stood there, arms crossed, staring at her.

"Really." She smiled to show him she was fine.

His expression didn't relax.

"You're beating yourself up over this, aren't you?" She stepped toward him and grasped his forearm. "It's okay. But if you really feel the need to make it up to me…"

His eyebrows rose half an inch.

"Do you have plans Saturday night?" she asked.

"Uh, no."

She tried not to smile at his uneasiness. He thought she was going to ask him out. Well, she was, in a sense, but probably not in the way he thought. "I have one of those 'having someone else there would be better' situations." They'd saved each other before, and she prayed he'd agree to this one lousy evening.

He smirked begrudgingly. "I'm getting excited already."

"My mom invited us over to meet the love of her life. Drinks, dinner, awkward chatter." She widened her eyes. "Please, go with me."

He lowered himself to the arm of the old love seat, grinning and shaking his head. "That's pretty harsh punishment."

"Will you do it?"

He studied her before taking a deep breath. "Why not? I could use a night of misery, myself."

"We'll call it even, then."

He'd be even more miserable when he found out Trent would be there, too, but she'd deal with that when it was too late for him to turn back. Like when they knocked on her mother's door.

"You realize this is going to be hell, don't you?" Carey asked Devin as they drove to her mom's house to meet her new boyfriend.

"Of course. You warned me."

She took a deep, silent breath. "Trent will be there."

He stared at her, and she braced herself to be kicked out of the truck and sent on her way. Instead, he raised his right shoulder in a half shrug. "We'll be fine. I'll ignore him."

He'd do what? Was the earth flipping off its axis and tumbling through outer space?

Well. She'd take the break, if Devin and Trent

could, indeed, ignore the animosity between them. The evening would be bad enough anyway.

She watched him as he concentrated on driving. God, he looked good tonight. He'd actually gone out of his way to look nice, which was rare. He wore a pair of khaki shorts and a white polo, which accented the golden color of his skin from time spent in the pool. He'd even shaved before he'd picked her up, and she wondered what it would be like to kiss him without all the stubble. Not that she didn't like his whiskers, but she had the urge to explore the clean-shaven planes of his face. His eyes darted toward her as if he sensed her staring at him, taking inventory.

"My mom will be in rare form," she said to distract him.

"Yeah. Should be interesting. I've never actually had an entire dinner with your mother."

Pretty sad, but it was true. In all the years they'd been friends, the most he'd experienced of the glory that was Penny Langford Name-of-the-Day Stringer was a passing "goodbye" as she left on a date or a man hunt.

"*Interesting* is one word for it. Although…she seems to be trying to get along with me."

"So it'll just be the four of us?"

"And her latest conquest, Phillip the Stud."

"With a name like Phillip, how can he be anything but studly?"

They shared a look, and Devin wagged his eyebrows, making her laugh.

As they pulled into the driveway of the tiny shoebox of a house her mother had rented since her last husband ditched her, the knot in Carey's stomach tightened.

Maybe inviting Devin was dumb, considering the mutual animosity between him and Trent, but she hoped if an outsider was present, maybe her family would leave her alone about the whole lack-of-a-father thing.

So much for trying to keep her blood pressure down.

She grabbed Devin's arm as they strolled up the walkway to the front door. "Wait," she said, pulling him to a halt. Her breast brushed his arm as he turned to face her, and she felt heat shoot up her insides. The desire to mold herself into him, to feel his breath on her lips, was almost overwhelming.

"Yes?" He glanced down at her chest as if he, too, had noticed the contact and its aftereffects.

Letting out a shaky breath, she took a second to remember what she'd wanted to say. "I…just wanted to warn you the whole topic of me being a single mom is still…touchy, to put it mildly."

"I won't mention it." He took her elbow as they ascended the concrete stairs.

"Well, look who's here," her brother said from the screened front door.

"Trent," Devin said stiffly.

Ah, perfect. The evening was deteriorating before they could even set foot inside.

"Colyer." Trent's chin notched higher in challenge and Carey wanted to push him out of the way.

Instead, she merely pulled Devin past her brother into the house. The air was stuffy, and not just because of the company. The temperature had to be at least ten degrees warmer than it was outside. Thanks to the thermal heater in her stomach, Carey was already over-heated.

"Hello, sweetheart," her mother called from the kitchen.

"Mom?" Carey walked out to the kitchen to find her. As she rounded the corner into the tiny room, they nearly collided. Her mom, in a pair of white linen shorts and a red sleeveless shirt with thong sandals showing off red polish on her toenails, looked even younger than usual and…happy.

"I'm so glad you made it."

She pulled Carey into an uncharacteristic hug. Over her mother's shoulder, Carey's gaze rammed into a hulking man who must have stood about six-five and four feet across. He wasn't overweight, just so large it didn't seem there was room for him in the miniscule kitchen. His graying hair was becoming, and his smile seemed genuine. Laugh lines surrounded his eyes. There was a grittiness around his edges that suggested he didn't do office work, and Carey remembered her mother saying he was in construction. His skin was dark, roughened from what she guessed was a lifetime of working out-doors. This man wasn't her mom's type at all.

She cleared her throat, waiting to be introduced to him.

"Carey, meet Phillip Weisbrenner. My beautiful daughter, Carey, and this is Devin…"

"Colyer," Carey reminded her.

They exchanged greetings, and Carey could barely take her eyes off her mother's beau. It wasn't only his looks that attracted her attention, but his manner, his overall attitude. He had an energy that suggested he enjoyed life. Based on her impression after the first five minutes, she suspected he was a well-adjusted human being, which was a whole new concept for her mom.

Nearly every other man she'd dragged home over the years had screamed complex unresolved issues. It had usually taken Carey about a week, max, to figure out exactly what was wrong with each one. Among her mom's collection there'd been at least one alcoholic, a freeloader and one with an ego the size of Texas. And those were just the ones she'd married.

She truly wondered how her mother had snagged this one. And how long it would take for the bliss to come to an end and her mom to find herself alone yet again.

"Why don't we go out to the backyard and get comfortable? Phillip has agreed to grill steaks. He can watch the grill while we talk."

Carey said a double prayer of thanks, both for the escape from the stifling kitchen and that her mom wasn't cooking. Before leaving the kitchen, though, she sent Devin out and grabbed a beer for him and a glass of lemonade for herself. A good hostess her mother would never be.

On her way out, Trent caught up with her. "I thought you told me you and Colyer weren't an item." His voice was friendly enough, but the question irked Carey anyway. Possibly because she wasn't sure *what* she and Devin were.

"We aren't. Like it's any of your business."

He watched her closely.

"What's it to you, anyway? Why all the concern about my love life? I feel like I'm under a magnifying glass all of a sudden."

He looked down at his feet. "I worry about you is all."

"Worry about me, fine, but don't act like a dictator. You've never been this way, Trent. Devin and I are close, as we have been for years. He's not going away." She started to walk off.

"He's not going to fall in love with you."

She couldn't believe what she was hearing. "Who said I want that?"

"You're going to have a baby. It's natural for you to want this guy to fall into the daddy role."

"Fall into the daddy role?" Carey had to fight to keep her voice from rising. "You think I'm trying to get Devin to marry me? You couldn't be further from the truth."

"If I'm wrong, I'm sorry. But that's how it looks from here when you suddenly start staying out all night with him."

"I was helping him take care of his grandpa."

Surprise registered on Trent's face, but Carey didn't care. He obviously had some kind of ax to grind, and she was the lucky grindstone.

"Kids?" Their mother's cheerful voice singsonged from the patio, signaling their absence had been noticed.

Trent started toward the back door.

"Wait," Carey said quietly. "There's one thing I want to get straight."

He stopped.

"Devin means a lot to me, regardless of what role he plays in my life. He's been here for me while you were in Alaska, out of touch. If you care as much about me as you say you do, you should be grateful to him, not hateful."

He stared at her as she strode past him to the backyard.

When dinner was ready nearly an hour later, Carey was shocked the evening was going so well. Her mother had made polite conversation about things other than herself, Trent and Devin were playing nicely for the most part, and she was discovering she genuinely liked Phillip.

She stood near him at the grill, holding a large platter for him to place the meat on. "You know my mom's a horrible cook, don't you?"

Phillip smiled back. "She mentioned that several times. I haven't had the pleasure of experiencing it firsthand though."

"These steaks look great." She started to carry the platter of beef inside when he stopped her.

"I'll take that. Pregnant women shouldn't have to lift a finger." His expression was kind as he took the plate. He was one of the few people who'd gotten past the idea that she was single and pregnant. Instead of acting as though her life was doomed, he'd shown interest in her baby, sharing stories about his granddaughter when she'd been an infant.

Minutes later, they sat scattered around the living room, eating off TV trays since the kitchen table could only seat four. The house didn't have a dining room. Carey frowned as she tried to cut her steak into bites, the tray wobbling back and forth along with the knife.

"All we need now is paper plates and plastic utensils," Phillip joked as he watched her struggle, then turned his attention to his own battle.

"We'll have more room soon," her mom said, and Carey looked up, puzzled by the comment. "You want to tell them?"

Phillip shook his head. "Your family. You share the good news."

Oh, boy. Carey instantly knew where this was heading.

"Phillip and I are getting married," her mom announced proudly.

Carey wasn't sure what to say. Congratulations seemed insincere, and best wishes were kind of pointless, considering her mother's track record. "Good luck" would be most appropriate.

Trent was quiet as well, and she could tell when she glanced at him he had similar thoughts. The silence dragged on, but she couldn't seem to form any words.

"Congratulations," Devin said heartily, and she breathed a sigh of relief. He stood and crossed the small space to shake Phillip's hand before resuming his place next to Carey. "When's the big day?"

Carey knew Devin didn't really care, but he came across as sincere, for which she was appreciative.

"Seven weeks away," her mom replied. "We'll have an outdoor ceremony at Phillip's home, which will soon be my home, too. I'm moving in with him in a couple weeks when my lease runs out here."

"Well, Mom," Trent finally spoke up, nodding at her. "Phillip, good luck." He got up to shake hands. "I know from experience, she's difficult to live with. But then, from what I've seen, most women are." The two men shared a laugh, and Carey wondered exactly what experience her brother had had of living with a woman—unless he meant her. The brunette from the Alaska pictures flashed into her mind.

When Trent sat back down, everyone seemed to focus on Carey, waiting for her to comment. "Phillip, you seem like a good guy," she said. She turned to her mother. "Hold on to him, Mom."

"I fully intend to." Penny wound her arm around Phillip's. She looked up at her fiancé and smiled. The warmth and affection that passed between them surprised Carey. She didn't remember ever seeing her mother share something like that with a man. Usually, from Carey's viewpoint, Penny's relationships were one-sided.

"We like to think we're finally old enough to figure this marriage thing out," Phillip said. "Banking on the ol' 'practice makes perfect' adage."

This man had potential. His feelings were obvious from the wide smile on his face and the light in his eyes. She only hoped it was real and her mother wouldn't end up disappointed once again.

An hour or so later, Carey, Devin and Trent decided it was time to leave the older couple alone. After-dinner conversation had been surprisingly pleasant, and maybe Carey was paranoid, but she figured the sooner they got out of there, the less chance there was for things to go south.

"Thanks for dinner, Mom," Carey said. "And for cooking it, Phillip. You'll complement Mom nicely in the kitchen. Or should I say you'll complement her nicely if she stays *out* of the kitchen."

"Listen to the expert," Trent said lightly. "She takes a couple of cooking classes and watch out world." He stepped toward Phillip and shook his hand. "Congratulations again, sir." Then he turned to Penny. "Fifth time ought to be the charm, right, Mom?"

Penny's grin froze, and panic flashed through her eyes. She glanced up at Phillip nervously, and Carey followed her gaze.

Phillip's brows dipped low on his forehead and he shot a questioning look toward her mom, who effectively dodged it.

Something was amiss here, and Carey didn't care to hang around and find out what. She moved toward the door, dragging Devin with her. "Bye, Mom, Phillip. Have a good night."

When she looked over her shoulder at the couple inside the door, she could tell they were going to have anything but. Carey had just started to believe her mom might have a chance at a happy ending.

LESS THAN two hours later, Carey sat at the kitchen table at Trent's. Her brother had gone out for drinks with an old friend, so she had the place to herself. Just her and a heaping bowl of mint chocolate chip ice cream drenched with peanuts and whipped cream. She had the rough draft of a brochure for her wedding photography business next to the bowl, intending to proof it.

She'd just dug her spoon in to savor the first bite when she heard a knock at the door.

She wasn't surprised to see her mother standing there, eyes red rimmed but dry.

"He doesn't want me anymore," Penny said in a quiet voice.

Carey backed up to let her mom in. She'd been through this scene many times before with her mother, but for once, she didn't feel angry. She wasn't sure why.

"What happened, Mom?" Carey led her to the table and they both sat.

"I hadn't exactly told Phillip how many times I've been married. He only knew about two husbands."

Carey shoveled a bite of dessert in her mouth before answering. "Uh…Mom? Why would you lie about something so important?"

"I didn't lie, really."

Carey hopped up. "Want some ice cream?"

Her mom nodded. "Not as much as you have though."

Carey took a bowl from the cabinet and scooped out a small serving. "How did you not really lie about having four previous husbands?"

She set the bowl in front of her mom and lowered herself into the chair again to indulge.

"He's never asked how many times I've been married. He asked me if I'd been married. I said yes. He asked about the man I'd been married to, and I told him about your father. And then I told him about Norm. Somehow the subject got changed, and we never finished the discussion."

"So he assumed they were the only two." Carey spooned some whipped cream out of her bowl. "You should've told him, Mom."

Her mother barely touched her ice cream, pushed it away. "I meant to. But there was never a good time. What was I supposed to do? As we walk out of a movie say, 'By the way, besides Robert and Norm, I've also been married to Jack and Ronald'?"

Carey shrugged. "You're asking the wrong person for relationship advice."

Her mother stood and paced across the kitchen. "I'm afraid there isn't any relationship left." Her voice was uncharacteristically quiet. Normally in breakup situations, she was in near-hysterics by now.

Carey was torn between feeling sad for her mom and wanting to shake her and say, "What did you expect?" Who could blame Phillip for bolting when he was hit over the head by such a whopper?

But she'd seen how different her mom had been around him. In past relationships she'd been blatantly insecure, paranoid, just waiting for the guy to walk out. With Phillip, she seemed more…grown-up. Less clingy. Like maybe she was finally learning how to do the whole love thing.

But apparently not. Because here she was, hanging out with her single pregnant daughter, and Carey couldn't shake the feeling that her mother would never learn. That she might as well give up on true love.

CHAPTER EIGHTEEN

"DON'T YOU DARE pack my Gwyneth Paltrow movies!"

"Why would I take any of those?" Carey said, looking up at Trent from the floor in front of the entertainment center. "If I were going to steal something, I'd take someone with talent." She rolled her eyes.

"Blaspheme." He perched on the edge of the couch and watched her sort through the mass of videotapes and DVDs the two of them had acquired. "So you're really going to do it, huh?

The friendliness in his tone surprised her. They'd hardly spoken since that dinner several days ago at their mom's house. "Do what?"

"Move out."

"Yep. I'm moving to my doctor's garage apartment—not far from here." She didn't know why she offered that tidbit, to appease him or reassure him.

"You don't have to go."

"Actually, I do." Jeeves crept up and stuck his front paws on her thigh.

"Have you given this serious thought, Carey?"

"Have you?" she asked. He surely couldn't believe

living with her and a newborn baby would be a good thing. "Do you know how many times a night a newborn cries?"

"I have a pretty good idea." An odd look settled on his face.

She stroked the cat absently, searching Trent's face. "Brother of mine, is there something you're not telling me? You got a couple of kids stashed away somewhere?"

He whipped his head up quickly, then forced a smile. "No." He joined her on the floor and helped her sort the tapes. The feline sauntered off, too good to be second in line for Carey's attention. "I'm sorry, Carey."

"For what?"

"For…everything, I guess. I haven't been myself."

"No, you haven't. You've been kind of a jerk."

He chuckled. "One of the things that makes you you. Total honesty."

"What's going on?" she asked, peering at him over the half-full moving box. "Something's different."

He sighed. "I'd rather not get into it."

"Not going to work this time. Tell me, Trent."

He became engrossed in sorting his movie titles according to genre, and Carey let him ignore her for several minutes. "It has to do with the brunette in the pictures, doesn't it? Erin?"

His head shot up. "What makes you say that?"

She held back her victorious satisfaction at his telling reaction. "I can just tell."

He leaned back against the couch, fiddling with a sci-fi flick with giant insects on the case. "I was engaged to Erin."

Carey thought her eyes might pop out of her head. *"You were engaged?"*

He nodded slowly.

"And you didn't tell me?" She crawled across the floor and planted herself next to him. "What happened?"

He tilted his head back, resting it on the couch, his eyes closed. "It didn't work out."

"Man of many words, would you care to elaborate?" His mood had suddenly become morose.

He opened his eyes and looked directly at her. "Not really."

"Tough," she said. "What happened to Erin?"

"She was perfect for me," he finally said. "She was up there doing the same thing…guiding fishing expeditions. She's a natural. Never met a woman who could fish like her."

"I've never met a woman who wanted to," Carey said dryly. "Anyway…so she seemed like your dream woman…"

He nodded. "I fell hard. We spent more and more time together and eventually became involved."

"You slept with her," Carey interpreted, knowing her brother wasn't the type to go to bed until his heart was into it.

"We were inseparable. I thought life couldn't get

any better." He paused. "Then she got pregnant. Since I was head over heels, it didn't faze me at all. I proposed and she accepted."

The news staggered Carey. To think she'd almost had a sister-in-law was one thing, but becoming an aunt…and she'd known nothing about it.

"She lost the baby at eleven weeks. Two weeks later, she told me she didn't love me, wasn't sure if she ever had. She'd been willing to marry me for the sake of the child, but since the baby was gone, she was ready to move on."

"Oh, Trent." Carey placed her hand on his arm instinctively. "That's terrible."

He didn't speak, merely nodded his head.

"How long ago was this? Is that why you came home so suddenly?"

"She went back to Virginia a couple of weeks before I came home. I tried to hang with it, tried to tell myself it didn't matter. But I couldn't do it. Everything reminded me of her."

"So you came back," Carey said unnecessarily, "and found your sister pregnant. That must have been a bizarre déjà vu."

"That's one way to put it. You were just about as far along as she would've been. If you were happily married, I'd be thrilled to death."

Understanding dawned on her. He'd done what he thought was the right thing by asking Erin to marry him. Leaving a woman to be a single parent was not an option in his mind. But of course, he had clearly loved Erin, too.

He was confusing her situation with his own. Proposing to Erin had been as natural for him as breathing. What he didn't comprehend was that she didn't love Jerod. She'd made a major mistake, but marrying Jerod, even if he wanted to marry her, would be an even bigger one.

"I'm sorry you had to go through that," she said sincerely. Erin had broken his heart. He was still hurting, and that had to be a large part of the reason he'd been such a bear to live with. "You know, the pregnancy is really the only part of my story that's close to yours."

"What do you mean?"

"I mean I made a big mistake. Terrible judgment. That's the reason I'm looking single motherhood in the face."

"Oh, so this is about you deserving to pay for screwing up?"

"No. I don't consider it paying, Trent. I'm going to have a baby—a girl, by the way. I love her already." She couldn't hide a smile. "I never in my life imagined having to raise a child alone, especially after growing up without a dad." She stood and paced. "It's not ideal. But it's my reality. I want to surround this child with people who love her and cherish her. I think it's wrong to force the father to stick around, either by marrying me or otherwise, just so she can say she has a dad."

Trent didn't look convinced.

"We both know Mom wasn't the best at being a single parent, but it could've been worse," she said.

"It can always be worse."

This wasn't the brother she used to know. Erin had done a number on him. He seemed older, wearier... jaded.

"Well," she said, realizing she wasn't going to convince him today that she was making a wise choice, "all I can say is that I'll do the best I can."

Trent was quiet while Carey closed the box she'd stuffed her movies and CDs in, rolling a strip of packing tape across the top. As soon as she set the roll of tape down, Jeeves hopped up to claim the box for his nap.

"This whole moving-out thing," Trent began. "You're not doing it just so you can spend more time with Devin, are you?"

She stared at him in disbelief. "Why can't you let that go?"

Shrugging, he answered, "I know you care about him, Carey. It's obvious. I can see why you wouldn't feel comfortable having him over here."

She threw her arms up in frustration. "For your information, I've never slept with Devin. This decision isn't about him. If you'd open your eyes, you'd see I'm trying to make the best decision *for my daughter.* Trying to be responsible. I'm not dwelling on what should or could have been and how things should've worked out with Jerod. I'm moving forward the best I know how. I suggest you try to do the same. You're stuck on the past, Trent. Devin hurt your little sister *years* ago. You still hold it against him. Erin stole your heart. You still wonder how you could've changed things, how you could've made everything all better. But you can't. Some things you just can't fix."

"I'm not trying to fix anything."

"Let them go, Trent. Be sad about Erin, but try to move on."

She plucked Jeeves off the box and took him with her to her room so she could pack the rest of her belongings. As she shut the bedroom door, she was strangely calm. Saying her piece felt good.

As she flopped on her bed, letting the cat scurry to the pillow, she realized she really was moving in the right direction. She felt sure of it. More sure of herself. In spite of Trent's disapproval, she knew she would do her very best as a single mom.

"COME ON, Carey, answer the door!" Devin stood impatiently outside the garage apartment he'd helped her move into the day before. It was just after 11:00 p.m.— usually Carey was a night owl. He was frantic to see her, but if he pounded any harder, he'd wake up the neighborhood. Her phone apparently wasn't hooked up yet, and her cell phone was turned off. Just when he needed her most, she was unreachable.

Finally, the outside light next to her door went on,

and she pushed the curtains aside to look out. He heard her unlock the door, and then it swung open.

"Devin? What are you doing here?"

He walked into the dark kitchen without a word, and she closed the door behind him.

"What's wrong?"

He sucked in a long breath. "Gramps. He…he's dead." It was the first time he'd said it aloud, and it was even harder than he'd expected. His throat threatened to swell shut with the effort of holding so much back.

"What?" The shock in her voice matched his reaction when he'd gotten the news.

"Tell me what happened." She took his hand in hers.

Devin moved toward her automatically, stood inches away, and he was glad it was dark, because his emotions were on overdrive. "I called him this evening several times and got no answer. I finally had a neighbor go over and check on him. She found him on the kitchen floor, next to a shattered glass of juice." His voice wavered. The thought of Gramps shuffling through the kitchen with his OJ, his oxygen cord trailing behind him, was too much. Imagining what had happened was unbearable. "He had a heart attack."

Carey wrapped her arms around his waist, pulling him to her. Grateful for the contact, he held on, lost, wishing she could lessen the pain.

"I'm so sorry," she whispered after several minutes. She sniffled. He'd only been semi-aware she was crying. "I know how important he was to you."

He nodded. There was nothing to say, nothing he could think of to make this go away. He wished for a phone call from the neighbor saying it had all been a mistake, that Gramps, the old man who meant the world to Devin, was alive and well.

Carey ran her hands up and down his back in an attempt to soothe him, and although he didn't think he'd ever feel good again, he didn't want her to stop touching him.

"What else did they tell you? Do they know when it happened?"

"This morning sometime. They think he died instantly."

"Then he didn't suffer." She said it softly, as if she was reassuring herself.

He wasn't comforted by the notion. They could say Gramps hadn't suffered, but who really knew? His grandpa might have been in pain all night. Maybe he'd had chest pains for hours before the big one. He might have known what was going on. He was stubborn enough to refuse to call Devin or to ask anyone else for help. He wouldn't want to be a burden. Devin squeezed his eyes shut. *Gramps, I would have been there for you.*

"That doesn't really help much, does it?" Carey said quietly. "Come in the living room."

As he followed her, he finally noticed what she was wearing by the streetlight shining through the window into the otherwise dark room. He assumed her shorts and tank were pajamas.

"Hell, Carey, you were asleep. I'm sorry to bother you."

"So? Sleep hardly matters when you're going through *this*."

"You're pregnant."

She took two indignant steps toward him. "Devin, I would've hurt you if you hadn't come over. Shut up about the sleep."

He understood her words were sincere. She didn't mind being woken up in the middle of the night because he needed her. For what, he wasn't sure. But knowing she understood what Gramps had meant, even just knowing she'd met the man, gave him a small measure of comfort. Being alone had never bothered him before, but tonight he needed someone. Not just anyone, actually. He needed Carey.

"Make yourself comfortable," she said. "Baby needs a bathroom break."

He stretched out on the couch, intending to make room for her when she returned since it was the only place to sit in the sparsely furnished room.

One of Carey's cats—he could never remember which was which—jumped up onto the back of the sofa near his head. He absently stroked the animal's fur.

In his overwhelming grief, he wanted to take care of everything for Gramps. Get things just the way he would've wanted them. Devin had several phone calls to make but he'd tackle that in the morning.

"Lean up for a second," Carey said, startling him. "Snicket, move over." The cat skittered to the cushion by Devin's feet. Carey sat in the spot where Devin's head had been, her legs in front of her on the old trunk that served as a coffee table. "Lie down again."

She pulled his head into her lap and began running her hands through his hair, rubbing his scalp gently. The only sounds were the soft whir of the window air conditioner and a cricket chirping faintly from some dark corner. Her lap made a firm pillow, and her warmth was calming, reassuring.

After a few minutes, he had to admit her fingers were working magic, helping him relax. They weren't getting rid of the ache in his chest, but he no longer felt frantic and out of control.

She leaned her head against the back of the sofa, her eyes closed. He would have believed her asleep if not for the continued light movements of her fingers. He allowed his eyes to drift shut as well, although there was no chance of falling asleep. His head and heart were embroiled in too much turmoil.

After a long while, her fingers did stop moving and Devin knew she was asleep. He sat up carefully. Staring at her for a long moment, he thought how tired she must be and then to have him wake her up so late. He hated to move her, but she wouldn't be comfortable here all night.

He made his way back to her bedroom and flipped the light on. The blankets on her bed were tangled and thrown halfway across it. Straightening them, he pulled them back so he could draw them over her once he got her in here. Then he turned the light back off and returned to the living room.

His arms under her knees and back, he balanced on the sofa with one knee as he lifted her. Four-and-a-half-months pregnant and she still didn't weigh much. As he stood with her in his arms, she mumbled something indecipherable and rested her head on his shoulder.

Moments later, he tucked Carey into bed and tried to leave. But he couldn't. The thought of being by himself nearly did him in. He kicked his shoes off and crawled under the covers next to her. Sliding close, he put an arm around her just for the human touch. Nothing more.

And he remained like that, not sleeping, trying not to think about guilt or grief, until dawn, when he crept out of bed and went home to start one of the most painful days of his life.

CHAPTER NINETEEN

WHOEVER SAID funerals served as closure for the living was full of crap. When you were drowning in guilt and regret, there was no closure.

Devin stared out the Excursion's passenger window at the scattered headstones, not really seeing anything. Carey had offered to drive from the church to the cemetery after the service, and for once, he'd readily given up the wheel.

"We should go," Carey said in a soft voice.

"Yeah."

He didn't move.

Devin couldn't bear the idea of the final goodbye. Not when he'd blown it so thoroughly during the last weeks of Gramps's life. He wasn't ready to let the man go. Wouldn't ever be ready.

He wished he could have even two months back to do over with Gramps. The old man had tried to tell him, as if he'd known his time was limited. He'd tried to make him see his career wasn't everything.

But Devin hadn't gotten it. Not in time.

Carey appeared outside his door and opened it.

Most of the group from the funeral were already gathered, waiting. Without a word, he climbed down and took Carey's hand. They made their way through the soggy grass in silence. After a night of violent storms, the day had dawned clear, but the air was so thick with humidity Devin could barely get a full breath. Or maybe that was the regret that squeezed his chest.

As they neared the burial plot, Devin glanced around, recognizing many of the faces of those who'd cared about his grandpa. The eighty-somethings, several seldom-seen relatives who'd flown into town, Jerod and his father, most of Jerod's sisters, even Uncle Jonathon. The one missing person was Landon, Devin's cousin. He'd been on a business trip in Europe and, by the time Devin had tracked him down, it was impossible for him to return to the States in time for the funeral.

After Devin and Carey made their way to the front of the group, the priest began speaking. Devin heard none of the words. He focused on the cold metal box in front of him, fighting the regret.

The minutes passed by and the brief ceremony neared an end. As the coffin was lowered into the ground, Devin forced himself to watch. "I'm sorry, Gramps." He couldn't bring himself to say goodbye.

A WEEK AFTER the funeral, Devin figured it'd be a good idea to get back to work. He'd been showing up in his office each day, but he couldn't name one thing he'd accomplished. In a numb haze, he'd been unable to concentrate on anything.

Monica, who'd been keeping the operation together single-handedly, appeared in his doorway, waited until he finished setting up a sales appointment. "I'm going to lunch. Want to join me?"

"Nah, I'm on a roll, relatively speaking. Thanks, though."

She looked as if she was about to say something, then shrugged and left.

Once Monica was gone, the silence seemed to grow. It had never bugged him in the past, but nowadays it felt so heavy, oppressive.

He clicked on the music library on his computer and set it to play some old hard rock from the eighties. Not a chance of anything weepy or depressing with that.

He was flipping through the latest *Info World* magazine, thrashing his head to the beat of the music, when he noticed Carey standing a few feet from his desk. He scrambled to find the mouse and click Pause. "If you didn't look so good, I'd take my damn key back from you," he said sheepishly.

"Nothing quite like Ratt." She shuddered. "Got a minute?"

"Got lots of minutes."

Carey leaned against his desk. "I brought something for you." Suddenly she seemed shy and unsure of herself. She held out a plain blue gift bag.

"What's this for?" Devin took the bag, puzzled.

"Just something I thought you might want. I hope it doesn't upset you."

He opened it and took out something hard that was wrapped in tissue paper. He pulled the paper off to reveal a picture frame. Smooth, dark red wood. He flipped it over and caught his breath.

He and Gramps at the birthday party. Their attention focused on each other instead of the camera.

Devin swallowed hard, overcome by bittersweet love and sadness. His grandpa was so real, so alive in the photo. It seemed impossible that Devin would never see him again.

"Carey…" he forced out. He felt moisture in his eyes as he looked up at her.

"Oh, God. I'm sorry, Devin. It's too soon…"

He sucked in air. "It's good. It's a wonderful picture."

"There were others with you two posing for the camera. They're decent. You both look great. But this one shows more, I think."

He stared at it again.

"You can see the love and the pride in his eyes," Carey explained.

Devin shook his head slowly. "I let him down in so many ways."

"Devin! You absolutely did not."

He shoved his chair back from the desk. Carey was too close. Leaning over, elbows on his knees, he rubbed his hands over his face. "I did. He told me I did."

"No. Gramps wouldn't say that. Wouldn't think that."

Devin told her about the dinner when Gramps had made it clear what he thought of Devin's inability to make it out more often.

"He thought you work too much," Carey said simply.

Devin nodded.

"That doesn't mean he didn't understand. Sounds to me like he was trying to help you, not himself."

"The bitch of it is that I had several chances after that to get it right. But I didn't make more time for him. Now I can't."

"He loved you, Devin. Look at the picture. It's there."

Devin studied it. "I know." He stood the photo up on his desk, lost in memories.

"I have to go," Carey said. "But I wanted to bring this over as soon as I could."

Devin rose and pulled her into a chaste hug. "Thank you, Carey. It's one of the best gifts I've ever gotten." He kissed her temple and breathed in her scent, felt her arms winding around him.

As she pulled away, she pressed her lips to his briefly—too briefly—and left.

He gave thanks silently that she was part of his life.

CHAPTER TWENTY

"THAT WAS Phillip on the phone." Penny poked her head into Carey's tiny, bare-walled bedroom, where Carey and her two cats stretched out on the bed under the ceiling fan in an attempt to cool off. "He wants to talk."

Carey sat up. The older woman's expression was amazingly calm, hopeful. She continued to handle the whole blowup with Phillip better than Carey would've imagined possible.

Her mom had been staying in the extra bedroom for a week and a half now. Ever since she'd had to move out of her rental. She and Phillip had spoken twice, but so far, he had yet to forgive her mother. To Carey's astonishment, her mom hadn't called him once in the month he'd been making her pay. She hadn't ranted on about her woes, although Carey could discern an underlying tension in her, which was understandable and expected. Her mother's maturity, however, as condescending as it sounded, was a surprise.

"That's good news," Carey said. "He's had a chance to think. Now he wants to talk about the future, I bet."

"God, I hope I don't screw it up."

"Mom, you know what you need to do. Just be honest with him."

"Do I look okay?" Penny asked. She wore denim shorts and a flowered T-shirt. Very casual. Non-threatening. "Is my mascara running from the heat?"

"You look great, Mom. Go get your guy." In her heart she wanted her mom to win this time. The woman had had more than her share of disastrous relationships and broken hearts, and, selfishly, Carey wanted the glimmer of hope. If her mom pulled this one off, maybe Carey had a chance to find a happy relationship, too, someday.

"See you later…maybe." Penny closed the bedroom door, and Carey listened for the sound of her car.

The apartment was startlingly silent. There were times in the past few days she'd wished her mom would go away, give her some peace. But now that she was alone, she felt trapped.

The heat didn't help. She'd come home from meeting with a prospective wedding customer to find her air conditioner had quit sometime early in the day. It felt like a sauna in here, even with the ceiling fan on high and all the windows open. Dr. Estes said he'd have it fixed first thing in the morning, after Carey had insisted she could handle it overnight. She was beginning to think she'd been wrong.

Fanning herself with her shirt, she trudged out to the thermostat in the living room. Ninety-two degrees. God almighty, this was absurd. She considered a shower, but…there was Devin's pool. He always told her she could come swim anytime. Besides, this place was lonely.

She dialed his number, digging through her purse for her keys. When his answering machine picked up, she hung up. She still had Devin's key. He wouldn't mind. Her sanity depended on cooling off. She went to the kitchen and added an ice cube to the cats' water bowl, leaving the fans on for the furballs. They'd probably sleep through the rest of the heat wave just fine.

Twenty minutes later, she looked out the sliding glass door that opened onto Devin's deck. Over the railing, she could see the far end of the pool below, illuminated by an underwater bulb. And then she spotted him in the water, facing away from her, resting with his arms hanging over the edge. In the darkness she could just make out the heaving of his broad shoulders as if from vigorous exercise.

She opened the door without a sound, without him noticing, and walked to the edge of the deck. With a splash, he dove under the previously calm surface of the water, pushing off the side. His body glided in her direction, his outline clear from the light behind him. He began swimming an even, graceful crawl stroke, and she started down the stairs. She took off her T-shirt and shorts and wrapped her towel around her swimsuit.

She loved to watch him swim. He did an underwater turn at the side closest to her and skimmed away, seemingly without effort. The gentle splashing mesmerized her, and she lowered herself to the cement a few feet from the pool's edge. A soft breeze rustled in the trees that grew around the perimeter of the yard. She inhaled deeply—chlorine, blooming flowers, dampness. Summer. A rare serenity seeped through her.

She counted his laps, knowing he wouldn't stop for some time. Devin challenged himself in the pool, just as he challenged himself in every other facet of his life.

Somewhere in the thirties, she lost count and patience. As he swam away again, she dropped her towel and lowered herself into the refreshing, cool liquid, thankful for the reprieve from the heat.

She stood in thigh-high water, directly in his path. He wore goggles, but apparently he didn't see her until he was a few feet away. He popped out of the water, sputtering, whipping the goggles off his head.

"Dammit, woman, are you trying to give me a heart attack?" He was breathing hard, watching her.

She tried not to smile. "You said whenever I wanted to swim…"

"You want to swim, huh?" She tried to dart away, but he caught her around the tops of her thighs and pulled her toward him. "Oh, no, you don't."

She attempted to get her footing, but he scooped her up before she could. He swung her toward the deep end of the pool and let go. She flew through the air as gracefully as a hippo and flopped into the water butt first. When she surfaced, she heard his low, devious laughter from the shallow end.

"You'll pay, Colyer," she said, attempting to sound tough. The smile on her face probably ruined the effect. "And don't you know you shouldn't throw a pregnant woman?"

She pulled herself through the water toward him.

"You're lucky you're pregnant," he said when she grabbed the wall next to him. "Otherwise I would have dumped you in headfirst from the roof."

"You should talk to someone about this violent tendency."

Devin laughed, feeling better than he had for days.

He watched from behind as Carey climbed one of the ladders. She wore a one-piece suit, bright yellow, as plain as could be. But something inside him tightened, speeding his pulse up.

Her wet blond hair draped over her back, pouring water behind her. He had the urge to touch her hair, to touch *her.* He dove underwater and skimmed the bottom down the slope of the deep end, as if to drown the feelings. *She's off-limits.*

He came up for air directly across from where she'd settled on the top rung of the ladder.

"What brings you out tonight? Isn't it past your bedtime?" he asked.

"For one, my mom went to Phillip's. The apartment seemed extra empty and quiet." She swished her hands through the water at her sides. "I think they'll work things out tonight. I'd bet there's going to be a wedding after all."

"Is that a good thing?"

"I'll be glad if they get married. I could do without the wedding itself."

She absently scooped water over her legs and arms. "The other reason I came over is because my air conditioner is dead. It's approaching boiling point in my apartment. Perfect night for a swim."

He nodded. He loved swimming late at night, usually in the buff. He was lucky he'd put trunks on tonight. "Boiling point, huh? Probably not ideal sleeping conditions."

"No, especially when you add in the pregnancy factor."

"Which means?" It was good to have the pregnancy hit over his head repeatedly. Annoying, but good.

"Heat is unbearable. I've been sleeping with the air set on sixty lately."

"No wonder it broke." He'd moved to the center of the pool, treading water a few feet from her.

"Just one of the many side effects of pregnancy hormones." She smiled sheepishly. "The heat thing is definitely not my favorite part."

"What is?"

"What is what?"

"Your favorite part of being pregnant?" The more

they discussed it, the less likely he'd be to make a stupid move.

She looked across the pool into the trees, serious. "I like being pregnant. The idea of having a little living being right here blows my mind." She ran her hand over her abdomen. "I'm never alone. She goes everywhere with me. I feel her move. It's…an amazing thing."

The idea of her cuddling an infant squeezed at something deep inside of him. Something best ignored, especially when he couldn't picture himself at their side.

"Another Langford woman." He shook his head. "God help us all."

She splashed him in the face then dove under, toward the shallow end. She burst from under the surface with a loud sputter, and he chuckled to himself. Graceful in the water she wasn't.

He lay on his back, floating along with his eyes closed as he usually did after a hard workout. Content. The night was perfect and he loved sharing it with Carey.

He had no idea she'd moved from the other end of the pool until he was suddenly yanked underwater by his feet. She let go of him, and he tried to grab her before she swam off but missed, probably because of the half gallon of water he'd swallowed and the other quart up his nose.

"You better watch out," he choked out when he finally stopped spewing chlorine.

An evil giggle assaulted his ears, and he swam steadily toward her. The playfulness in her eyes ignited his raw desire. He'd always loved the expressiveness of her eyes.

He wasn't about to let her get away with a sneak attack though. He lunged toward her and grabbed her, cradling her in his arms.

Stupid move.

Her arms flew around his neck, and she gazed up at him, her lips puckered in an attempt not to smile. The top curves of her ample breasts were exposed, the creamy smoothness of her skin accented by drops of water. He longed to touch his tongue to each droplet, longed to taste her.

"Put me down, Dev. I'm not supposed to roughhouse."

"Don't worry. I won't throw you." He walked down the sloped floor, the water deepening with each step.

"No dunking." She was trying to sound stern, but she kept laughing.

"Sure, Care." He kept walking. The water covered her chest now.

"I'll drag you down with me!"

"Wouldn't be the first time."

Two more steps and her head was underwater. He let go of her, but her arms clung to his neck, and before he knew it, her body slid over his, pushing him horizontally under the surface with her. He expected her to let go, but instead she locked her grip. Struggling to move the weight of both of them, he couldn't set his feet on the slippery slope, so he had to use his arms to pull them both to the shallow end.

She let out a wicked laugh as he finally got his feet securely on the bottom of the pool, keeping his knees bent so he was submerged to his chest. She released his neck and stood up between his knees.

"Which one of us were you trying to drown that time?" Damn if he couldn't erase the feeling of her body stretched out on top of him, moving with him. The contact had made him rock hard. He stood, fully aware his reaction to her would no longer be hidden by the water. He moved toward her until mere inches separated them. Her smile faded as she gazed unwaveringly into his eyes. The playful mood had vanished, and the magnetism between them was undeniable, overpowering.

CHAPTER TWENTY-ONE

UNABLE TO RESIST any longer, Devin bent and kissed her.

He tasted her familiar mouth and caught the slightest hint of berry scent in her hair. Her breath was hot in spite of the cool water. She responded to his touch without hesitation and his chest tightened with emotion at the realization she was willing to give him whatever he wanted.

He wanted everything.

He ran his hands over her bare shoulders and up into her hair, urging her head closer if that was possible.

She grasped his neck, and he plunged backward into the water, carrying her with him until they were submerged to the shoulders. Leaning against the pool wall, he pulled her until she was straddling his lap, his lips never leaving hers.

His hardness pressed against her exactly where he imagined burying himself, separated only by the thin yellow material of her suit and the bulky cotton of his. She strained against him as if she couldn't get close enough.

He had to slow this down or making love to the

woman of his dreams would be over in two minutes and two seconds.

He peeled one yellow shoulder strap down several inches until her breast was free of the suit. Running his palm over it, he relished its fullness, her nipple already erect. He lowered his mouth to the rosy tip and ran his tongue around it. Carey let out a low moan and her head fell back. He teased her nipple, then slowly trailed a line of kisses up to her beautiful neck.

When their lips met again, any semblance of patience or moving slowly had disappeared, and they explored each other's mouths fervently.

Devin slid a hand across her inner thigh and ran it gently between her legs, feeling her heat. She writhed against his hand. He pulled her suit aside enough to push a finger inside her, and she inhaled sharply. The squirming of her pelvis against his hand told him she wanted him as badly as he did her.

His breath was ragged in his throat and his heart raced. He took his hand from her with the thought of stripping the bothersome suit off her. He ran his hand up toward her shoulders.

The blatant roundness of her belly under his fingertips stopped him cold.

He couldn't do this.

There was no denying Jerod's baby between them.

Devin trailed his hand up to her shoulder, hoping she hadn't noticed his hesitation.

He pulled his head back to look at her, emotion

nearly choking him. He grasped her arms loosely, easing away from her, and sucked in a slow, silent gasp of air.

Her eyes popped open. "What's wrong, Devin?"

He pulled her into an embrace, the backs of his eyes stinging.

Dammit!

If he took Carey's body and her heart, then he damn well better be prepared to take her baby, too.

Which wasn't going to happen.

"Devin?" Obviously confused, she slid away from him.

He shook his head, missing the warmth of her body already. "This isn't right."

"What isn't right?"

God, he hated himself at this instant.

"I can't handle anything but casual right now."

It wasn't an outright lie. He couldn't handle a relationship with her right now, and with her, it was all or nothing. But if he told her he was struggling with the baby's paternity, it could have serious repercussions on their friendship. He couldn't lose her.

"I'm sorry. My life is too messed up right now. Getting involved wouldn't be fair to either of us."

Maybe someday he'd be man enough to get past the Jerod thing. Maybe once the baby was born, he could forget who her daddy was.

"I care about you," he said. "But we're not ready for this."

She exhaled slowly. "Devin. I get the picture. You

can shut up already." Her voice was strong and steady, almost had a teasing tone. Almost.

He was a damn clod. Without another minute's hesitation, he eased to the side of the pool and climbed out to the pavement, getting his towel from the table. Eager to put as much distance as possible between them.

He ached with sadness even as his body still pounded with desire.

He sat in the wooden patio chair, drying himself.

Carey, still in the pool, had submerged, maybe to cool her engines, too.

When she finally surfaced, she didn't spare him a look. He craned his neck up gazing at the dark sky. His blood still thrummed through his body at high speed and he was sweating despite having just gotten out of the water.

He heard her footsteps on the pavement as she walked past and picked up her towel, but he didn't look at her. Then she jogged up the stairs. He jumped up, unable to let her leave angry.

"Carey."

She paused at the back door just as he reached the top step.

"Wait."

Her face was blank.

"You okay?"

"I'm fine, Devin." She opened the door. "See you later."

SHE WAS such a fool!

What was she doing kissing him in the first place? It didn't matter who initiated it, she'd wanted it all. Wanted it badly.

Snorting in self-disgust, she reached into the shower in her closet-sized bathroom and turned the water on.

Devin was one hundred percent right they couldn't be together. How could she forget when her tummy stuck out a mile? It should have been as noticeable as a toddler screaming, "Mama!"

Oh, at first when he'd backed off she'd been... *humiliated* was a good word. *Annoyed, hurt,* you name it.

But now that she was home, now that she'd had several minutes to cool off, get her blood to stop centering deep between her thighs where he'd touched her and gather her wits, she felt like kissing Devin's feet in gratitude. Platonic kisses, of course.

But he didn't have to know she was thankful. He didn't have to know anything at all about how she felt.

She tossed her damp suit in the sink, then climbed into the shower.

She could still be angry at the mixed signals—or rather the complete one-eighty—Devin had thrown her way. Seriously, if a female did what he had, she'd be called nasty names.

He'd gotten her so worked up she would've followed him anywhere, given him anything. She'd never

ever felt like that before. Not even with Jerod, and she'd thought he was a good lover.

She had to get her head screwed on straight. Motherhood loomed. To be a good mom, she had to get herself under control. At times that seemed as though it should be simple.

And then there were all the times she was with Devin.

IF BLACK was supposed to make a person look thin, Carey would hate to see herself in any other color right now. The maternity dress she'd ended up buying for the wedding was not flattering. Monica had sworn she looked great when she'd tried it on, but she just didn't see it.

She'd had limited time to shop once Phillip and her mom had patched things up—sixteen days, to be exact.

Most of the long-lost relatives and acquaintances her mom had dug up to attend yet another wedding had no idea Carey was pregnant. She dreaded the inevitable questions about her rounded belly.

Carey finished pulling her hair up in a style off her shoulders, knowing she'd be dying from heat before the vows were spoken, and made her way down from Phillip's spare room. Glancing at the clock on the living-room wall, she realized the ceremony would start in less than forty-five minutes. Thank God. She was ready to have it over with. She felt completely out of her element with these people, three-quarters of whom she barely knew. It was nice that they'd come from out-of-state to support her mom again, she guessed, but she wasn't in the condition to be a good hostess, or daughter of the bride, as the case was.

"Picture time, honey," her mom called. Carey pasted on a smile.

Later, she watched her mother and Phillip exchange vows from the first row and couldn't deny their bond was deep. She longed for her camera to catch the moment on film; there was no way the crabby photographer they were paying would capture their expressions from the distant spot she'd camped out in.

Carey saw love there, security and partnership. She gave in to a smile, her throat tight, though she had vowed long ago never to cry at her mother's wedding again.

THE RECEPTION was in full swing, and a host of forty- and fifty-somethings boozed it up and danced like fools in the backyard. Carey felt dizzy and a little nauseated, probably from the heat and choking humidity. She'd taken refuge on the front porch, sitting on a wooden bench in the dark, to escape the noise.

"There you are," Trent said as he came out the front door. He'd shed his jacket and his shirtsleeves were rolled up. "Saw you disappear a few minutes ago."

"Got a little hot," she said, moving over to make room for him. "So…Mom really looks happy."

He nodded. "Blows my mind. Good for her, I guess."

They sat in silence for several minutes, and she listened to the locusts buzz in the trees. She still felt dizzy, exhausted. She didn't feel comfortable enough in Phillip's air-conditioned house to find a quiet room to hide in, and she wasn't up to making more meaningless conversation with the other guests.

"Colyer going to make it to the reception?"

She shook her head. "I didn't invite him."

"When are you going to tell me what's up between you two?"

"There's nothing to tell."

In truth, she and Devin hadn't had a lot of contact since the night in his pool. The little interaction they'd had was stilted and uncomfortable. Neither of them seemed to know how to act.

She felt Trent watching her, and it made her uncomfortable.

"I think you care more about him than you'll admit."

"Since when are you Dr. Lonely Hearts?"

He smiled. "I will never profess to know much about love, but I do know you. I can tell you care about him. A lot."

"How I feel about Devin is irrelevant. I have other things to worry about right now."

Trent didn't say a word, which meant he didn't believe her.

"I know you think I should wander out into the big world and track me down a husband and father for my baby, but it's not going to happen. I'm trying my damnedest not to put my wants above the baby's needs."

"Have you ever thought you'd be a better mother if you were happy and content?"

"Yeah, I've considered that." She rolled her eyes even though he couldn't see it. "Sounds fabulous. Now tell me how to be happy and content."

"Follow your heart."

She looked at him doubtfully. "Now you're spouting Hallmark-isms?"

"Answer me this. How *do* you feel about him?"

She sagged against the bench, twisting a strand of hair around her index finger and thanking God it was too dark for her brother to notice she was blushing. "He's been good to me since I found out about the baby."

"Are you two closer than just friends?"

"What are you asking me? Have I had sex with him? I told you before, I haven't." Her cheeks heated up and she felt sweat bead on her forehead.

"You can't deny there's some interest."

"Interest?" *Ha.* More like a ton and a half of dynamite centimeters from an unprotected flame.

He crossed his legs and put his hands behind his head. "I may be a dense guy, but there were serious undercurrents between the two of you at Mom's house."

"So?"

"You see him all the time. You can't tell me neither of you notice the energy in the air when you're together."

She leaned forward on the bench. "Yes. Okay. We've kissed. Yes." She turned toward him. "Happy now?"

His slow grin infuriated her. "Why are you fighting this?"

"I've told you. I'm going to be a mom. Now isn't a good time for me to screw up a relationship."

"Maybe you wouldn't screw it up."

"Hmm." She tilted her head and placed her index finger on her chin as if in deep thought. "Yep, I'd screw it up."

"Has Colyer told you how he feels?"

She shook her head. He hadn't said a word, and she wasn't convinced she wanted to know Devin's feelings.

"You make it impossible to have a conversation with you, you know that?" Trent asked.

"Now you know what it's like to talk to *you*."

"Seems to me there's a hell of a lot more brewing between you and Colyer than you'll admit. You're being a chicken. Hiding behind the baby excuse. You've seen Mom screw up a million and one relationships and you're scared to death that's what you'll do, too."

She stuck her tongue out at him. "Anything else, Mr. Outdoorsman-Turned-Shrink?"

"Nah." He grinned. He was having a grand old time with this. "Just that. Being careful's good, but…you've known this guy for years, Carey."

"You want me to have sex with Devin?" *If only he knew.*

"I want you to admit your feelings for him. If you're so sure you can trust him, then trust him."

"Maybe it's not him I don't trust. Maybe it's me."

He stood and took two steps to the porch railing, then turned and leaned against the banister. "So you chose badly with the dad. Look how many times Mom's screwed up. Then look at her tonight. If she'd run scared from this guy, she never would have gotten it right."

"Why are you trying to convince me I love a man you don't like?" Talk about ironic.

"I never said the L-word. Interesting you should choose it though." He looked smug, but also affectionate. "If I could pick who would make you happy, Colyer wouldn't be my first choice. But if he's the one who does it for you, if he can treat you well, I'll get over it."

"I think I liked you better when you weren't talking to me."

He ignored her, completely into his speech now. "You've made changes, I'll give you that. Lots of them. A photography business. Your own place. Hell, you've learned to make toast without burning it." He chuckled. "I'll give you credit for all that, Carey. But…"

Always a but.

"Take the last step. Take the love that's staring you in the face. Don't be such a chickenshit."

She smiled, amused. "Words of wisdom from my dear brother. 'Don't be such a chickenshit.'" She leaned over to peck him on the cheek because she knew he meant well.

"I'm going on a cake run," she said, standing. "Want to join me?"

He shook his head, and she wound around the side of the house to take refuge in a plate full of sugar.

She wasn't being a chickenshit; she was trying to be responsible.

AT QUARTER TO ELEVEN the party was winding down. Guests were scattering—some to bars, others to hotel rooms or home.

Carey's body felt like lead, and she'd ditched her shoes hours ago. She'd finally surrendered to the temptation of the air-conditioning and was camped out in a deep, cushy armchair in the front room.

People worked their way through to the door, saying their goodbyes to her mom and Phillip. She watched them go, two by two. Couples. All of them. Aunt Lorraine and Uncle Harvey. Mr. and Mrs. Friedrickson. Joel and Clara Stubers. Lots of others whose names she couldn't remember. Now she knew how Noah must've felt watching the animals board the ark, two by two. But at least he had his own "other half" to cuddle up with.

Some of them came to wish Carey luck on the upcoming birth. More than one of them shot her a look of sympathy on their way out, and if she wasn't so bone tired, she might have chased them down and beat them with her abandoned shoes.

Her mother disappeared into the kitchen, and Carey decided it was past time to leave herself. If she sat here much longer, she might be convinced to wallow in her post-wedding, woe-is-me, I-want-to-be-part-of-a-couple musings. It *had* been a happy night, but the wedding had tugged on her emotions more than she intended. Weddings and pregnancy hormones did not mix.

She followed her mom to say goodbye. "Great party, Mom."

"It went well, didn't it?"

"Perfect." She sidled up next to her mother at the counter. "I think you finally did it."

"Did what?" Her mom drained the last wine from her glass.

"Found the right one. Phillip is super."

Joy lit her mother's face. "He is, isn't he? I have good feelings about this marriage."

Carey took a thoughtful breath. "You know, I wasn't sure you'd ever find the right man. I'm sorry if I've been less than supportive over the years…."

Penny put her arm around Carey, and she returned the unfamiliar gesture. "I wish I could have found Phillip when you were a child. I think he would have been a good father. Would've made a difference in your life."

Carey shrugged and smiled. "I do okay on my own." She hugged her mother. "I'm happy for you, Mom."

When they pulled away, Penny's eyes watered. "I hope you find someone just as perfect for you, Carey. I mean that."

"You know, I've always thought we were so different. You're so free with your love. I'm…not. But I think we actually do want the same thing."

"Love," her mom said, smiling through tears.

Carey's own eyes teared up then. It wasn't so much the emotional moment with her mother as it was sadness and loneliness.

Carey backed away slowly, wished her mother a good honeymoon and headed for the front door.

CHAPTER TWENTY-TWO

CAREY'S CAR was trapped in Phillip's driveway by three other vehicles. Her shoulders slumped as she stared at the offending heaps of metal. She could either go inside and make a fuss or she could just sit down and wait.

Wandering toward the side of the house closest to the driveway, she found a concrete bench surrounded on three sides by rosebushes. The flowers' sweet aroma permeated the still-warm air as she lowered herself to the hard surface.

From her perch, she could see guests as they left, but she was hidden in the shadows. A couple strolled down the driveway, arm in arm, laughing and discussing the wedding. Engaged, Carey thought. Something about the way they held on to each other and the intangible air of promise about them. Carey smiled, imagining them taking notes for their own big day.

Another couple, older, maybe in their fifties. They held hands and talked so quietly that Carey couldn't make out their conversation. Married, happily, for a long time. She could tell by their familiarity—they seemed to anticipate when the other would speak, take the next step.

She felt an intense longing for that kind of intimacy with another person. Was there room in her heart for more than just a baby? Was there another person on this earth who could, indeed, love her child as much as she did?

If such a person existed, it had to be Devin.

He was the most caring man she'd ever known. Practical, stable, funny, fun. Generous. He knew what it was like to grow up as she had, with a less-than-stellar family life. They understood each other. At some point when she hadn't been paying attention, he'd become her lifeline, her support, the person she was closer to than anyone else.

He was perfect—for her. She suddenly realized she had a goofy smile on her face, and that's when it struck her what a blind moron she was.

Maybe Trent was right. Maybe...she did love Devin.

Holy crap.

Did she...?

And she knew. Her heart expanded, feeling so light, she thought it might flutter out of her chest. Her grin got goofier and she nearly laughed out loud.

She loved Devin.

No wonder she'd been ready to jump into bed with him and have wild, crazy sex—or make sweet, passionate love—whatever he wanted.

Then she did laugh, looking to make sure no one else was around to have heard her.

In light of such a monumental realization, she had a decision to make. She could try to stay away from Devin for the rest of her life. Or she could take a chance on her feelings.

Don't be a chickenshit.

She *was* being a coward. She was a fool to fight her feelings. Trent was absolutely right.

Devin wasn't Jerod. Not even close. She'd never had such a need to open herself and her life up to a man, to become so vulnerable.

She wanted to trust him.

Ached to trust herself.

She could sit here and fret about what he might think or she could charge to his house and put her heart on the line. Tell him how she felt. Take a chance on herself.

Only one car remained behind the Bug. She hadn't even noticed the other drivers leaving. She stood and walked to her car, feeling more energetic than she had all evening. She got in and maneuvered around the Town Car behind her in a creative twenty-five-point turn.

Now that she'd made her decision, nothing would keep her from Devin.

CAREY POUNDED on Devin's front door again, even though she doubted he'd appear. This was the fourth time she'd knocked.

Without waiting, she dug her keys back out of her purse to let herself in. He was in there. Through the tall, skinny window at the side of the door, she could see the faint flickering light of the television at the back of the house.

Once inside, she kicked her horrible shoes off and went to the family room. Mostly likely he'd fallen asleep watching sitcom reruns. She'd wake him. This was too important.

Sure enough, she spotted his bare feet hanging over the end of the sofa. Walking around it, she paused to take in the sight of this man she wanted to be with for the rest of her life.

He didn't wake up. His arms were crossed on his bare chest, his head propped at what had to be an uncomfortable angle on the end cushion. He wore cut-off jean shorts and nothing else. Carey's heart nearly burst just from looking at him.

"Devin," she said in a low voice.

He stirred, but didn't open his eyes.

"Devin, wake up."

He scowled, eyes still closed, and turned onto his side, mumbling something she couldn't understand.

Carey lowered herself to the edge of the sofa and put her hand on his waist. "Devin."

Finally his eyes popped open and he startled a bit when he saw her so close.

Grinning, she stood. "Morning, Sunshine."

Devin glanced toward the window, his brow furrowed, then eased up to a sitting position. He checked his watch. "Looks like it's the middle of the night. Why are you here? And why so damn cheerful?"

"Such a charmer when you wake up."

She ambled to the big, matching armchair and sank into the overstuffed cushions.

"Could we talk?" Her voice sounded tentative even to her ears. She cleared her throat and added, "Without the TV on?"

He stared at her seeming not to really see her, then aimed the remote and clicked the television off. The room became dark.

He didn't seem happy to see her at all. Maybe she should just leave. Sleep on it, see if she still felt the same way in the morning, and, if so, talk to him then. This atmosphere was not ideal.

"Devin."

"What do you need?" His voice wasn't rude or hostile. He didn't act angry. He was just…detached. Apathetic.

"Do you mind if I turn on a light?"

Without answering, he clicked on the floor lamp and she blinked until her eyes adjusted to the brightness.

"Have you been drinking?" she asked without thinking.

"Nope. Just sleeping. A drink's not a bad idea, though."

She jumped to her feet in a burst of energy driven

by antsiness. "You'd definitely be more pleasant if you were drunk. Either that or passed out."

He looked up at her as she stood directly in front of him, and finally, he appeared to focus on her and realize there was another living, breathing being in the room with him. The corners of his lips rose ever so slightly. "Touché."

Devin watched Carey flop ungracefully in her fancy dress next to him and his spirits rose a tad. What the hell was this woman up to? It was after midnight.

"Why are you here, Carey?" She was too close. Too tempting.

She pulled a leg up under her. "I figured you were dying to hear all the details of the wedding." Her words dripped sarcasm.

"How was it?"

"It was…actually pretty good. Happy. Real." She smiled, although she wasn't looking at him, but rather off to the side at nothing. "I had a good talk with my mom. Borderline bonding. There may be hope for us."

There was more contentment in her expression than he'd seen in a long time. She'd never said as much, but he suspected it really bothered her to have a poor relationship with her mother. The urge to pull her to his side and tell her he was happy for her nearly overwhelmed him, but he held himself back.

When she grasped his hand, he didn't take it away. Her mood switched from amused to serious in the time it took him to blink.

Carey took a slow, lung-expanding breath. "So, um, have you ever had one of those lightbulb moments where something suddenly becomes crystal clear to you?"

"Ye-e-e-ah." His reply was stretched out, as if he was suspicious of what she was going to reveal to him. "I guess so."

"I had one tonight."

"At the wedding?"

"Afterward. Outside in the rose garden." She ran her fingers nervously over the back of his hand.

He didn't speak, which made it harder to spit this out.

She took another deep breath, glancing at the ceiling. "I was sitting there watching all the couples leave the wedding. Thinking how nice it would be to have someone to go home with on a permanent basis. And…" She swallowed hard.

"And?"

"I couldn't get you out of my mind."

His face didn't change at all. He just stared back at her.

"I know I'm hard to deal with sometimes and I drive you crazy when I fly by the seat of my pants and you wish I'd be more careful about everything and—"

"Carey. Breathe."

She did. Her chest rose as she sucked in air until she couldn't fit any more in.

She pulled herself toward him and pressed her lips to his, tentatively at first. He seemed to hesitate for a moment, but then he responded and the kiss escalated to white-hot. She slid onto his lap and wound her hands around his neck, not breaking the contact between their lips. Which seemed just fine with him.

Her heart pounded and she felt light-headed. This wasn't going to be so difficult.

She could feel his hardness up against her thigh and she was thrilled to think they would soon be together, physically and emotionally. She wasn't even nervous about making love with him—it felt completely right.

But first things first.

She pulled her mouth away from his reluctantly. Rested her forehead against his.

"Devin?"

His breath was ragged and his "yeah" came out as a croak.

"What I figured out is that I love you." Her words rushed together, but she didn't care. She'd said it.

Judging by the look of alarm on his face, she shouldn't have.

CHAPTER TWENTY-THREE

DEVIN WORKED his way out from under her and paced across the room as Carey's heart sank into her gut. He obviously didn't feel the same way about her, so she'd just ruined everything between them.

She pulled her legs up as close to her chest as she could get them—which wasn't very, thanks to her belly—and tried to form a ball with her body. She was afraid to speak. Afraid to breathe.

Refusing to look directly at him, she sensed he was leaning against the cabinet on the opposite wall, his back toward her. "Devin?"

He didn't answer.

Didn't need to.

She rose slowly, bone-deep weary in every cell of her body. Her throat felt scratchy and dried up. "I shouldn't have said anything. It's clear you don't feel the same. I'll leave."

"Don't."

She froze. His back to her, he stretched his arms over his head, resting them on the top shelf of the entertainment center.

His wide, golden shoulders rose with a heavy sigh and, in spite of the difficulty of the situation, she longed to run her hands up his muscular back and feel the heat of his flesh.

"It's not as easy as you think," he finally said, turning. He took several steps forward and stopped about six feet in front of her. He ran his fingers through his hair and then grasped the back of his neck. She noted his motions as if she was watching a movie she wasn't part of.

"I do feel the same way, Carey."

His eyes pierced hers and she felt tears flooding them. Her throat ached...she sensed a "but" coming.

"I love you." He dropped both hands to his sides. "Dammit. I do."

She looked at him in confusion. He seemed to be arguing with himself.

She couldn't bring herself to ask what the "but" was.

"I want you so badly, Carey. I lie awake thinking about you at night, thinking about what it'd be like to have you in my bed. To wake up by your side every day."

He paced as she held her breath.

She couldn't take the agony. "What is it, Devin? Just say it." A tear fell down her cheek.

He looked down at the floor. "I just can't...the baby...I'm...trying really hard."

The baby. It all made sense in a split second. *The*

baby. It wasn't his. It was Jerod's, and he couldn't handle that.

How could she ever expect him to?

"God, I've tried to deal with it. Tried to find a way to accept your little girl as my own."

Tears seared her eyes and poured over onto her burning cheeks. He couldn't have said anything less fixable than that.

The regret that she'd managed to bury for weeks now, the remorse over her poor judgment toward Jerod, came flooding back. With that single mistake, she'd condemned herself to a life without Devin.

"I want to love that baby growing in your belly as much as I love you. Maybe someday I'll be able to…"

She shook her head slowly, the anguish centering in her chest. "Not good enough."

"I'm sorry." His voice was gravelly with emotion. "It hurts me like hell, too."

The room seemed to close in around her. She had to leave now. "I have to go," she said flatly.

She shuffled to the front door, walking away from the man she'd thought was the best thing ever to happen to her.

Wrong again.

HER BELOVED Bug offered nothing in the way of comfort or reassurance. Carey sat in the driver's seat for several minutes, trying to stop crying long enough to drive.

Devin didn't come out of the house to tell her it was a misunderstanding. To convince her that he'd find his way to loving her baby.

Sucking in a deep breath of thick, damp air, she forced herself to start the car and head home. Biting her lower lip until it was raw, she managed to pull the car into the driveway outside her apartment three minutes later. Her head hurt. But it was nothing compared to the pain in her heart.

She reached the top landing and dizziness made her grab for the railing. She held on for all she was worth. The air was suffocatingly still. She stood there, immobile, trying to regain her bearings.

Finally, she was able to let go and she jammed her key into the lock, then stumbled inside. She made a beeline through the kitchen toward the couch and collapsed.

God, the pain.

How stupid could she be?

What pissed her off the most was that two months ago—two *hours* ago—she'd learned to accept that she would raise her child alone.

Then she'd dared to imagine having a loving, supporting husband to stumble down the path with her.

In a matter of minutes, the illusion had been ripped out from under her, and while someday she would probably be glad she'd found out sooner rather than later, at this very moment, ignorance seemed like bliss.

As she rolled to her side, another wave of dizziness

swept over her, and she grasped the side of the couch in a futile attempt to make the world stop spinning. The headache resurfaced with a vengeance.

Something was horribly wrong with her body.

She thrust her trembling hand out toward where she'd dropped her purse, hoping her phone was inside. Maneuvering herself to a semi-sitting position was a chore, but she pushed up on the arm of the couch anyway.

She called her doctor's home phone, praying he was there, just steps from her back door. He would make everything okay.

He wasn't home. His wife told her he was at the hospital and that she'd have him call her right back. The phone rang within minutes, and when she opened her eyes to pick up the phone, she had trouble seeing clearly. Spots danced in her vision. It was the doctor. In tears, she reported her symptoms to him, the very symptoms he'd warned her to watch for a few weeks ago, willing him to tell her this was normal and that it would subside soon.

No such luck.

He ordered her to get to the hospital immediately. He was gravely concerned about her blood pressure.

For once Carey longed to have her mom take care of her. She nearly dialed her new phone number. But it was her mother's wedding night and Carey didn't want to ruin it for them. Instead, she called Monica, who answered on the second ring, clearly still awake. Carey tried to explain the problem without blubbering.

"Don't move," Monica said. "I'll be there in fifteen."

The line went dead, and Carey closed her phone. Squeezing her eyes shut in an effort to deny any vision problems, she curled up in a ball.

She would die if anything went wrong. Her love for the child was overwhelming. Her future was so tied up in bringing this little one into the world and giving her a happy childhood, she couldn't imagine anything else now.

She'd already suffered one loss tonight. There was no way she could survive another.

IT HAD BEEN dawn for more than an hour when Devin emerged from the shower and threw on clean clothes. He hadn't bothered to go to bed. He'd known there was zero chance of sleeping.

Every muscle in his body screamed, and he hadn't even pulled one of his usual killer pool workouts. He'd merely sat in his family room and watched Carey walk out of his life. He'd brooded on the sofa for hours, unable to muster the energy to try to swim through the ache.

He lumbered down two flights of stairs to his office, not because he thought he'd get a damn thing done. He didn't know what the hell else to do with himself. Without bothering to flick the lights on, he went to his desk and collapsed into his chair.

The look on Carey's face haunted him.

It killed him that he was too weak to be what he wanted, what Carey needed.

She loved him, for God's sake. Carey. The woman he'd wanted for nearly half his life. And he'd rejected her out of…what? Jealousy? Pride? What, exactly, kept him from trying?

Hopeless and weary, he stared at the photograph of him and Gramps. Gramps, whom he'd let down.

And now he was letting Carey down. And himself. This time it wasn't work getting in the way, but his own damn hang-ups.

You'll be much more content with yourself if you give everything you've got to your relationships.

His grandpa's voice rang out so clearly in Devin's mind, he actually turned to make sure he was alone.

What the hell would happen if he actually made an effort to forget about Jerod? If he focused on being the best father to Carey's little girl? If he simply just *tried?*

CAREY WAS nowhere to be found.

Devin had gone to her apartment after spending a good two hours at the lake, sitting on the dock, mulling over the realization he'd had in his office.

What it came down to was that he had to do this. He believed he could. He'd disappointed the most important man in his life by not trying hard enough, and hell if he was going to disappoint Carey. Or himself.

He'd spent his time on the dock imagining the baby, thinking about being a father, picturing how it would be to wake up several times a night to help Carey feed her. He hadn't let himself think about his cousin. Jerod had turned down the chance to be in Carey's and the baby's life.

His loss, Devin's gain.

Devin had knocked on Carey's door three or four times, willing it to open. He'd tried Trent's house. He'd tried Carey's cell phone but could tell from the immediate voice mail that it was turned off. He'd even broken down and tried to track Carey's mother's new phone number but had had no luck. Apparently Phillip's phone was unlisted. Damn inconvenient when Devin had a future to go after.

At a loss, he tried Monica's cell phone for the second time as he drove from Trent's house to who-knew-where.

"Hello?"

"Thank God you answered. I was beginning to think I'd entered some kind of black hole."

"Devin. I was just about to call you. Carey's in the hospital."

Suddenly afraid, his stomach tightened into a knot. He swore crudely. "What happened? Is she okay?" Panicked, he pulled onto a side street to get out of traffic. "What hospital?"

"I took her in late last night. Her blood pressure was sky-high. She's at General. Room 408."

"Shit." Committing the room number to memory, he turned the car toward the hospital. "What's...how—"

"They've been monitoring her all night and it's gone down a bit. Not enough, but they want to give her a few more hours to see if it lowers some more. If not, they'll be forced to do a caesarian."

"Shit, Monica. Shit, shit, shit." He banged his fist on the steering wheel. The compression in his chest intensified.

"Calm down. She's going to be okay."

"You don't know that."

"The way it's lowered is a good sign."

It was because of him. He knew it deep in his gut. It'd been less than ten hours since she'd left his house. The pain had done this to her. Pain he'd caused because he'd been too dense to know what he really wanted. And needed.

"What if they have to do the caesarian?" he asked, a sharp ache spearing his temples. "Can the baby...make it?" His voice was a raspy whisper, foreign to his ears.

"She's twenty-six weeks along. The baby needs to stay in as long as possible."

"But...can she make it?"

"The baby? Yeah. A lot depends on her weight and lung development."

"Like what? What depends on those things?"

He heard Monica sigh. "Devin, you need to ask the doctor these questions. I didn't get a lot of information myself. I was with Carey and her mom and Phillip most of the night, and I didn't want to upset her more than she already was."

His heart hammered out of control. He broke out into a cold sweat. She couldn't lose the baby.

"Where are you now?" he asked.

"I'm heading home to change clothes. We're meeting Kyle's family for his birthday lunch. I was hoping you could stay with her."

"On my way. I hope the sight of me doesn't send her blood pressure back up." He swore to himself again.

"She wouldn't let me call you last night. What's going on between you two?"

"I don't have time to go into it. I need to get to her."

He got on the freeway driving toward downtown, his mind completely focused on Carey and the baby.

"You can't leave me hanging, Devin," Monica said.

"I have to go." He hung up on another plea for information.

Minutes later, he shot into a parking space and jumped out. It was all he could do to keep from sprinting inside. Logically, he knew there was nothing he could do, but he was desperate to set eyes on Carey.

The door to Room 408 was closed, as were most in the labor and delivery hallway. He opened the door slowly. Carey appeared to be asleep, so he moved noiselessly across the room and sat in a chair by her side. She didn't stir.

The sight of her hooked up to machines had a startling effect on him. He'd never been squeamish in his life, but something about Carey being in any kind of danger made him feel like he'd been suckerpunched.

Rubbing his hands over his eyes, he took a deep breath and sat forward, his elbows on his knees, just inches from her. There was no indication of the battle her body fought.

God, please. Let her be okay. Let them be okay.

Her blond hair was tangled. Shadows underlined her eyes. Her lips were parted slightly, and they appeared dry, chapped.

He'd never loved her more. He ached to hold her and soothe her blood pressure down far enough to give the baby more time.

He hated to imagine the alternative. Carey would be shattered if anything happened. He couldn't bear to think of her pain….

Or his own.

The strongest urge came over him—the urge to fend for the child, to keep her safe, to give her the love and security Carey was so focused on providing.

DNA be damned…it didn't matter anymore. What mattered was the child's survival.

He had to make Carey believe his heart was open. To her *and* to their baby.

A FEW MINUTES later, Trent walked into the room gripping a foam cup of steaming coffee. Carey hadn't woken up yet, so Devin merely nodded in greeting.

Trent stood at the foot of her bed for several seconds watching her. His concern was written all over his face. Then he caught Devin's attention and silently invited him to the hallway where they could speak without wakening her.

Hesitating for a beat, Devin wondered if Trent was out to cause trouble, maybe try to make him leave so Carey didn't get more upset than she already was. For once, Devin wasn't sure he could blame her brother.

He followed Trent outside the room and eased the door shut behind him.

"She know you're here yet?" Trent asked.

"No. I just got here. She's been asleep the whole time." He braced himself.

"My mom and Phillip are in the cafeteria. They'll be back up soon."

Devin nodded.

"She cares about you."

Devin slowly turned to meet Trent's gaze head-on. He didn't say a word, wanting to see where he was going with this conversation.

"She didn't want you here last night."

Devin nodded. "We had…a disagreement."

"Any woman who protests that much about having a man visit her in the hospital is in love."

Devin gave a half-hearted chuckle. "Something like that."

"Look, I don't know what's going on between you two, but I do know she really cares about you. And if that's so, then I'll give you the benefit of the doubt. That is, if you really care about her."

Devin sized him up. "I care about her."

"Hurt her and you'll hear from me."

"I have no intention of hurting her."

Trent nodded once. "Let's go back in and make sure Sleeping Beauty's behaving herself."

Making peace with Carey's brother could very well turn out to be the easiest part of his day.

CHAPTER TWENTY-FOUR

DEVIN KNEW the exact instant when Carey woke up, even though she didn't immediately open her eyes. He'd been staring at her for almost an hour, willing her body to heal itself. He slumped on an uncomfortable vinyl-cushioned chair and his feet rested on the bottom side rail of her bed.

Her eyes flickered open and focused on him for a split second, then shut again. He watched her face, and the distress he saw there ripped at his insides.

He stood and leaned over her. "Carey." His voice sounded gravelly, as though he'd just woken up. He only wished this were a bad dream and he *could* wake up.

Her eyes eased open again, but she didn't speak.

"How do you feel?" he asked.

In slow motion, she licked her lips and cleared her throat. "Scared shitless." Her raw honesty choked him up. He read unmitigated fear in her face.

Sitting on the edge of the rock-hard bed, he grasped her hand, aching to do anything that would help her. "Do you need something? A drink of water?"

She nodded, and he jumped up to fill a cup from the pitcher on the table. As she maneuvered herself upright, he held the cup to her lips.

"I wish you'd let Monica call me last night. I would've been here in a second."

It suddenly occurred to him that maybe it was best the way things had happened. If he'd spent the night in a vigil by her side, he might not have figured out his future was with Carey.

"Didn't want to bother you." She seemed like a stranger, ill at ease with him near.

Devin dropped the subject. This wasn't the time to scold her for anything. Now was the time to help her get better.

He wanted to tell her everything he'd figured out in the past few hours about being a father to her child, but he didn't dare bring up any of their personal problems here. Not now. Not in the state she was in.

All he could do was sit here holding Carey's hand.

He regretted he'd taken so damn long to see the light. Why couldn't he have figured it out before last night? If he had, if he'd been able to take Carey into his arms when she'd told him she loved him, she might not have wound up here in this cold, sterile room, fighting for her health and her baby's life.

He tried to swallow the lump in his throat. He needed to be strong for Carey now. To help her believe everything would turn out okay.

As soon as she was stable and he could take her

home, he hoped he'd be able to convince her they had a future together.

Carey closed her eyes again. Devin was the last person she wanted to see. It hurt too much. She fought against the tears forming beneath her eyelids. Didn't he realize how much the sight of him tormented her? The pain of last night was as fresh as if it'd just happened.

But she wasn't about to admit it.

She had to put him and the turbulence he caused in her heart to rest, had to block them out, because her tiny baby was depending on her body for a few more weeks in the womb.

Carey focused on breathing deeply and evenly, hoping Devin would move off her bed, figure she was asleep. When she finally heard him shift to the chair again, she turned over carefully, attempting not to jostle any of the monitors and cords she was hooked up to.

Her baby had been her priority for weeks, and now the child was all she had. She resumed her deep breathing and alternated breaths with pleas to the powers that be that her little girl would be okay.

HOURS LATER, the nurse finally worked up Carey's discharge papers. Her blood pressure had gone down significantly, thank God. Dr. Estes had sentenced her to full bed rest for the remainder of the pregnancy. She had no idea how she'd manage lying around for ten weeks, but she'd do it somehow if it would give the baby more time to develop.

She'd never been so overcome with relief.

Devin hadn't left her side since he'd arrived. She wasn't sure how she felt about that. She'd finally sent her mom home to get ready for her honeymoon. Carey had called her a few minutes ago to tell her and Phillip to go ahead and get on the plane.

"Doc wants you in bed or on the couch all the time. You can get up to pee," the nurse said harshly. It was an act, Carey knew, because throughout the day, the older woman had proven she was a sweetheart with her caring attentiveness. "You'll need someone to take care of you. No cooking, no walking, no working, no sex." She trained a meaningful look on Devin, and Carey resisted the urge to correct the nurse's assumption they were a couple.

"Don't worry," Devin said. "She won't lift a finger."

The nurse went over the discharge papers with her—with them, actually, since Devin hung over her shoulder like a meddling grandmother. Carey signed them and moved to the edge of the bed to get up and dress.

Devin handed her the clothes her mom had brought in, his gaze fixed on her protruding abdomen. Instead of the frown she expected to see, the corners of his mouth actually turned up. "She's getting huge," he said.

She placed a protective hand on her stomach and

couldn't help smiling down at it, imagining the baby who was responsible for her increasingly cumbersome middle. "Grow away, baby," she whispered. The sadness caused by Devin's presence was greatly outweighed by her relief to be going home with her baby still inside her.

Once she'd pulled her clothes on in the private bathroom, she went back to sit on the bed, waiting for the nurse's return as she'd been ordered to do.

"You're supposed to lie down," the nurse said gruffly as she charged back into the room pushing a wheelchair.

"But I'm leaving—"

"Watch her," the nurse said to Devin, but Carey could see a spark of mischief in her eyes.

"I suppose it's out of the question for you to let me walk to the car."

"In the chair," Devin said, his voice stern. His expression softened when she met his gaze though. "Enjoy the ride." He wasn't acting like the man who'd turned her away last night.

Once they were in his SUV, silence settled around them, and the events of the night before taunted Carey. She couldn't ignore reality now that they were out of the sterile hospital.

"Where are you taking me?" she asked.

He glanced over at her. "To your apartment so you can pack your bags."

"I'll stay there until Trent can come get me."

"I'm not about to leave you alone. Either you can pack your bags and stay at my house, or I'll wait with you."

She sighed. Arguing about it wasn't worth the effort or the upset. He could hang around if he wanted to, but she intended to ignore him.

The more she was around Devin, the harder it would be to remember… It would be far too easy to let herself believe everything was hunky-dory if she let him take care of her. No matter how tempting the delusion was, her heart couldn't afford it. She wished she hadn't given her mom the go-ahead quite yet. Carey hadn't been thinking about who would get stuck waiting on her.

He reached across the front seat and grasped her hand. "We need to talk."

Rehashing the dead end they'd arrived at last night was the last thing she needed. She couldn't afford to get worked up. "Please, Dev. Let it go."

"Will you give me a chance, Carey? I promise I won't do anything to upset you. Please."

"I don't want to drag out everything again. There's no point."

"We have some new ground to cover," he said, and she couldn't miss the faint smile on his face.

Intrigued, she sat back and stopped arguing. She was curious enough she'd hear him out, although there was very little he could say to change their situation. If she felt her stress level rise, she'd call Trent or Monica to get her out of there right away.

As they pulled up into the driveway, Devin spotted

a familiar car parked in the street. Instead of the annoyance and combativeness that normally struck him at the sight of his cousin, he felt strangely calm, albeit protective of Carey.

"What's he doing here?" she asked, apparently noticing Jerod, too.

"We'll find out. Try to stay calm."

He got out and walked around to her side to help her down from the high seat. Jerod approached from the street. Instinctively, Devin put an arm around Carey's waist.

"Hello, Jerod," she said as he neared.

"Carey." He nodded at her. "Devin."

"What's going on?" Carey asked.

"I'd like to talk to you…to both of you, actually. Could we go inside?"

Devin and Carey exchanged a brief, puzzled look and she nodded.

"Carey just got released from the hospital," Devin told him, hoping he'd get the clue not to upset her.

Jerod's eyes widened. "Everything okay?"

"Blood-pressure problem," she answered. "It's okay now."

They made their way up the long flight of stairs, and Carey dug around in her purse for the key. She finally located it, and Devin took it from her and unlocked the door.

"Let's go in the living room so Carey can relax," Devin said. "This won't take long, will it?"

Jerod shook his head.

Carey sat at one end of the sofa and Jerod took the other end. Devin remained standing and noticed that Jerod held on to a file folder.

"What's going on?" Carey asked.

"Well," Jerod began. "This is awkward, but what the hell. I'm heading to Oklahoma City to be part of a new station we just purchased. It's a fresh challenge, and frankly, there's no reason for me to stay here."

"Congratulations," Carey said, still looking confused.

"Thanks. Anyway, I'm feeling a little strange about leaving you here with loose ends. I know you don't want anything from me," he added quickly. "But…" He shrugged. "I'm pretty sure I'm missing out somehow. Never thought I'd feel that way. But you've made your wishes clear, Carey, and I intend to honor them."

Devin's dislike of his cousin eased ever so slightly at that moment. "What's in the folder?"

Jerod looked up at him, seeming to size him up. "It's none of my business what's between you two. Doesn't matter, I suppose. But I saw how close you were at Grandfather's funeral." He glanced at Carey. "I've had an attorney draw up paperwork for me to give up all paternal rights."

Devin wasn't sure he'd heard right. Both he and Carey stared at Jerod.

"I don't want you to worry about me having a

change of heart, whether you're with Devin or some-one else. You and I didn't work out, and I might be the loser in that. But. Anyway."

Jerod stood and set the folder on the makeshift coffee table. "I hope that helps you in some small way, Carey."

Devin couldn't help smiling as he looked at Carey. Tears pooled in her eyes. When she met his gaze, he raised his eyebrows in question.

She nodded briefly and started to stand.

"Uh-uh," Devin said, putting a hand out to keep her on the couch. "Bed rest."

She sniffed loudly. "Jerod. Thank you. Kind of odd circumstances, but I appreciate what you're trying to do."

He tried a smile that didn't quite work, then nodded. "I need to go. You'll be one hell of a mother, Carey."

Jerod went outside and Devin followed him, telling Carey he'd be right back.

Once out the door, Devin spoke. "Thanks, man."

"I hope she's okay...."

"She will be. I'll make sure."

Devin stuck his hand out and Jerod shook it.

"Good luck," Devin said.

"You, too." Jerod looked at him strangely, then started down the stairs.

Halfway down, he stopped and turned back to Devin. "You going to marry her?"

"Sure as hell going to try."

Jerod grinned nervously. "Don't invite me to your wedding." Then he took off the rest of the way to his car without looking back.

DEVIN WENT BACK inside, relieved to return to the cooled air after baking in the late-afternoon sun that beat down on the landing outside.

Carey still sat on the sofa. "About that talk. Do you want to rest first?"

"Hell, no. I've been resting all day."

Carey eyed him as he went into her bedroom. Both cats had apparently been camped out in there because they came shooting out at once.

When he returned, he carried a pillow and a fuzzy blanket. She allowed him to fuss over her, arranging the pillow on the sofa's end and holding the blanket up in front of her, despite the fact she sat upright.

"Down," he said.

She complied, stretching out on her side and allowing him to cover her even though she wasn't cold. She was dying to know what he wanted to say. He seemed way too upbeat for it to be bad news.

He sat on the floor, inches from her face, pulling his knees up and resting his arms on them. He took his sweet time to begin speaking, and the suspense drove her crazy.

"Speak," she said. "Say what you want to say before my blood pressure spikes again."

"I'm not sure where to start…"

"The beginning's good."

He drew out a breath, and Carey took in the rugged profile of the man she loved too much. He was close enough she could almost count his eyelashes.

"I had a moment of reckoning this morning," he finally said, still not looking at her. "It finally hit me that the thing I want most in my life is you."

Hope reared inside her and she hardly dared to breathe.

He folded his hands together and cracked his knuckles. He was nervous, which touched Carey immensely.

"You scared me to death today." She could see him struggle to swallow, and he lifted his face. "I love you so much, Care. Seeing you in that hospital knocked the wind out of me. Confirmed how much a part of my life you already are." He reached under the blanket and took her hand. "You...and that little girl."

Her heart thumped in her chest, and she grasped his hand tightly.

"I kept thinking how awful it would be if anything happened to her." He paused as if he had to search for the right words to say. "It would be awful if I could never hold the baby you've been carrying for months."

She understood exactly what he meant, because the same what-ifs had haunted her for the past eighteen hours or so. Her throat tightened in spite of her attempt to stay even-keeled.

"She's become such an inherent part of you. I want you, Carey. All of you. Your laughter, your drama... your daughter. I want her to be *our* daughter."

He rubbed the back of her hand absently. "I swear to you, I wanted this before Jerod dropped his little bomb."

"I know," she said. "I could tell something had changed before he showed up. I just didn't dare to hope..."

He squeezed her hand lightly and his eyes bored into hers. "He's history. He doesn't want the child, but I do."

Tears flooded her eyes as she stopped resisting the hope. "Are you serious?"

He nodded. "More serious than I've ever been."

He propped himself up on his knee, grasping her hand with both of his now. "I want to marry you, Carey. Want to marry you and the baby and be a family."

She saw it in his eyes. Knew it in her heart. If he had any lingering doubts, he would never talk about marriage.

She sat up, not letting go of his hands. "Don't you dare tell me to lie down right now," she threatened. "You have to be sure about this, Devin. One hundred percent sure."

He rose to sit on the couch next to her, his blue-gray eyes not leaving her face. "I've never been so sure about anything." He raised her hand to his lips and pressed a tender yet compelling kiss to the back of it. "Be my wife, Carey." His voice had dropped to a near whisper.

She burst out in something between a laugh and a sob. "Yes! If that was a proposal, this is a yes!" Joy made her feel lighter than air, which was saying a lot, considering how heavy she really was.

He leaned over her, pushing her onto her back. "That was a proposal." He kissed her full on the mouth. "And there's no backing out now. You and the baby are stuck with me." He kissed her again, propping himself up on his knees to avoid smashing the baby in question.

"I want to marry you soon. Want to give the child my name, if that's okay."

Okay? It was a dream come true. For years, she'd yearned for the perfect family she didn't have, never once guessing she already knew the right man to make it possible. "I think that would probably be just fine."

"Probably? Just fine?" He raised one eyebrow.

"Definitely. Perfect."

She pulled him down to seal the deal with a long, soul-baring kiss.

"Welcome home," he said softly. He slid down her body and placed gentle kisses on her abdomen. "And to you, too, little girl. Can't wait to meet you."

EPILOGUE

"YOU...ARE...MINE, sucker," Carey said as she reeled in a hefty bass. The fish flopped against the boat at the water's surface. "Okay, Dev, you're up." She bent and pulled the net out, holding it in his direction so he could take the fish from the line.

"I've got more important things to take care of right now," he said to her. His voice softened, changing to syrupy baby talk. "Isn't that right, Princess?"

Holding the pole with the frisky fish as steady as she could, Carey turned enough to see her husband doing diaper duty on their eight-month-old daughter on the back bench seat. She'd convinced Devin to trade in the fishing boat for a larger, family-friendly one. She couldn't help smiling. She'd never get tired of watching him with Carla. Something about the gentleness of a sexy, muscular man goo-gooing over a baby turned her inside out.

The blasted fish demanded her attention as it thrashed about. Gritting her teeth, she captured it with the net and brought it close enough to study where the hook jabbed at its mouth. She looked over her shoulder again and was treated to a view of Carla's bare behind, legs flailing in the air as Devin cheerfully cleaned her up. "Damn," she muttered to herself. She could see the hook, had watched Devin take them out countless times now, but she'd never done it herself.

Finally, squeezing her eyes most of the way shut, she opened the fish's mouth and twisted the hook out. She rushed to the livewell and dropped the slimy creature in with a shudder. "Did it."

Devin chuckled. "I never thought I'd see the day when your mommy would take a hook out," he said to Carla.

"I could say the same about you and dirty diapers." She grinned when he shot her a shamed look. She knew he still regretted his initial doubts about being able to love the baby, but she'd gotten over it long ago—the second he'd proposed, in fact.

They'd never looked back on that dreadful night when she'd been rushed to the hospital. She'd spent the next two months being pampered by Devin, who had become involved in every aspect of planning for the baby. He'd even spent an entire weekend painting the room they'd made into a nursery and then repainting it when Carey decided the yellow she'd chosen was too dark.

When she'd suggested naming the baby after his grandpa, Carl Thaylor, he'd been overcome with emotion.

Life was better than she'd ever thought it could

be. Devin's work was going gangbusters. He'd recently expanded by taking on a second security specialist, and Monica still assisted him, even though she was expecting her own baby in less than three months.

Carey's photography business was growing as fast as she wanted it to right now. She averaged about two weddings per month and still took some freelance assignments when she could arrange to have Devin or Monica stay with Carla. It was ideal—enough work to challenge her and keep her fresh, but not so much that she couldn't bring up her daughter herself.

Trent and Devin were no longer hostile toward each other. They could all spend time together without any disagreements erupting, with the exception of Carey and Trent arguing over whether he needed to get married and have his own kids. He tended to lavish tons of attention on Carla, which Carey secretly loved. But she still maintained he needed his own babies to fuss over. She aspired to be an aunt soon. She just had to find a sister-in-law first.

Carey's mother had kept her promise to help with the baby, even though Carey hadn't ended up a single mother as she'd expected. She and Phillip were willing, doting babysitters whenever Carey and Devin needed an evening alone. As she'd suspected, Phillip had done wonders for Penny.

Devin carried Carla to the driver's seat of the boat and sat down across from Carey, upholding his side of a very serious conversation about fish with his daughter. "Business," he said in his indulgent voice, "is okay. It feeds the bank account. But fishing…it feeds the soul."

Carey rolled her eyes. "You're poisoning her mind." She leaned forward. "Don't listen to him, girly. Fishing is nasty, smelly boy stuff."

"So much for feminism," Devin muttered.

"She can stay home and run Daddy's business."

They laughed together, and Carey decided she couldn't wait any longer to tell him her news. "Speaking of business…it's a good thing CMT is doing so well now."

"Why do you say that?"

She watched him play with Carla's toes, thinking for the millionth time what a good father he was. "Because it'll get pretty expensive to keep two in diapers."

He whipped his head up, his lips hinting at a smile. "Did you say *two?*"

She nodded.

"As in Princess here and a sibling?"

A wide grin spread across her face, and her heart melted at the excitement in his voice.

"That's what I meant. I'm seven weeks pregnant."

They hadn't been able to consummate their relationship until after Carla was born, but they'd made up for lost time since then.

He howled in happiness, and the sound echoed over the water.

"Way to scare the fish away, Ace," she said, her elation overflowing.

"Forget the fish. You're going to be a big sister, Carla."

The baby gurgled in delight, as if she understood her daddy.

Devin leaned forward and kissed Carey long and hard, until a giggle from their daughter pulled them apart. They both glanced down at Carla to discover she had a death grip on the fishing pole.

Carey laughed. "Looks like someone's ready to fish. Are you going to drop a line in?" she asked Devin.

"Hell, no. I've got me the catch of a lifetime. Let's go celebrate, girls."

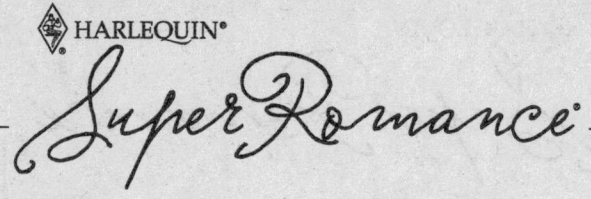

THE OTHER WOMAN

by *Brenda Novak*

A Dundee, Idaho Book

Elizabeth O'Conner has finally put her
ex-husband's betrayal behind her. She's
concentrating on her two kids and on opening
her own business. One thing she's learned
is that she doesn't want to depend on any
man ever again—which definitely includes the
enigmatic Carter Hudson. It's just as well that
he's as reluctant to get involved as she is....

By the award-winning author of
Stranger in Town and *Big Girls Don't Cry*.

On sale May 2006
Available at your favorite retailer!

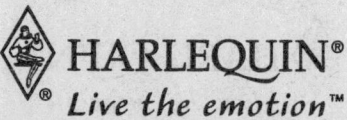

HARLEQUIN®
Live the emotion™

HARLEQUIN®

Super Romance

LEARNING CURVE

by Terry McLaughlin

(HSR #1348)

**A brand-new Superromance
author makes her debut in 2006!**

Disillusioned high school history teacher
Joe Wisniewski is in a rut so deep he's
considering retirement. The last thing he wants
is to mentor some starry-eyed newcomer, so
when he gets an unexpected assignment—
Emily Sullivan, a student teacher with a
steamroller smile and dynamite legs—
he digs in deeper and ducks for cover.

On sale May 2006
Available wherever Harlequin books are sold!

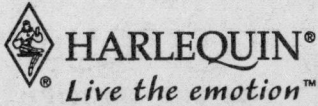

HARLEQUIN®
Live the emotion™

ATHENA FORCE

**CHOSEN FOR THEIR TALENTS.
TRAINED TO BE THE BEST.
EXPECTED TO CHANGE THE WORLD.**

The women of Athena Academy are back.
Don't miss their compelling new adventures
as they reveal the truth about their founder's
unsolved murder—and provoke the wrath of a
cunning new enemy....

FLASHBACK
by Justine DAVIS

Available April 2006 at your favorite retail outlet.

MORE ATHENA ADVENTURES
COMING SOON:

Look-Alike by Meredith Fletcher, May 2006
Exclusive by Katherine Garbera, June 2006
Pawn by Carla Cassidy, July 2006
Comeback by Doranna Durgin, August 2006

If you enjoyed what you just read,
then we've got an offer you can't resist!

Take 2 bestselling
love stories FREE!
Plus get a FREE surprise gift!

Clip this page and mail it to Harlequin Reader Service®

IN U.S.A.
3010 Walden Ave.
P.O. Box 1867
Buffalo, N.Y. 14240-1867

IN CANADA
P.O. Box 609
Fort Erie, Ontario
L2A 5X3

YES! Please send me 2 free Harlequin Superromance® novels and my free surprise gift. After receiving them, if I don't wish to receive anymore, I can return the shipping statement marked cancel. If I don't cancel, I will receive 6 brand-new novels every month, before they're available in stores. In the U.S.A., bill me at the bargain price of $4.69 plus 25¢ shipping and handling per book and applicable sales tax, if any*. In Canada, bill me at the bargain price of $5.24 plus 25¢ shipping and handling per book and applicable taxes**. That's the complete price, and a savings of at least 10% off the cover prices—what a great deal! I understand that accepting the 2 free books and gift places me under no obligation ever to buy any books. I can always return a shipment and cancel at any time. Even if I never buy another book from Harlequin, the 2 free books and gift are mine to keep forever.

135 HDN DZ7W
336 HDN DZ7X

Name	(PLEASE PRINT)	
Address	Apt.#	
City	State/Prov.	Zip/Postal Code

Not valid to current Harlequin Superromance® subscribers.

Want to try two free books from another series?
Call 1-800-873-8635 or visit www.morefreebooks.com.

* Terms and prices subject to change without notice. Sales tax applicable in N.Y.
** Canadian residents will be charged applicable provincial taxes and GST.
All orders subject to approval. Offer limited to one per household.
® are registered trademarks owned and used by the trademark owner and or its licensee.

SUP04R   ©2004 Harlequin Enterprises Limited